A THOUSAND
SHALL FALL

A Thousand

Shall Fall

THE SHILOH LEGACY SERIES ★ BOOK TWO

BODIE & BROCK THOENE

TYNDALE HOUSE PUBLISHERS, INC.
CAROL STREAM, ILLINOIS

Visit Tyndale's exciting Web site at www.tyndale.com

TYNDALE and Tyndale's quill logo are registered trademarks of Tyndale House Publishers, Inc.

A Thousand Shall Fall

Designed by Dean H. Renninger

Edited by Ramona Cramer Tucker

Published in 1992 by Bethany House Publishers under ISBN 1-55661-190-0.

First printing by Tyndale House Publishers, Inc. in 2006.

Scripture quotations are taken from the Holy Bible, King James Version.

Library of Congress Cataloging-in-Publication Data

Thoene, Bodie, date.
  A thousand shall fall / Bodie & Brock Thoene.
    p. cm. —(The Shiloh legacy ; bk. 2)
    ISBN-13: 978-1-4143-0121-1 (pbk.)
    ISBN-10: 1-4143-0121-9 (pbk.)
    1. Shiloh (Ark. : Imaginary place)—Fiction. 2. Depressions—Fiction. 3. Country life —
Fiction. 4. Arkansas—Fiction. I. Thoene, Brock, date. II. Title.
  PS3570.H46T48 2006
  813'.54—dc22   2006001567

Printed in the United States of America

11 10 09 08 07 06
 7   6   5   4   3   2   1

For
Chance, Jessie, Ian,
Titan, and Connor,
with love.

Prologue

The gold case of the old Rockford pocket watch lay open beside the huge stack of manuscript pages heaped on the old man's desk. Soft ticking provided a gentle rhythm behind the urgent scratching of pen against notepaper. The watch hands swept across the ivory face, as if to remind the writer that time was passing too quickly for him. And time *was* running out. Only a thousand pages of his life had been written, and surely it would take ten thousand more to tell the whole story!

He paused and glared at the watch. No, it was not the timepiece that was the enemy but Time itself. The old man cocked a bushy eyebrow and tugged his drooping mustache as he recalled how he had come to carry the watch, the heavy gold watch chain, and the California-minted ten-dollar-gold-piece watch fob. It was one of the children's favorites—a tale they never tired of hearing—but the old man had not yet put the story down on paper. He had held off writing it, as though he could bribe the watch and slow down the steady forward movement of its hands.

"And when I've written about you, old friend," he often whispered to the timepiece, "then I'll shut your golden case and send you to Jim to carry. I shall lay down my pen at last, and you may mark the hour of my passing as just another tick of your cycle."

The watch made no promise in return, as though it did not care if the story of the pocket watch and chain and fob were ever written.

But there were other tales to tell.

The dark eyes of the old man flitted to the black, fist-sized paper-weight that prevented the wind from scattering the legacy in the heap of papers before him.

It was the story of this stone that the old man now struggled to re-count. The most important story of his eighty-six years was in that hunk of iron and nickel in stone! It had saved his life when he was twenty-six years old. It had given him the gift of sixty more years to live. It had made possible the sons and a daughter and grandchildren to gather at his knee and beg, "Tell us the story of the star, Grandpa Sinnickson! Tell it again!"

For sixty years he had hefted up the stone and cried, "Well now, chil-dren, listen up! This may look like just a black rock to you, but it's more than that. It ain't gold, but it's more than gold. This ain't an ordinary stone—no sir. This is a star! Yessir, you heard me right! A star! Straight from heaven it came, blazing across the sky on the darkest night of my life. With a tail of fire a mile long, it screamed down to earth and saved my life in a most miraculous way. Listen up now, and I'll tell you about it. For it is the truth, and I stand alive here as witness to it."

And then his grandchildren would pass the star from hand to hand. The eyes of young and old grew wide at the story of danger and death and the miracle of the falling star.

Perhaps of all the stories, this was the most often repeated. This was the most important tale to be written down because it had made all the rest of his life possible. . . .

The shrill whistle of the Hartford train echoed across the valley of Shiloh, interrupting his reverie.

The old man peered at the watch a moment. "Late again," he grum-bled, snatching up the timepiece and striding to part the curtains of his bedroom window.

Just above the golden tops of the autumn trees, a dark gray plume marked the progress of the locomotive. Far across the valley, the row of birch trees trembled and swayed as if to bow toward the train.

"The boys are playing in the trees again," the old man muttered. Glancing at his watch again, he whispered a warning: "You're late, boys. Get on down. Get home before your father gets wind you're having a good time. Hurry home now, boys!"

As if they heard his distant heart, the two small boys in the birch trees began their descent. Bending the slender trunks low, they rode the tree-tops to the ground and tumbled onto the field.

The old man mopped his brow in relief as he watched the two red-shirted figures dash up the hill toward home. Perhaps their father, who had no timepiece, would not know they were late.

For a long time the old man stood at the window and stared across the dusky fields at the birch trees. He had planted those trees with his own hands. A tall, straight row of birch trees for his grandsons to climb and ride. Too bad their father did not believe that small boys were created to climb and whoop and laugh.

Samuel Tucker would leave a legacy of harshness, of distance and cruelty, for his sons. It was for this reason that their grandpa, the old man, worked day and night on the tales of his own life.

Clicking the watch face closed, he turned from the window and returned to his task. Filling his pen with ink, he tapped the nib on the blotter. It was easier to tell the story aloud than it was to put it down on silent paper, so he whispered the words as he wrote at the top of the page:

"For Grandson Birch

From Grandfather Andrew Jackson Sinnickson:

Already I have written one thousand pages, yet I find I have come only to my twenty-sixth year. This may be the most important tale of all my legacy, however, as in it I learned by the miracle of a falling star how God delivers those who trust Him. Read on, Birch, for it is a story you seem to not tire of. Perhaps one day you will have children of your own whom you may read these words to. Then you will tell them early what I have learned late: A thousand shall fall at thy side, and ten thousand at thy right hand; but it shall not come nigh thee. . . ."

THE
FOWLER'S
SNARE

part one

Just as war is
waged with the
blood of others,
fortunes are made
with other people's
money.

ANDRE SUARES,
1906

CHAPTER ONE

Old Glory

SEPTEMBER 24, 1929

Moonshine whiskey and cockfights—the two ingredients spelled *money*, plain and simple. Prohibition had proven to be a profitable enterprise. Not a county in the entire nation remained untouched by the sale of illegal liquor at illegal sporting events held deep in some secret, wooded glens or back-road barns. The law knew, but hard cash or a stake in the profits silenced them. From near and far, men came to see the mortal combat—sometimes between cocks with razor-sharp metal spurs strapped on their legs, sometimes between pit bulls raised from puppies for the sole purpose of battling to the death before a roaring crowd.

On still other occasions, those within the fighting pit were men—convicts, specially chosen from among their fellow prisoners for strength, endurance, and brutality. Their masters were guards who urged them to fight in the prison yard. The champion received extra food and special privileges.

There were no rules in such fights. Leg-irons, fists, and teeth were all equal weapons. Like ancient gladiators, they fought until one man lay unconscious in the ring of torchlight. Sometimes the loser lived. Sometimes he did not. But the winner was expected to fight again at some future date. The law did not even need to be bribed, because it was the lawmen who sponsored the fights and gloried in the profits.

Sheriff Myron Ring had discovered a champion among the human refuse of his Oklahoma chain gang. Ring had seen him take on three white men in the prison yard one sultry afternoon. Ordering his officers to stand back, the sheriff had let the battle take its course. In the end the black man remained standing, and Sheriff Ring knew he had found something that would draw crowds in Kansas, Missouri, Arkansas, and Oklahoma.

Twenty-two times in two years the fighter they called Cannibal had defeated his opponent, making Sheriff Ring a man of substance.

Cannibal had never fought in this part of Arkansas before tonight. Chained hand and foot like a ferocious beast, he lay in the back of the pickup that rattled along the wagon track on the way up the Poteau Mountains. Two guards rode with him, their shotguns aimed at his scarred face and thick, muscled body. Sheriff Ring would take no chances of Cannibal jumping out and running for it as he had done before. Tonight the take promised to be tremendous. The local champion was young and fresh. He had already beaten fourteen opponents, killing three. Odds on the match were dead even. The men here in Arkansas believed their fighter would win, but then, they had never seen Cannibal.

A small caravan of Oklahoma lawmen followed close behind the sheriff's Model T Ford truck. They had brought their hounds as usual, so if anyone unfriendly questioned their purpose, they could claim they had come to Arkansas to hunt. But twenty miles deep into these hills, no one had asked them yet. They swilled their sour mash whiskey openly in the moonlight until they swayed with the lurching vehicles and shouted drunkenly to one another in celebration of what was to come.

"Cannibal gonna show these dumb Arkies! Their nigger ain't nothin' to ol' Cannibal!"

A shooting star streaked a fiery path across the sky—an omen of a great victory tonight.

Still ten miles to go to the old barn. Nearly all the party was drunk, except for Sheriff Ring and Deputy Bigger, who drove the second truck . . . and Cannibal, of course.

The road grew more narrow and treacherous. The rocky shale fought against the spinning tires. It was plain that this road was not meant for Henry Ford's mechanical contraption. This was horse-and-mule country.

Sheriff Ring leaned out the window and shouted at the gun-toting guards, "You two got them scatterguns cocked?"

"Shore we do, Sheriff!" came the slurred reply.

"Then uncock 'em! We hit a rut, you gonna blow the head right off my business."

The sheriff was right. An accidental discharge of the shotguns aimed at Cannibal's head would ruin the chances for tonight's match. The guards eased the hammers down with a click, then passed around the brown jug one more time. As the truck bumped over a pothole, corn liquor spilled from their mouths, eliciting curses. Never had there been such a jarring ride. Sure to ruin a man's back. Sure to dislocate something. It was lucky there was enough moonshine on board to make the trip more tolerable.

The road reared up a steep incline to the right. The headlamps skittered across the shadowed ruts and swept over a dark embankment where the hill tumbled down a rocky slope. Voices were raised in raucous song.

The sheriff leaned out the window of his truck one more time to make sure his orders about the cocked weapons had been obeyed. "You boys done what I told—?"

At that moment, the tires of the pickup began to lose their argument with the road. With a sound like escaping steam, the truck slid sideways toward the embankment and the darkness.

There was not even time to scream before the truck launched over the empty air. Headlights scraped wildly across trees on the far side of the valley, then tilted down to illuminate the ground at the moment of impact.

When the dust cleared and the shouting stopped, the sheriff, dazed but unharmed, staggered out to survey the damage. Broken axle. Fenders and running board ripped from the vehicle. The barrel of one shotgun bent in two. The arm of a guard broken. It was a miracle no one had been killed.

But Cannibal was nowhere to be found!

They called the oil field Old Glory, and to the rich oil barons of Oklahoma, it was indeed a glorious sight to behold.

Like a barren, leafless forest, hundreds of great wooden derricks sprouted and grew sixty feet into the air, yielding a harvest of thick black sap to fuel the rattling Model Ts and feed American furnaces and factories.

The roar of the engine houses and the groaning of the bull wheels were never still. But the clank of pipe and traveling blocks and tongs was as sweet as birdsong to the ears of the new tycoons. The stink of sulphur and oil was as fragrant as the foreign perfumes that wives and daughters purchased in their travels to Paris, France, and Vienna, Austria. Rigs operated around the clock in the Old Glory field while the oil kings slept soundly, knowing they would wake up richer in the morning than they had been the night before.

While the owners dreamed, crews of roughnecks made their living in the stench and the filth of Old Glory. Derrickmen, pushers, floormen, and mudmen wrestled with pipe and tongs and hoist controls, coaxing the black goo from the earth's crust. For these men, there was little glory attached to the field. But at least they had work, and that was something. Some of them still had dreams of their own as well. Dreams that took their thoughts far from Old Glory, well No. 49.

Tonight the rig was lit up like a giant Christmas tree in the darkness. Lights were strung from every beam and powered by a generator. No doubt the derrick could be plainly seen all the way to Tulsa.

From his place high inside the rig, Birch Tucker could easily spot the lights of the city. He could see things up here that the floorman and the driller could not see. Perhaps that was why he did not mind working forty feet above the floor while balancing on a narrow plank called a fingerboard. As derrickman, it was Birch's job to attach new lengths of pipe to the clamp below the traveling block when it was hoisted high into position. It was a job that some would consider dangerous, but, Birch explained to his wife, Trudy, he had climbed enough trees in his life to be used to the height. And he sure did like the view up here.

It was not the view that got his attention this evening, however, but the smell of rain. A breeze had sprung up from the north, strong enough to rattle the long pipes in the pipe stand and cut through Birch's heavy jacket.

He squinted past the glowing bulbs toward the sky. Stars were still visible, but streamers of clouds snaked across the heavens. Something big was coming. Birch felt it more than he could see it. And an oil rig was no place to be when a thunderstorm broke.

Down in the noise and the fumes and the glare, the rest of the crew would not know what was coming until it hit. Birch had seen enough to know that storms blew in out of nowhere in these parts. He wanted to be somewhere else when this one arrived.

But Birch had little time to worry about the thunderstorm. Moving headlights turned from the main road onto the dirt lane that snaked through the Old Glory field. From the speed of the automobile, Birch knew immediately who was driving.

A different kind of storm was moving in on No. 49, it seemed.

For a second, Birch considered dropping something to warn Murray Hawkins, the driller, that a most unpleasant visitor was coming. But he didn't have to. Hawkins had evidently spotted the headlights, too. He shook his head and looked up toward Birch. Raising his hand in a signal of frustration, Hawkins continued with his work as the bright red Reo roadster squealed to a stop.

Damon Phelps, son of the oil tycoon, staggered out of the car. Moments later a chic flapper in a fox cape wriggled out of the passenger side of the vehicle and tiptoed through puddles of goo to stand and twitter at the side of her wealthy young beau.

Glory well No. 49 belonged entirely to young Damon—a college-graduation gift from his daddy. The boy brought visitors out to the well at all hours of the day and night. He had told his father that he intended to be close at hand when she finally came in. This well was to be the beginning of his own fortune. Some rich men gave their sons racehorses, but Old Man Phelps figured his boy ought to have an oil well.

Damon began his usual tour of the rig. The flapper trudged gingerly after him to the engine house and poked her head in as though she were fascinated by the great clanking engine pulling the hoist. Removing a silver whiskey flask from his pocket, Damon raised it in a toast to the well. He took one long swig before passing it to the girl, who drank as deeply as he had. Tonight Damon did not speak to the crew—a relief to the men, Birch knew. Birch himself was usually glad to be up on the fingerboard when Damon Phelps came around.

But tonight was different.

In the distance, Birch could see the lightning rolling in ahead of the front, blinking on and off like silver neon behind the clouds. The wind had picked up, tugging hard at his jacket. From the look of the lightning, the storm would break in a few minutes.

There was nothing to do but shut down the drilling and take shelter until the worst passed over. Maybe later they could resume their work in the rain, but until the lightning moved on, remaining on the rig was foolhardy.

Below him, Birch spotted Damon pointing up through the two-by-twelve planks toward Birch's perch. Damon had a way of making his pretty little guests believe that he had built the rig and hired the crew himself. The truth was, the boy was terrified of heights and had never worked a day in his life.

The lightning flashed brighter. Birch could distinctly see the spark flare and branch a half dozen times as it reached for the ground.

"It'll be here in five minutes," Birch muttered. He reached for a wrench and dropped it as a signal to Hawkins to look up: *"Something is not right. . . ."*

Hawkins shifted the hoist controls into neutral and peered up at Birch, who swung from the fingerboard onto the wooden ladder. Birch pointed at the sky. Hawkins nodded and raised his face to the wind. Now he could smell the storm, too.

Birch began to climb down, then stopped halfway as the angry shouts of Damon Phelps penetrated the rumble of the idling engine.

"What do you think you're doing? Hey! You're getting paid by the hour, and if you want to keep your job . . ." This fury was directed at Hawkins, who motioned toward Birch and then pointed skyward.

Birch took another downward step as Damon ran to the bottom of the ladder, shook his fist at Birch, and cursed. "You're not being paid to take breaks whenever you feel like it!"

Cupping his hand around his mouth, Birch replied, "Well now, Mister Phelps, there's lightning heading this way in about a minute."

As if to emphasize the truth, a brilliant light flashed behind Birch, illuminating the entire field with a silver glare. The rumble followed an instant later, drowning out the rest of Birch's words.

But clearly the storm did not matter to Damon. He had come all the way out here to show his girlfriend *his* well, and no filthy roughneck was going to ruin the show.

"Listen! If you want to have a job, you'll get back up that ladder right now!" Furious, Damon put one foot on the floor of the rig as though to stand guard and prevent Birch's descent. "Get up there or you're fired! And don't think I don't mean it!"

Another flash erupted to the right. The rumble seemed to sway the giant rig. Birch held to the ladder, poised midway between the crown block and the ground. He did not move up or down.

Damon glanced at his girlfriend, who seemed to be enjoying his display of power over the employees. Pointing at Birch, Damon said angrily, "You've got ten seconds, mister! Get back to work or—"

Birch felt his hair stand out from his head at the violent approach of the lightning bolt. The air crackled around the derrick as Birch pressed himself against the wooden ladder and prayed that he was not touching metal.

The explosion was deafening, as though a bomb had struck the rig. Bright blue-and-white electricity surged through the crown block, splintering the wood. Lightbulbs popped as the lightning replaced the tamer current with a deadly fire. Coursing through the cables, the charge hit the pipe rack and traveled down to the floor of the rig, seeking a conductor to the ground. Young Damon Phelps, with one foot on the rig and one on the ground, formed a perfect bridge for the lightning to pass through.

Damon did not have time to count to ten. He was dead in an instant. His girlfriend was knocked twenty yards. Hawkins, who was at the hoist controls, was unharmed. Birch descended the ladder without a scratch. The silver hip flask in Damon Phelps' hand was blackened, and a thin vapor escaped from the opening as the alcohol evaporated. The young man's other fist was still clenched and cocked slightly skyward in defiance.

The flapper moaned in the puddle of oil where she had landed. "*Dayyyyy-monnnnn!*"

Hawkins ran to aid her.

Scanning the rig, Birch was relieved to see that no one else had been touched by the bolt.

Leo Johns, floorman on the rig, towered over the body of young Phelps. He shook his head solemnly as the rain began to fall. "If I hadn't put down them tongs a second before . . ."

Birch knew what Leo was thinking. He might have died, too.

Hawkins glanced at the dead man. "It might as well have killed us all. Anybody but young Phelps!" He cursed, then caught himself, looking fearfully upward.

Birch remembered that the last word of the young man had been a curse.

"He's right," Leo agreed as Birch removed his coat and placed it across the face of the tycoon's only son. "Anybody but the kid, and the old man wouldn't give it a thought. You know it's true. Bury the dead, but don't shut down the rig. Widows and orphans out on the street! But Old Man Phelps'll blame us, you know. We better start lookin' for another job, and that's the truth."

There was no need to rush off and call an ambulance. The bolt of lightning had been seen for miles around. Within minutes twelve pairs of headlights were snaking toward Old Glory well No. 49 as every crew in the field rushed to see if anyone had survived.

A hundred men soon milled around the scene, shaking their heads as they gaped at the rig, the body, and the muddy, sobbing girl who sat on the running board of a crew truck.

Birch did not know how Phelps got word of the accident, but suddenly he was there, dressed in his dinner jacket. Instantly the whole field hushed. Somewhere the squeak of the jack lines sounded, but no man spoke as Phelps looked hard and long at the bright red roadster and at the shaken girl.

And then, somehow, the old man just *knew.*

The crowd parted for him as he staggered toward the rig. A path opened, leading him to the motionless form sprawled in the mud. His eyes widened, and he swayed as though he would fall.

Birch reached out to support Phelps's arm, only to be shoved away.

"Don't!" Phelps shouted, then moved through the pelting rain until he stood above his son. His shoulders sagged. He looked up at the splintered crown block as if to retrace the path of the lightning through the rig and through Damon to the ground.

A long silence passed until at last Phelps exploded in rage. "Who was the derrickman!" he bellowed, whirling to face the spectators.

"Me." Birch stepped out from the men.

"You didn't see it coming?" Phelps lunged as if to strike Birch.

Hawkins moved between the two men. "He saw it, Mister Phelps. Tried to shut her down, too. The young mister told us if we shut her down, we was fired. And then . . ."

Birch saw the thoughts that flashed through the old man's mind by his changing expressions. *Well, of course. It makes sense, doesn't it? I know my own son, and it sounds like something he'd do. Fool kid! I always thought he would grow out of it one of these days. . . .*

Phelps blinked at Birch, then winced. "Where were you when it hit?"

"On the ladder." Birch glanced at the spot.

"My . . . son—" Phelps's voice cracked at the word—"he told you to stay up?"

"Yessir."

"And then he came here . . . to the bottom of the ladder?" The voice tightened as Phelps pieced the sequence together.

"That's the way it was, Mister Phelps."

"If you'd obeyed him!" Phelps grabbed Birch by his soaking shirt. "If only you would have . . ." He slapped Birch hard across the cheek.

Birch flinched but made no move to defend himself.

"You see!" Phelps shook Birch by his shirtfront until the buttons of Birch's shirt popped off. "If only you would have stayed up there like my boy said, then he wouldn't have been so close! He wouldn't be dead! You hear me? It would be *you*, not him! You're the one who ought to be lying here!" He shoved Birch away and stood before him with fists clenched.

"Well, I ain't dead," Birch replied quietly.

"You're . . . fired! Get out of my field! Get off my land! You hear me? Pack up! Out of here by tomorrow night!"

"Mister Phelps—," Hawkins began in defense of Birch, but Birch put a hand on his arm.

"It's okay. I was figurin' on leavin' anyway." Birch spoke in a soothing voice.

"Draw your pay!" Phelps started in again, more enraged that his order did not seem to hurt Birch. "If I see your face around here, you'll wish you'd been struck by lightning! You hear me? You will be dead!"

The old man's rantings followed Birch as he trudged through the pelting rain toward the field office. Glancing back over his shoulder, he saw the fractured derrick. It was tilted slightly to one side, and the glowing embers of the crown block were still smoking like the snuffed wick of a giant candle. At the foot of the rig, Old Man Phelps knelt in the mud beside his broken dreams and wept aloud.

Lifting his face to the rain, Birch let it wash the filth of the Old Glory field from him. He welcomed the cold sting against his skin. By now, no doubt, word would have wakened every family in the camp. Trudy would have heard that well No. 49 had been struck, and she would be waiting for news. Waiting to hear if he was still alive. Waiting to know if all their dreams had come to an end. . . .

"I'm alive, Trudy," Birch called joyfully in the darkness. "True! We're goin' home!"

CHAPTER TWO

The Fall of Camelot

Golden light emanated from the windows of St. Francis Hospital in Philadelphia. Standing outside on the sidewalk, nine-year-old David O'Halloran thought the place looked more like a castle than a hospital. The ivy-covered, redbrick facade took the form of towers and turrets in his mind. Inside, knights and royal ladies feasted and danced and drank flagons of honeyed mead, just like in the stories his mother had told him. The king and queen laughed at the jokes of the court jester and ate without silverware, throwing scraps of food to the hunting hounds lying at their feet. At such a party it was impolite not to belch loudly after supper.

David liked that thought. Whenever his mother told him that part of the story, he would gulp down air and let loose a magnificent and kingly belch. It made his mother smile. . . .

He let his eyes trace the silhouette of the building to the corner room of the west wing. On the third floor, a shade was half drawn, as if to keep the light from escaping. Or was it to keep out the darkness of the night? David's mother, queen of storytellers, the Guinevere of his imaginary Camelot, lay in that very room. David pictured her in a wide canopied bed with heavy red-velvet curtains tied back with golden ropes. She could pull a tassel if she wanted anything, and servants would rush to her bedside to brush her golden hair and plump her pillows, to feed her tapioca pudding and ice cream and hold a flagon of mead to her lips.

"Queen Irene," they would say, "is there anything else you wish, m'lady?"

Then she would smile serenely, beautiful in the golden light. She would nod the way queens were supposed to nod. *"Send up Prince Davey, will you? It's visiting hours, and I want to hear everything that happened today in school. He is in fourth grade, you know. I used to teach fourth grade."*

It was almost as though David could hear his mother say all that. Standing in the shadows outside St. Francis, he could see everything that happened in that corner room. He could hear her ask for him. *"Visiting hours . . ."*

David slung the rucksack of books over his shoulder and joined dozens of other pilgrims climbing the steps of St. Francis, where each night a feast of hope and despair was held at every bedside.

The long, narrow lobby of the hospital was crowded with men and women visitors. It smelled of cigarette smoke and antiseptic and cafeteria food. In the lobby everyone spoke in hushed tones, as if the place were a church. Sometimes faces smiled at one another over the top of David's head, but David noticed that the eyes of the visitors looked anxious. Or busy. Or angry. Grown-up eyes during visiting hours never matched the smile.

The clacking of a typewriter and the buzzing of a telephone made more noise than the voices. Worried voices came out of those who asked for room numbers for the first time. "Pardon me? Can you tell me which ward . . . ?" David could always hear the first-time visitors before he spotted them at the reception desk. People always sounded that way the first time they came to visit at St. Francis. They just weren't used to the place—that was all.

But David was used to it. He had been scared the first time they told him he could come see his mother, but he wasn't scared anymore. He knew just the way to go. *Wait by the elevator while everyone crushes out cigarettes in the metal, sand-filled ashtray. Watch the arrow of the dial above the door swing from four to three to two and then . . .* bong! *The brass doors slide open and people crowd in. Watch out for careless elbows, high-heeled shoes, and heavy wing tips. Watch the doors slide shut, blocking out the view of Jesus hanging on a cross on the wall.*

Wait. Second floor. Doors open to another cross. People get off. No one gets on. The doors slide shut, and the elevator hums upward to the floor where Queen Irene waits for me. Another cross on the wall opposite the elevator. Turn left past the nurses' station and then . . .

The nurses behind the tall counter in the center of the corridor looked up as David passed. Sister Anne, the black-robed nun beside them, smiled gently and passed a clipboard to Miss Noonan, the heavyset nurse who never smiled.

"David?" Sister Anne stepped out and blocked his path. She leaned down until her face was level with his. Beads of perspiration hung on her brow and dampened her wimple slightly. She placed her soft, plump hand on his shoulder as if to take his rucksack. He saw that her pale blue eyes were worried, like the grown-ups in the lobby, like the first-timers. David knew the smile was not real. She was not happy to see him. But he let her take the book sack from him.

"Hiya, Sister Anne." He drew a deep breath and looked past her toward his mother's room. The door was closed. Why was the door closed?

"Hello, David. . . ." Her eyes darted toward the three nurses, who just stood there staring at him. White hats. White dresses. White stockings. White shoes. All very close together, as if they were not three nurses but one motionless statue in the niche of the church, staring at David and Sister Anne.

"Why is the door closed?" David asked out loud.

The rucksack was placed on the floor, and again Sister Anne put her hand on his shoulder as though to hold him there. "Father John is with your mother now."

David pressed his lips together and nodded once in relief. "Can I go in?"

Sister Anne squeezed his shoulder briefly. "Your mother is not doing . . . well tonight."

Ah. Another bad spell. There had been more of those lately. They didn't let David go in when she was having a bad spell. Sometimes he just waited on the long wooden bench in the hall until his mother felt better. Then he got to kiss her good night.

He stared at his rucksack. "I can wait. I can do arithmetic. Long division. If I wait, she will wake up and ask for me, and I can kiss her good night."

Pained glances passed between the three statues and Sister Anne. "David . . ."

"I won't get in the way."

"David . . ."

"I won't be a bother."

"Of course you won't." Sister Anne sounded like she might strangle. She threw a desperate look toward one of the nurses. "Go try to reach David's father again, will you?"

One of the nurses broke formation and rustled toward the telephone. David knew she would only reach Mrs. Crowley.

Sister Anne led David to the bench. She placed the book bag like a sack of potatoes on the floor of the corridor. "Have you heard from your father, David?" she asked gently when they sat down.

"He sent Missus Crowley a wire from Cincinnati." Mrs. Crowley was the housekeeper who stayed with David all the time since his mother had gotten so sick. Brian O'Halloran was almost always off selling office supplies these days.

"Did he say when he would be back?"

"Pretty soon." David stared at the closed door and tried very hard to conjure up the pleasant image of Queen Irene on her plumped pillows in the canopy bed. But reality crowded his mind, pushing out the image of her golden hair and deep blue eyes and smooth, fair skin.

Breast cancer. Her arms are like toothpicks, her beautiful hair cropped short like a boy's. Her cheeks are hollow and gray, her once-clear eyes sunken and full of pity.

It was not self-pity David saw in her eyes but pity for him, because she knew how much he needed her!

"I want to see my mother!" he suddenly demanded, springing to his feet and pulling his arm free from Sister Anne's grip.

She overtook him in a stride and grasped his arm again, spinning him around. "Not now! You promised you would not be trouble . . . remember?"

"When can I see her?" He did not cry, although his throat was closing, making it hard to talk quietly.

"Not . . . now!" She led him back to the bench.

David did not fight her. He sat down and stared hard at the toes of his shoes. Always the toes were the first to wear through because of marbles. David liked to kneel in the rough gravel of the playground and shoot marbles. His mother hated it because it wore out the toes of his shoes. He wished now they were not so scuffed, not almost worn through. He did not want to do anything tonight that would make his mother unhappy. *Not tonight!*

Something was up. This was not like the other times. Something different, something terrible, was happening behind that closed door. Sister Anne had never stayed right beside him like this. Her hands were clasped as if she were praying, but her eyes were wide-open as she looked toward the crucified Christ on the opposite wall. It was like she was looking out through a window, David thought.

"Maybe you should do your arithmetic," Sister Anne said after a long time. "You know your mother always likes you to have your schoolwork done."

David fetched his book bag without reply as Sister Anne sat very still on the bench. Taking out his notebook, he opened to a page of long-division problems that he had copied from the blackboard. He had imagined his mother helping him with homework tonight. Sometimes she did that during visiting hours, and it seemed to make her happy.

Often David let her help him even when he already knew the answer. He knew she liked it, so he pretended.

This was a place to pretend, after all. St. Francis was no castle. Irene Dunlap O'Halloran was no queen. She was David's mother, dying in a hospital.

He did not ask Sister Anne to help him with his math.

Hours ticked by.

Visiting hours were over. Still, they did not tell him to go home. The door remained closed.

The plump nurse walked by many times in a hurried way. She stopped once and leaned very close to Sister Anne. "Mister O'Halloran is on the way from the station."

Sister Anne sighed with relief, as though she had not breathed for a long time. "Thank God."

She could not know, David thought, that Brian O'Halloran was David's stepfather and that he hated David and David hated him. David's real father had died and Irene had married Brian.

Brian is coming. This was not good news.

David did not call him Dad; he called him Brian. And Brian called David a lot of things—none of them pleasant.

David finished his long division and put away his books. "Can I see my mother now?" he asked, his voice creaking in a weary way.

Sister Anne patted his hand and stood. "I'll ask Father John." She turned to the nurse. "His father will be here soon. Do you suppose it will be all right?" She rustled to the closed door, opened it a crack, and peered in.

Slipping through the crack, she disappeared. A moment later she reappeared with her face very pale. Her eyes drifted to the clock, to the Christ, and back to David.

"Father John says you may come to your mother's bedside," she whispered in a holy-sounding voice, the same kind of voice the new visitors used at the hospital reception desk when they asked which way they should go to find somebody. Worried.

David did not just want to go to his mother's bedside; he wanted to show her his math problems and tell her about the two agate shooters he had won in the marble game. But there was something behind the door that made his heart pound hard and his knees feel weak. He took his book bag all the same. The marbles in the pouch clacked together as his heels tapped on the polished floor. Sister Anne pushed back the door for him and held it. He stood outside her room for a moment. His legs simply could not take him farther.

Who is that old woman lying on the bed? Not my mama! The soft glow of the bed lamp made her look yellow. Her damp hair was matted, the same color as her complexion. Her once-active hands were lying across her chest as though she were already in a coffin.

David pushed past Sister Anne, moved toward the bed, and rested his hands on the white-iron rail.

Father John stood up from the chair at the head of her bed.

"Mama?" David croaked.

"She is medicated," Father John answered. "Sleeping now."

Honeyed mead . . . they put it to her lips and made her drink it all down so she would not hurt. Morphine, they called it.

David knew all about it. Sometimes it gave her bad dreams, and she cried out for David and for David's father—his real father, Max, who had died before David was born.

Her breath was very shallow, as though she were in pain.

"Does she hurt?" David asked. *Dying. Dying. Dying . . .*

"No," Father John replied. "I don't think so."

"Will it hurt?" *Dying. Dying. Dying . . .*

"She is peaceful." Sister Anne stepped up behind him and encircled his shoulders with her arm. "Not in pain anymore, you see."

Not anymore . . . was that why they had not let him in before?

David studied her features, relieved that he could still see some remaining beauty. How proud he had been of his beautiful mother at school! All of his friends had commented how lucky he was to have such a pretty mother who was also a teacher—everyone's favorite teacher at Public School 129 in Baltimore.

That was last year. Now they lived in Philadelphia, and no one knew his mother was a teacher. No one knew she had been beautiful. Now she was just sick. What was beautiful seemed to shrink and fade day by day, until David had to look very hard to see what once had been.

"Mother?" He leaned his cheek against the cool rail and wished she would open her eyes for just an instant or move her hand toward his when he talked to her. "Are you there, Mama?"

No reply. Shallow, fluttering breath.

"She is in a very deep sleep now," said Father John as he sat down again. The bed lamp reflected in the lenses of his wire glasses, hiding his eyes from David. Father John tugged at his white collar as though it were too tight around his neck.

David wondered if the man felt like he was choking, too. "Will she wake up soon?"

Why did he ask that? He knew she would not wake up. He knew. *He knew.*

The door opened behind him. The smell of sour whiskey and cigarette smoke announced the arrival of Brian O'Halloran. A muttered curse confirmed that he had not expected to see Irene like this. Not like this. It had been only two weeks since he had left on his sales route, after all.

"Look at her!" he slurred to the priest. "She's dying."

David did not turn to face his stepfather. Brian O'Halloran was drunk. He seemed not to notice David standing there between him and Irene, as if David were part of the room, part of the bed—a piece of Irene clinging to the iron bars and slowly dying with her.

"How'd she get so bad so quick?" Brian's massive shadow swayed over the bed as he took a step forward.

"Two weeks is a long time, Mister O'Halloran," said Father John gently.

Didn't Father John notice the reek of bootleg whiskey? Did he think Brian slurred his words and swayed in the center of the room because of grief? Yet Father John spoke kindly to this man—as if Brian O'Halloran had really loved Irene and David. As if his dark heart were breaking at the sight of his poor wife dying.

"I got back soon as I could," Brian shot back defensively. "Got to work to pay for this, you know." The shadow of his arm swept over the room.

David flinched as though Brian might strike him.

"Doctor bills. Hospital. Stuff like this isn't free, you know. Got back as soon as I . . ." Brian stared at Irene. "She used to be beautiful," he whispered. "Will you look—"

Father John rose slowly. "Perhaps we should talk in the hallway." He took the shadow of Brian O'Halloran out of the room.

Sister Anne came to stand beside David. Again her hand rested on his shoulder. He wanted to tell her not to touch him, because she would make him cry. But he kept his silence, and the nun did not say anything either. David was glad she did not try to make him leave. For once the fact that Brian was drunk had worked in David's favor. Father John and Sister Anne would not make David go home with his drunken stepfather.

The light from the hall shone into the room as Father John reentered. "David, I've sent . . . your father . . . home in a taxi. Perhaps it would be best if you go back to the convent with Sister Anne to sleep until morning. I'll stay with your mother."

David shook his head slowly. He touched his mother's hand. It was surprisingly warm. Still soft. The one thing about her that had not changed at all.

"Her hands are the same," David murmured, grasping her fingers and pulling her hand to his cheek. "I want to stay with her. To see her off. You know?"

Yes. They knew. He had been here every night for visiting hours. From the time the doctors said there was no changing things, they had let David come. No matter that he was a kid. They let him come and be with her every evening, and it had made this inevitable night easier to face. Last rites had already been performed.

"Well then . . ." Father John resumed his seat.

Sister Anne pulled up a chair for David to sit in. He rested his face against the bars of the bed and held his mother's hand.

Prince Davey, Irene Dunlap O'Halloran called her nine-year-old son. He waited at the bedside of his queen until, at 2:34 AM on the morning of September 25, 1929, she slipped away and left him utterly alone.

✳ ✳ ✳

It was the hour of Wall Street in New York City.

A sea of bowler hats and pin-striped suits and fine wool overcoats from London surged toward the entrances of the world's financial centers. The crowd was so dense that the street itself seemed to be moving.

At the top of the street was the delicate spire of Trinity Church, still holding its own beneath the avalanche of skyscrapers towering above it. Here was some proof of what America had come to believe: God and Mammon could, indeed, peacefully coexist.

The doors of Trinity Church were closed today. But at the base of the granite-and-glass skyscrapers, revolving doors spun like fan blades, sucking up human beings and spewing them into banks and offices and the New York Stock Exchange. Beneath the sidewalks, under the soles of perfectly shined shoes, lay vaults containing the world's largest reserve of gold. Banks brooded over the tons of ingots like old hens over their eggs. Twenty-ton gates of steel, tear gas, and jets of scalding water guarded the treasure like dragons.

It was, no doubt, the same old gold melted down from the idols of the Incas and shipped to Spain. It had been passed to the Dutch, then to the English, and somehow managed to recross the Atlantic. Now, although the faces of the ancient golden gods had been wiped away, the stuff itself was still worshipped. Here on Wall Street the effigies had changed, but rich and poor alike still bowed down before it. The eyes and hearts of all Americans—and all the world—looked to Wall Street as the new Holy of Holies. Bankers and grocers and tramcar operators read the market report as an oracle of their future. They praised its daily gains and paid their tithes to buy stocks in their dreams of prosperity.

Simply said, America was drunk on the spirit of Wall Street. God and Mammon dwelt peacefully together because Mammon had become god.

✳ ✳ ✳

A chill wind swept through the Financial District of Manhattan this morning. Max Meyer pulled up the collar of his London-tailored overcoat as he weaved through the crowd of brokers to the shoeshine stand on the sidewalk outside Sisto and Co. Bankers. Here, at No. 64 Wall Street, the buttonwood tree had stood where the first brokers had established a stock exchange in the late 1700s. Today the site was still the place where items of market news might be unofficially discussed and a lucky financial columnist might pick up bits of gossip and tips that could lead to headlines.

Max believed in luck. Part of his market-news-gathering ritual each day was to stop at the shoeshine stand of Joey Fortuna to have his shoes polished to a high sheen. At ten cents a shine and a nickel for a tip, Max was often rewarded with gossip from the twenty-two-year-old shoeblack, who had a long list of impressive customers. Joey was given tips of a different kind by his wealthy clients, and like nearly everyone else in the country, he also speculated in the market.

"So how's it going this morning, Joey?" Max hefted his foot onto the stand.

"Mornin', Mister Meyer." Joey unceremoniously smeared black goo on shoes that already glistened. "Pretty good. My next-door neighbor made a killin' on that tip Mister Keenan gave me about RCA."

"Yeah? How'd you do?"

Joey shrugged and frowned. "I shoulda done it early. Shoulda bought. It went through the roof and then down again, and I waited too long to take profits at the top. But Mister Harris from the House of Morgan says copper is the thing. Anyway, it's old Missus Fernelli who gets the dough from RCA, and I'm still dealin' in shoe polish."

"Plenty of chances," Max said with a grin, but he did not believe it. The RCA deal had been part of a large pool of wealthy buyers who had purchased thousands of shares to drive the stocks skyward. Then when the little investors had begun to buy, the pool members sold at a massive profit, and the stocks plummeted again.

"Yeah. Well, I shoulda bought RCA. Coulda made a bundle."

Max patted him on the shoulder. "You were smart to sit that one out," he consoled. "The stocks were way overvalued. Lots of little guys lost their shirts on that one."

"Well, the big operators cleaned up . . . and Missus Fernelli." Joey slapped the cloth over the shoe with a rhythm. "So what about Consolidated Copper? What do you think?"

"Steer clear of that one, too, Joey," Max advised. He knew what he was talking about. "You know what they say . . . what goes up must come down. It's too high already."

Joey scowled. "You gonna print that?"

"I already did. It's in the column this morning."

"The big boys ain't gonna like it . . . you advisin' against them." The shoeblack shook his head with the rhythm. "They're callin' you a monkey wrench in the gears around here, that's what."

"I've been called worse." Max laughed, enjoying the secondhand report about his unpopularity with certain big names in the Financial District.

Joey laughed too. "Don't I know it! I've heard you called worse plenty of times myself."

Thirty-two-year-old Max Meyer had come a long way since his childhood on Orchard Street. Wall Street was a universe apart from the poverty and squalor of the old neighborhood, yet Max had found a different variety of squalor planted firmly in the hearts and minds of the men who controlled the finances of the entire world. Manicured nails and tailored suits were a thin veneer covering ruthlessness and self-interests so profound that Max believed these men could topple the financial superstructure of America—and beyond. He often sounded these trumpet blasts of retreat in his column to the delight of the bears and the rage of the bulls of Wall Street. To many elite brokerage firms, Max Meyer's opinion was a plague akin to the Black Death. But even so, every man faithfully read his column each day.

Max had married well. His wife's family had banking connections in the highest echelons of society. Social dinners and charity balls had been his introduction to the great names of the financial world. At first suspected, then mistrusted, then accused of treachery and betrayal for his columns, Max had often peeled away the image of respectability among the wealthy manipulators. Needless to say, his stories had not gone down well at the family gatherings in Newport. Eventually, his wife had left him and had been killed in a car wreck three months later—leaving Max a widower, technically, without the taint of divorce.

His powerfully built frame turned the heads of fashionable flappers lunching at the Ritz. His dark hair and flashing brown eyes evoked whispered comments about the Rudolph Valentino of Wall Street. For the chic Manhattan women, the fact that he was not an Arab sheikh but a Jewish interloper brought up on Orchard Street did not matter much. The daughters of the rich and famous chose dinner with Max Meyer as their favorite form of rebellion against their fathers. And Max found their dinner conversation even more useful to his purposes than a chat with Joey Fortuna at the shoeshine stand.

"You sure about that Consolidated Copper mine stock?" Joey gave the right shoe a final swipe.

"Positive." Max flipped him fifteen cents. "That one's a sleigh ride, Joey. Somebody's gonna get hurt."

Max had the sense that maybe everyone in the market could get hurt. The entire market had been a sleigh ride lately, and a wild one at that. The bulls claimed it was going up like an elevator to the sky. The bears growled that it couldn't last, and they played the game accordingly. As for Max, he now had his finger on the pulse of Wall Street. With a 10 percent commission on all the Cunard Line transactions, he would make money regardless. If clients bought, he cleared a few dollars. If they sold, he made a few. Like owning a floating craps game, he got a piece of the action regardless of the winner. He was not wealthy yet, but the prospect was certainly there.

Joey looked at his coins and furrowed his brow. "Too bad about copper. I was hopin' to make it big and retire early."

"Plenty of chances." Max admired his reflection in the shoes.

"That ain't what you been writin' in that column of yours, Mister Meyer. You know they call you Chicken Little around here?" Joey gestured toward the sky, which had not fallen in spite of the grim predictions of Max Meyer. "Now you're tellin' me I got plenty of chances to strike it rich." He tossed a nickel into the air and caught it. "So? Gimme *one tip*, Mister Meyer, whadda you say? What's hot? What's goin' up? Tell me what to buy, and I'll hock my polish and sell my stand and pawn my mother's weddin' ring."

The kid was grinning, but Max knew he was serious behind the banter. Max leveled his gaze on the bootblack and shook his head. "You want a tip, Joey?"

"Yeah! There ain't a guy in New York who wouldn't buy if *you* said buy, Mister Meyer."

"Okay, here's my tip. Right off the press. Straight out of Max Meyer's financial column for the whole country. And I'm going to give it to you straight, Joey, because you shine my shoes so well every day."

Joey was nearly panting, like an eager puppy waiting for a bone. "Thanks, Mister Meyer . . ."

Max patted him on the shoulder. "My advice is—" he jerked his thumb skyward—"the sky is falling, Joey. Sooner than you think."

"Huh?"

"Stay out of the market. Keep your stand and your polish and your good sense. It's a lot more than these big-time operators are going to have when this house of cards tumbles down."

Genuinely disappointed, Joey's face conveyed a look of betrayal, as though Max really knew the direct path to wealth but simply refused to give out the secret. "If you change your mind, will you let me in on it? Will you, Mister Meyer? You hear of a sure thing—"

"I'll be sure and get my shoes shined before I make a move, Joey. And I'll let you in on the deal." Max lifted his face to the wind. "I sure will do it."

This seemed to cheer Joey a bit. A raindrop splashed on his cheek, and he gathered up the tools of his trade and dashed beneath an awning as Max crossed the street.

Max cast one glance back at the young man, wishing he honestly did have a tip to give Joey. But every sign pointed to the fact that a great storm was coming to Wall Street—a flood that could carry away both rich and poor in its current.

The shades behind the glass front doors leading into the First Petroleum Bank of Oklahoma were pulled down, as were all the window shades. The doors were locked, but taped very neatly in place was a printed card, edged in black, that read *Closed Due to Funeral*. Underneath, in small print, it added, *We are sorry for any inconvenience.*

Damon Phelps Sr. stared morosely out the window of the Cord automobile, wishing his driver had taken a different route. Coming from the graveside of his only son, did he have to be reminded that this day of official mourning was also costing him money? Phelps realized that as the chairman of the Petroleum Bank as well as the head of Phelps Petroleum, closing the bank and shutting down the rigs had been the only "right" thing to do.

Only half a day on the rigs, he thought with some satisfaction. *Those crews better be back at work right now.*

The driver pulled the Cord around to Phelps's private entrance at the rear of the bank and scurried to open the car door. Phelps scowled. The driver was wearing a black-felt armband. Everything conspired to remind him of his loss. Everything! Well, Damon Phelps Sr. was not going to let it ruin an entire business day. After an interminable parade of sympathizers had finally been ejected from their home, Phelps had told his exhausted wife that he was going for a drive to clear his head. But he had been planning to go to his office all along.

The driver unlocked the entry, then handed the key back to Phelps.

After holding the door open for his employer to enter, he returned to the car to wait. Phelps closed the door behind him and locked it carefully before turning to face his two astonished assistants.

"Mister Phelps," said Senior Vice President Tell, "we were not expecting you in today, sir. A very moving tribute, and the flowers were—"

"What's the market?" asked Phelps, gruffly cutting off the flow of sympathetic murmurs. He pushed past Tell and Assistant Vice President Penner to a table beside his oak rolltop desk, where a sheaf of paper covered with columns of figures was displayed.

Phelps caught the raised eyebrow that the tall, skinny Tell gave the short, stout Penner.

"Up all across the board," Tell reported quickly. "Consolidated Copper announced a new joint venture in Chile, and the shares are up ten dollars already from the $110 we paid last week. RCA is also moving nicely."

Phelps brushed aside the details. "Where do we stand?" That's what he really wanted to know.

It was Penner's turn to respond. "As of this moment, we are $211,000 to the good."

This was good news, particularly since only $25,000 of the original investment had come from Phelps's personal account. Tell and Penner had even less of their own money involved.

The remainder of the original $75,000 investment had come from the bank's depositors. Not that they knew about it, of course.

It had come to Phelps in a flash some months before. The market was making gigantic leaps—30 or 40 percent a year—and the depositors were only promised 3 percent on their savings. Why should the Petroleum Bank be satisfied with making only 7 or 8 percent loans when it could cash in? If only the board of directors had agreed, none of this secrecy would be necessary.

Phelps shrugged as he inspected the balance sheets and quotations. It did not really matter to him. If the stick-in-the-mud fools were left behind, so be it. There was more than one way to skin a cat. So far, Phelps and his two assistants had come up with four different ways to use the deposits of the Petroleum Bank to buy stock without asking anybody for permission. And the plan was working!

CHAPTER THREE

Devil's Backbone

SHILOH, ARKANSAS

It was difficult to tell the make and model of the automobile beneath all the household goods tied on every available surface. Tent and camp stove were tied to the hood, along with luggage and the baby's cradle. Pots and pans dangled over the left fender and clanged a warning at every rut and bump in the road. Mattresses were rolled up and tied across the cloth top.

A tall, lean man in a straw hat sat behind the wheel and peered out through the bug-splattered windshield at the same road he had left home on ten years before. Then he had been riding a horse. Now his wife sat beside him with a baby boy on her lap, two sons in the backseat, and all his worldly goods heaped on top of the 1925 Model T Ford. All in all, he made more of an impression coming home than he had made leaving.

Pungent woodsmoke mingled with the sweetness of the pines that crowded along the gravel highway. The leaves had turned early this year, promising a harsh winter. To the south, the Poteau Mountains stood rank on rank, clothed in brilliant reds and purplish reds from the dogwood, the sumac, and the black gum. The slopes of the Sugar Loaf glistened in pale yellows and golds among the stands of sycamore, hickory, and birch.

In the fields, the cotton and corn were already harvested. Pumpkins lay in bright splotches against the thin, rocky soil. Patches of wild persimmons took over the untilled fields. Possums climbed the persimmon bushes to gorge themselves on the firm ripe fruit, and little farm boys hunted them for meat and pelts.

All these pleasant memories had called the heart of Birch Tucker back home to Shiloh, Arkansas, to take up on the family farm where his father had left off when he died last spring. He was coming home from the forests of oil rigs, home from the unrelenting stench of sulphur and crude oil—crude oil in the streets, on the clothes, in the hair, in the pores of a man's skin.

Boardwalk brawls and boomtowns were no way for a man to raise a family. So Birch Tucker was bringing his wife, Trudy, home. He would teach little Tommy and Bobby and Joe how to hunt possum and how to plant corn and how to milk a cow. For ten years, Birch and Trudy had saved for this day, lived on this dream, looked forward to coming down this road and saying at the end of it, "Well, boys, we're home."

The tracks of the Rock Island Line followed the highway. A distant whistle blew, stirring the boys to hang out the side of the car as the great locomotive gained on them.

"Faster, Dad!" Tommy cried. "Don't let him beat you!"

"Come on, Dad!" Bobby joined in. "To the water tower!"

Half a mile ahead, the water tower on the Rock Island loomed above the treetops. Birch knew the train had already begun to slow for its scheduled stop to take on more water. It would be a small matter to beat the train and satisfy the boys that their father was a hero.

"Don't you speed up so, Birch!" Trudy looked panic-stricken as Birch yanked down on the accelerator level on the steering column and the car leaped over a rain-soaked rut. Pots swung up and clanged down. The baby looked surprised, then shrieked with laughter as his brothers thumped the leather seats and urged their father on faster, faster!

"He's giving up, Dad!" Tommy shouted.

"Slow down, Birch, or I swear I shall get out and . . . walk!" Trudy's face was white with anger.

Birch grinned at her and adjusted the accelerator lever for more speed as his boys whooped their approval.

"You'll kill us all, Birch Tucker! Birch! Slow down, or you will murder your family! Murder us all on the happiest day of our lives!"

"I always wanted to die happy, True," Birch called above the noise of banging utensils and groaning wheels and the shriek of the train whistle and the howling boys.

"Our things. Our stuff!" She gestured toward the flopping suitcases and flapping canvas tent. "It will all fall off! Birch! Birch! I demand that you . . . slow—"

"You're walloping him, Dad!"

"Go! Go faster! Look! He'll never catch us now."

Birch reveled in the approval of his sons—and this was only over a race with a locomotive. Just wait until he took them on their first possum hunt!

He hollered with them and ignored Trudy, who sat in rigid disapproval. Her pretty jaw set, her eyes straight ahead, she clung to the laughing baby as they were jostled off their seat to land with an undignified whump. Outnumbered, she was, by her sons and husband, who had lived too long in boomtowns where there was at least one race a day down Main Street.

"You got him! You beat him! He ain't coming on no farther! Look at that, Bobby! Look what Dad did! He broke the train, that's what! It run fit to bust, and he busted it!"

Birch straightened in the seat. He readjusted his grip on the wheel and peered out to make certain they had not left a trail of household goods down the center of the highway. Nope. Everything was intact, everything fine—except for Trudy, who had lost that pleasant, wistful homecoming look. No matter. She would get over it once she saw the house for the first time. Once she got a good look at the fields and the barns and the kitchen . . . well, True would forget all about the race with the locomotive.

Grimy little-boy hands reached up to thump Birch proudly on the back. The baby rocked on his mother's lap as an indication that this jumping of potholes was something he wanted to do again soon.

Trudy tugged his blue knitted cap down over his ears and laid the back of her hand against his ruddy cheek. "Cold as ice," she snapped. "And the faster you go, the colder the wind blows. He'll catch the croup and then—"

Birch interrupted her. "Look yonder, True." He pointed to where a single plume of smoke rose over the trees to mark some dwelling place just out of sight of the highway. "That's my cousin's place, J.D. Froelich. Our farm was—is—not far from his. Just beyond a little church and up the hill from there."

The cloud of her irritation broke and dissipated. "So close as that?"

It had been a long time since Birch had seen the fingers of smoke that rose from the hills around Shiloh. Still, he could remember the name of each family warmed by those fires. He pointed to an empty place in the sky where the Tuckers' smoke had once been. Where it would soon be again.

Just ahead the road dipped down into the James Fork Creek and reappeared on the opposite bank. Birch slowed and turned down a rutted lane flanked by barbed-wire fences and worn-out fields with traces of the summer cotton crop remaining. A covey of quail, offended by the rattle of the automobile engine, scurried across the lane and into the brush beside the creek. Here and there the road disappeared entirely beneath a thick blanket of autumn leaves. The spoked wheels churned them up and spewed them out behind the Ford in a cloud of colors.

Around a stand of trees, a broad expanse opened to the left. To the right, a well-kept Victorian-style farmhouse stood with its back steps only a few dozen yards from the James Fork Creek. The white paint was fresh and bright. The windows reflected the pastures, the trees, and the sky. A wide veranda circled the house. Trudy could make out rocking chairs flanking a small table on the porch. Two dogs rose from where they had been sleeping beneath an enormous elm tree in the front. Like the quail, they were also offended by the noisy contraption heading toward them. They bristled and barked and called for their master.

A moment later, tugging his suspenders over his red long-handles, the short, plump figure of Cousin J.D. emerged from the house and squinted at the wheeled mass of household goods swaying down the road.

"It's J.D., all right, True," laughed Birch. "But he's lost most all of his hair and got more belly on him than last I saw."

Cows in the pasture bellowed unhappily at the noise and lumbered uphill to escape it. Birch leaned far out the window, and with one finger on the steering wheel, he waved and hollered, "It's me, you old coot! Hey, J.D.! It's Birch, boy!"

A shout returned from the porch. J.D. stuck his head in the door and called for someone to join him. He shushed his dogs, who did not shush. In his stocking feet, he hurried into the yard, where he laughed and shook his head and called the name of Birch as though he could not believe the prodigal had indeed come home to Shiloh!

As Birch leaped from the car and embraced Cousin J.D., Trudy and the boys were silent and shy for the first time since they had left Oklahoma. Here was a part of Birch's life they had never shared. Had they ever seen him embrace a friend with the same joy he now embraced this stranger?

"Maybelle! Maybelle! Mayy-bellle!" shouted Cousin J.D. over his shoulder. "Get out here, woman! It's Birch! Birch done come home!"

A short, plump female scurried out of the little house. Her slightly graying hair was done up in a careless bun on top of her head. It canted off to the right, and wisps fell across her flushed face. She rushed forward to join in her husband's embrace of Birch, and all the while tears of joy streamed down her cheeks. "Glory!" she cried. And then again, "Glory be. J.D.! Do you see who this is?"

Bobby and Tommy remained in the backseat of the car, solemnly watching this demonstration between J.D., Maybelle, and their pa. All the while, their daddy had been talking about Shiloh this and Shiloh that and going hunting with J.D. for possum. But never until this moment did they ever think of Shiloh as a place actually populated with real people who knew Birch. Cousin J.D. had always been just a hero in a story, like in the books their mother read to them. Could this little, short, bald man really be the cousin who had scaled mountains and swum raging rivers and shot the biggest possums and hunted the meanest coons?

"I figured he'd be a giant," Tommy whispered.

Trudy's mouth curved in a slight smile. Indeed, the tales of Shiloh were legendary. Like Canaan of old, it was peopled with giants and blessed with milk and honey. Or so Birch had always said. And one day, Birch had promised, he would be their personal guide to this magical place.

✳ ✳ ✳

Birch had completely forgotten that he had a wife and sons watching and waiting in the car behind him. Neither J.D. nor Maybelle seemed to notice either. They took him by the arms and led him up the steps and onto the veranda.

They were within a few steps of the door when Birch came to himself and remembered that he had left this place as a bachelor, but he was returning as a husband and father.

"True!" he said, pulling away.

J.D. and Maybelle stared at him as though he had lost his mind. "True?"

"Trudy! My wife . . . and my boys." He swung around and motioned for them to tumble out of the car.

✳ ✳ ✳

J.D. and Maybelle stared curiously, politely, at the people who had drawn their own dear Birch from the familiar circle of his family.

So this is the woman . . . the one Birch married after ol' Sam threw him off his land. Well then. What do you know? And these young children are the offspring of that union. Handsome boys. Each of them. Handsome. Glory! How they all three favor Birch at that age! Astounding. Three little replicas of Birch—willowy, lanky, with fair hair and blue eyes. These three do not look even a little bit like their dark-haired, brown-eyed mother. No, not one bit. Well, well, it is easy to see that they are family!

And so the boys were readily accepted into the circle of what had been Birch's life.

Trudy, however, remained apart and hesitant. *A shy little thing,*

Maybelle observed. Birch's wife stood with a polite smile on her face as J.D. hefted each of the boys up in turn and proved that although he was short and stocky, he truly was built like a bull.

"I can tell you," J.D. said, "it's a pity your grandfather never knowed you boys! One look, and he woulda know'd your daddy made him a whole nuther batch of little Tuckers!"

Maybelle inclined her head to Trudy. "Won't you come in and warm yourself? My, it's cold this mornin'. Did you have a pleasant journey from Oklahoma?"

✳ ✳ ✳

The ridge was known by the old-timers as the Devil's Backbone. Local legend had it that old Lucifer—Satan himself—had tried to push his way up through the earth in that place and was held down by the prayers of a Methodist circuit rider. Of course, the Baptists told it a different way, and the Presbyterians yet another.

In such a matter it was best not to name denominations. The fact remained that Devil's Backbone was ten miles long from neck to tailbone. Shale and limestone poked out of the thin soil, giving the ridge an ominous appearance that made little boys pray that the devil would stay put when they passed by. Thick stands of scrub oak made it a natural home for wild turkeys and quail. And for those who were grown up enough not to be afraid of treading on Lucifer's vertebrae, it was a prime spot for the taking of game.

Sheriff Ring stood on a rocky promontory at the eastern tip of the spine. The ridge fell away into a wooden hollow cut out by a small confused creek. The world beyond was a wonder of scarlet and yellow, but the sheriff was not out this morning for the view. His A.J. Aubrey 12-gauge double-barrel shotgun was pointed at the enormous track of a bear's paw as the bloodhounds sniffed the ground for the scent of the convict they had been tracking for over a week.

"Yessir, Sheriff Ring, that convict of yours is keepin' company with old Lucifer, all right." Red Watts, the local tracker, dug at the paw print of the bear with a stick. "Leastwise, he's followin' just as close as he can git to that bear." He shook his head in amazement and then pointed to the track of a man's foot. It, too, was large. "That boy's got quite a foot on him, don't he?" He chuckled. "Big fella, is he?"

Sheriff Ring nodded once. "Big enough. Six foot five. Never could find shoes to fit him at the prison farm. He's near as big as that bear y'all call Lucifer, I reckon."

Red snorted. "Nobody's that big this side of perdition. This here is all his territory. That old bear claims the Devil's Backbone for his own. Prowls around here like he's the son of Satan. He's been known to kill a man who irritates him."

Red gave another sidelong glance at the man's footprint. "That boy we're chasin' is either mighty smart or dumber than a stone. No tellin' when old Lucifer's gonna turn on him. I seen that bear wipe out a pack of dogs with one swipe and then go after a mule. An unarmed man in chains wouldn't be nothin' for old Lucifer to whip."

He pointed to the stripped branch of a chokecherry bush. "Bear's been feedin' there." Then he gestured to a place where the grass was crushed. "That boy sat himself right there to rest and wait for Lucifer to finish breakfast. You see there? Neither of 'em was in a hurry. Bear watchin' the man. Man watchin' the bear. Then old Lucifer scratched his back against that oak over there—"

Red examined tufts of brown fur stuck to the bark. "And when he done his mornin' business, off he took. Yonder." He pointed to the ridge. "And that boy went on after him." He scratched his head. "What you reckon this convict is up to?"

"Maybe hopin' the bear will have enough and turn on the dogs. Maybe hopin' we'll be misled. Confuse the noses of the hounds. *Which scent is the bear and which is the man?* I suppose that's what he's about."

"My dogs will follow that bear to hell and back. They don't care about your convict. But if he stays behind that bear, my dogs can track him better than anythin' with four legs and a nose! I've been after that bear *three times* this summer! He's slowin' down—all fat and ready to sleep through the winter. We might just have a chance to overtake him and catch you your convict in the bargain."

Sheriff Ring eyed Red's dogs with some suspicion. They were not trained to hunt men like the posse dogs. What if they were led astray? What if they pulled the bloodhounds off the trail? "You know this country pretty good?" Ring said by way of testing.

"Better than any man around these parts, I reckon. My family's been huntin' for four generations up on this here mountain. Pappy, grandpappy, and all the way back—come in with Dan'l Boone and been huntin' ever since." He frowned at the footprint. "Ain't never hunted no man, though. That's your department. Don't reckon I care to shoot a man. If it comes to it, you can do that sort of killin' without my help. Suppose you need me, though. This place is pure perdition if a man was to get hisself lost!"

The sheriff's dogs seemed listless compared to the fresh hounds of Red Watts. Black-and-tan hounds and redbones, they snorted up the dust eagerly and wagged at Red when he said the word *dogs*.

A week on the run had worn the posse bloodhounds down. Even Old Grandee seemed uninterested in picking up the hunt again this morning. Maybe it would be good to let Red's dogs take the lead today. Stir up the blood. Make Old Grandee jealous and eager to move again.

But what would put a spark back in the sheriff's deputies? More than once since the weather turned cold, Ring had heard them mumbling about "home" and "lost causes."

"You take the lead today," Sheriff Ring said. "But mind your hounds follow the man as well as the bear. This nigger is smart. Down to his big feet, he's *smart*! He ain't followin' that bear just for company."

Red straightened up and whistled to his hounds, who sprang to attention and instantly surrounded him. A jumping, yipping mob, they awaited orders. Red took out a twist of tobacco from his leather pouch and cut a plug for himself and one for the sheriff.

"Don't you worry none about my dogs. They been hankerin' all summer to sink their teeth in the flank of the devil. They'll track old Lucifer *and* find your convict in the bargain."

CHAPTER FOUR

The Prodigal's Return

There was not an end table or windowsill in Maybelle's parlor that was not covered by photographs. Old tintypes pasted onto china plates displayed the serious faces of Birch's grandfathers and great-grandfathers. Old teak frames held images of Birch's father and mother on their wedding day. And then another of Birch with blond curls, looking like a girl on his mother's lap. Then there was the brother, Robert.

"And this here is who you was named for," J.D. said proudly as he passed the serious photo to little Bobby. "Always said it was a good thing to name a child after somebody in the family who died young. Keeps the name goin', if y'all follow my meanin'."

Everyone did follow his meaning. Bobby looked solemnly at the face of his dead uncle and shuddered.

Tommy piped up. "Baby Joe is named for my Grandpa Joe who lives in Montreal. But he ain't dead. He just moved out of Fort Smith because he said folks there was backward bigots, and he went north to open another store."

Trudy flushed at the unwelcome revelation of her father's opinion of Fort Smith. She smiled and shrugged, nudging Tommy, who took it as a signal to continue, even though it was not.

"Now me? I'm named after a hero. Yessir."

J.D. seemed interested. "Well, that's nice. But I always figured your daddy was gonna name one of his kids after me. J.D.—Jefferson Davis. After the Confederate president, that's who I'm named after. But they call me J.D. for short."

"Is that 'cause you're so short?" Bobby asked.

Birch nudged Bobby. "No, it ain't," he shushed him.

Tommy beamed, the center of attention. "Part of my name is Jefferson, too."

"You don't say!" J.D. puffed up with pride. "Well now, Birch. That's right good to—"

"But I ain't named after the Confederate president nor anybody else except Thomas Jefferson Canfield. My daddy knew him in the war, and he was the biggest hero, too. Won the French Legion of Honor, and he was a preacher. He might be dead. White folks run him off, my daddy said—"

Maybelle's eyes bugged. "*White folks?* You don't mean he's a . . ."

J.D. was frowning, as if he'd just realized that, in spite of the Jefferson part of his own name, he had been passed over in the naming of Cousin Birch's sons. "You didn't name this child for a . . . Nigra?"

Well, this was just almost too much, Trudy could tell. J.D. snapped his suspenders and rocked back on his heels. Maybelle scurried off to fix the tea, and Trudy sent the boys out to play in the yard.

Tommy poked his head back in the door. "I got a picture of him, too, gettin' his medal in the war. He ain't short like you, I reckon. Big as a bear." The door clicked shut on Tommy's proud face.

J.D. spent the next several minutes straightening all his family photographs, with his back to Trudy. By the time he turned toward her, he had somehow managed to fix a smile on his lips.

At his invitation, she and Birch followed him into the kitchen.

It was as pretty a kitchen as Trudy had seen in a long while—like something out of a Sears and Roebuck catalogue. Above the sink a window looked out toward the James Fork Creek. Through the glass pane, the rush of the water sounded soft and peaceful.

Like kittens lapping milk from a saucer, Trudy thought.

The men rambled on in a boisterous way. They talked and laughed about this old memory or that. Birch asked about skinflints and bent old men he remembered hobbling into the church. Some had passed away, but many, surprisingly, were still hobbling on or rooted in their pews or tilling the soil of the land where they had once been young like Birch.

Mostly, it seemed to True, folks in Shiloh lived to be old—unless they died very young or were killed in an accident or a war.

Maybelle heated the kettle for Trudy to have tea. For Birch and J.D. she made a fresh pot of strong coffee. Maybelle's real name was May-Belle, she explained as she poured the tea. And then she waited for Trudy to pronounce it properly, just so there would not be a misunderstanding. When Trudy repeated it, Maybelle raised her eyebrows slightly at the faint hint of a foreign accent.

"Well," she said. "It don't matter, just so long as you spell it right. M-A-Y, like the month. And B-E-L-L-E . . ." Here she giggled and plumped her wispy hair. "Like a Southern belle, don't you know?" With that announcement, Maybelle shifted her attention instantly to the men's conversation. "Old Man Potts? He done jumped down a well and killed hisself."

"But why?"

"Who can say? Got mad at his kids over somethin' and wrote a note tellin' them where he could be found. Sure enough . . ."

Trudy watched through the kitchen window as Tommy and Bobby went exploring by the creek. They were framed like a picture in blue calico curtains as they picked their way down to the edge of the stream, where a rock dam had been built and a water pump installed to bring water right up to the house.

Trudy was grateful to watch her sons and imagine them with cane fishing poles over their shoulders come summer. Baby Joe was sound asleep on a quilt in the sitting room. The warmth of the house after the long, breezy drive had almost instantly lulled the child to sleep.

And so Trudy sipped her tea, careful not to scald her mouth. She tuned out the raucous laughter of the family reunion and contented herself to sit in such a wonderful kitchen. It had been so long since she had enjoyed even a moment of this kind of luxury.

Her eyes lingered on the blue china cups hanging from little hooks beneath the shelves where real china plates and bowls and saucers were stacked. Such plates were acquired one by one from the peddler's wagon of the Jewel Tea Company. Trudy had never seen so many matching pieces all together on one shelf. Maybelle had been buying tea for a long time.

Trudy lifted the cup and inhaled the steamy aroma. Maybe now that they had a real home, she could collect her own set of china from the tea peddler. Maybe ten years from now some young mother would stop by the house where she and Birch lived and would sip Jewel tea and admire Trudy's collection.

On the opposite wall was an enormous Wherle wood-burning cookstove. Six-holed, blue-polished and nickel-plated, it had a warming oven in the top and a hot-water reservoir to the side. It was, like the kitchen, a thing of beauty. Trudy imagined the cooking of jams and the canning of vegetables and using all six burners at the same time to create a feast surpassing any other.

Birch's voice penetrated her daydream. "That stove, Maybelle. Did you go and talk this old miser into finally buyin' you a stove like Mother's?"

There was a nervous laugh, a shifting of weight in the pressed-back oak kitchen chairs.

"Well . . ." J.D. chuckled like a woodpecker hammering a soft post. "Since you wasn't here, Birch . . . I mean, there wasn't nobody else to help your daddy when he was failin'. And so . . . Maybelle, you know . . . she took care of him, and he . . . well, he willed her your mama's kitchen things." He gestured toward the stove. And then the table and chairs. And last of all toward the Jewel Tea china plates and cups and saucers.

The smile on Birch's face was still intact. Of course. That was only right. After all, Maybelle had treated the old man like one of her own family.

"Nobody ever collected as many plates as your mama did," Maybelle said.

Trudy saw something in her husband's eyes that Maybelle and J.D. did not see. He fixed his gaze on the china and blinked hard.

"She was proud of that china," Birch said. He did not ask what was left of the kitchen in the old house. Trudy could see that he was a bit surprised, but it was only right. Yes. He squared his shoulders and gazed out the window at the boys and smiled.

"Well now," J.D. continued with renewed courage, "things at your old place ain't what they was, Birch. You shouldn't expect that they are."

The smile on Birch's face wavered. "I've been gone a long time. I wasn't welcome in my father's house, as you know. Ten years is a long time. Lots of water gone down the James Fork since then."

"The house is still standin'," J.D. began awkwardly.

That was the good news, Trudy supposed.

Maybelle joined in. "But your daddy didn't work the fields for three years since he was smitten. And the house . . . well . . . he sort of let it go. Sold off the furnishings one piece at a time. The mules and the equipment, too. But he didn't die in debt. Paid for the funeral in advance, he did. And not owin' any man a penny."

Another exchange of looks.

J.D. took over. "The house'll bear fixin'. The fields are about grown up with persimmons and scrub-oak saplings. You know about them things." A shrug. "But you own it all now, Birch."

"Delbert Simpson is bank manager now. Maybe you can get yourself a loan on the place for the livestock and such." Maybelle said this with a falsetto voice that quavered until she cleared her throat. It was plain to see that she and J.D. had been dreading giving Birch the full story.

"We will not be needing a loan," Trudy said firmly.

Maybelle and J.D. blinked in surprise. "Oh?" they asked at the same instant.

"We've been savin'," Birch explained. "True has been savin'. We wanted to buy a place. Would have done it, too, even if this hadn't happened. . . ." Birch looked proudly at Trudy. "Show 'em, True. Go on— show 'em what we got."

Trudy hesitated. She looked past the blue curtains and wished she were out with her boys at the creek. "Birch . . ."

"Go on," Birch insisted. "Take it out. Show 'em how much we saved. They're family . . . same as the boys."

There were curious, hard smiles fixed on the faces of J.D. and Maybelle as Trudy took the envelope from her handbag and pulled out a black leather-bound savings passbook. She laid it on the table beside her teacup. She did not nudge it toward the couple even when they crowded in to see the amount printed neatly in the last column.

"Whew! Birch! Birch, boy!" exclaimed J.D. "Near two thousand dollars you got there!"

Maybelle studied Trudy with cautious respect. "I been told you people are clever with money, but this is more than I would have expected."

J.D. roared his loudest laugh. He thumped his hands on the table. "Tell me the truth, now. Have you been bootleggin'?"

Trudy straightened in her chair. "He has not! He *earned* it. Saved it. Twelve hours a day in the oil fields." The indignation was thick in her voice, the foreign accent easily discernible.

"There now—" J.D. was still laughing—"no offense meant. Call her off, Birch. I can tell you got you a real stern character here."

Trudy blushed. She wished she had not defended Birch's honor. J.D. was only joking. No need to be insulted. After all, he was family. He had cared for Birch's father and taken care of business. No doubt he deserved the stove and the china.

"Come Monday we will transfer this to National Bank in Hartford." Birch glossed over the flare-up. "And we can start all new. Livestock and kitchen stove and whatever else."

"I've got that good team of your daddy's. The grays. They're a matched pair. A lot of good years left in them if you'd like to buy. . . ."

A flash of resentment flickered in Birch's eyes. Trudy watched him carefully. He tapped his fingers on the tabletop, a sure sign of irritation. J.D. and Maybelle did not know this about him. They chatted on about the team of mules without regard to the drumming fingers and the questions Trudy knew were playing in Birch's head.

"Well now," Birch said. "I just don't think so. Those two was gettin' up in years when I left home ten years ago. By now they must be among the halt and the blind."

"I'd give you a good price," J.D. offered.

"What did you pay for them?"

"Well . . . I took 'em off your daddy's hands. Fed 'em for free . . . it seemed only right. . . ."

Birch smiled. "I'll pay you whatever you paid my daddy for the mules, if you still got the bill of sale. Other than that, I don't relish the idea of feedin' a couple of old-timers who must be near thirty years old."

Another laugh from J.D. "I always was too good-hearted. Didn't want to see them mules goin' down from neglect. So I brought 'em here."

"I don't want them," Birch said quickly, but there was a sudden stiffness in his posture.

After they'd collected the baby and the boys from the creek, Trudy and Birch packed them all in the car once again.

Birch thumped J.D. on the back. "Good to see you, J.D.," he said, smiling just as if everything were all right.

But as Trudy got in the car, she knew different. She had seen the drumming fingers. Birch was hers, after all. These people might have known him when he was a child, but they had forgotten about the fingers. They had forgotten the way Birch kept right on smiling at an adversary, right up until he landed the first punch. Pats and thumps and handshakes aside, there was blood in his eye.

Trudy watched him scan J.D.'s fields for livestock and look into the open barn door at farm machinery. She noted how his gaze lingered on one thing and then another, and she knew these things were familiar to him.

As the car clattered away, they all waved as if this were the warmest, most perfect welcome a prodigal son had ever had.

But Trudy knew the truth from the way Birch's head was tilted to one side and the way he set his jaw as they drove past the team of old mules in his cousin's pasture. She put her hand on his arm as if to say, *"Steady now, Birch. Remember the boys. . . ."*

He nodded in reply and shrugged, grateful that she understood everything without being told. Then he shifted gears and pointed to the banks of the James Fork.

"That's the best fishing hole in Arkansas, boys," he called to his sons. "Catfish nearly big as this automobile."

Tommy and Bobby scrambled to peer at the rocks where the creek tumbled down into a broad pool. "Ain't no catfish that big, Dad," Bobby admonished his father.

"When I was your age, they seemed that big to me." And then Birch began a long recital of fishing in that very hole with Cousin J.D. and his brothers. "And skinny-dipping in the summertime!" He pointed to where a mossy rope hung from the branches of a water oak at the edge of the creek.

Trudy knew Tommy and Bobby were imagining themselves swinging far over the water and then letting go at the highest arc. In their minds, they had come to paradise—the Eden of boyhood, where their father had grown up.

Trudy glanced over her shoulder at the enraptured expressions of her sons. They did not see—could not know—the pain that mingled with the joy of this homecoming. The prodigal had returned, but there would be no father waiting to embrace him.

The road curved gently, following the sweep of the creek. Just ahead and to the left was a small white building surrounded by buggies and buckboards and a few automobiles. The clamor of singing voices and a wheezing organ drifted over a forest of headstones in the cemetery beside the building.

"Circuit rider's here this week." Birch slowed a bit, and for a moment, Trudy thought he would stop. The music called to her heart:

"'I come to the garden alone while the dew is still on the roses. . . .'"

Trudy watched as Birch's eyes swept the markers in the cemetery for a new stone, the place where his father was buried. He would not speak of such things to his sons, Trudy knew, but sadness flashed across his face. Not all stories had happy endings.

"What's this place, Dad?" Tommy's eyes scanned the living forms through the windows even as Birch searched the silent congregation in the graveyard.

"A church," Birch said as if it had never been *his.* "Shiloh Methodist Church." He raised his arm to point beyond the church to where the road forked. There was so much he could not talk about. Not now, anyway. But Trudy knew the unspoken things in her husband's heart.

The singing followed them as they chugged past. Faces swiveled from songbooks to look and wonder who was going by. Trudy did not raise her hand to wave, even though the urge was strong. She would know them all soon enough, and they would know that Birch Tucker had brought his family back home to the old place. They would no doubt comment that they had witnessed the homecoming on a Sunday morning.

Birch guided the car up the right fork in the road. He had told Trudy all about this place. Up a hill to the left was the general store. Far distant across the James Fork was the Shiloh Baptist Church. The clouds broke for an instant, and a beam of sunlight shone down on its white-clapboard walls and steep green-shingled roof. There were no buggies tied around the church. Apparently their circuit-riding preacher was in some other little church this morning. They passed the red building of

Shiloh school next, and the boys stared at the empty structure and deserted playground with apprehension.

So this was Shiloh. Small farms and neat houses. A schoolhouse. Two rival churches and a general store with post-office boxes tucked in between the cracker barrels and the sardine cans. It was just as Birch had described it, as though he had carried a picture in his mind of the buggies around the church and the sun breaking through the clouds just as he turned up the fork. Half a mile farther, Trudy knew, they would come to a rise. At the top of the hill was the home Birch had loved. The home Birch had tried to return to . . . but his father had been too bitter, too drunk.

Again he glanced at her, and she saw everything in his eyes. It was too late for Birch and his father. All his hopes of reconciliation lay buried back in the graveyard of Shiloh Methodist Church. Crumpled letters on the floors of a dozen shacks in a dozen boomtowns had never been mailed. Would Birch have been welcomed home again if he had sent those letters? There was no way of knowing now.

"*Too late,*" the engine of the Ford seemed to say. "*Too late. Too late. Too late.*"

When the grade of the road reared up before them, Birch pulled to the side. The house was at the top of this hill and around the bend. For a minute Trudy wondered if he would turn around and leave this place without making the final climb to his boyhood home.

He swallowed hard, then mastered his emotion. "Out, boys. I'll race you home."

Bobby and Tommy tumbled out and took their marks while Birch swung the car around so he could back it up the hill. There was no other way to get the old Ford up the slope. The gas tank was beneath the front seat, and attempting to drive forward up a steep hill meant that the fuel would not flow to the engine.

Birch hung out the window and slid the gear into reverse. Trudy shouted for the race to begin, and the boys disappeared up the hill and around the bend before Birch had driven even halfway up.

The road at the top of the hill was too narrow to turn around, so Birch drove the last fifty yards to the house in reverse.

Tommy and Bobby were already on the wide veranda of the deserted house by the time Birch pulled onto the gravel drive. They peered into the dirt-caked windows and exclaimed at the bigness of the empty rooms inside.

Birch sat quietly watching them. Trudy was grateful that the boys were on the porch. That someone living and familiar and smiling was calling out joyfully to Birch from the deserted and hollow-looking place.

Birch set the brake and switched off the ignition. He clasped his hands over the steering wheel and sighed. "J.D. was right," he muttered. "It will bear fixin', all right." He shrugged apologetically. "It wasn't this way when I was a boy, True. Looks like she ain't had a coat of paint since I left."

Trudy took in the old house at a glance: Victorian—one story, with steep gables and a wide, covered porch all around. A stone foundation, with white paint peeling everywhere. The screen door hung from one hinge at the top, and weeds grew where flowers must have been planted once. Dead leaves covered the roof and filled the corners of the porch. But the walls were straight. The ridgepole of the roof was level. Not one window was broken out.

The house was situated on a hill that sloped into a broad valley flanked by the James Fork Creek on the far side. From the creek a thick wood climbed low hills and finally swept into the scarlet mountains beyond. A thick stand of birch trees marked the south boundary of the farm.

While Birch gazed forlornly at the big empty barn and the broken chicken coop, Trudy took in the sweep of the fields and the clouds as they scudded across the tops of the mountains. Was there ever a place as beautiful as this?

"Oh, Birch!" she cried. "It is everything you said it was and more."

He frowned. "It's a broken-down—"

"A real home for us! A real home for the boys!" It was everything they had saved for all these years. Everything she had dreamed of through ten years of oil towns. With two thousand dollars they could buy paint, tools, shingles for the roof, a milk cow and mules, and a plow to work the lower field in cotton. They could put everything right again in no time!

Bobby and Tommy spread their arms like little birds in flight and leaped from the porch. "Look! Lookit here, Dad!" They ran to where a swing hung from the low branch of a hickory tree. Together they jumped on it and swung high.

"My daddy put that up for me and my brother, Bobby," Birch said, never taking his eyes from the boys. His mouth curved in a smile at last. "Ah, Trudy. It was good here, I tell you. It really was."

"And it will be again," she insisted. "Don't worry, Birch. We've come home now, just like you always wanted."

CHAPTER FIVE

Bear Hunt

It was slow going for Sheriff Ring and the posse in the Poteau Mountains. The biggest hound, Old Grandee, snuffled at the dust purposefully, while the younger dogs whined and worried through the brush flanking each stagnant pool.

Sooner or later, Sheriff Ring knew, the convict would make a mistake. Just one heel mark on the soft bank of the dry creek, one broken cottonwood branch or scrap of fabric on a bramble bush. Nothing else would be needed to confirm that Cannibal had passed this way.

But there was no sign. No scent. No clue. After a time the patches of water broadened and deepened into a real stream. At the end of his tether, Old Grandee pulled the sheriff through the middle of the tiny creek as he swept the exposed rocks for the convict's scent.

The sheriff's feet were cold and wet inside his boots, but he would not give up. He was a white man in oiled boots chasing down a black convict with bare feet. He would not be outsmarted or outrun!

He had heard the stories of his grandfather, a bounty hunter who tracked down runaway slaves in the old days. The old man had recited every clever trick and deception practiced by the forefathers of the man Ring now tracked. There had been times when the runaways kept pushing on until they dropped dead in their tracks. In the end, it was the bounty hunter who remained standing. He would cut off the ears of the dead slave and take them back to the plantation owner with the tale: "That nigger would not be brought back alive. You're better off with him dead. Tack his ears up on the barn door for the others to see. You'll not have any others runnin' off."

Sixty years later, Sheriff Ring was practicing the same methods his grandpappy had used. Mostly patience and perseverance were what was needed in such a case. Sooner or later the Cannibal would step wrong. He would sit down on a stump and give up, or he would die. Either way, Sheriff Ring intended to carry on the tradition his granddaddy had begun. In the end, the white man in boots would put his foot on the neck of the barefooted black fugitive.

The house felt as if it had been empty for a hundred years.

Birch stood in the center of the front room and stared hard at the marks on the bare board floors where table legs and chairs had stood.

It must have been a beautiful place once, Trudy thought as she studied the blue-floral print on the cracking wallpaper. *It must have been as beautiful as Maybelle's kitchen.* She could imagine tea being served in the blue china cups and the sweet aroma of Jewel tea brewing.

Squares where pictures had hung on the walls were still bright and clean-looking, in contrast to the faded paper.

Birch did not speak as he let his eyes move from empty square to empty square and then to a corner where a bookshelf or a small china hutch might have stood.

"It must have been real pretty here, Birch," Trudy said, shifting baby Joe on her shoulder.

"When Ma was alive . . ." He frowned at a patch of wallpaper where her picture must have been. "You know, I never thought about it. Never noticed the pictures or where the sofa was. If you'd asked me yesterday where everythin' was, I couldn't have rightly said. But now, Trudy . . . there's nothin' left here at all, but I see everythin' so clear!"

He walked slowly toward the kitchen. His boots made prints in the thick dust left behind by a summer without habitation. He crossed his arms and stood framed in the doorway, as though he could go no farther. His shoulders hunched forward as he shivered.

Trudy joined him at the threshold. She was startled by the forlorn little space that had once held the grand stove and the Jewel Tea china. "It was good to see the things at your cousin's house. Good to know what it was like here . . . before." She tried to sound cheerful in the face of Birch's anguish.

"Me and my brother bought that stove for Mother. Ordered it right out of the Sears and Roebuck. Shipped it from St. Louis and picked it up ourselves to save two dollars' shipping." He gave a short, bitter laugh.

"We hauled it up here in the wagon . . . just a couple of years before I left for the war."

Baby Joe was stirring, threatening to wake up. And where would Trudy put him when he did? One minute on this floor, and he would look as if he had tumbled down a mountain. "We'll have to sweep, Birch," she said in a businesslike voice, pulling him back from the edge of melancholy. There was so much to do.

Birch seemed almost grateful for this yank back to the present. "Now I'm glad you made me pack everything. I'd have left the broom behind, and then what?"

He turned abruptly and strode onto the porch. Outside, Bobby and Tommy were hollering down the well. Birch warned them not to run off. There was work to do before their new home would be fit to live in. Before they could even move the cots and mattresses through the door, the house would have to be swept clean, he told them in a fatherly voice.

They both replied with a polite, "Yessir." And then as he rummaged for the broom, they continued hollering their names down the well.

Birch held the broom over his shoulder like a soldier's rifle as he joined his sons and gestured to the Poteau Mountains on the far side of the valley. "Now listen to this," he said as though the echo in the well were nothing at all. He cupped his hands around his mouth and shouted, "Birch! Come hooome!" And then the mountains echoed the cry back to him a dozen times. *Come home . . . come home. . . .*

The boys looked at their father in awe. The secrets he knew about this place!

He pointed as the last echo faded away. "You gotta aim right over yonder, boys. Right in that little holler. It'll call back to you."

Trudy sat on the front step and nursed baby Joe while Birch swept the floor clean for a start.

The boys stood on the brow of the hill beside the broken chicken coop and shouted their names and vied for who could get the most echoes out of one shout. *"Tom-my! Tom-my! Tom-my-my-my! Bobby! Bob-by! Bob-by-by-by!"*

Never once did Birch call the boys away from their idle play. That was the difference, Trudy knew, between Birch and his own father. The boyhood of her husband had been no boyhood at all. From the time he was seven, Birch had been in the fields, guiding the mules while his father held the plow steady behind. The row of birch trees had served as his markers to keep the furrows straight. If Birch led the mules off even a fraction, he paid for it by picking his own birch stem and bending over a stump to receive lashes. When the cotton bolls were white for harvest, Birch dragged a long cotton sack down the rows with the stoop-backed men.

No, Birch had never been a boy, but he had told Trudy that he was determined his sons would be everything he had not been allowed to be. So together, he and Trudy scrubbed the floor with lye soap and corn shucks until every trace of stain was bleached away and the place smelled of disinfectant.

And all the while, as Birch listened to the laughter of his sons outside, he chuckled along quietly as though he were out there with them. Now stooped on hands and knees beside the soapy bucket, Birch's boyhood heart was shouting echoes into the hollow.

The stillness of the woods exploded.

Across the slopes of the Poteau Mountains, underbrush crashed and dry leaves crackled as the line of men and dogs advanced. Two dozen snarling hounds strained against their leads and dragged their cursing, puffing masters along behind.

The scents of bear and convict blended into the smell of a single beast to be tracked down and ripped to pieces.

Red Watts's hounds had hunted in these same woods a hundred times. When they lay beneath the porch and dreamed dog dreams, they twitched and yipped through visions of this place. Apparitions of possums, raccoons, and deer made them growl in their sleep, but when the image of the great bear appeared, they woke up ready to fight. This morning they took the lead, making the posse's hounds look like a pack of tourists following after.

The bear, which had been quick and lean all summer, was slower now. Fat and sleepy, he lumbered through the underbrush. He could not scent the hounds or the man smell downwind. He paused to tug the chokecherry limbs down to his mouth, then let the tree snap back upright without ever seeing that another creature was watching. Behind him, a black bearlike man in chains paused when Lucifer paused, always cautious of the direction of the wind. . . .

The man, not the bear, first sensed the approach of the hounds. While the wind was still in his face, he turned and looked down the slope as the forest seemed to stir across a front. Birds rose, disturbed by something unfamiliar. When the man in chains was certain of what was coming, he stepped upwind of old Lucifer. He waved his arms and crashed the iron cuffs together like cymbals.

Lucifer's great head swiveled, his small black eyes staring at this unpleasant interruption. A man. Dark and ragged, lean and wild, flapping like a scarecrow in a garden. Strong with a smell only half human, as if he had smeared himself with the droppings of a bear. . . . Lucifer snorted a warning and raised one paw.

The chains crashed louder. "Git! Git! Hoo-wee! Git on, ol' granddaddy! Git on back the way you come! Go on! Go back the way we come up! You don't smell 'em yet, but the hounds is comin'! Go fight 'em! Git!"

This man-thing blocked Lucifer's path. Where had it come from? Had it spoiled all the chokecherry trees up ahead? The bear snarled and growled, waving both paws. The man-thing backed away. Still upwind, his scent offended Lucifer's senses. Another snort. The bear lowered himself on his haunches, then turned from the stinking man-thing and his chains. There were lots of berry bushes back down the trail that Lucifer had passed up. Plenty to eat without being bothered by this noisy creature.

Lucifer sniffed and turned away. Lumbering back the way he had come, he could smell the odor of the man-thing wafting on the wind behind him. The scent drove him directly into the line of approaching men and hounds.

CHAPTER SIX

Sunday Visit

It was Sunday morning all right, but David O'Halloran had not gone to church. Still in his pajamas, he lay on his bedroom floor and read the comics in the Sunday paper.

He thought for just a moment about working on his stamp collection. His mother had taught him how to sort and label and organize stamps in his stamp album. She had shown him how to read postmarks, and her excitement about foreign stamps and the exotic lands they conjured had rubbed off on him.

Then he shook his head as if to clear his mind of the unwelcome idea. The stamp collection represented his mother's life. Her death was too close, too raw. Maybe later he would go back to the stamps. Maybe someday. But not today. Not now.

Maybe somewhere far away his mother was scowling down at him and chiding him with voiceless words for skipping Mass, but he did not feel guilty. He had no ride to church. Brian O'Halloran was in the next room, sleeping off his hangover. He had not been sober since Mama died. David thought his stepfather's binge was just an excuse to stay drunk. The good Irish cops on the beat would not haul him in for drunkenness. They would look at Brian with pity and tell themselves the poor man's wife had just died, and what else was Brian to do in order to forget his sorrows?

There had been a fine wake for Irene. Toasts were read and glasses raised to her short life and her memory. But David knew the truth of it. No one here in Philadelphia had really known her at all. Maybe only David knew her. At least he knew enough to know that she would not like it that he missed Mass this morning. She would have wanted him to find his way to church even if Brian was too drunk to take him.

The hoots and whistles and wheezes of Brian's snoring told David that it might be a long time before he woke up. Until then, David had an odd sense of exhilaration about his freedom. There was no one to tell him what to do. No Mrs. Crowley, no Father John . . . just himself and the Sunday funny papers. He slurped down half a glass of milk and took an enormous bite from the peanut-butter sandwich he had fixed himself for breakfast. He chewed with his mouth open just because he could do it, and there was no one to tell him not to.

So this was what it was like to be half an orphan. He glanced angrily at the wall that separated him from Brain. Since Brian was not his real dad, didn't that make David a full orphan, with all the rights and freedoms due a kid who had no real parents to love him and boss him around? He wished that Brian were back on the road again, out of his life altogether. If David had to be lonely, it was something he wanted to do without Brain O'Halloran around. Better to be altogether alone than to have to hide the dreadful loneliness from a man who would only ridicule him for it.

But here he was, thinking again instead of reading. He got up and went to the window. All the trees in the neighborhood had turned. Oranges and golds stood out against the slate gray sky. Leaves rained down to cover the ground like a lumpy brown skin. Up the block he could see Marty Davis and his sisters raking the leaves with their father. They heaped them into a pile, then ran and squealed and jumped, scattering the leaves. David watched them do it over and over. He smiled as he watched, imagining what it would be like . . . remembering what it had been like just last autumn with his mother.

He wished that she would have waited until winter to die. Winter made the world a sort of blank page. Cold and white, it did not make a boy think about the colors of leaves raked up in a pile. She should have waited until the world was not so beautiful. Another month, and the world would have been as cold and still as she was. He had prayed that she would wait just one more month to die, but she had not waited. God had not heard his prayer, and he felt cheated somehow. Why was the world so beautiful when she was gone? How was it that families still played in the leaves and went to church and kept on as if nothing at all had happened?

David caught his own reflection in the mirror. Why did he look the same when he was half an orphan? Glancing at the open newspaper, he was vaguely surprised that he could still read the comics and enjoy them. His mother had been buried only a few short days before. Had he actually smiled? Was he so heartless that he longed to go out and romp through the leaves this morning?

He did not know what was expected of him; how he should act or what he was supposed to feel. He felt numb and pained in turns, like when his hands got numb from making snowballs and then hurt as they started to warm up again.

Nothing made sense. He wished his mother were here so he could ask her what he was supposed to do now. But if she were here, there would be no question to ask.

Brian moaned and coughed—a sure sign he was waking up. David dressed hurriedly and carefully replaced the comics in the newspaper as though he had not read them. Brian hated it when anyone touched the paper before he did. To read the Sunday paper before Brian was a sure guarantee of a beating if David was caught. He placed it on the kitchen table and, grabbing his baseball and mitt, slipped out the back door, careful not to let the screen slam shut. Noise in the morning was another invitation for Brian to use his belt, especially after he had guzzled so much booze.

David walked carefully through the leaves, trying not to crunch them under his shoes. It was amazing the things Brian O'Halloran could hear when he had a bad hangover: loud breathing, chewing cornflakes, scooting a chair over the kitchen floor. The list was endless and probably included walking across dry leaves on the lawn. Brian would be happier if David was out of the house, David knew.

Like a little ship bobbing toward a lighthouse, David found himself moving directly toward Marty Davis and the enormous heap of maple leaves. Up the block, Ralph "Oink" Johnson rounded the corner and raised his hand to hail David.

Then Oink's face clouded. David knew what his friend was thinking. Maybe it was not polite to holler at a fella whose mom was freshly dead.

So David shouted, louder than usual, "Hiya, Oink!" Just like nothing unusual had happened last week.

Oink looked shocked at first. He scratched his big round face and half smiled. "Well . . . hi . . . David. Whatcha doin' out?"

David looked longingly at the heap of leaves. "No school today. You wanna do somethin'?"

Marty Davis stood staring at him, holding the rake motionless just above the leaves as if David were a ghost, or as if David had died instead of his mother. As if David should not look so *normal.* . . .

"Hiya, Marty," David said in his most cheerful voice.

Marty replied with a very soft "Hello."

The heads of Marty's parents leaned together for a moment. They were talking about David with sad, buzzing voices. Then, very cheerfully, they both spoke at once. "Good morning, David. Would you like to help with the raking?"

Brian O'Halloran never once poked his head out of the house to see where David might be. If he had done so, he would have seen David talking, whooping, jumping, and raking, just like all the other kids. And if Brian had sat on the porch with the Davises, he would have heard them whisper, as David did, "Poor child. He just does not realize what has happened. . . . Can't understand about his mother . . . certainly taking it well. . . ."

David hooted and laughed and jumped harder than the others. But the whole time he wished his mother were near to tell him how he was *supposed* to act. How he was *supposed* to feel. Sometimes he saw the other kids looking at him strangely, almost fearfully.

Even though he was smiling and laughing, David was hating the day, hating the colors, and hating the kids who still had moms waiting for them at home.

Birch rigged the small camp stove in the front parlor, running the stovepipe up through the chimney. The crackle of the fire and the sweet woodsmoke made the old house seem more welcoming somehow—more like home, filled with ten thousand fresh memories.

Fanning the kindling, Birch studied the tongues of flame. The little stove had warmed them at a hundred campsites, and he had never once let himself dream that he would build a fire here in this room. This place. Home. This was fire enough to warm this one room tonight. They could all sleep in here, snuggled down beneath the quilts.

He closed his eyes and imagined what his mother might have said to see them here. *"Glory be, Birch! I'm so proud of these grandchildren! You done so good, Son!"* How she would have loved to see them all together in this room! How she would have fussed over Trudy and the boys!

The thought made him smile . . . and also raised a lump in his throat. Birch had not missed his mother this badly in all the years since she died.

As though she had heard his thoughts, Trudy came quietly to where he knelt and placed her hand on his shoulder. Then she handed him his Bible. The pages fell open to a sealed envelope containing the last letter Birch's mother had written him. Ten years had passed since she died, but he had never opened the letter. It marked Psalm 91, her favorite passage. A dozen times through the years, when things had seemed hopeless, Birch had opened his Bible with the intention of reading the letter.

Instead he had always found himself reading the psalm and finding his comfort there. And so his mother's last words to him remained sealed, like gold in a bank account that he refused to spend unless even his faith ran dry.

"Don't you have a visit to make?" Trudy's voice was soft, treading lightly around the tender places in his heart.

"I reckon so." He touched the envelope addressed to PFC Birch Tucker from when he was in the trenches in France. "How'd you know what I was thinkin' of?"

"I have been thinking about her since we came through the door. Thinking what a grand woman she must have been to have raised a man like you." She stroked his shoulder.

"Ten years, and the best I've done for you and the boys is a rented house, boomtowns, and—" He gestured toward the camp stove. "Not much she could be proud of, I'm afraid."

"Oh, Birch! I'm not talking about *things*. I'm talking about *you*! And she *would* be proud! And proud of our sons." Trudy knelt beside him. "Ten years she's been waiting for her son to come home. And now you're here, and just listen. . . ." She leaned against him as the voices of their boys and the creak of the swing brought life into the house.

"Ten years. It don't seem so long ago, does it, True? But it's a big part of a lifetime. So much can happen. It's hard to believe that she was gone before the boys were even born . . . before I ever met you."

"Hmmm. She would have loved this . . . the boys out there in the yard," Trudy said wistfully.

"And she would have loved you." He touched her cheek. "Funny. I have always imagined that somehow she had met you. That she held our babies and had such joy from my family. I keep forgettin' how long she's been gone. I don't think I really knew how long until we got here this mornin'. Now I'm lookin' around and rememberin' how it used to be . . . the good times before Pa took to the drink. We had everythin' growin' up here. We've missed so much, you and me and the boys, movin' from place to place. And all along, *home* was right here. If only Pa could have . . ."

Birch placed another stick of wood on the fire and waited for it to blaze up.

"We've had one another." Trudy's brown eyes warmed him, easing the ache.

"I reckon we have some catchin' up to do."

"Your heart has some catching up to do right now, Birch. I saw the way you looked out over the churchyard and wondered where your mother was. Go on now. It's all right. Go find her and sit for a while.

I have lots to do here. Go tell her you've come back to the place your heart never left."

And so Birch trudged the mile back down the deserted lane to Shiloh Church. Without the noisy rattle of the Model T engine, Birch could hear the soft rushing of the James Fork Creek on his left and the clear call of a covey of quail in the brush on his right. Sights and smells and sounds of home swirled around him with such familiarity that it seemed as though he had never left Shiloh. That he had simply awakened from a dream about oil derricks and cities built of tents and air that reeked of sulphur and hot oil. He had pictured Trudy here a thousand times, imagined his sons climbing the same trees he had climbed, shouting and laughing just the way he had done with his brother. Now it seemed hard to believe that he had only imagined such things.

Was there really so much catching up to do? Or had Shiloh simply held a place in time for Birch to step in and take up where he had left off?

Up ahead, sunlight broke through the clouds and light dappled the shingles of Shiloh Church. Except for one horse and buggy, the place was deserted now. All the congregation had gone home to Sunday suppers of fried chicken and apple pie. Birch knew in his heart that even the Shiloh Sunday menu remained unchanged. He scanned the deserted church grounds and remembered potluck suppers and tubs of iced watermelon and long plank tables laden with food. Everywhere he looked, he visualized faces of friends he had not thought about in years. And the questions plagued him: Why had he waited so long to come home? Why had he run so long and so far from the bitterness of his father?

Trudy was right. He had carried Shiloh in his heart all the time, never realizing that it was still there. Still the same place. Still *home.*

Birch reached the gate of the cemetery and stood outside for a moment. He touched the ornate wrought iron and remembered walking through it as a child when his grandfather had died. People had come from all over the county to pay their respects. The place had been packed with men in black suits and women in Sunday dresses, wearing black armbands and broad hats to shield against the hot sun. Birch had grown weary and leaned hard against his mother as the preacher preached on. The pine box had been lowered into the ground and covered with dirt. A potluck had followed, and then life had gone on. Shiloh had rocked back into place as though it did not notice the absence of Grandpa Sinnickson. . . . *Timeless. Unchanging. Shiloh.*

Birch scanned the forest of headstones in search of the granite angel that marked his grandfather's resting place. Surely Birch's mother would be nearby. Pointing skyward, toward Grandpa's special star, the angel seemed to beckon him.

The hinges of the gate groaned as Birch entered the enclosure and wound his way around other markers. He scanned the engraving on the stones, surprised at the people ten years had depleted—people he had always imagined as alive and well. He mentally erased them from his roster of neighbors and shook his head as though he could not imagine Shiloh without this old character or that young man.

In this place all the changes in Shiloh could be measured. Beyond these gates, however, lay the rush of the James Fork and the call of the quail and the cotton and corn and the houses and the young folks making new children to replace the lost ones. A new crop of children had been born in ten years, and none of them would remember the old-timers buried in this yard. Faded photographs and old family stories would never make the new children believe that there were real people buried here . . . people who had once been just as alive as they. Like the set of a play, the stage itself remained unchanged. Old players slipped away to take their places among the silent congregation on the other side of the gate. New players were born each year to toddle and babble and squawk at Sunday potluck dinners as the whole process began over and over again.

The words of the psalmist replayed in Birch's mind:

As for man, his days are as grass: as a flower of the field, so he flourisheth. For the wind passeth over it, and it is gone; and the place thereof shall know it no more.

For Birch Tucker and the folks of Shiloh, this was not a morbid thought—merely a statement of fact. Life was beautiful, but it sure was short. Any man who thought otherwise was a fool. *"Eat your fill of fried chicken at those Sunday potlucks,"* the wise old hearts would whisper, *"but take care to remember those asleep in the yard across the fence!"*

People of the land knew the parable about planting and harvesting. They knew good soil and rocky soil from firsthand experience. It was a very small step from a furrowed field to thoughts about mortality. Dying was a part of living—inevitable, inescapable. Not something to dread, but certainly something to prepare for.

Birch knew his mother had packed her spiritual bags long before she passed from this place into heaven. *"Gonna be home with Jesus someday, Birch. Don't you worry none about me. My soul is ready for the journey. Hallelujah!"*

At Birch's feet, three black-granite markers offered the only physical proof that his family had once been on the potluck side of the fence. Father . . . Mother . . . Brother . . .

SAMUEL CLARA ROBERT

The ground around Sam Tucker's grave was still scarred from pick and shovel. Patches of yellow grass struggled to regain control of the churned-up earth. Birch remembered his mother saying that a new grave had the look of grief about it, but after a while the grass grows and the ground settles down—just about the same time folks' hearts begin to mend. Birch stooped and pulled a tar weed from his father's grave. There could be no mending of hearts between father and son now, no matter how green the grass grew over this place.

Birch turned away and fixed his eyes on his mother's headstone. It was plain, befitting her plain life.

CLARA TUCKER
b. June 19, 1872
d. Sept. 28, 1918
Beloved Wife, Mother

Birch could see his own reflection in the face of the stone. Hat in hand, he smoothed his hair and stood like a schoolboy waiting for his mama to notice and inspect him.

"Hello, Mama," he whispered. The breeze stirred the dry leaves in the water oaks, offering a sound like distant applause. "I've come home. To stay this time." The brittle clapping of the oak leaves cheered him on. "Brought my wife, Trudy. My three boys, too. I named one of the boys Robert. We call him Bobby . . . after Bobby."

He glanced toward the grave of his younger brother and for the first time imagined what it would be like to lose a son so young. "I thought you'd like it if there was still a Bobby Tucker tearin' around in this world."

A quail called and was answered by another in the field.

He told her about Tommy, too, then paused. "Named the baby after Grandpa Joe, Trudy's father. I bet you know all this already. . . . I'll bring 'em all down to meet you soon. The house is a wreck, but me and True will put her back in shape in no time."

He looked toward the church. "I surely have missed this place, Mama. I don't intend on leavin' here again. I just wanted you to know . . . I'm a real happy man. The Lord's been real good to me and True. Reckon your prayers have somethin' to do with that."

Birch opened his Bible to Psalm 91 and held up the envelope. "You see? I've still got your letter. Haven't read it yet. Hope I never have to. Hope I never get so down that I have to open it. I've just been savin' it like a word from heaven." He pondered the sealed envelope a moment before replacing it. Then he began to read the words of the psalm aloud as the gentle Shiloh autumn wind played like a song above him.

Time slipped away without Birch ever realizing how long he had been standing there. Strange how a man can think and think and never notice minutes drifting into hours. But Birch Tucker had a lot of catching up to do. Ten years was a long time to wander—a long time for a mother to wait to hear all the news.

CHAPTER SEVEN

Empty Heart

"He's a smart one, this Cannibal of yours," said Red Watts. "I know these hills like the back of my hand. Every bush and crevice and hole in the ground. Wouldn't figure no convict could stay on the loose this long."

Sheriff Ring raised his face as if to smell the wind. Some scent, some sign—anything to give him a clue. "He was from these parts, if I remember rightly. Mount Pisgah."

Red squinted across a mist-shrouded valley. A tree-covered hill sloped upward. "Pisgah is over yonder. Ain't much there now. Share-croppers got run off some years back. Ain't nothin' there for him to go home to, if that's where he's goin'." He turned his gaze to the rocky shale of Devil's Backbone. "But that *sure* explains it, now don't it? I reckon he knows these hills like the back of his hand, just like I do."

Ring stared off toward small ribbons of smoke rising over the scarlet landscape. "He ain't too smart to be worn out. And he *ain't* gonna outlast us, no matter what he thinks." He glared at the sunken flanks of his hounds and the unshaven faces of the twelve men who remained in the posse.

Red turned over a stone with the toe of his boot. "And he ain't so small that he can hide under a rock. There's only so many rocks in these hills. You'll find him, Sheriff. Dogs can tell the difference between the scent of a man and that of a varmint, all right. Cannibal's been followin' after this bear, tryin' to confuse the dogs, see?"

The dogs did indeed seem confused. They had continued to follow the lumbering animal for miles. At last old Lucifer had turned on them and fought. One dog was dead from the battle. Three others licked their wounds and whined at the enormous carcass of the brown bear. It had been shot by half a dozen guns and lay in a bloody heap beside the boulder where it made a stand.

Red scratched his head in thought. "Sure is a shame to let that meat go to waste. Yessir. I *sure* do hate to kill a critter and leave it to rot!"

"We ain't huntin' no bear!" Ring snapped. "Ain't been out here for a week to kill a bear. *Leave it!*"

Nudging the brim of his cap, Red shook his head. "There ain't that many bears left in these here hills to let go to waste. A real shame, I say. The missus would be right pleased if I came home with something to show for all this bother."

The sheriff narrowed his eyes angrily, certain that the tracker was about to forego the reward offered for Cannibal for a more certain reward. Fresh meat. "Can't say you've been much use to me anyhow," the sheriff said. "It was your hounds that led mine off the scent of the man."

Red defended his animals. "They ain't been trained to hunt men. We just hunt critters in these parts. They're the best huntin' dogs in Logan County. They ain't supposed to follow the scent of a human. But a bear . . . now that's somethin' else again."

"Then take them! And take *that!*" Ring gestured angrily at the brown heap. "And may you choke on all the lead in it, for all I care!"

Red was unperturbed by the anger of the Oklahoma lawman. It was evident he had seen men in worse moods than this after a weeklong hunting trip. Lack of sleep and days on the trail without success had a way of making grown men irritable.

"Don't mind if I do. A bear in the hand is worth two bears in the bush, my ol' pap would say if he was here. Hoo-boy! Leastwise my missus can't say I come back empty-handed."

Sheriff Ring pretended not to hear the glee in the voice of the deserter. "We'll have to go up a ways. Find where Cannibal broke off from the bear."

"The trail will be cold by now." Red shook his head as if to say it sounded like an impossible task.

Ring swore at him and whirled around, kicking at a redbone hound that belonged to the tracker. "Get these lapdogs out of here! Take that carcass and get out of my way! If it weren't for your mutts, my hounds would be ripping the throat out of that nigger by now!"

Red shrugged, still not bothered by the sheriff's outburst. "Like I says, they ain't trained to hunt men."

"Well, that's all the game my hounds hunt. Track and kill, or run until they drop. He won't outlast 'em. Cannibal ain't nothin' but a man—a man in chains, at that! He'll wear out, and then I'll have him." Sheriff Ring fixed his eyes on the nearly dry streambed down in the hollow. The morning sky reflected in pools linked by a trickle of water. "There! That's where he's got to!"

"Reckon you could be right." The tracker rubbed his stubbled chin.

"Could be?" the sheriff roared, and his words echoed across the valley. He grabbed the shirtfront of the laconic trapper and pulled him close as though to strike him. "I can *smell* him. He's gone down there. I can smell his black hide. His blood and his sweat!"

Red Watts nodded fearfully, remembering the legend . . . remembering that his feet rested on the Devil's Backbone . . . certain that he was seeing hellfire in the eyes of Sheriff Myron Ring this morning. "I reckon you know what you're talkin' about, Sheriff." He hung in the sheriff's grip a moment, then gently pushed himself free and whistled for his dogs to gather around him. "I reckon you know the smell of a man runnin' for his life just about as good as these here dogs smell the fear of a critter on the run."

His words seemed to placate the sheriff. Ring turned away and clapped his hands once, calling his men and bloodhounds to attention. He pointed to the little valley. "He's gone thataway. He's got no bear scent to cover his trail now. Old Grandee can sniff out a man's track in muddy water. We got him in a corner now, boys."

Red chuckled. "If he knows these parts like you say, he might have a trick or two up his sleeve."

"He's got no sleeves left," Ring growled.

"Well, if that be the case, if he hides in the Poteau Mountains, he'll plumb freeze to death." This seemed a likely possibility, the way the weather had turned so cold the last three nights. "If he follows that creek, he'll be right on up in the Poteau wilderness, and y'all will find him stiff as an old board, I reckon." Red patted his panting dogs and grinned at the fallen bear. "So, you don't need my services no more." He tipped his cap. "I'll be gettin' back, then."

The convict had not heard the baying of the hounds since the boom of a dozen rifles announced that the bear had finally confronted dogs and men. Now that fight was over. It would only be a matter of time before Sheriff Ring found the trail in search of Cannibal's scent.

There was no time to rest. Though his lungs were seared, he could not stop to catch his breath. Carefully he picked his way through the muddy pools of the stagnant creek. The chain of the leg-irons had broken the first night of his escape. His ankles chafed beneath the iron cuffs, but at least he could take a full stride, stepping from pool to pool in an effort to conceal his scent from the bloodhounds. The bear had given him precious time. While the posse stopped and scratched their heads in confusion, he could put a few more miles between himself and them. And if he could make it to the Poteau Mountains . . .

This was his country. He knew each creek and bottom like the face of his own mother. It seemed he had hunted in these hills a thousand times as a child. Never had he imagined that one day he would be the one who was hunted!

The weight of the leg-irons pulled his bare feet deep into the muddy creek bottom and held him back like a mired ox. Men with boots and guns would pursue him on firm ground. They would study each pool for signs of his track. They would call the hounds to sniff the mud, and soon enough, Cannibal would hear them bay once again!

He fought the panic that threatened to overcome him at that image. Battling his own exhaustion, he forced himself to think about tired dogs and footsore men who wanted only to return home.

How many days and nights had he been running? How often had he managed to throw them off his trail, only to have it discovered again a few hours later? Cannibal lost count of how many times he had dared to hope that they would give up and turn back.

But Sheriff Ring was a hard man and cruel. He would not give up easily. Either he would return with his convict bound and chained, or he would be certain that the one he called Cannibal was dead. What the sheriff could not know was that his prey had determined from the first night that he would not be taken back alive.

These woods were his home. He would not leave this place ever again! Like the great brown bear, sooner or later he would turn and fight, and then he would fight no more forever.

It was cold outside. The wind whistled down from the Poteau Mountains to rattle the dry leaves in the rain gutters and ridges of the roof. Small squares of light from distant houses gleamed across the dark valley.

The tent canvas was rolled out on the floor of the front room for a makeshift carpet, and the mattresses were placed on top of that. Until a proper stove was bought, they would all sleep together in front of the camp stove.

Trudy closed the bedroom doors and laid another quilt on Bobby and Tommy. Baby Joe was snug in his cradle at the foot of their mattress.

Birch came in through the kitchen and warmed his backside by the little stove. "Chilly out there. Unusual for September."

Trudy climbed beneath the covers. "It's a tight little house, Birch," she said quietly. "Listen to that wind, and we're still snug and warm. Not a draft—"

"We'll get a proper parlor stove first thing tomorrow. And a cookstove." He scratched his head, then wondered out loud how he would get everything home from Hartford. "We'll need a wagon. And mules and harness."

"Before the stoves?"

"Before anything." He jerked a thumb in the direction of the barn, where the old Ford was parked. "Automobiles might be fine for cities, but a man without a mule is helpless in Shiloh."

"After the wagon and the mule and the stoves?" Trudy was smiling at him as she pulled the covers back and patted his pillow. The list of things they needed to make this place livable was endless. Every time Birch thought of something, he thought of something else he needed to get before he could get the last thing.

Birch slipped between the blankets and curled up against her. "Plow. Hoes. Maybe a cream separator for the milk cow."

Trudy took his hat from his head and found he had a stocking cap on beneath that. "Did you put the cow on your list yet?"

"No. And chickens. Rhode Island reds. Good layers." He wrapped his arms around her. "Everything new, True. Everything I've always wanted for you and the boys. We'll even buy you a set of dishes. Who cares about the tea peddler? Brand-new china cups and saucers. Real plates. And a china hutch to put them in, too." He kissed her gently. The soft light from the kerosene lamp shone on his rugged face.

"And a bed, Birch. Maybe a real brass bed with knobs on the posts? And wallpaper? Curtains, too. I can make the curtains." She looked at the newly scrubbed windows. They were tall and reflected the light like mirrors. In the windows the room looked clean and new and beautiful.

"And what else do you want? Tell me, True."

She let her fingers play on the back of his neck. "Only you. Here. With my children around me. Any more than this, and I will break with joy."

As Birch studied her in the soft light, she saw her reflection in his eyes. He blew out the light and kissed her with the friendly passion that comes with years of loving.

"Welcome home, Birch," Trudy whispered as he laid his head against her shoulder and slept.

* * *

A thin bar of light seeped under the door of David's bedroom, carrying the voice of his stepfather through the darkness like a knife.

"He's not my kid, anyway."

David heard the clink of glasses as the bootleg gin was poured and passed around the poker table where Brian O'Halloran sat with five other men.

"Poor kid," said the voice of Mr. Ryan. "Poor little kid. His mama ain't hardly dead, and you just home . . ."

Brian scoffed at Ryan's sympathy. "Don't shed tears for the kid. He's got no heart. Tap that scrawny little chest, and it's hollow in there, I tell you. Not a tear for his old lady. Not one."

"Somebody deal . . . come on, will you?"

Brian hardly missed a beat. "Not that I'm surprised. His mother was one coldhearted dame, I can tell you. Married me to give the kid a name. Got herself in the family way with some Jew in the old neighborhood and spotted me as a likely candidate after he ran out on her."

"Will you deal the cards, Brian?"

"So . . . out of the goodness of my heart . . . well, I was drinking with her brothers and here she comes. A real looker, I think to myself . . . so I marry her. Got her and the kid. A couple of cold fish, I tell you."

"Well, it didn't slow you down with the dames, did it, Brian O'Halloran?" Much laughter followed.

"Why should it?" Brian replied. "She knew enough to get herself pregnant and then forget everything she knew about making a man happy. I would have had the marriage annulled, except her brother said he'd kill me. Who would blame him, since there was a kid involved—which everyone figured belonged to me."

The conversation turned to more serious business—how many cards to throw out, how much to bet, who was bluffing. Full house? Pass the booze. Somebody open a window. Somebody else turn on the radio. Anybody want a sandwich?

David sat up in bed and hugged his knees to his chest. He stared at the light beneath the door as though it were an enemy, as though the light itself were his stepfather. He had told those men everything! They thought that David's mother had been cold and unfeeling and that it was okay for her to be dead.

David tapped his chest where his heart was supposed to be. It did not sound hollow. He placed his palm hard to feel the thumping. He had a heart. But Brian was right. David had not cried when his mother died. Not then. Not at Mallory Brothers Mortuary. Not at the grave when Father John said the last prayer and Sister Anne put her arm around him. It wasn't that he didn't want to cry. But something inside had dried up. There were no tears for David to cry. Even though he knew he was supposed to.

Maybe there was some other sort of heart that had died in David when his mama died. Maybe Brian was right about that part of it. But Brian was wrong about David's mother. She hadn't been cold—she had cried plenty of times! David had heard her the nights Brian came home drunk. He had yelled and called her names. He had hit her and then come in and whipped David with his belt while she fought him and cried for him to stop. The neighbors had called the police, and after that Brian came home and said he had been transferred to Philadelphia and they were going to move. Then David had cried because he did not want to leave his school and his friends.

Well, that was the end of the tears. Brian had called him a baby. Brian said that only babies cry, so David stopped. Now he was just permanently angry. There did not seem to be room for anything else in him. When his mother died, the hole inside him filled up with hating Brian O'Halloran. This was much better than crying for his mom, David thought. He dreaded the sadness that lurked everywhere around him. He knew that if he ever let it come in and push away the anger, the sadness would sit on his chest at night and choke him to death. He did not want to hurt. Did not want to think about his mother. It was much better to sit in the dark and hate Brian through the walls.

"Hey, how about I bet the kid? Anybody want a cute little kid? I'll see your five bucks and raise the kid. No kidding. Take him."

Nervous laughter.

"You've had too much to drink, Brian O'Halloran. Lay off it, will you?"

"Raise your own kid, O'Halloran. Nobody else wants him."

Brian boomed. "*Nobody!* So that's it. A bachelor again, free as a bird, except I'm stuck with this kid."

"Shut up. He'll hear you."

"Nothin' he ain't heard before, I bet," said Mr. Ryan.

Then David heard chairs scrape back and the gamblers saying they'd had enough cards for the night. Brian told them to stay—said he was kidding, just trying to make the best out of a rotten situation, blowing off a little steam. Didn't a man have a right to blow off a little steam, after all?

The poker game was over, just the same. David was pleased that other people—grown-up men—had gotten sick of Brian O'Halloran's big mouth. He delighted in Brian's misery as he heard the gin bottle clink against Brian's glass and he finished the bottle alone in the front room.

David snuggled into his bed and pulled his blanket up around his chin. He blinked sleepily at the bar of light seeping across the floor as his stepfather made pitiful, muttering noises about "poor losers" and people who had "no sense of humor." Finally, David drifted to sleep with a sense of contented revenge filling the space where Brian had said a heart should be. . . .

It was well on toward morning when the door to David's room crashed in, flooding the darkness with light from behind the massive silhouette of Brian O'Halloran.

David sat up with a start. He cried out, uncertain if he was having another nightmare. Brian's thick belt swung from the arm of his shadow like a serpent caught by the tail. The strong aroma of bathtub gin filled the air.

This is no dream! David thought wildly.

"You little Jew skunk! You've been nothing but *trouble* since the day—" The arm and the belt rose and lashed down hard against the foot of the bed.

David covered his head and curled up in a ball as Brian jerked the blankets onto the floor. "Don't, Brian! Please, don't!"

"If it hadn't been for *you*—" the blows began in earnest—"Irene and me . . . we coulda . . . had something! I'll *make* you cry! Heartless little Jew . . . I'll *make you cry!*"

CHAPTER EIGHT

Conspiracy

The meeting in Damon Phelps's private office had been going on for only five minutes, but neither Senior Vice President Tell nor Assistant Vice President Penner expected it to last much longer. Phelps was not a man who required lengthy consideration before making decisions. For investments, as with locating wildcat oil wells, Phelps operated more on gut feelings than anything else.

Neither assistant was surprised when Phelps looked only briefly at his oak-paneled walls and then made up his mind. "No, not yet. I know that a bunch of old widows keep cash in their deposit boxes and leave the keys with us. But just sweeping new bank deposits into the market is enough for now and easier to hide."

Tell and Penner naturally agreed. No one ever argued with Damon Phelps. They may have had pangs of conscience about their activities, but both were in too deeply to retreat now. Tell's wife required expensive medical treatments, and he justified participating in the thefts by that need. Penner simply could not afford his new sixty-thousand-dollar house and the lifestyle he enjoyed on a bank vice president's salary.

Phelps's own motivation for what the three were doing was even less complex. He enjoyed it, and he felt he had the right. His oil business had already made him wealthy, but he viewed the bank deposits in the same way that he saw his oil-field equipment and the human crews. When Phelps ordered them moved to a new location, they went. Phelps thought that money deposited in the Petroleum Bank should behave the same way.

The black candlestick telephone that was his private line buzzed discreetly. Penner answered it. "Mister Phelps's office, Penner speaking. . . . Who? . . . Yes, Mister Riley. You want what? . . . Just a moment please." Penner held the mouthpiece against his chest and waggled the receiver in the air. "This is Mister Riley, Mister Keenan's assistant," he reported to Phelps. "He says that the market in copper is edgy, and he wants more margin for the consolidated purchase."

Buying on margin was like buying a house with a mortgage. Phelps bought stock with 10 percent down and borrowed 90 percent from the broker to complete the purchase. Mike Keenan must believe that the price of the stock was about to fall drastically, since a call for more margin meant that he wanted to protect himself by requiring a greater cash payment.

Phelps exploded in a burst of profanity. "Tell that little pip-squeak that we have always bought on a margin of 10 percent down, and not a penny more."

Dutifully reporting this response back to the broker's assistant, Penner apparently got yelled at from the other direction as well, because he held the receiver away from his ear. "Mister Riley says he needs to speak with you, Mister Phelps."

"Tell him to go—no," Phelps corrected himself, "tell him I only deal with the Boss, not with flunkies. Have Keenan himself call me if it's so important."

The message delivered, Penner hung up the phone. The three conspirators were reviewing the next planned trades when the private line rang again.

"Mister Keenan calling for you, Mister Phelps," Penner announced.

"Keenan!" bellowed Phelps into the phone as if he had initiated the exchange. "What's this about more margin? Yes, I know the Feds want to get tough on buying on credit, but they mean that for the suckers, not for big operators—what?"

Tell and Penner watched with alarm as Phelps's complexion passed crimson on its way to plum. "Listen, you, you're not the only broker who—what's that? A pool in copper? Pulling out when?"

The word *pool* had caught Phelps's attention. He had been part of the RCA pool, the secret group of large investors who had successfully driven the price of RCA stock upward. A sudden sell-off had made the small group an obscene profit off the hordes of little people who had scrambled to buy the overvalued stock.

Tell and Penner both breathed relieved sighs as Phelps actually sat down again in his desk chair and his color returned to its normal scarlet flush. "That's mighty white of you," he said at last. "Yes, sell at the market. That's right, at the current price. Now, you will call again to explain the other? Right, right. We'll go to work on it right away. Good day, Keenan."

Phelps hung up and sat silently. At last he said, "There's been a pool running the copper price up, but it's pulling the plug today. Keenan warned us, so we're out at the top. Tell," he said to his senior VP, "there are big doings. Bigger than anything we've seen so far. We need to see how much we can really get together. You and Penner inventory the safety-deposit boxes tonight. I'll want the figure first thing tomorrow."

The bubbling noise on the trading floor of the New York Stock Exchange rose and fell the way a breaking ocean wave roars and then recedes. A flurry of activity around the horseshoe-shaped Post Twelve spoke of renewed interest in radio, the glamour stock of the 1920s. At Post Two, steel was trading at over two hundred dollars a share as gray-uniformed messengers came and went in controlled haste . . . and so on, through the eighteen posts at which America's corporations were bought and sold to the tune of five million shares every trading day.

From the press box in the visitors' gallery on the Broad Street side of the Exchange, Max Meyer watched the ebb and flow. He needed to stay in touch with the primitive rhythm of this marketplace. Otherwise, his columns, even if long on facts, would be short on perception. Everybody was always trying to feed Max information about some stock or other, but a sense of the deepest level of Wall Street came only from being there and watching it happen.

Max was recognized and greeted by other members of the press, whose beats also covered financial doings, but he discouraged conversation. After all, he was there to gather impressions, not to gab.

One of the first items on Max's personal agenda was to scan the trading floor for brokers he knew. The columnist could often tell the condition of stocks handled by these specialists from their activity or the lack of it.

Max located his first benchmark in the person of William Wadsworth at Post Five. Willie was always easily identified by his shock of white hair. At eighty-six, Willie was the oldest trader on the floor. The octogenarian specialist in railroad stocks was nodding and taking notes and bouncing on the balls of his feet . . . a sure sign that the Rock Island Line, or some other rail company, was making a profit for some happy investor.

Next Max located the round, rumpled form of Mike Keenan at Post One. Mining and oil stocks were his area of expertise. Keenan was widely acknowledged as one of the most successful and most ruthless traders on the street.

There seemed to be some difficulty at Post One. As Max watched, one of Keenan's red-haired Irish assistants was waving his free arm angrily and shouting into a telephone. In another moment the man stared at the receiver before slamming it down. A consultation followed with Keenan at the center of a huddle of his flunkies.

Harry Beadle, another reporter, scooted over and followed Max's gaze down to Post One. "Ah," Harry said, "keeping an eye on your new partner, eh?"

Max ignored the jibe. Just because Keenan had found one of Max's ideas to be interesting and had said so in print, the rumors were flying. But anyone who really knew Max realized that he could not be on the take. He offended everyone with his comments about "overvalued stocks" and "the bubble that has to burst sooner or later."

"Hello, Harry," Max said. "I wonder what's up with the Irish Brigade?"

As both writers watched, Keenan himself picked up the telephone. There was a lengthy conversation. While still talking, Keenan nodded to the red-haired assistant, then made a throat-slashing gesture, the signal for an order to sell.

"Must be the copper pool," Max muttered. "They're gonna pull the plug on copper."

"Yeah?" queried Beadle, grinning. "Can I quote you?"

Max stood up, his story idea for tomorrow's column forming rapidly. The opening lines were writing themselves in his head and only awaited confirmation by the stock ticker back in his *New York Times* office. "Yeah, Harry," Max responded, "and you can print it if you don't mind putting *my* name in *your* story."

Harry laughed. "Hey, in a few more days we'll be out on the ocean being pampered, thanks to you and your partner down there." He jerked his thumb back toward Keenan. "I'm already so grateful, I promise to put *both* your names in—and spell them right, too."

"Looks like rain today, David."

Mrs. Crowley wiped her hand on her apron and placed a bowl of Cream of Wheat on the table beside a cup of steaming Ovaltine.

"David?" she called again and turned back to the sink to clean up the stack of dishes that had remained unwashed while Brian O'Halloran had been home. Now he was on the road again, and Mrs. Crowley muttered as she fished half a wet cigar from the clutter. "He'll just have to get married again. Men! Live like pigs and . . ."

David looked one last time in the mirror. If he pulled his baseball cap to the right and low over his forehead, he could hide the bruise on his forehead and eye.

"Day-*vid*! Breakfast will be ruined!"

"Coming, Missus Crowley." He lowered his head and slipped into the kitchen while her back was turned so she would not notice the cap. While the pots and pans clanked, he slurped down his breakfast, hoping to dash out the door before she really looked at him.

"Your poor dad . . . ," Mrs. Crowley began. "All alone with a boy to raise."

Of course, Mrs. Crowley didn't know anything at all about Brian O'Halloran. Seventy-two years old and alone in the world herself, Mrs. Crowley had been hired to help with the housework when Irene got sick. Later, the old woman had just taken over. Laundry. Cooking. Shopping. She scooted around the six-room brick house without ever really seeing David. Not that her eyes were bad. She could spot dust on the windowsills and find a bit of lint on David's jacket or a thread dangling from his sleeve. She was swell at ironing and sewing buttons on.

But all the same, she never seemed to look at David's face. He wondered if she would recognize him if they passed on the street. Probably she would spot his clothes and remark on the fact that he could get his knickers dirty quicker than any child she had ever seen. But did she know his eyes were green? His hair blond? His face quite thin and pale these days?

The Ovaltine tasted good. He smacked his lips, and the old lady turned.

Immediately her eyes narrowed. She had evidently spotted his ball cap. Wearing a cap indoors was a great crime, according to Mrs. Crowley. "What do you think you are? A Jew? Only Jews wear hats indoors. Your mother would be spinning. . . ."

David put his hand to his cap and held it there as she reached to snatch it from his head. "No! It's for the World Series! We're all wearing ball caps in honor of Philadelphia! It's bad luck to take it off!"

Well, that stopped her. Mrs. Crowley was a great fan of the Philadelphia Athletics and their manager, Connie Mack. She sure wanted the team to beat the Chicago Cubs.

"Who made up such nonsense?" she demanded, hands on her broad hips and a scowl on her weathered face.

"Mister Mack said it himself." David did not raise his head. He spoke between bites, hoping she would not hear the tremor of a lie in his voice. "Yeah. A bunch of kids was down at Shibe Park hanging around and Connie Mack himself said that everybody should keep his cap on for luck." This was a pleasant lie. David could picture the tough athletics manager talking to a group of fellas at Shibe Park. David wished he had been there or that he had painted himself into the tale.

"Oh, so Connie Mack himself said so, did he?" She sounded skeptical, but she did not grab at his cap. Instead she walked back to the sink. Perhaps the cap indoors was okay if Connie Mack said so.

"That's what they told me," David offered, scraping the bowl and finishing off his Ovaltine with a slurp. "I gotta go. . . ."

He was up and into the bedroom to fetch his book bag, then out the door before any more could be said. And she never noticed the shiner. He sighed with relief.

The baseball-cap story had worked with her, but it wouldn't work at school. But that was all right, too. This morning, before he left, Brian O'Halloran had taken a look at the bruises caused by his fists and his belt and had given David a good lie to tell at school. "Tell 'em you were carrying out the trash and you tripped and fell down the back steps."

It sounded believable enough. Except that Mrs. Crowley would have known it was a lie because the trash can was full, and David had not carried it out. It was important that David keep his stories straight. That he give a good account of the bruises on his face and arms and back. If he ever told the truth, Brian had warned him that David would be called a liar, and Brian would make him sorry he ever opened his mouth. David believed the threat and feared another beating much more than he feared the sin of lying.

The air smelled like rain. Clear and damp, a breeze rattled the leaves in the trees as David hurried up the sidewalk to meet his friend Ralph Johnson. The nickname Oink suited him well, because he was as big around as Fatty Arbuckle in the movies.

Oink waited dutifully on the corner. David was sort of a hero to Oink because he could run faster than anyone at school and play marbles better and did long division with an ease that made their teacher smile with pleasure and pat David on the back.

"Hey, Davey!" Oink breathed hard, as if he were out of breath, even when he was standing still. "What . . . how'd you get the shiner?"

So much for the shadow of the baseball cap. "Carrying the trash out for my ol' man and I fell down the steps. What a mess."

"Yeah." Oink peered at the blue bruise with admiration. "Looks like you was fightin'. Like Dempsey or somebody."

Shiners were a badge of honor in the neighborhood if they were won in battle. David wished that Brian had thought of a more interesting lie . . . *"Fell off your bike . . . out of a tree . . . hit a triple and slid for third base and got a knee in the face . . ."*

"Yeah. I bet Dempsey don't take out the trash at home," David replied, sticking to the original story. Nobody would doubt something so ordinary and dull as falling down the steps. Now Oink would tell it for him. Maybe David would not have to explain again all day long.

Willie Faber joined them down the block. "Hiya, Davey! Hey, Oink! What happened to you, Davey?"

Panting, Oink replied, "He fell down the steps carrying out the trash."

"Oh." It was not worth talking about. On to important matters. "Hey, they already got the ticket booths set up down at Shibe Park," Willie said. "My dad is gonna take me and Fred to the Series. You goin'?"

Oink shrugged. "My dad says a regular guy who don't have a lot of money can't hardly get a ticket." He panted and wheezed. "My dad says a fella's got to be practically rich or real quick to get a ticket."

It was true. Ticket scalpers were already advertising that the white purchase slips that allowed a fan to buy two grandstand tickets for $3.50 were worth as much as $25 each now—a week's wages for an ordinary man.

Willie Faber's dad had made a bundle playing the stock market, so he could afford such extravagance. Oink's father was neither rich nor fast on his feet. And David's stepfather? If ever Brian O'Halloran had the good fortune of acquiring a World Series ticket-purchase slip, he would sell it to the highest bidder and spend every last cent at the nearest speakeasy.

David nudged Oink. "Me and Oink are going. Right, Oink?"

Oink's eyebrows plowed upward in surprise. "Huh?"

David continued. "Yeah. Me and Oink are going for free."

"What?"

"We got us this secret place where we can go see the whole Series. Bring our own soda pop. Don't have to look over the heads of grown-ups either. And if Hornsby knocks one out of Shibe Park, you know who's gonna catch it?"

Willie glanced unhappily at David. "Not you."

"Nope. *Oink!* Oink is gonna catch it." David slapped Oink on the back and laughed. Then he narrowed his eyes, the shiner making him look tough. "Where are you sitting, Willie?"

"Behind home plate." Willie puffed up.

"You can't catch anything there. Not even foul balls. They got the net all the way up. Rotten seats."

Willie was insulted. "Better than some knothole through the fence. Coppers'll come along, and you'll be kicked out."

"Who said anything about knotholes? or fences?" David replied, nudging Oink, who started to appear worried.

"Yeah? Where you goin' to be then?" Willie demanded.

David shrugged. He had already told a million lies today. What harm would one more lie do? "You know those houses on Twentieth Street, the ones right across from Shibe Park?"

"Yeah? So?"

"We got connections." David gazed upward, toward a rooftop. He had heard the controversy about spectators on the rooftops of houses across from the ballpark. "We're going to see the whole Series from up on a roof. Right behind right field, too. Ha!"

Willie glowered at Oink, who looked really agitated at the news that he was expected to climb onto a rooftop and balance there like a flying hippo.

"How you gonna get Oink up there?" Willie snapped. "He'll bust through the roof."

"Not this roof," David said with a confidence that made Willie Faber shut up. It made a good story, didn't it? Something to talk about right up until the day the Series started. And who would ever know if David really watched from the roof or not? Oink wouldn't admit to anything. David was certain of that.

Oink looked doubtful. "I dunno. . . ."

"Sure. We're gonna have a rope and tie one end to the chimney and the other end around Oink so he don't slip."

This seemed to reassure both Oink and Willie. The three boys walked the rest of the way to school in silence. David would not have to tell the tale again. Willie and Oink would tell it for him. Friends would come up to him in the school yard and ask if they, too, could come along and climb the roof to see the World Series. He would shake his head and say, "Sorry. Only me and Oink." And the two of them would be the envy of everyone at school.

Rocks in the bottom of the streambed tore at the bare feet of the fugitive. The water was over his knees, and the current had suddenly grown swift. Every step became a stumble. His legs ached from the bitter cold. His muscles trembled, and his teeth chattered like the beak of a woodpecker on a tree trunk. And he was tired. So tired. If only he could lie down on the bank of the stream and sleep awhile. To close his eyes and shut out everything!

He glanced toward the embankment, where heaps of dry leaves made a soft bed. He could not hear the hounds. Had he finally managed to throw them off his trail? Was it safe to stop and rest a few minutes before pushing on?

The thought held him captive, and he stood motionless for a moment. Water rushed around his knees, seeming to push him toward the bank. Above him, the wind stirred the leaves, carrying the scent of woodsmoke to his nostrils. He could not remember ever being so hungry. The pangs gnawed his stomach, pulling his mind away from the temptation of the leaves.

To sleep was certainly to be captured. The convict knew his pursuer was a patient, methodical man. Sooner or later he would pass by this place. Sooner or later the nose of Old Grandee would pass over those leaves. One whiff of Cannibal's scent, and all would be lost. They would know for certain he had come this way. They would press on and push ahead and close the gap Cannibal had gained when the old bear had turned and fought the posse for him.

But could they keep on coming forever? Weren't they men, like he was? Didn't they need sleep and food as he did? Soon it would be dark. Soon . . . surely they would camp somewhere and let him sleep for an hour or two of undeclared truce.

He shook his mind clear, reminding himself that the temptation to sleep was the sentence of death. He backed a step from the embankment and turned his face upstream.

Somewhere far behind him, the report of a rifle sounded, echoing across the narrow valley and into the mountains. The sound was like a whip to his soul, forcing him to take one more step through the icy water and then another and another.

Sabre Oil! The idea of being in a pool to drive up an oil company's stock inflamed Phelps's imagination. What better way to combine both his areas of self-professed expertise than to profit from the stock market and the oil business at the same time?

Broker Mike Keenan found a receptive audience when he explained the workings of the new pool to Damon Phelps. "Sabre is a small company, just beginning to be traded on the Big Board of the New York Exchange," he said. "The oil fields they are developing are in South America. Who's going to run down there to check? We start buying. A few well-timed articles by our newspaper shills, and it won't take long before the minnows will notice that a stock that was available for ten dollars a share is suddenly double that. We'll let it run up to five times its value and then pull the plug. The little fish will never know what hit them, and we'll walk away with a profit of 400 percent. What do you say?"

Phelps could not say anything but yes, and he could not say it fast enough to keep from stuttering in his excitement. "How much will we need to get in?"

"We want to keep this short and sweet," Keenan told him. "Not too many partners. We need about three million dollars to work with to really control things. Three million dollars split five ways . . . how does six hundred thousand strike you?"

Swallowing hard, Phelps could not bring himself to voice any doubts. He was thinking how the sum mentioned was triple what the conspirators had made so far in all their dealings. They would have to take all the cash out of their other holdings, and they would still need to come up with more. Phelps's share in the pool in RCA stock had involved only fifty thousand dollars—a tiny drop compared to what he was being asked for now. On the other hand, the radio pool had stopped with a modest 100 percent profit. After paying Keenan's brokerage fees, the Petroleum Bank embezzlers had only realized forty thousand dollars of gain.

What else could he say? "Count me in. Yes, six hundred thousand is no problem at all."

CHAPTER NINE

The Race

The boys had begged Trudy not to enroll them in school today. Couldn't they wait until after the trip to Hartford? She agreed, but at a price—Sunday suits and tight shoes.

"But, Ma, it ain't even Sunday," Tommy protested.

"It *isn't* Sunday," Trudy corrected, handing him his newly pressed Sunday suit.

"That's what I said." He pouted, glaring at the black coat and knickers. "It *ain't* Sunday, so how come—?"

Trudy silenced him with a threatening look, then whirled on Birch, who had mostly been trying to stay out of her way. "You see the sort of grammar he picked up at that school? *Ain't,* he's saying! I told you he'd pick that up if we—"

Birch smiled broadly. "He ain't gonna hear no better around here either, Trudy!" He ducked and scooted out the door, and she gasped as though he had been swearing.

"And me with a teacher's certificate, too." She turned back to Tommy, who was also smiling at his father's use of the unholy *ain't.* "And that's enough out of you, young man. Put your Sunday suit on. We're going to Hartford to the bank office, and I won't have my sons looking like scarecrows and talking worse."

It was plain to see that she was cross this morning, so Tommy offered no more argument, even if the suit was too small in the sleeves and the knickers too short. Neither did he mention that Bobby's suit, which was a hand-me-down from Tommy, was too big for him. The sleeves covered his hands, and the knickers hung down to midcalf. But no one dared mention such minor points. Not this morning.

Since before dawn Trudy had been scrubbing and ironing and digging for the shears, then calling everyone, one by one, for haircuts. She would not go to the Hartford bank unless every man jack of them had their hair cut, she declared! This was even before breakfast. They had eaten their oatmeal with scratchy bits of new-mown hair in their nightshirts. It was enough to make them grateful for the bath she made them take in the tin tub on the back porch. Even baby Joe got himself shorn and scrubbed all over in a bucket of warm water.

It was plain to every male in the house that Trudy was nervous. No arguments. No back talk. No using improper grammar, even as a joke.

"First impressions," Trudy said as she brushed her navy blue wool skirt with the lint brush and then presented the brush to Birch to do her back and shoulders. Front or back, first impressions were important. They were going to live right here, five miles from Hartford, for the rest of their lives. It wouldn't do to be remembered for lint and ragged overalls.

They stood like a row of soldiers for her inspection—eyes front, expressions deadly serious. They dared not speak blasphemies against collars and Sunday shoes and ties.

A loose thread was discovered hanging from Tommy's too-short sleeve. She hefted his arm and cut the wayward thread with her teeth.

"Whew," Bobby said, looking genuinely relieved. "I thought she was gonna bite you!"

At this, Birch snickered and then saluted. "Well, General," he addressed Trudy, "you got a hankerin' to bite anybody, or are we goin' to town today?"

At that word *go*, baby Joe squealed. Trudy raised her chin haughtily as if she would not dignify such a remark as that. "I will do more than bite if you boys do not act like gentlemen," she warned. Then to Birch, "And that goes doubly true for you, Birch Tucker! No spitting on the sidewalks. No roughhousing with the boys."

He nodded, then nodded again. "You know what you need?" he asked when she finished the list of what gentlemen do not do in bank offices.

"Birch! The list of what we need is already from here to Hartford."

He put his hand on her cheek. "You need a little girl, that's what you need. So you can put all this fussin' into fixin' her hair and starchin' her petticoats. Then me and the boys here could just be boys."

Bobby and Tommy agreed with solemn nods. Sometimes their mother took these fits of making everyone look like models in the Sears catalogues. Usually it was every time they moved to a new town. But all towns were the same. Men chewed tobacco and spit on sidewalks and said *ain't*. And the ladies had their sewing circles and dolled up their little girls and didn't worry about what the men did.

Trudy did not like the comment about her needing a girl to fuss over. She brushed Birch's hand away and yanked on Tommy's sleeves as if she could make them longer. "Don't you go telling me what I need, Birch Tucker. Just get the Ford and mind what I say. It's first impressions people remember most."

He shrugged in surrender. Then, as he and Tommy and Bobby crowded out the door to fetch the Ford, he said loud enough for her to hear, "Give people too good of an impression at first, you're bound to disappoint them later." Down the steps and in the yard he said still louder, "Now as for me, I always used to wear my overalls to a brand-new place. That way when folks caught sight of me in my Sunday suit, they were always surprised." He grinned at her over his shoulder and mimicked the high voice of a woman. "Oh, my, my! Don't Birch look fine when he's all brushed and curried?"

There was nothing on hand to throw at him that wouldn't dirty his suit coat, so Trudy resolved that she would hold her temper. There was nothing else to do. She had cleaned her troops and shined them up bright. Let the day bring what it may. She had at least given the effort her all.

Turning, she caught her own reflection in the window. The skirt was too long for the fashion, but this was not New York, after all. Who would notice such a thing? Her shoulder-length chestnut hair, thick and shining, was tied at the back and parted to one side.

At thirty-two, Trudy's complexion was olive and still smooth and young. Her brown eyes were clear and direct, businesslike. Today was a day for business, and she was dressed for it.

The Ford coughed and chugged out the barn doors in a cloud of blue smoke. Birch drove it right to the front steps so Trudy would not have to cross the yard and risk getting her shoes dusty. He set the brake and tipped his hat, then descended to take the baby and open the car door for her. The perfect gentleman.

Tommy and Bobby sat erect in the backseat. Their mouths were tight and their hands folded in their laps as though they were sitting in a church pew. Even baby Joe sensed the importance of this trip to Hartford. His wide eyes were serious as they headed down the drive and out onto the lane that led to the main highway.

Birch did not look at the little church as they passed it. He honked the horn as they chugged by Cousin J.D.'s place. Never mind the gray mules in the pasture or the plow in the shed or the hooks all hung with harnesses and bridles that had once belonged to Birch's father. Today there would be a new harness. Young, strong mules. A double-shovel plow. Dishes and table and chairs and real beds! This day was the culmination of every dream—ten years of doing without so that every penny might be saved.

The wind slipped in through the window and blew away Trudy's tension. Excitement rattled on the breeze, and dreams came alive and ran beside the spinning spokes of the Ford.

Baby Joe began to dance on her lap. Bobby and Tommy bounced on the leather seats and chattered about the new milk cow and the mules they would ride and maybe even a hunting dog to help them track down the squirrels they would hunt! Their carefully pomaded and parted hair began to stick up in the wind. Their bow ties cocked off at an angle, and their shoes came unlaced. But such irregularities in perfection could be easily fixed once they reached Hartford. Trudy relaxed and thought about dishes finer than Maybelle's.

Then the high, shrill whistle of the Rock Island locomotive wailed its challenge behind them. She had made her water stop and had a full head of steam up for the run to Hartford Station. Twin plumes of smoke and steam billowed into the sky like the breath from the nostrils of a giant dragon in pursuit of the little Ford.

With one voice, Bobby and Tommy shouted the warning to Birch: "Don't let her catch us, Dad!"

At the same instant Birch reached to crank up the accelerator lever, Trudy called, "Don't you dare! Birch Tucker, don't . . . you . . . *dare*! I shall get out and walk!"

Birch threw his head back in a laugh as the little Ford leaped over a pothole and doubled its speed to a roaring thirty-five miles an hour. "You'll have to jump then, True," he bellowed, " 'cause I'm not slowing down for you to get out now!" The fire of competition burned in his eyes.

Plain old fury burned in Trudy's, she knew.

The engineer leaned far out the window and waved to the boys as the locomotive gained on the Ford. The whistle screamed again.

"Faster, Dad!"

"She's gainin' on us!"

"Faster! Faster!"

"Birch Tucker, don't you dare touch that! Don't you dare touch that lever again, or I'll—" Trudy whirled to demand that the boys pull their heads in from the windows. "Bobby! Tommy!" Baby Joe bounced with exhilaration on her lap. The wind whipped the bow ties to stiff ribbons streaming out behind mud-splattered collars and shirtfronts. The boys' open, cheering mouths caught the spray from rain-filled ruts. There was no dampening the delight of Bobby and Tommy as Birch slipped the accelerator up higher and the muddy highway spit back in disapproval. The left sleeve of Birch's suit received a brown rinsing; he seemed not to notice. Trudy's hairpins worked their way loose from their hiding places, like so many twigs protruding from a nest.

"Oh," she cried. "Oh! Oh! Birrrch!" No longer was she wailing about hair or mud-caked suits. She shouted because just ahead the highway dipped down a slope into the James Fork Creek! The road ran through the water for twenty feet and then emerged on the other side! There was no bridge for automobiles. This was mule country, after all. Had Birch forgotten?

The locomotive engineer had his hand to the throttle. He saw the James Fork coming just ahead, but his trestle bridge would carry him straight across the water without a break in stride.

Neither did Birch slow down—until it was too late. For one smooth second, the Ford glided in midair as it leaped over the lip of the road.

And then, like a just-christened battleship descending the dry-dock ramp for launching, the little ship splashed into the creek. A wave rose over the hood and through the open windows to drench the passengers before the car chugged and gasped and died in the center of the stream.

The engineer hooted his whistle in farewell and continued serenely on to Hartford. Passengers on the train stared out at the little family marooned in the middle of the James Fork. Trudy could see men and women alike point and howl with laughter. These were passengers on their way to Hartford. End of the line. They would be there when Birch and Trudy and their once perfectly groomed offspring drove through the center of town.

So much for first impressions. Water dripped from Birch's drooping hat brim. The boys looked as though they had rolled down the bank of the creek and then up the other side. Baby Joe wailed his unhappiness at the sudden icy bath. As for Trudy's recently lint-free blue suit . . .

Birch simply gripped the wheel. He did not look at Trudy or the evil serpent-train that had tempted him and enticed him to such a terrible fall. It slithered away. The back of the caboose was crowded with passengers who had darted back to stare after the marooned automobile.

"We'll beat 'em next time," Tommy said in grim encouragement to his father.

Trudy swiveled in her seat and leveled a wet and angry glare, warning that nothing of the kind would ever happen again.

Tommy's eyes widened with fear. He hunkered back in his seat and blinked at her. Never had he seen his mother so angry and wet in her

Sunday clothes. The phrase *wet hen* whispered through his mind, but he did not say the words out loud. Bobby took the cue from his older brother and did not open his mouth, lest it get swiped around to the back of his head.

Without a word, Birch removed his boots, rolled up his trousers, and climbed out on the running board to see what damage had been done. No broken wheels. Spokes intact. The Ford had survived, even if Birch might not.

Trudy looked grimly downstream. Leaves floated past them and swirled away. Birch muttered hopeful things about how he had forgotten there wasn't a bridge and how he figured he'd learned his lesson and he'd never race the Rock Island again because tracks were smooth and the highway wasn't anything but a gravel path through a pitted wilderness.

The Ford engine started just fine, but the tires had sunk into the streambed just enough so they all had to take off their shoes and wade through the chilly waters to get back on the shore.

Only as the Ford pulled out of the water did Trudy trust herself to speak. "Birch"—her voice trembled and cracked—"you cannot suppose that we shall go on to Hartford today. You will turn the automobile about and take us back home . . . immediately."

Birch obeyed without an argument.

Damon Phelps listened attentively to the latest scheme to make more money available to the embezzlers. Behind the round spectacles that magnified Penner's already owlish looks, Phelps could see the little man's eyes sparkle with enthusiasm.

"Two hundred fifty thousand dollars in loan money," Penner said. "Neat as anything. Mister Tell approved loans for very important people here in the area. Except they never asked for any loans, so they don't know they are missing anything when we take the money and invest it."

"And," explained Tell, "our clerks don't suspect a thing, since all they see is that we are giving personal attention to some extremely significant clients. By choosing highly placed individuals, we eliminate any possibility that our tellers could mention even the slightest hint of our loans where it would matter."

"Brilliant," Phelps admitted. He actually chuckled. "And who are the dignitaries who are now unknowing customers of the Petroleum Bank?"

Ticking them off on his fingers and reciting the names in a singsong voice like a nursery rhyme, Penner listed, "The mayor, the sheriff, five councilmen, three judges, and the coroner."

"These are all written as simple interest loans, repayable in, oh, anywhere from thirty to ninety days," explained Tell. "That way, they don't all come due at once. In fact," he concluded, "all we have to do is pay the interest out of our profits and then renew the loans. We are actually going to make money for the bank, Mister Phelps."

Phelps roared his delight. "Not nearly as much as we'll make for ourselves! But tell me, what about signing the documents?"

Penner beamed modestly. "I took the liberty of examining some old real-estate records. Do you know, not one of those men has a signature that is the least bit difficult to copy?"

"And if the bank examiners want to review the applications," Phelps asked, "what then?"

Tell was smiling the broadest smile possible for his thin, normally dour face. "It is the most believable part of all. We indicated that all of these leading citizens intend to use the loan money for speculating in the stock market!"

CHAPTER TEN

The Fugitive

Birch looked worried when he told the boys to run along and play for a while. Trudy had been altogether too quiet on the drive home.

"Whew," Tommy said under his breath. "Dad's in trouble!"

The narrow dirt lane followed the downward slope of the hill away from the house. Gravity urged Bobby and Tommy into a lope as they ran toward the frantic baying of hunting dogs moving toward the opposite bank of the James Fork.

"Dad said we're not to cross the creek," Bobby warned his older brother as they reached the flat field bordering the creek.

Tommy did not slow his gait. While the hounds tracked their prey, Tommy tracked the hounds. "That way." He pointed through the birch trees and beyond the creek. The voices of the dogs rose in a chorus.

"Dad said we're not—"

"Go on back, then," Tommy called scornfully over his shoulder. "I wanna see 'em. Most likely a raccoon."

Bobby kept pace with Tommy and considered the stories his father had told them about hounds battling to the death with raccoons in the water. "Okay, we can watch. But I ain't crossin' over."

Tommy cut through the persimmon thicket as the baying grew even louder. "Comin' right to us!" he said happily. "Now we're gonna see somethin'!"

The trunk of an enormous fallen oak easily spanned the width of the creek in a natural bridge.

"Look there!" Tommy continued. "Near wide enough for a horse to cross it."

"Well, I . . . I ain't no horse," Bobby protested as the mud from the creek bank oozed over the tops of his shoes. "Dad said . . ."

"Dad said don't cross," Tommy retorted as he climbed onto an exposed root and grasped another root above his head to haul himself onto the massive trunk. He smiled at Bobby through the tangle. "So we won't cross it. Just sit on it, up here where it ain't muddy, and wait until them hounds come from the other side. Why, look!" He gestured upstream and then toward the distinct voices of a dozen dogs. "I got the best seat ever. Sit in the mud if you like. See what Mother says about that." He balanced easily out to the center of the log to sit and wait high above the rushing creek.

Bobby looked at his muddy shoes and imagined what Mother would say when he got home. Muddy shoes would be a grave offense if he went home and walked on her clean boards. The roots of the water oak were high and dry, on the other hand. If he only went halfway across the James Fork, that would not be considered going across the creek, would it?

He picked his way through the roots, climbing them like a ladder to the broad platform of the trunk. Tommy had chosen a place on this side of the middle. That way if anyone asked if he crossed over he could truthfully say, "No, ma'am. We stayed on our own side."

Bobby joined him, straddling the log as if he were riding a horse. His legs stuck straight out on either side. He thought maybe two horses could cross this old tree without much trouble.

"You know what—" Bobby started to tell Tommy what he thought, but Tommy jabbed him in the ribs and glared at him for silence.

✳ ✳ ✳

"You want to scare the critter away?" Tommy whispered to Bobby, imagining the raccoon would be headed right for this very tree trunk to cross onto Tucker property. They were coming! Right here to the bank of the creek! Maybe they had been hunting all night in the mountains, and now Bobby and Tommy were here to witness what would surely be the end of the chase. There was no way an animal could get shed of a pack of hounds baying like that. There was blood in their voices! The James Fork was the battlefield, and Tommy and Bobby were going to see firsthand what their father had been telling them about hunting in these parts.

The voices of the hunters called out to one another as heavy boots crashed through the thicket:

"We got him now, Ed!"

"No place for that coon to go but into the open fields!"

Bobby nudged Tommy knowingly. So it *was* a raccoon they were after. Tommy put a finger to his lips for silence.

One of the men screamed a wild war whoop. "We got him! Listen to them hounds!"

Another voice shouted, "You're a dead'un! Ain't nobody ever got clear of these dogs!"

Half a dozen more yells echoed back in the hollow until it sounded as if a whole army were smashing down to the bank of the James Fork.

"What's he sayin'?" Bobby asked, gripping the sleeve of Tommy's canvas coat.

Tommy shushed him. The hounds were very near. Their shrill howls carried the sound of death before them. The voices of their masters matched those of their dogs in bloodlust. Tommy was not so sure he liked this anymore. Again and again the men taunted the hunted animal with the nearness of its death. They jeered at it as though it had human understanding of the panic of its flight. The men sounded crueler than the dogs. The dogs seemed only an extension of their masters' brutality.

Suddenly Tommy imagined the lone creature as it fled before this mindless army, and he found himself hoping that the animal would somehow outwit the men and their hounds.

"Let's go." Bobby's face reflected the same unnamed dread, as if he did not want to see the end either. Yet he remained rooted to the tree trunk.

Tommy did not respond. The brush on the opposite side of the banks trembled like an approaching wave. The baying drowned out the peaceful rush of the water flowing beneath the trunk. He resolved that when the raccoon broke into the clearing, he would cheer for it to escape. He did not like the unseen men attached to such terrible words. He had heard men talk like that in the oil towns—wild, insane, hungry to hurt something or someone. Mostly those men had been drunk. But these men, the hunters, were drunk in a different way.

"Come on!" Bobby tugged Tommy's sleeve again. "They're comin'!" Suddenly it was as if they were the ones being chased. What man or beast would not run from men and dogs such as these?

"I have to see." Tommy pulled himself free of Bobby's grasp. "I gotta see what happens!"

"Please," Bobby said. His freckles stood out on his pale skin. "Let's run home! Let's—"

The brush broke in a dozen places at the edge of the creek. The wild baying continued as a pack of redbone hounds and blueticks and black-and-tans ran to the water and sniffed and howled and circled and darted up and down a dozen yards from where Bobby and Tommy sat, wide-eyed. A red hound plunged into the water and brushed the current with his long nose as if he could somehow find the scent. Another and another broke into a yipping whine as they tracked the scent to the rim of the James Fork and then charged toward the fallen log as if they would jump onto it and devour Bobby and Tommy as replacements for their lost quarry. The boys jumped to their feet as six cursing men emerged from the brush.

They carried guns of all varieties. Their coats were filthy from the chase. Their hat brims drooped over scowling faces.

"They lost the scent. . . ."

"No place for that coon to go!"

"The dogs'll pick it up on the other side!"

"I'm gonna blow his head clean off when I . . ."

They called their dogs by name and scrambled down the bank. Only then did they notice Bobby and Tommy on the log.

"Hey there! It's a couple of young'uns!"

"You there! Boys! You seen a coon come on by here? cross this here creek?"

Tommy spotted the sheriff's badge on the coat of the tallest man in the group. "No, sir. No raccoons," Tommy answered in a serious tone.

The sheriff spoke. "We're talkin' about a nigger, boys." The hounds still scrambled in the mud, searching for the scent. "Escaped the road gang. Had leg-irons on, too. Couldn't have swum this creek. Had to cross it there." He pointed to the very place where the boys stood.

Bobby clutched his brother's coat again, but Tommy paid him no mind.

The sheriff called a big red hound to his side. "C'mon, Grandee. Get up there." The dog leaped onto the log bridge and sniffed his way to the boys. They backed up from the probing nose, mindful not to fall in.

The sheriff jumped onto the log and easily walked out to the middle. He peered down into the deep, swift water. "You hear what I'm askin', boys? You seen a nigger runnin' thisaway?"

"No, sir," Tommy replied, keeping a watchful eye on the dog. So this is what they had meant when they shouted to one another. Not a raccoon at all, but a man! A black man in leg-irons! Tommy was glad they had seen nothing of the kind.

"Where you boys live?"

The sheriff's eyes were cold and gray. He was missing most of his back teeth, so his cheeks were sunk in. He had the same amount of beard as Pa had once when he was sick for three days and didn't shave. And he smelled of rank sweat and old tobacco.

"Up yonder." Tommy pointed toward the birch trees behind them.

"Well, get on up there, then!" the sherriff snapped. "We got a nigger cannibal on the loose. Been all over the countryside. Now go on before he spots you and decides to have you for supper! Get on now!"

Tommy tore his eyes from the red hound to the face of the sheriff and then to the group of men and dogs combing the bank of the creek. With a shudder, he nudged Bobby back toward their own shore.

"Grandee'd smell his black hide if he came across here," the sheriff called to his men. "He ain't come this way. Couldn't get away from this nose."

"If he swum the creek, he's dead! Ain't nobody swimmin' the James Fork with leg-irons this time of year."

"Clem, take your hounds up thataway!" the sheriff ordered. "Jones, we'll go downstream with Grandee. He's a tricky one, that buck. Maybe he waded a bit and then took out cross-country again!"

The angry, swearing voices and the whine of the hounds followed Bobby and Tommy back through the persimmon thicket and the stand of birch trees, finally fading into bits and pieces of conversation carried on the wind.

The boys ran across the field to where the lane sloped up again to the house. Tommy grasped a rail of the split-rail fence and stared off to where the hunters were. He felt sorry for the man they hunted. The sheriff and his men were enjoying what they were doing too much, it seemed.

"We ought not tell Ma and Pa what we seen," Bobby said. "They wouldn't let us go down there no more if they knew."

Tommy bit his lip and squinted as he considered what his brother said. Sometimes Bobby had some good thoughts, even if he was only seven and a half. As a nine-year-old, however, such a decision should be left to Tommy.

"They'll find out."

"But suppose that convict feller is a . . . cani . . . can . . ."

"Cannibal."

"What's it mean, Tommy?"

"Means he eats people."

Bobby put his hand to his throat and looked all around. "We can't tell Ma that! She'd load us up right now and *whoosh*. . . we'd be right back to Oklahoma, livin' in a tent again. I say we don't say nothin'!"

"You heard that sheriff. He's dead. Tried to swim the creek in leg-irons." Tommy raised his chin slightly as he pictured such a desperate struggle. Cannibal or no, he still pitied the man. Nobody cared if he was dead. They hoped that was the case, it seemed. Even if he hadn't drowned, he was as good as dead. The sheriff would shoot him on sight, and the hounds would tear him to pieces. The matter was settled. No use getting Ma all upset. "We should keep our mouths shut," Tommy said with authority.

And they shook on the bargain.

"Birch! Ho!" The kitchen door flung open and the voice of J.D. Froelich invaded the house without waiting for an invitation. "Birch boy!"

Trudy's mouth was set in a thin, angry line as she hung up the damp clothes on lines strung across the front room. She closed her eyes for a moment of irritation as J.D. entered the house as though it were his own. Trudy knew she would not only have to be polite to Birch's cousin, but even pleasant. She did not feel up to either.

"I am in the front room," she called, not pausing as she draped Tommy's jacket over the line.

"Front room!" J.D. bellowed. "Looks more like a Chinese laundry! Lordy! It's a good thing Birch's mama ain't alive to see what a mess is here." He peered around Bobby's long johns at Trudy. "Now that woman could keep a house."

Trudy managed to fix a patient smile on her face. She resisted the urge to say that no one could have kept this house with the flock of vultures waiting to descend and take everything in sight. "Birch is out . . . in the barn."

"What's he doin' out there? Has he heard the news?" At this, J.D. held up his shotgun for Trudy to see.

"He's taking inventory."

"Inventory?" J.D. scratched his bulbous nose and tugged at his stocking cap. "What's to inventory?"

"Nothing," Trudy replied sharply.

J.D. raised his eyebrows. "Well now, Miz Trudy . . . well now . . ." He hefted his shotgun. "Y'all might just be real lucky you got nothin' out there to steal. Otherwise you'd have got home, and the whole barn would be empty."

"That barn *is* empty." She reached around J.D. to take a damp shirt from the wash basket.

"I mean you might have been stole blind."

Trudy did not reply that this had happened long before their arrival, apparently. "Yes, I see." Clothespins wrestled with the fabric and the line as Trudy thought how much she would like to snap a pin on J.D.'s mouth. "Birch is making a list of everything we don't have for anyone to steal."

J.D. was silent. Had he understood her clearly?

"He's out in the barn," she said again.

J.D. did not go find him. He propped his shotgun against the wall and warmed his hands by the camp stove. "Well, I come to warn him." He rubbed his hands together as if he were washing them in the warmth of the stove.

"Warn?" It was too late to warn Birch about unscrupulous relatives, Trudy thought. But she held her tongue.

"There's a nigger got loose a while back from the chain gang. They think he's drowned in the creek down there, but until they find a body, there ain't no way of knowin' for sure."

Trudy clutched a pair of knickers to her as she considered J.D.'s words . . . then J.D. himself. He was a coarse little man. It was hard to believe that he was in any way kin to Birch. She would change the locks on the doors—not because of an escaped convict but because she could not tolerate the thought of J.D. walking in any time he wished without so much as a by-your-leave. "What's the man done?"

"I told you. He done escaped from the chain gang." J.D. looked annoyed.

"Is he a murderer?" She returned to her task.

"If he was a murderer, he'd be hanged long since. Don't put no nigger murderer on a chain gang." J.D. seemed irritated by the question.

She could guess what he was thinking: How was he to know what the man had been jailed for? "Is he dangerous?" she asked.

"Desperate, more like it. Been runnin' nearly ten days. Starved, I reckon—that is, if he ain't drowned in the James Fork. You didn't hear them hounds?" His eyes sparkled at the telling of it. "The posse went up and down the creek on both sides. This is the closest they got to catchin' him, I hear. His footprints went right down into the water. They found blood on the bank. And neither footprints nor blood ever come up no place else on the shore."

"Blood? Has he been wounded?"

"Leg-irons. A man can't go far without them things cuttin' right into the ankles. Slows him down so the dogs can get him. But this one went right down into the water, and the dogs can't find no trace." J.D. frowned at his weapon. "There ain't no dead body gonna pop up neither. Those irons'll weight him to the bottom just like cement on the feet of a bootlegger in Chicago."

Trudy went to the door and called for Birch to come. She did not want to hear more news. Not today. She held the door open for J.D., who did not budge. Then she said to him in a quiet voice. "This is exciting, isn't it, J.D.?"

"Ain't it though?" He laughed. He evidently hadn't heard the disapproval in her tone.

"What will you do if he isn't drowned? if he comes to your place?"

J.D. snatched up his shotgun. "They'll have one less nigger on that there chain gang, I'll tell you!" He grinned hopefully. Perhaps he was imagining bagging his game. "We never have nothin' like this happen in these parts. Keep your boys close to home. Birch has a gun, don't he?"

At that, Birch entered the house and ducked under the line. His face showed the strain of Trudy's displeasure about this morning. He managed a weary smile for his cousin and then a sideways glace at Trudy. One look at her expression, and he put his arm around J.D.'s shoulders and led him outside to the back porch.

Trudy could see Bobby and Tommy pitching rocks into a target on the side of the chicken coop. Without thinking why, she called them into the house as Birch spoke quietly to J.D. outside. Only after they had come inside to stand before her did she realize that she was less afraid of an escaped convict than of J.D. Froelich's way of talking and thinking. She did not want her sons to witness the eagerness with which J.D. anticipated shooting a man.

★ ★ ★

The news that Cousin J.D. brought canceled the vow of silence taken by Tommy and Bobby. In an unending stream, they related the story of men and dogs and the escaped cannibal. At least now they no longer had to hide their fear. The story was repeated over again like a tall tale told around a campfire.

The doors of the house were locked tight. Birch lay on his back with his old Colt revolver in its holster at his side. The boys had long since fallen asleep after an evening of wondering about the fate of the convict and wondering if he might not spring from behind the bushes at the side of the outhouse and carry them away as hostages.

All trips to the outhouse that night had been made with Birch, who stood patiently by as protector. "Ain't nobody gonna come near this privy unless he had to, boys. If he ain't drowned in the creek, then he ain't coming here to get suffocated, neither!" he told Trudy. All the same, nobody wanted to go out there alone, so Birch shivered and stamped his feet from the cold. When he came in, he added to his list a fifty-pound bag of lime to dump down the toilet.

Birch had seemed absolutely unconcerned about the convict. Until now.

"Are you awake?" Trudy asked in a sleepy whisper.

"Uh-huh."

"Why?"

"What a question, woman!"

"He won't harm us." Trudy patted Birch on the chest.

"I got my gun."

"We've got nothing anyone would want," Trudy said with assurance. "Even if someone stole the bankbook, you know the money couldn't be transferred by anybody but you."

"I'm not worried about that."

"Then what? You've already been robbed blind of what's yours—and by your own kin." There! She had said it out loud. "If that convict comes this way, just send him down to J.D. and Maybelle. Whatever he takes will be twice stolen; that's all."

Birch laughed as he thought about the truth of her words. "Yes. J.D. would love the chance to shoot at somebody, at that."

"And there's the difference between him and you. J.D.'s waiting down there in the dark and just praying that poor drowned criminal drags himself out of the James Fork so he can shoot him full of holes. And you're lying here wide-awake, praying you won't have to shoot anybody."

"I suppose you're right, True."

She could feel him relax beneath her gentle hand. She kissed his cheek, his ear, his neck, forgiving him for racing the Rock Island locomotive today.

"You're always right," he said softly.

"Mostly." She smiled against his face. "Except when I'm not."

All was indeed forgiven.

He kissed her. "I know something that would help me sleep," he said in a whisper.

"Hot milk?"

"We got no milk cow."

"Well then, we'll have to think of something else."

CHAPTER ELEVEN

Last Will and Testament

Mrs. Crowley brought her radio to the O'Halloran house because she said she was here more than at her little one-room flat. Such a fine house ought to have a radio, she said. It was too quiet without one.

David lay on his stomach on the worn floral rug in front of the enormous old Majestic radio. The music of *Dixie's Circus and Novelty Band* made his arithmetic homework seem more bearable. And Mrs. Crowley was right. The house did not seem so empty when the radio was on. The old housekeeper knitted and thought her own thoughts and smiled sometimes at some faraway memory.

The old Majestic was not nearly so fine as the radio David's mother had purchased last year. Only three dollars a week—that's what his mother had paid for a brand-new Kellogg three-screen grid radio with cathedral sound.

Mrs. Crowley's radio whined and wailed with the voices of the singers and comedians. When the atmospherics were fussy, it faded in and out unpleasantly. But it was something, anyway. Better than the silence that had filled the evenings after Brian O'Halloran had sold Mama's radio.

Well, why should Brian care if there was a radio in the house? He was hardly ever home anyway. His long absences had been perfectly fine with David and his mother. Every evening she would turn on the stock-market report at six o'clock and listen while she washed the dishes and David worked on homework. She did not own stock, but she was interested in what was happening, all the same. Pretty boring stuff as far as David was concerned, but she listened to it avidly, sometimes shushing

David if he interrupted news about this tycoon or that Wall Street mogul. Their lives, she said, were like fairy tales, weren't they? Poor boys became millionaires and married the daughters of royalty. It was better stuff than movies, she said. Maybe the most interesting program on the radio.

David did not listen at all until *Dixie's Circus and Novelty Band* came on at seven o'clock. Then he listened to Harry and George and Littman's entertainers . . . stories and music right on through until *The True Story Hour* came over the air at nine o'clock sharp. That had always been the signal for David's bedtime. He would take his bath and climb into bed and wait until the program was over. Then his mother would come in and tuck him in and read to him. She was a better storyteller than the radio. David told her she should have been a radio queen, and she had laughed at him and blushed.

Those had been pleasant days, with Brian on the road most of the time. Even when David's stepfather came home to drink and sleep and fight for a few days, David had consoled himself with the fact that things would get back to normal soon enough. Brian would leave again, and all would be right with the world.

Then Irene O'Halloran got sick and Brian sold the radio. David had been able to listen to parts of his favorite programs during visiting hours at the hospital, but evenings at home had been so quiet. Too quiet. Old Mrs. Crowley must have thought so, too. So she had borrowed David's wagon, and with the help of David, Oink, and Willie, she'd wheeled the old Majestic a mile and a half uphill and down and lugged it up the front stairs without breaking even one tube! Even Brian O'Halloran had been impressed when he got home. He privately called her a "game old broad," but to her face he called her "thoughtful."

So here they were. *Dixie's Circus and Novelty Band* twanging over the airwaves in spite of an approaching storm. David could almost imagine his mother in the next room . . . almost.

There was a knock on the door that tapped in rhythm to the beat of "When the Saints Go Marching In."

Mrs. Crowley glanced up and peered toward the lace curtain that covered the glass panes in the front door.

David could see Father John's white clerical collar. The unexpected arrival of the priest reminded him that things were all different. There might be homework to do, music on the radio . . . but David's mother was not here. And Father John had been with David when she left. The clerical collar jerked David back to the stark reality of the present.

"It's the father." Mrs. Crowley made as though to get up, but David knew better.

"I'll go," he said when the knock sounded a third time.

Father John was smiling as David opened the door. He touched the brim of David's baseball cap, playfully tweaking it to one side. When the priest's smile faded, David knew he had seen the dark bruise on his face.

"Evening, David," he said in a solemn-sounding voice. "You been fighting?"

David self-consciously readjusted his cap and stepped aside to allow the priest to enter. "No, sir," he replied, not wanting to lie to a priest, but uncertain if he was telling the truth. After all, it had been Brian O'Halloran doing the fighting, not David.

"Where'd you get the shiner?"

Mrs. Crowley stood up and gaped at David in amazement. "Yes! Where?" Then she turned to Father John. "Come in, Father. I . . . we were just listening to the radio." She snapped it off and waddled toward David, snatching off the cap and leaning close to examine his face. "And when?"

"I fell out of a tree," David lied. "It's nothing." He took back his cap and returned to his books on the floor while Mrs. Crowley made pleasant talk with Father John about how difficult it was to keep track of a small boy and how one could not be around every minute to make sure he was where he needed to be. She took the priest's hat and hurried into the kitchen to put the kettle on.

Father John eyed the big radio. "Your mother told me that your stepfather . . . Brian? That he sold your radio."

"This is Missus Crowley's." David assumed that the priest had come to visit the old woman. After all, priests did not stop by to visit with kids.

"She brought it here to the house, did she?"

"Me and Willie and Oink . . . that is, Ralph Johnson . . . we helped. Brian says Missus Crowley is a game old broad."

Father John glanced toward the door of the kitchen. "That she is. You've been lucky to have her on hand, too."

David did not reply. He tapped his pencil on his open arithmetic book. He did not feel lucky. Not at all. Sometimes he even thought that he could do perfectly well on his own. Make his own breakfast. Live on cornflakes and peanut-butter sandwiches for the rest of his life. Mrs. Crowley was okay for an old lady, but that was as far as he was willing to take it.

"I guess so." He pretended to study his multiplication problem.

Mrs. Crowley rattled cups in the kitchen.

"She keeps the house good for us. My mom said so."

Father John cleared his throat. "Yes. Well. With your father on the road, it must be difficult."

David glanced up at the priest. "Not so bad." David turned his attention back to the arithmetic book. "I've got the radio."

Did Father John know that David liked it a whole lot better when Brian was gone? Did he know that David had been lying about how he got the black eye?

"David?" Father John leaned forward, and the rocker squeaked. "Come here, will you?"

David obeyed, coming to stand in the circle of light in front of the lamp. He was careful not to step on Mrs. Crowley's knitting. Father John lifted the brim of the ball cap and looked—really looked—into David's eyes. Not like Mrs. Crowley, who had gone the whole day and not seen the bruise. And David could tell that Father John knew he had lied. The priest touched David's cheek with his finger. "Tell me what happened."

"I . . ." David ducked his head, not wanting to speak the truth out loud. He felt as though Brian O'Halloran could hear him through the walls and across the miles. "I hit my face . . . when I fell." He was lying, just as he had been all day. Only this lie was not fun like the one about climbing up on the roof to watch the World Series.

Father John took David's small hands in his big ones. He stuck his chin out a bit and narrowed his eyes to show that he was thinking. Then he unbuttoned the cuff of David's shirt and rolled up the sleeve until the purple bruises were revealed. On the forearm were the distinct marks of five fingers where Brian had picked David up and hurled him to the floor. Three stripes crisscrossed his upper arm, and the very clear outline of a buckle was unmistakable.

"David . . ." Father John rolled down the sleeve quickly as though he could not bear to see more. He embraced the boy, who stiffened at his touch.

"He didn't make me cry," David spat. "He couldn't! I told him to go ahead and kill me. But I didn't cry!"

Father John's eyes were moist behind his glasses. His deep brown eyes shone sadly as he looked at David in the same way Irene had looked at him in the end. "I was afraid of this. Your mother . . . told me he was . . ."

"Don't do me any good now, does it?" David pulled away. What was the use of all this? "If you tell him I told, it will be worse next time, and then he'll just move away. Take me away where nobody knows us. That's what he did with Mama."

Father John drew a deep breath. "Yes, I know all about that, too. David? Your mother made some provisions for you . . . a request to the church, actually. She asked that you be placed in the care of the church. Do you understand?"

"You mean like some kind of orphan?" David's tone was flat. He focused on the toes of his shoes and thought about playing marbles at school. About Oink and Willie and the fellas and how he had just made friends and now would have to start over again.

"I have spoken with Mister O'Halloran."

"Brian?"

"He agrees."

"I'll bet he does."

"He thinks that you'll be better off with us than . . ." He swept his hand around the nearly empty room. His eyes lingered on the radio.

David felt panicked. "Me and Missus Crowley get along okay."

"Missus Crowley agrees with the decision as well."

"She knows?" No wonder she didn't make a fuss about him wearing his hat. The old coward! She'd known they were going to lock him up in an orphanage all along. No wonder she didn't say anything all day, and now she was hiding in the kitchen!

"She is elderly. Not even your relative. What else is there? You can't remain in the care of a housekeeper indefinitely." Again the finger rose to touch the edge of the bruise. "And there is this . . . David. You don't want to live with *this*, do you?"

"I want my mom!" David shouted, backing into the Majestic. "That's what I want!"

Father John mopped his brow and shook his head slowly. "Yes, boy, I know. And she knew. And she placed you in the hands of the church because she knew her own hands would be out of reach. Beyond helping you now." His voice was soothing.

David felt suddenly tired. "My friends! What about school? I'm doing okay. I'm doing real good. I haven't cried. I don't bother nobody."

There was no clanking in the kitchen, so David knew that Mrs. Crowley was listening. Would she talk about him later in the neighborhood? Would she see Willie and Oink at the market and tell them how he begged? The thought made him shudder.

David stared past the form of Father John, toward the kitchen door. "When do I have to go?"

"We thought you could finish the week at your old school." Father John sounded relieved at David's resignation. "Say good-bye to your school chums. Let them know where you'll be and get their addresses, too, if you like, so you can write letters."

David nodded. Everything had been arranged. All set. "I guess so. Okay." The clock on the wall approached nine o'clock. Time for *The True Story Hour* on the radio. Time for David to go to bed and wait . . . for someone who was never coming in to say good night.

* * *

There were choices to be made. Terrible choices. What to take away to St. Joseph's Children's Home and what to leave behind.

For David, such choices had to be based on what fit into the small metal footlocker that Father John left at the house. Every boy at the home had his own footlocker, into which an entire world of possessions must be stashed. The lockers slid easily beneath the iron cots in dormitories that housed twenty-four boys to a room. There was no extra space for frivolous toys or the mementos placed carefully on top of David's chest of drawers. His baseball bat just barely fit inside the locker. His glove and ball took the place of a sweater that his mother had knitted for him.

And then he sat on the floor of his bedroom and held the sweater while he thought of her hands and the clacking of knitting needles. Out came the baseball glove, and the sweater was packed neatly back in place. The books she had read to him lined the bottom of the locker like an uneven floor. All the L. Frank Baum books about a wondrous land called Oz. Dorothy and the Cowardly Lion and the Tin Man grinned beneath his small stash of treasures. He set aside his cast-iron replica of a Model T in favor of his mother's thick volume of *Great Expectations*. She had promised to read it to David when she got well again. She had promised!

Mrs. Crowley was off at the market buying bitter chocolate to bake him a going-away cake. The old woman felt guilty, David knew, because she had known all along about the children's home and the little cots and the footlockers. She had acted as if nothing was wrong. As if David would have his old familiar room forever, and nothing would change even though his mother was dead. Her act had been a lie, but David could not feel angry at her because he was an expert liar himself.

He still had not told the fellas that come Monday he would not be at school. Poor Oink was still puffing around the playground and bragging about how he and David were going to perch on a roof to watch the World Series. David thought it would be better to let him go on thinking that until David vanished . . . and the dream vanished with him.

He stared at his baseball bat. Maybe he would put a note on it. *I, David, leave this bat for Ralph Johnson, also known as Oink.* Like a will.

This was a good idea. He let his eyes skim over his jumble of belongings, picking out the best stuff and thinking which of his friends would like to have each item. This was something he could do. He could line up his trucks, his kites, and his stamp collection and label everything he loved so it would go just where he wanted it to go. Somehow this decision made him feel better.

It was growing darker outside. He switched on the lamp and then went into the room that had belonged to his mother. No one had slept in there since she had been gone. Brian never opened the door. He slept on the couch when he was there. Mrs. Crowley didn't even bother to dust it. His mother's belongings were still in place, just as she had left them. Only now she was jammed into a box and stuffed underground.

David opened the top drawer of his mother's bureau, and perfume—sweet and clean smelling, just like her—filled the room.

He closed his eyes and laid his hand on the neatly folded stacks of slips and chemises and pastel cotton blouses she had worn through the summer. He almost felt as if he were touching her, and he wondered why he had not done it before.

On the dresser was a crocheted doily that she said her grandmother had made in Ireland. She loved that little thing. It was the only thing she had inherited from her grandmother, and she had cherished it. On top of the doily was a mother-of-pearl brush and comb and a matching mirror. Beside that was a small heart-shaped crystal perfume bottle, still half full of perfume. David picked it up and squeezed the bulb, sending a puff of his mother's perfume into the room. The scent, so faint from her clothing, now penetrated his senses. "Mama," he breathed, shutting his eyes and inhaling her fragrance. Gently he replaced the bottle on the doily.

What other treasures were in the dark mahogany chest? David slid open the second drawer: folded skirts. The third: sweaters and three long-sleeved blouses that she had worn when she was a teacher and when she was beautiful. Seeing those clothes again made David remember everything, just like seeing it at a movie theatre rolling across the screen. He closed the drawer reluctantly and then pulled out the bottom drawer.

A jumble of photo albums and shoeboxes held together with ribbons filled the drawer. David sank to the floor and sat cross-legged before the heap. He opened the ragged cover of a heavy black album and saw his own baby face smiling up at him, labeled *DAVEY—9 months*.

There must be a million of these pictures, he thought, flipping slowly through the pages. His mother was forever snapping photographs, telling him to stand still and smile.

Behind every photograph of him was his mother's command: *"Davey, smile!"* He smiled now as he remembered. The album took him back to New Jersey—Atlantic City, at the beach . . . building sand castles . . . getting sunburned so he cried all night and his mother plastered him with tea bags to ease the pain. Then Baltimore, at Grandma's flat before she died two years ago . . . Uncle Bob before he sailed off in the Merchant Marines.

And then there was "the old neighborhood," as his mother had called it. The pictures slipped back before his time. The handwriting switched to that of David's grandmother, and the labels beneath the photographs all started with the name *IRENE . . . Irene—19 years old . . .* so pretty and young in her old-fashioned dress and high collar. Irene at Coney Island, eating a Nathan's Famous hot dog! Oh, the stories she had told him about Coney Island and Nathan's!

David noticed the places where photos had been removed from the pages of the old album. Blank black squares with faded paper all around. These were the pictures where the face of his father—his real father—had once smiled out.

David had never seen a photograph of his father. His mother told him Max had died. But Brian O'Halloran said that he had just left Irene . . . left her alone with David.

With a shudder, David closed the book. He traced the gold writing on the cover: *Family Memories.* What would become of this book now? There was no family left to care for these faces. Only David was left to love them. He frowned and set the book to one side. He would find room for it in his tiny locker. Even if he had to give his Louisville Slugger bat away to Oink, he would manage to cram the photo album into his box.

"What else . . . ?" He lifted out a worn-out shoebox and placed it on his lap. When he pulled at the ribbon, the top tumbled off, revealing letters in envelopes that were yellowed with age and dog-eared from the reading. At first he gasped with excitement at the discovery that the stamps were not American but from faraway France. And with postmarks from Paris and Nice and Marseilles. A stab of pain shot through him as he remembered how his mother had taught him to notice things like postmarks and dates, to find unusual stamps to fill his collection. Then his eyes moved from the postmarks to the neatly inscribed name on the return address: *Max Meyer.*

"Max," David whispered. He touched the ink as if to be sure that he was not imagining. His father . . . *real* father . . . had been called Max. *Max Meyer.* David had heard the name, but this was the first time he had ever seen it written. Or maybe this was just the first time he was old enough to recognize it written out longhand. Hadn't he seen his mother rummage through this drawer? Certainly the bundles of letters had all been here! Yes! But they had never held any interest for him. Not like the picture album. And unlike her precious books, his mother had never once offered to read him his father's letters.

There were dozens of letters in the shoebox. Dozens of envelopes, each containing something his real father had written to his mother! How could David find room to take them with him?

The back door to the kitchen banged open and then shut. "Day-vid!" Mrs. Crowley shouted breathlessly. "I'm back! They were all out of chocolate, but I'll make you angel food if you . . ." She trudged down the hall, looking into his room. "David? Where have you gotten to?"

He did not reply. He stuffed the letters back into the shoebox and crammed the album into the drawer, closing it before the old woman poked her head through the door.

She sniffed. "Into your mama's perfume?" She eyed him without disapproval. There was a hint of pity in her voice. "Well then—" she frowned and nodded—"I suppose you have a right. She was your mother, after all."

"What . . . what will happen to Mother's things?" David remained on the floor.

"I suppose . . . Mister O'Halloran will do something with them. It's none of my business unless he asks me to help with it."

"My baby pictures?"

"They're yours. Take them if you like. He'll never miss them, I'll wager."

David had already planned to take the album. And the letters. And the doily that his mother cherished and maybe even her comb and brush set and the last of her perfume. His own stuff seemed of little importance to him compared to the things his mother had considered special family treasures. Maybe he could wear two pair of knickers to the children's home instead of wasting precious space in the footlocker with his clothes. And probably it would be a good thing to leave his bat for Oink. After all, they wouldn't be going to see the World Series together, would they?

The phone at Max's elbow rang. He ignored it until he had finished typing the sentence he was on, then tucked the receiver between shoulder and chin. "Meyer," he said, scanning what he had just written.

"Maxie," said the cheerful voice of Harry Beadle. "Were you planning to cover the lunch at the National Business Conference?"

Max glanced at a calendar page thumbtacked to the wall over the typewriter. "To hear Roger Babson give the same talk for the third year in a row? I don't think so. Besides, Harry, why do you care? Babson is a bear, same as me. Not a cockeyed optimist like you."

"Me and the rest of the country," Harry corrected. "But, I don't know, Max. Word is that this time Babson has some new stuff. He isn't giving out an advance text either."

Max stopped rereading his column to listen with greater attention. Usually speakers freely passed out advance copies of their pet theories and shopworn commentary. For an economist not to have a press release meant that he wanted to keep his remarks secret until after the intended audience heard them first.

"Okay," agreed Max, "I'll be there."

★ ★ ★

Babson's speech was as dull as Max had feared. In an unrelieved monotone, the little professor reviewed again the reasons why the long-running bull market could not continue.

"Working families are putting all their income into stocks, then borrowing more than they can afford and buying even more. People from foreign countries have done the same thing. England, France, Germany . . . none of their economies can stand the further drain of capital into this nation's stock market. They must and they will raise interest rates, and then gold will reverse its movement and flow out of this country and out of the stock market. Prices will drop."

There was the sound of fake snoring from close by Max's table. Max knew that the words were true. But after three years of the same remarks, the rampaging bull was still unchecked. Babson and those who took him seriously looked like fools.

The speech moved on from the reasons for the coming market drop to the signs that it would happen soon. "Production of steel continues to rise, but automobile purchasing has slowed. New-home buying is sluggish. Inventories are up from half a billion dollars to eighteen billion dollars in one year. People have stopped buying. What does this mean?"

"It means," grumbled a man whose gray suit bulged all around his overstuffed frame, "that people are being sensible. They are using their paychecks to make real money in the market instead of frittering it away."

"Shh!" hissed Max.

If Roger Babson had heard the critical comments, he gave no sign and continued the unemotional pace of his remarks. "If people stop buying, what will support the profits on which dreadfully inflated stocks are trading?"

"Rubbish," muttered the heckler, louder this time. "The American economy has never been stronger." A general murmur of agreement hummed through the crowd. It was clear that this talk of a faltering misstep on the road to universal prosperity had few supporters.

"The price of farm products is falling."

"Good," called the heckler. "I can buy more stock if I spend less on bread and bacon."

"But . . ." Babson faltered, uncertain now about continuing.

"Professor Babson?" Max called out suddenly.

"Yes? What is it?" Babson looked relieved that someone had addressed him by name.

"Give us something concrete. How big a drop?"

"Yeah," agreed the heckler. "Stick your neck out. How bad will it be?" he sneered.

The buzz in the room continued. Everyone knew that economists never gave predictions in clear terms. No doubt Babson would figure out some way to wriggle out of committing himself.

"I should say . . . sixty to eighty points."

A ripple effect of silence began near the speaker's platform and spread outward as Babson's words sank in.

"Would you say that again, please?" Max urged.

"Certainly. A loss of 25 to 30 percent of the value of the leading stocks is imminent."

Max's column, carried in the *Times* the following morning, was no more than one voice among hundreds. The Associated Press bannered the story: "Leading Economist Predicts 60- to 80-Point Plunge."

CHAPTER TWELVE

High Finance

Even though the text of Professor Babson's speech was widely reported by the wire services and carried by newspapers all across the country, it was largely ignored in the offices of the Petroleum Bank.

The three embezzlers were too busy admiring the contents of a polished glass dome that sat like a shrine on its own special oak pedestal. Inside the shining bowl was a newly installed stock ticker. Tell and Penner—worshippers before the altar of Mammon—stood in reverent silence beside this latest innovation in high-speed investment information.

Phelps inspected the brass mechanism inside the dome and nodded for Penner to switch it on. Immediately a thin strip of white tape began spewing out of a narrow slot in the globe and spiraling down to pile up on the dark carpet.

"Now," said Phelps with satisfaction, "now we can keep a close eye on things. We can spot trends just as good as those slick New York johnnies in their fancy suits."

Penner retrieved the end of the tape from the floor. "Look at this, Mister Phelps. A good omen, sir. The very first trade that came off the ticker is for Sabre Oil!"

The chairman of the Petroleum Bank shrugged as if to say that even machines acknowledged his financial wisdom. "What is the quote?" he asked, confident that it would show additional profit for the operators of the pool.

"It's—," Penner began, then stopped. In a questioning tone he said, "Mister Phelps, this thing must not be working right."

"Why? What's wrong with it?"

"It says that Sabre Oil has dropped, sir! It's trading at five dollars lower than yesterday!"

Phelps almost knocked Tell down in pushing past him to reach the phone. "Get me Keenan," he demanded when he was connected with the Exchange. "What do you mean he doesn't have time to talk? Tell him Damon Phelps wants to speak with him right now. *Now, immediately*, do you hear?"

In the pause that followed, Penner ventured to pick up the ticker tape. All the prices seemed to be lower than the previous day. The whole market was in a tailspin! Penner almost remarked as much to Phelps, but the assistant vice president got a glare of such anger and hatred for having even touched the traitorous tape that he promptly dropped the spiral of figures and backed up against the wall.

When the broker came on the line, Phelps was practically frothing at the mouth. He was so busy cursing and ranting that he heard nothing of what Keenan said until the broker threatened to hang up and leave Phelps to stew.

"What do you mean, calm down? This whole thing is blowing up in our faces!" Phelps shouted. "How can we cover—I mean, what can we say to our clients?"

When he got off the phone, Phelps was again in control, but not altogether his usual confident self. Keenan had claimed the drop was just an overreaction to a negative speech made by some professor. The market was still on a limitless upward track, and Phelps's ticker would prove it the very next day. In fact, Keenan asserted that this temporary drop was the perfect time for the pool to buy additional shares of Sabre Oil so the profit would be even greater when it came time to unload.

Hartford at last! The road rose and fell in a series of oceanlike swells. Each little hill was topped by a small brick or frame house facing another house just across the road.

The train track veered off to the left to pursue its own course into town. Across the tops of the trees stood an enormous water tower with the name Hartford painted on it.

Twice curried, combed, and shined up, the Tucker family had started all over this morning just as if yesterday had not happened at all. Birch had driven the highway at a reasonable speed. They had set out an hour later than the day before, lest they chance to meet the Rock Island train on its early route. They forded the James Fork Creek carefully and slowly, and this time the little Ford proved itself worthy of its name.

Bobby's too-big knickers had shrunk a bit in the night as they dried on the line strung across the living room above the camp stove. They fit him perfectly now. Tommy's already too-tight Sunday suit had also drawn up and clung uncomfortably to him like a second skin. But, like his father, he did not complain.

Nor did anyone use the vile word *ain't* today. Not even Birch, who used it regularly and without thinking about it. Trudy had mostly given up correcting his speech, but after yesterday Birch's grammar came right out of *McGuffey's Fifth Eclectic Reader*. It was almost a miracle how well behaved the boys could be after only one reckless adventure and a long night of remorse.

Trudy thought to herself that all things truly did work together for good after all, but she dared not repeat such a verse to her errant brood lest they repeat it back to her after their next wild ride. She kept it quietly and pleasantly to herself, but she was smiling as they turned left onto Hartford's Main Street.

On the corner was a movie theatre with a big sign advertising Garbo in *Flesh and the Devil*. Trudy glared at such a shocking title and drew the attention of her sons to the gristmill and the windows of shop fronts and to the stone letters set into the brick cornices of each of the buildings. Beginning with Siemon's Mercantile, each of the structures on the left side of the street bore one letter of the town's name until HARTFORD was spelled out proudly. Below the letters was the date the building had been completed. 1920. Hartford was a recently rebuilt town, and its bricks were still clean and new-looking.

"Well now," Birch said in a puzzled way, "this does not look like the Hartford of my childhood. They've torn everything down and put up new, looks like. Maybe a tornado? . . . Well, she's a prosperous-looking place, if anyone asks me."

No one asked. A number of automobiles were parked along the two-foot high curbs in front of dozens of stores. There was a building where furniture was made. Birch looked the place over closely and then pronounced that they would most likely buy their furniture right there because it would be better to give local folks business instead of ordering out of Fort Smith.

Just up a side street was a livery stable and a few mules and horses milling in corrals. Perhaps he could find a used buckboard for sale there. Hartford had two cafés. Birch explained that the Baptists usually ate at one and the Methodists at the other. There were not enough Presbyterians or Catholics to support a third, so those folks just went wherever they liked the blue-plate special for the day. Next to the café patronized by the Baptists was the barbershop. This place, which had been run by old Mr. Dee ten years ago, was neutral ground. Plenty of politics were discussed in that old chair, but the men of Hartford had always kept their religious differences to themselves when Barber Dee laid his razor to the strap.

These bits of insider information Birch related to his wife and sons as they moved slowly up the street. The brick facing on the buildings might have been all new, but Birch figured that the folks inside the buildings were just the same as they had always been.

"Too bad we gave the boys haircuts at home," Birch said. "I'd have liked to show them off to old Barber Dee . . . if he's still there."

To this, Trudy replied regally that her sons could still meet the barber, but without the extravagant waste of money. Birch simply gazed wistfully at the barber pole and the crowd of old-timers talking in an animated way inside the shop.

And then he pointed out the bank—big round columns supporting a broad overhang. The place looked like an antebellum mansion, only smaller. The name Hartford First National Bank was chiseled in stone above and painted in gold on the window and repeated once more on the door. There was no missing this establishment.

Trudy clutched her handbag as her heart beat a little faster. She opened the latch just to look at the savings book one more time. For nearly two weeks she had been carrying their wealth with her—sleeping with the envelope under her pillow, tucking it into her bodice when she went about her tasks. She had been ever mindful that someone could hold them up and take all their cash, but this savings account was absolutely guaranteed to be transferred only in the name of Birch Tucker. Her single fear had been of misplacing the passbook somehow. Now that worry was going to be resolved. Birch and Trudy were about to become solid citizens and bank depositors in Hartford, Arkansas!

When the Ford coughed to a stop, Birch opened Trudy's door and helped her descend onto the firm soil of Hartford. This was no dream, he couldn't help but think. It was really happening at last!

Even Bobby and Tommy and baby Joe sensed the importance of this moment. They stood quietly beneath the colonnade and stared at the arch of gold letters on the window. Trudy had delayed enrolling them in school so they might be a part of this occasion. All the turmoil of yesterday was forgotten as Birch opened the bank door and stepped aside for his family to enter the marbled halls of high finance.

The inside ceiling was high, supported by still more columns like those outside. The lower floor was occupied by a row of tellers' windows along the far wall and desks surrounded by waist-high partitions near the windows. Up one flight of stairs was a balcony with a wrought-iron railing, where the actual president of First National Bank sat at his huge desk. From this lofty perch he could watch over his little flock of employees with an eagle eye. He had a perfect view of the nimble fingers of the tellers as they counted every dollar and cent out of their cash boxes. The echo of each conversation carried the details of transactions up to his sharp ears. With a nod he could signal to his loan officers one way or the other his final decision on this or that.

Birch remembered well the dour-faced old miser on the balcony. His paunch was much broader now, and the flesh of his scowling face had slipped down a bit farther, but Mr. Henry V. Smith was still president as ever. No one knew what the *V* in his name stood for, but most townsfolk called him King Henry V. If the old man knew of his moniker, he did not seem to object to it. But no one had ever dared to call him that to his face.

King Henry leaned forward in his creaking leather chair to examine the family who entered his courts. He did not like to see small boys in the bank. He made a quiet *harrumph*, which caused the tellers to look up nervously.

Bobby and Tommy needed no further word of warning about behavior. Like the secretary's rattling typewriter keys, the whole place crackled with tension.

Trudy shifted the baby on her hip and removed the Petroleum Bank savings book from her handbag as Birch scanned faces for his old friend Delbert Simpson, who, according to Cousin J.D., was now assistant bank manager.

Simpson spotted Birch first and rose from his desk to greet Birch in the way that was proper for assistant bank managers to greet old friends. "Well, if it isn't Mister Birch Tucker! Birch Tucker and his *most* lovely family! Welcome to First National Bank of Hartford, Mister Tucker." Though smiling at Birch, Delbert Simpson's eyes darted up to the balcony.

"Why, Delbert! You old coot! Look at you! Look like that collar's gonna strangle you! You wear that every day?"

Simpson laughed nervously. No doubt he wished for everyone to believe that, as assistant manager, he not only wore his suit to work but only took it off to change into another. And if no one else believed it, Mr. Simpson at least hoped that King Henry V would.

"Well, Mister Tucker. You've come back to these parts." Then he whispered, "And what a welcome, eh, Birch? Escaped convicts drowning in

the James Fork, I hear." He held open the swinging half door and ushered them back to his desk. "And this is Missus Tucker. How do you
do. . . ."

Birch thrust the savings book into his old friend's hand. "We have
come to open an account." He smiled proudly as Delbert's face registered surprise. No use rehashing the unpleasant incident of the day before in front of the boys.

"I see. I see you have. Well now, this is fine." He looked up at the loft
and then, as if he was scratching his head, he placed two fingers on his
forehead. *Two thousand dollars,* he signaled King Henry V.

When a pleased-sounding *harrumph* echoed down, Delbert relaxed a
bit. He said under his breath, "Lordy, you've done good, Birch. I heard
you were stuck in the James Fork yesterday. Glad you got out." He
glanced up and raised his voice immediately. "We here at Hartford First
National are pleased you've come to us. May I recommend a savings
account?"

"Glad to see you stuck it out, Delbert," Birch whispered. "When I left,
you were sweeping the place."

There was no perceptible change in Delbert's expression, and Birch
wondered if sweeping might not still be among Delbert's duties as assistant manager.

"It will take thirty working days for your account to transfer from Petroleum Bank, of course. Perhaps then you'll want to establish checking
as well."

Trudy leaned forward in her chair. "But there are purchases we need
to make right away. Thirty days?"

Another *harrumph* sounded from the balcony, warning Mr. Simpson
that this was not a charity ward.

"I *am* sorry, Missus Tucker. That is standard policy. Thirty working
days to transfer an account. Especially out of state. This is from
Oklahoma." He tapped the little book. "The world is filled with con men
nowadays. Standard practice."

"It's okay, True," Birch murmured. "We can open credit accounts as
long as we show the savings book, see?"

"No," she insisted. "This is not what we were told. This passbook is as
good as cash money to a bank, they told us in Tulsa. Only much safer to
carry, they said. We have only to fill out the forms, they said, and the
matter would be easily settled."

Delbert's eyes widened in dismay. The customer was balking. "Well
now, Missus Tucker, that may be true in Oklahoma, but here in Hartford
. . . this is a different state. It will take time."

Trudy looked directly at Birch. "Shiloh is smack between Hartford and Mansfield. I say we go to the bank in Mansfield, where no doubt they will transfer our funds from Tulsa without question."

She rose and snatched the savings book out of Delbert's hand as the noises from the balcony sent a furious message to Mr. Simpson that he had better not let two thousand greenbacks go out the door to Mansfield, or else.

Delbert Simpson put a hand to his stomach. His face was very pale. "Just . . . one . . . uh, one moment and I will . . . it's beyond my authority. But I'll just be a minute." He gestured toward the desk of the king and coaxed the savings book out of Trudy's grasp. Then he scurried away. His shoes clanged hollowly on the wrought-iron stairs, and his voice could be heard nervously explaining the situation to Henry V, who knew it all already.

Silence reigned.

Tellers, clerks, and customers lowered their own voices, hoping to catch some sliver of information that might be taken to the cafés and the barbershop to be discussed.

Growls could be heard emanating from the balcony, but until Mr. Simpson padded back down to the floor and wiped sweat from his brow, no one knew the final decision.

"Our bank president, Mister Henry V. Smith, has indicated that we may present you with a letter of credit that you may draw on until your account clears through the usual channels. If there is anything irregular . . ."

"There isn't," Trudy said confidently.

Simpson narrowed his eyes in response. Birch could tell what he was thinking. Trudy's slight foreign accent and her assertiveness were most unusual. She was pushy.

"Yes. Well. I don't doubt your word, Missus Tucker, but we would be a mighty foolish bank if we just accepted everyone's word for everything, wouldn't we?" He didn't look at her; his gaze was fixed solidly on Birch. "If anything should happen to be irregular with this account, you understand that you will be responsible to repay with interest to this bank whatever amount you draw on the letter of credit." He thumped his hand on his desk like an auctioneer's gavel. "That is our final offer—take it or leave it."

"It's a long way back to Mansfield, True," Birch whispered in her ear. "And we might get no better offer there."

Birch could tell from Trudy's expression that she did not like this simpering little assistant or the overlord in his nest on the balcony. She did not care for the bank in the least. But it *was* a long way back to Mansfield. She nodded reluctant agreement.

"Good," Birch said, extending his hand to Delbert. "Done."

But Delbert was not quite done. Another growl from above reminded him not to accept Birch's hand until the terms were quite clear. He acted as though he did not see Birch. Turning to the boys, he said sweetly, "Bet you young'uns would like a soda. Bet your mama'd take you right over there to the drugstore for a soda while your daddy and the bank finish up this business."

"Sure. Sure," Birch urged Trudy and the boys. "This is men's business. Go on now." It was more an order than a request. The Petroleum account was solely in the name of Birch Tucker, after all. The bank could not be expected to know how Trudy had saved every penny and done without to acquire such a handsome amount. Or that Birch would have freely spent it all.

The look Trudy gave Birch made it all clear: No, she did not like the attitude of little Mr. Simpson and King Henry V. Still, it was a man's world, so she herded her little flock gracefully out of the sacred halls of Hartford finance and left Birch to complete the business.

CHAPTER THIRTEEN

Digging for Treasure

It was a morning for miracles.

The sun was out after three days of threatening skies. The newsman on the radio said the canvas tarpaulin was being rolled back off the playing field at Shibe Park, and Athletics Manager Connie Mack would have the team out in force practicing today.

David ate his cold breakfast of cornflakes and considered this news. He thought about the bright sun. About the fact that Philadelphia was in the World Series and that he might never have a chance to see them close up and in person if he didn't do it today. Never mind that they would be practicing. Did it matter if they were just running bases and tossing the ball around? Since they were only practicing, maybe there wouldn't be so many coppers around to run a kid off from watching. Maybe David could see Connie Mack close up . . . maybe ask for the autographs of great players like Jack Quinn, the veteran spitballer; or Eddie Collins, who everybody said was washed up—everybody except David and Oink, that is.

And did it matter if David played hooky? Who would care after the last school bell clanged on Friday? He poked at the final cornflake floating in his milk like a little boat. "Abandon ship!" he said in a high voice as the flake sank. "It's Moby Dick!" He scooped up the flake and downed it with a whalelike bite.

Mrs. Crowley scowled from behind her ironing board. "Get going." She did not like children to play with their food.

In response, David deliberately smacked his lips after devouring the cornflake whaling crew and then sucked up his milk right out of the bowl.

"You'll be late, David," she warned, banging the flatiron hard on the board.

David wanted to jump up and tell her he was sure enough going to be late to school. As a matter of fact, he wasn't going at all. But if he told her his plan, she might call Father John, who would come get him early and haul him off to the children's home today instead of waiting.

"See you after school, Missus Crowley," he said politely. He took his mitt and his baseball with him out the door. Stashing his book bag in the oleander bush, he retrieved his lunch and two nickels and hurried off to meet Oink at the corner.

It might have been okay for David to play hooky because he was leaving anyway. But Oink wasn't moving anywhere. He wasn't being dragged off to a Catholic boys' home. He could stay here forever at Public School 129. People would care if he ditched class—people like his teacher and his parents and the principal. Everybody would have something terrible to say when he finally showed up after being gone all day to Shibe Park with David.

Later, as he and Oink paid their nickel to the tramcar driver, David supposed that he should not have temped Oink to go. Everyone knew that there was one thing Oink could not resist: temptation! He had tried to lose weight a thousand times, but just wave a candy bar under his nose and he couldn't help himself! Down it went, and Oink's mother ended up moving the buttons of his trousers over one more time.

"We're going to get nabbed," Oink puffed as they took their seat.

"Shut up, will you?" David snapped at his companion. "Act normal, and no one will know the difference."

This was another problem poor Oink had. After yielding to temptation, he was immediately overcome by guilt and fear—guilt because he was, indeed, guilty; fear because he always got caught.

"The driver's looking," Oink whispered through the side of his mouth.

"Shut up," David warned. "He's looking at you because you're looking at him. Cut it out. We won't get caught."

This was a lie. Oink would be strung up and roasted when the escapade was over. David knew it. Oink knew it. But Oink wanted to be lied to. He wanted to believe they wouldn't get caught playing hooky and that the day would be just like David said.

"You think we can get in the park?" Oink wiped his sweaty palms on his frayed knickers.

"Sure." David had not yet figured out how. It was clear that his friend could not climb over the fence or shinny up a pole. They would have to walk through a gate and through a door and into the stadium some normal, nonathletic way.

"How?"

David glanced nonchalantly out the window at the massive statue of William Penn on top of city hall. Penn never told a lie, they said. That's why he was up there in bronze, and David was sentenced to life in an institution. But it was too late for David to stop lying now.

"I got it all figured out," David reassured his comrade.

"Ain't gonna make me climb a fence, are you?"

"Relax. I told you, I got it all figured out."

Oink's cheeks were red. "You sure we ain't gonna get arrested or anything?"

"Ha!" David scoffed at the idea.

He could tell that made his friend feel better. It was good when fears were ridiculed and disaster made light of.

Oink ate a sandwich as the tram trundled on. He lifted the bread and examined the lunch meat and the pickles and the mayonnaise, then shoved it into his mouth with the same vigor as David had finished off his last cornflake.

Perhaps this would, indeed, be a perfect day. After all, how often could Ralph "Oink" Johnson finish off his lunch twenty minutes after he had finished breakfast? He seemed to feel better once he had eaten the sandwich. He smiled pleasantly, and his eyebrows went up in interest as he watched the other unlucky schoolchildren trudging off to class. The lives of the good and honest and obedient little children could not be compared to the joys of these two wicked hooligans. For just a moment the sin of hooky felt joyful and free and worth forgetting what the future might hold for them.

"This is really fun," Oink said, looking pleased.

The new stock ticker was still chattering away, but the chairman of Phelps Petroleum was ignoring the loops of paper now piling up on the floor. He had barricaded himself in his private office at the same moment that the opening bell rang in the New York Exchange. Tell and Penner had tried to follow him into the inner sanctum, but he had curtly shown them out and locked the door.

For three hours of the three-hundred-minute trading day, Phelps had scrutinized every single trade and covered an entire legal pad with his own notes on stock-price changes.

The very first sheet was labeled SABRE in block capitals. The first few entries on the page were deep slashes where the pencil cut into the paper as Sabre continued to trade at well below the expected level. Slowly, as the day wore on, Sabre's price began to rise again. Little by little, the oil company stock rose, as did the entire general picture of the market.

After one hundred eighty minutes, Phelps ringed the name of the oil company with several approving swirls and pushed his chair away from the clicking machine. Sabre Oil had regained the entire amount it had dropped the previous day and was, in fact, several dollars per share ahead. It was clear that Keenan had been right. The so-called Babson Break was only a temporary setback caused by that stupid doomsayer and some crazy newspapermen who had trumpeted his words.

Phelps stood and went to unlock the door into the rest of the bank. From their close proximity and the guilty looks on their faces, it was plain that Tell and Penner had been hovering around the door. "Come in," he said gruffly. He did not ask them to be seated, nor did he himself sit down again. Instead, he began at once to bark his conclusions and orders. "Market's back up."

Penner tried to look nonchalant as he dabbed his forehead with a handkerchief.

"But," Phelps continued, making Penner freeze with the hankie on his face like some distraught heroine in a melodrama, "I've got to go to New York."

Phelps reminded the other crooks that they had all their eggs in one basket. With the fake loans coming due soon and the other juggling that had gone on, it was absolutely essential that nothing go wrong now. They had to have the profit from Sabre. The pool needed to get wrapped up successfully and soon.

"Even this gizmo isn't good enough," Phelps complained about the ticker. "I'm still too far away. So, I'll go see to it myself . . . make sure it's being run right. In the meantime," he instructed, "no new trades. If any of the grannies want into their boxes, tell them the vault has just been fumigated and it'll be a week or so. Or bust a key off in their lock. Stall them until you replace the cash."

"Should we discourage withdrawals from savings?" Penner wanted to know.

"No, you imbecile!" roared Phelps. "Do you want to start rumors? Pay any request for cash without question."

"What about notes and out-of-state transfers?" Tell asked.

"Delay those all you can," he ordered. "There can always be something not done right, or some form we forgot to send the first time. Take care of the local folks right away, but as for the others, they can just twist in the wind awhile."

✵ ✵ ✵

Harry Beadle poked his head into Max's office. "The Dow is now *up* 5 percent, Max. Some big slump, huh?"

"Leave me alone, will you, Harry? I don't need you to say I told you so. Strangers laugh at me on the street. People I haven't heard from in ten years have been showing up at my office to accuse me of *causing* the drop."

"You can't say you weren't warned," Harry said. "Just be glad that the wire services got fooled, same as you."

"But everyone seems to think I started it. Some wit hung the nickname Prophet of Loss on poor old Babson, and today I find that title pinned to *my* door."

"Well," Harry comforted, "look at the bright side. When we're sailing on the *Berengaria*, nobody can get at you."

"Yeah," said Max glumly. "I just hope I still have a job when I get back. And people I don't know better quit picking on me."

✵ ✵ ✵

If David and Oink had done nothing at all other than ride around Philadelphia on a tram, the day still would have been perfect. The sight of Shibe Park looming up from Twentieth Street, however, was something like arriving in paradise.

There were the fabled houses with the rooftops where David had promised they would watch the Series. They looked like ordinary houses—redbrick, three stories. Normal houses with stoops and steps and windows with curtains. Climb up those steps and look out those windows, and there was the back side of Shibe Park. Climb a bit farther to emerge on the rooftop, and there was a clear view across right field! The thought of it was like heaven.

Oink screwed his head around on his thick neck and pointed down the row of houses. "Which one of those places, Davey? Huh? Where will we go on game day?"

David scanned the residences for a likely looking rooftop as the tram rattled away. He pointed to the tallest house in the center of the block. It looked as if it would have the best view of the playing field. He knew that as Oink imagined it over the next few days, his cheeks would flush and his eyebrows would rise above his ecstatic expression.

"That one," David said.

Oink opened his mouth in amazed delight. "Yeah? You mean it, Davey? From up there a fella can see all the way to home plate, I bet!"

"Into the press box," David assured him coolly as they trekked toward the ballpark. "And no crowds either."

White ticket booths were set up outside the park. Long lines of fans stood patiently waiting to present the penny postcard that allowed them to purchase their two grandstand tickets for the Series.

Oink eyed them with disdain. "Willie's dad had to pay twenty-five bucks apiece just to get the purchase permission slip. Huh! Then he had to wait in line out here to buy the tickets. And we get to see the game for free!" he added proudly. "Just because he's rich don't mean he's got any brains. My dad said so. My dad said some of the dumbest people he knows are rich people. You gotta be really smart to be poor. Gotta be figurin' out stuff all the time so's you can have fun." He clapped David on the back to congratulate him on the brilliance of the rooftop seating and also for the nickel tram ride and playing hooky.

They might be broke, but boy, what a day this was!

"Yeah," David agreed. "I'd rather be smart than rich." He glanced at the men standing in line. "Although it's easier to be rich."

"Naw, it ain't!" Oink argued. "It ain't easier at all. We ain't gonna have to stand in any old line. Just look at 'em! You got it figured, Davey. You got brains!" He proudly jerked his thumb back toward the house. "And I got a rope. Found it out back in the gardening shed." He turned to walk backward so he could view the rooftop and the chimney. "Just like you said. Tie one end around the chimney and the other round me." He patted his girth. "Just like we were window washers at city hall."

David wished that Oink would shut up about it. After all, it wasn't really going to happen. Just like when they had dreamed up a treasure and said it was buried down at the old deserted Whitley house. They had spent a day looking for clues. A day prowling around the place. A day gathering supplies: shovels and picks and food. And then they had sneaked out at night and dug and dug and dug until finally they ended up with a great big hole in the ground and a lot of dirt.

The way poor Oink was going on about the rope and the roof and the dumb rich people standing in line, David was beginning to feel guilty.

"Shut up, Ralph," he said as his friend babbled on about how he would catch a home-run ball by leaping off the roof, and David could pull him back up like a fish on a line.

"Huh? How come?"

David inclined his head toward the blue-uniformed cop standing by the gate into the park. "He could hear you talking."

Oink lowered his voice in a guilty "Oh yeah." Then he whispered, "How we gonna get in today? How we gonna get past him? Are we really gonna meet Connie Mack?"

"Shut up, will you?" David warned, as if he really did have a plan. As if Oink's big mouth could ruin the plan.

"Oh," Oink said with genuine guilt. He stopped his babbling and simply walked beside David with the quiet trust that David would do everything he said. David would get them into the ballpark today to see the great Philadelphia ball team practice. David would get the autographs of Connie Mack and Jack Quinn on that baseball he carried. David would get them back on the tram afterward and home again, and no one would ever know they had ditched school. Ah, David was a miracle worker who could pull it all off without a hitch!

The boys approached the longest line of ticket buyers. Men in pinstriped suits and shiny shoes mingled with factory workers who had managed to get their purchase slips cheap and early. The queue snaked around the stadium. The buzz of conversation filled the air with bits about the coming Series or business or the stock market or how much the scalpers were getting for tickets these days.

David squeezed through the line between two men in business suits.

"What're you kids doing out of school?" The voice was amused, not hostile. "Playin' hooky, you two?"

David replied confidently, "Looking for my dad." He yanked Oink hard by the arm and dragged him away along the fence.

Even the small bit of questioning had nearly made Oink faint. His eyes were wide and suddenly glassy with fear and guilt, his cheeks red. He was puffing again as if something were after them.

"Davey!" His voice trembled. "Davey! They noticed us!"

"Shut up!" David hissed, giving his arm another hard jerk. "You look like we robbed a bank. You think they ain't going to notice if you're so scared you wet your pants? *Smile!*"

Oink showed his teeth. His eyes bugged out wide like they were propped open with toothpicks. "How's ziss?" he asked through his teeth.

It was lousy—more like a leer than a smile. "Just shut your mouth and don't look at anybody," David warned as they passed yet another entrance guarded by a cop.

"Hey, you there!" shouted the cop, stepping after them.

"Keep walking," David warned Oink, who was wheezing loudly.

"You kids!" the cop called again.

"Keep going," David croaked. Oink's breathing was interrupted by groans of terror. David stuffed his mitt and ball into his shirt.

"Davey!" Oink squealed.

The copper was upon them. He snatched up Oink by his collar, choking him as he wailed and clung to David, who fought to free himself.

"Hey you! Playin' hooky, huh!"

"Davey!" cried Oink. "He's got me!"

"Run for it!" David tore himself loose from Oink's clawing fingers and dashed through the crowd of ticket buyers.

David heard the laughter of the grown-ups as he darted across the parking lot and made for the Twentieth Street houses and the bushes. He also heard the dreadful cries of Oink as he called out for David to rescue him and shrieked, "He made me! He made me come! I didn't wanna do it! He made me!"

Vaulting over a fence, David crouched down between the box elders and the rough boards and peered out between the cracks. Ralph "Oink" Johnson was being led away like some sort of criminal. The cop held him firmly by the back of his jacket and propelled him forward like a giant weeping beach ball on legs. Nobody seemed interested in pursuing David. They didn't need to chase him down. Oink would tell everything. By now the cop had David's name, address, and phone number. No doubt Oink was spilling his guts about the fact that they had ditched school and that it had been David's idea and that they were going to sneak into the ballpark to see Connie Mack.

As if to verify David's suspicions, Oink swung his arm up to point at the rooftop of the house on Twentieth Street. So he was even telling the cop about their plans to watch the Series from the roof! *The rat!*

For a moment David half believed that Oink had ruined their great plans for viewing the game. Then he remembered that the whole thing had been made up anyway. Oink's confession simply got David off the hook. Now there was no way that Oink could expect to be escorted up to a rooftop and tied to a chimney! He would think he had blown the plan apart himself by squealing and would not blame David when it did not come to pass.

With some relief, David turned around and leaned his back against the fence to wait until it would be safe to come out of hiding. He removed his mitt from his shirt and stared at the scuffed cover of the baseball.

It would have been swell to have gotten the autograph of Connie Mack on the ball, he thought. Or maybe Jack Quinn.

He tossed the ball into the air and caught it with a snap. All the time he had been hoping for a miracle. Hoping that everything he told Oink would really happen. Funny how disappointed he felt that none of it came true. Sort of like digging for buried treasure and ending up with a big hole.

CHAPTER FOURTEEN

Luck

It was not a brand-new wagon Brother Williams offered for sale around back of the barn, but it was new enough. It still smelled of linseed oil, and the green paint on the box was barely scratched. The name *FAMOUS* was painted in red on the side of the wagon box. It looked to Birch as if it had been ordered from Sears and Roebuck, unloaded from the train, and then left to sit awhile here behind the livery stable.

Brother Williams, proprietor of the stable and owner of the wagon, spit tobacco juice and eyed the merchandise as if he were seeing it for the first time. He circled it, peered under the bed at the axle and red leaf springs.

"See for yourself, Birch." Brother Williams sniffed. "Ain't hardly a scratch on this here wagon. Aged hickory wood, poplar wood sides on the box, and grooved pine on the bottom. Extra gear brake. Three-inch tires and riveted rims." He patted the word *FAMOUS* and spit again. "Can't do no better. There she sat down in ol' Fred Pickett's barn from the day he took her home till the day he died. 'Bout the only freight she's hauled was Fred's body when they brought him in over yonder to the mortur-eery."

Tommy made a face and Bobby's eyes widened as they considered traveling in the very wagon box where Mr. Pickett's body had lain. It took the edge off their eagerness to own this particular wagon, even if it was pretty.

Birch, however, seemed unimpressed by the information about the wagon's unfortunate freight history. He seemed unimpressed by the wagon itself, even though the price was half of what it would have been brand-new. He stuck his hands in his back pockets and circled it slowly. His eyes were all squinty, and he chewed on his lower lip. Tommy had seen his father do enough trading that he knew part of this was for show. Birch did not want Brother Williams to think he was too interested in the wagon, after all. There was still bargaining to do.

"Well, what'll it be, Birch Tucker? Your ol' daddy could sure spot a bargain when he seen one." Brother Williams gave a big laugh, as though he had a thousand memories about Birch's daddy.

Bobby trailed his father as they circled the wagon again and squatted to look beneath it one more time. Tommy peered over the side and imagined the dead man all wrapped in canvas. He hoped his father wouldn't buy this wagon. First they had a dead convict on the bottom of the creek back home, and now they were about to purchase a vehicle whose only use had been as a makeshift hearse. But Tommy did not speak his concerns out loud, lest he interrupt his father's negotiations.

"I got me other fellers looking at this here wagon," Brother Williams warned. "You don't buy it, somebody else is sure to."

Birch took out his pocketknife and knelt down again to scrape at the paint on the bottom of the wagon. Tommy knew his father was checking to see if the wagon really was this new or if it had merely been re-painted.

"Suit yourself." Brother Williams shrugged. "I got nothing to hide."

Birch looked puzzled. The wood was obviously new and clean beneath the paint. It had not been refurbished. Could it be that Brother Williams had renounced his former ways and suddenly gotten honest? Well then, things had indeed changed over ten years if that was the case.

Birch stood slowly and tapped his fingers on the metal rim of the wheel. "There's one thing got me stumped, Brother Williams," Birch said. "How come you're selling this wagon so cheap?"

Brother Williams laughed. "Well now, Birch boy, I'll raise my price if that's what's botherin' you. It seemed a fair price to me."

"How long you had this wagon back here?"

"Not so long as all that . . ."

"And how come you haven't sold it before now?"

From the hayloft of the barn came a low chuckle from Boomer Hugo, the slow-witted stableboy who had been around the place as long as Birch could remember.

"Just been waitin' for the right time," Brother Williams insisted. He ignored the ever-increasing laughter in the loft above them. "Been thinkin' I might . . . might wanna keep her myself."

Now Boomer Hugo's chuckle became a mighty roar of hilarity.

Birch looked defiantly at Brother Williams, who glared grim faced toward the hayloft. Even Bobby could tell there was something about this wagon that was not being told.

Birch stepped back and hollered toward the hatch in the loft, "Boomer! Boomer Hugo! Come on; show your face!"

"Boomer, get on with your work!" Brother Williams countered.

Birch gave Williams a slow smile. "I ain't buyin' this wagon from you, but I might buy it from Boomer." Then he cupped his hands around his mouth and hollered up again. "Boomer! Come on. Show your face!"

The loft had become deathly silent. Boomer had made a mistake, and he knew it.

Brother Williams spit angrily. "Get on out here, Boomer, before I give you a lickin'."

A timid voice called slowly from the loft, but no face appeared. "Ain't you gonna give me a lickin' anyway, Brother Williams?"

Birch replied with a warning glance at the trader. "Nobody's gonna give you a lickin', Boomer, not as long as you tell the truth."

"Is 'at so, Brother Williams?" Still only Boomer's voice.

"Well, it's all over now, anyway," Williams muttered. Then he shouted to the invisible Boomer, "Tell him."

Birch asked, "Why hasn't somebody bought this pretty wagon, Boomer?"

Silence.

Boomer might talk, but he would not come out in the open. "Do I tell him, Brother Williams?"

"Tell him, tell him!" Williams muttered under his breath. "That's what a man gets taking in a homeless half-wit."

"Tell me why nobody likes this wagon," Birch questioned again.

" 'Cause that there's a bad-luck wagon," Boomer said in his most eerie voice. "Dead man's wagon. First Mister Pickett done hanged hisself outta that wagon. Then the bootleggers bought her and got theirselfs shot dead by them federal men and hauled to the mortur-eery same as ol' Pickett. Ain't nobody wants a bad-luck wagon."

At that, Brother Williams took off his hat and threw it at the wagon. "And I ain't never gonna get rid of her neither. Took her all the way into the saleyard at Fort Smith, but the story got there ahead of me. Nobody'd buy her. I ain't never seen a wagon with so much history for bein' so new."

Birch crossed his arms across his chest and eyed the luckless vehicle. It was indeed a *famous* wagon. "I might still be interested."

"You *what*?" Astonished, Brother Williams fetched his hat and patted the wagon.

Tommy and Bobby backed way up and prayed that they had misunderstood their father.

"That's right. But first I gotta take a look at your mules. Need a good team to haul this wagon if I take her."

"Yessir! Yessiree! Always said you had a head on your shoulders, Birch Tucker."

Birch nodded his agreement. "But I want Boomer to show me your stock. No offense, Brother Williams. It's just I always got on real good with Boomer. He's got an eye for a good mule, I always thought."

"As the Hebrews left Egypt, drivin' their flocks and herds afore 'em, so Birch Tucker leaves Hartford," Brother Williams muttered as he watched his FAMOUS bad-luck wagon and his two best mules depart at the head of a line of three additional hired wagons loaded up with the bounty of the little town. The story of Boomer and the wagon was repeated all around town and discussed at length in the barbershop.

"That ol' Birch, he's a smart man. He told them young'uns of his that if they told their mother about that wagon, they'd get a good hidin'!"

Much laughter filled old Dee's barbershop. Everyone knew that Brother Williams had also warned Boomer not to say anything, but the truth always had a way of coming out, all the same. Eventually Trudy Tucker would find out about the bodies stacked like cordwood in that wagon, and she'd be the one giving Birch the lickin'. Just to make sure the wagon did not end up back behind the livery stable, Brother Williams had made Birch sign a paper saying *No Return*.

Half the merchants of Hartford ended up standing in line at the bank of King Henry V that afternoon to collect cash from the letter of credit. It had been an altogether good day for business. Good to have Birch back in the county. His young'uns were well mannered mostly and his wife was tolerable, although she talked like a foreigner and carried herself a bit high-and-mighty for the wife of a plain farmer.

There were other things whispered about Trudy Tucker as the day wore on. Everybody in town reopened the old gossip about when Birch left home for this woman. It was plain to see she was pretty enough to entice a man away from his father's house, but now the question was whether Birch was a happy man being married to a woman who was so pushy and strong-willed in matters of business purchases. After comparing notes, it was discovered that Trudy Tucker had not paid the full price for even one purchase.

Eyebrows raised at that information. Well, it just proved what she was, didn't it?

From the dusty window above the rust-streaked kitchen sink, Trudy could see the white line of the birch trees against the backdrop of straight, dark pines. She watched as the birches bent from left to right— not from any wind but from the puffing of two small boys high up in the branches.

Bobby straddled a branch and rocked the whole tree like a giant rocking horse. Tommy, who was most like his father, climbed higher still and bent the limber trunk toward the ground, then rode it up straight and tall again. All the while their shrieks of laughter echoed from the field and multiplied in the hollow until it sounded like the laughter of two dozen boys down there—a whole baseball team of shouts and challenges and joy! But it was only the two of them, making do with invented adventures until a real baseball team could be found. The birch trees trembled with laughter, too. Had these old trees, planted by Grandpa Sinnickson the year Birch was born, been waiting solemnly for Birch to bring his own sons back to ride them?

Trudy still wore her coat. It was cold inside the house, but soon enough it would be warm. Two burly young men from the hardware store helped Birch carry in the cookstove. It was not nearly so grand as the stove that had been here before. It was only an Acme Charm and had less chrome and a smaller hot-water reservoir, but it was everything Trudy had ever wished for.

She did not turn at the sounds of their scraping and clunking.

"Well, look here, Mister Birch! Your stovepipe fits first rate!"

"It's good luck when your stovepipe fits, did y' know?"

Then there was the sound of opening and closing the metal rolltop warming oven and the door to the firebox and every round eight-inch lid.

"She's a good'n all right!" Birch said, his voice sounding satisfied. And then he called, "You can look now, True!"

Only then did she turn away from the celebrating birch trees. "Oh," she sighed, reaching out to run her hands over the cold cast iron that would warm her family and cook their meals. "Oh! *Look* at it! Oh!"

Well now, here was a tale to carry back to the barbershop. Mrs. Trudy Tucker was actually shedding tears over a stove! No man among the hired moving crew had ever seen the likes of it. That woman had dickered and fought to get the price of that stove down three dollars with delivery thrown into the bargain. She had declared that it was not such a fine stove that she couldn't find twenty like it cheaper; then she had started to walk out of the store. Just like the Acme Charm stove didn't mean a thing to her. And now here she was, bawling for joy because the stovepipe fit right off and because the thing had raised legs that she could sweep under. That was a woman for you!

The workmen, with their grimy, soot-blackened faces, viewed her emotion with embarrassment. They doffed their hats and wrung them in their meaty paws. They lowered their voices.

"Where should we put that there chest of drawers, Mister Birch?"

"What do we do with the sofa and chair and the parlor stove? The pipe don't fit the parlor stove, Mister Birch. . . ."

Birch left Trudy to her Acme Charm and went to sort out the confusion. Bedroom furniture, dining-room table and chairs were all piled in the center of the front room. Chairs were upside down on other chairs, bed frames stacked against the wall. The barn was a mess of plows and feed and seed and all the things a barn should be full of. It would take days to get each thing put into its proper place.

Birch looked at the sky. It got dark early in October, and it was more than an hour by wagon back to Hartford. "You got everything in out of the weather?"

"Yessir, Mister Birch. You'll have to get yourself another length of stovepipe for the parlor." The big Irishman threw a worried glance toward the continuing sniffles in the kitchen. "But we done moved the stoves right in place for you."

"Well then, you boys better be gettin' along back to town or you'll be caught in the dark." He paid them each a dollar for a good day's work and sent them on their way.

The Irishman snapped the dollar bill in a pleased gesture. "Even if we was caught in the dark, leastwise we won't be drivin' that there bad-luck wagon!"

Birch cleared his throat in a noisy warning that no more should be said about the FAMOUS wagon so close to Mrs. Tucker.

The Irishman glanced toward the kitchen, nodded, and winked. "Oh . . . sure," he whispered. "Might be too much for the little lady, 'specially after that there convict drowned down yonder yesterday."

In an instant, Birch had the man by the elbows, propelling him out the door and down the steps. "Thanks, boys!" he said in an overly cheerful voice. No doubt the teamster was correct. Better that Trudy concentrate on weeping for joy over her new stove than spend another night thinking about the events of yesterday and the truth about the bloody history of the wagon in the barn.

Birch was relieved to hear her still happily sniffling in the kitchen when he reentered the house.

From his hiding place behind the fence, David had watched enviously as ticket buyers came and went all day. The line shuffled forward but never seemed to get any shorter. Baseball fans would not stop coming, David knew, until every place in the grandstand was filled for every Philadelphia game.

Late in the afternoon a wind came up, pushing a layer of gray clouds across the sky like a giant tarpaulin covering the blue. Maybe it would rain, but still the lucky stiffs came to the ticket booths to trade in their purchase slips for tickets. The first raindrop splashed on David's cheek just as twenty black umbrellas popped open along the ticket queue.

The rain finally drove David out of hiding. If the cop across the street spotted him, he did not consider that capturing David was worth getting wet for. He remained at his post beside the entrance of the stadium and did not budge when David boarded the tram and paid his nickel with two dozen new holders of World Series tickets.

Every man on board the moving tram had white envelopes out to compare the seat numbers in the grandstand and talk about what seats were good and which ones were not so good. David could easily have joined into a conversation about batting averages of the players or who was the best spitballer in the big leagues, but nobody was talking about baseball—only about seats and scalpers' prices and the fact that two box seats were better than money in the bank right now. David pretended that he was not interested. He took out his mitt and tossed his ball into the air.

"Hey, kid," said a dowdy, bank-clerk-looking man. "Where you gonna be sitting?"

"You kiddin'?" called another man in workman's dungarees. "This kid is pitchin', ain't you, kid?"

There was good-natured laughter and someone mussed his hair, knocking his cap to the floor of the tram. "I'm sitting in the . . ." David stooped to retrieve his cap. He blinked at the small white envelope on the black-rubber flooring. *A Shibe Park ticket envelope!* He reached for his cap at the same instant the bank clerk scooped up the envelope.

"Here, kid," said the man, extending the treasure to David. "You dropped this." He thrust it into David's upturned hat.

David gawked at it and opened his mouth to protest when the tram clanged to a halt and the bank clerk exited with half a dozen other men, each pocketing his own World Series admission.

Two rings of the bell and the tram lurched forward. New passengers swung into place as David sat waiting for someone to snatch the envelope from his hat and call him a thief. No one did so. Commuters got on and commuters got off. David stared at the white thing in his hat and realized, *It must be empty.*

Only with that thought did he dare to open the flap. *Admit One. Shibe Park—Seat F, Box 15.* David groaned slightly and touched the top ticket to make certain he was not dreaming. *Box seats? Could the writing mean box seats? Box number 15? Right above the dugout?*

He glanced up sharply, expecting to see someone on board with a pained and frantic expression. Somebody had lost these, David was certain, but perhaps that somebody had gotten off the tramcar. Careless! Foolish! Angry! The former holder of these box seats would be tearing pockets apart and retracing his footsteps all the way back to Shibe Park. David pulled the two passes out and held them tightly like a winning hand at a poker game. If the person who had dropped them was still inside the tram, no doubt he would notice.

"Hey, kid!" A young factory worker smiled. "You got Series tickets, huh?"

"Yeah." David did not smile. He was waiting for the owner to pounce and roar.

"Where you sittin'?"

David glanced around at a number of newly interested faces, then displayed the stubs. "Box number 15. See? Right above the dugout. Seats F and G."

The factory worker whistled low. Other men who knew nodded approval. "Don't get no better than that, kid. Not unless you sit right in the dugout with Connie Mack himself."

No one pounced. No one roared. David's ears were ringing, and he felt light-headed as he slid the admissions back inside the envelope and tucked them into his shirt pocket, over his heart. He kept his hand there. He could feel his heart thumping away. There was something there after all, no matter what Brian O'Halloran had said.

It was nearly dark by the time David ran toward home. Drunk with excitement, he dashed up the steps two at a time and banged open the front door. He had forgotten all about his earlier transgression. Forgotten he had ditched school. Forgotten about the apprehension of Ralph "Oink" Johnson . . . he had even forgotten that his mother would not be home to hear of his good fortune.

"Mom?" he shouted, exploding into the parlor. "Hey, *Mom!*" A quick look around the room. Mrs. Crowley's radio sat in the corner. The clock ticked in the silent void. Only then did the truth come crashing back on him.

He stood panting in the center of the room as Mrs. Crowley scowled around the frame of the kitchen door.

"So it's you!" she snapped. "I thought maybe you weren't coming back." She eyed him angrily. "Missus Johnson called."

"Missus Johnson . . ." Oink's mom. She would be on the warpath. It all came back clearly to David.

"The school called, too . . ."

"Sure."

"I told them you would not be coming back and frankly, after your enticing young Ralph into playing hooky today, they did not sound disappointed that you were leaving. Saves them a session with the paddle, I'd say!"

David lowered his eyes to the toes of his shoes. Maybe the teachers wouldn't mind if he left, but Oink would miss him. And Willie and the rest of the fellas. No more chances to win their marbles back. "Is Oink . . . I mean Ralph . . . is he in trouble?"

The old woman's eyes squinted behind her glasses. "What do you suppose?" She sniffed indignantly and took a step into the room. David imagined she would grab him by the ear and drag him to his room, but she did not. What was the use, after all?

"I suppose he got a licking," David said.

She snatched his hat from his head and thrust it into his hands. "Don't you think you're going to get away with such shenanigans at St. Joseph's Children's Home. No sir! And you won't get away with *this,* either. I've called Father John already. He is on his way here right this minute to fetch you," she fumed. "I don't know how they expect me to keep an eye on you all the time. I couldn't follow you to school every morning, could I? Well, you're better off at the home—that's all I can say. Better off where you can be supervised."

"Yes, ma'am," David said quietly. He had forgotten why he had been so happy a moment before. What was it? What had happened? His hand touched the stiff envelope in his pocket, and the memory came back to him. Everything except the happy feeling. That was entirely gone. After all, if he was going to the children's home this very night, then how could he use the tickets?

"You'll get a talking-to and probably more." Old Mrs. Crowley seemed pleased that he was in trouble.

"Can't I say good-bye to the fellas?"

"You were supposed to do that today. And tomorrow. Well, now the school won't have you back, and it's your own fault." She looked at him through steely eyes. "You'd better go finish packing if you haven't."

"I'm done."

"Well then?" Hand on her hip, she waited for him to leave the room.

He turned to see her glaring at him down the hall. "Missus Crowley?"

"Well, what is it?"

He peered in his room toward the row of neatly labeled belongings on his bureau top. "I got this stuff for the fellas . . . all my best stuff, see? To give to Oink and Beany and Willie, too. I put their names on it. Could you tell them to come get it?"

For an instant there was a flicker of something soft on her face before the coolness returned. She nodded curtly to his request. "A bunch of junk, if you ask me. Their mothers won't want them hauling it home. But I'll tell them it's here, all the same."

"Thanks." David closed the door behind him. He sat down heavily on his groaning bed and took out the World Series tickets. What would he do with these? If he could only be free another week . . . if only. He would have taken Oink to the game and maybe then he really could have gotten the autograph of Connie Mack. But Father John was coming. So what was the use of finding such a wonderful treasure?

CHAPTER FIFTEEN

The Hollow Oak

Far away, across the treetops and the brow of the hill, came the whistle of the Rock Island locomotive.

"She's on the afternoon run back to Fort Smith," Tommy called to Bobby. The whistle shrilled again. Tommy threw his head back and imitated the sound, then laughed out loud with joy because he already knew so much about the train. They had raced the great steam locomotive twice already. Now it was like an old familiar friend. From the branches of his birch tree, Tommy could just see the plume of smoke as it rose to blend in with the low clouds. "She's stopping to take on water," he told Bobby with authority.

Bobby crowed his own train whistle in response and rocked his tree as though he were on a fast horse, galloping along beside the train.

Tommy could not remember ever feeling this good. Trains had always seemed to him nothing but black smoking hulks taking people and things far away. But Shiloh had its own train. It had most likely carried everything Mama and Dad bought in Hartford. It had chugged past this place with cookstoves and beds and double-shovel plows and dumped it off in Hartford to wait until this day when Mama and Dad would bring it all home to Shiloh.

This same train would pass the farm and holler "Howdeeeee" twice a day from now until forevermore. Tommy decided he would never get tired of the train or the whistle that floated over the valley.

The afternoon haze thinned in the west. The sun gleamed through low clouds in the sky like the great copper gong at the Chinese restaurant in Tulsa. Most all the families of the oil workers ate there on payday.

Tommy had often peered in at the gong and been quietly angry at his mother because she never once let Dad splurge and take them to eat there. They were saving, she said firmly, and if they ever wanted to have a place of their own, then Chinese restaurants were off limits!

Today Tommy was glad he had never tasted egg rolls like his school friends had bragged about. What was happening up at the house made every missed fortune cookie worth missing!

He imagined his friends filing past the gong and gulping down a strange-tasting supper, then going back to the boomtown sheds where everyone lived in the oil towns. He would not trade Shiloh for all the Chinese gongs in the world!

Tommy sat still on his branch and listened to the peaceful rush of the water of the James Fork. He scooted to face away from the sun. Through the trees he could see the bank of the creek where the convict had drowned. Bellowing men and baying hounds had concealed the lapping of the water beneath their curses.

Today, however, it was like an entirely different place. The gentle voice of the James Fork called to Tommy in his perch. Would he like to come see for himself if there were paw prints and boot tracks in the mud? Was the warning about a loose cannibal true? If he and Bobby leaned close to the water, might they catch a glimpse of something dark and sinister far beneath its surface?

The voice of the James Fork was almost audible. Bobby must have heard it, too, for the boys locked eyes in agreement to the unspoken thought. Together they shinnied down the smooth white bark of the birch trees and struck out through the persimmon patch toward the fallen oak tree that spanned the waters.

The banks of the deep, rain-swollen stream were a muddle of confused tracks. Tommy squatted to study them as he had seen his father study the tracks of deer on a hunting trip. But there was nothing so delicate as the print of a deer hoof here. Big, waffled-soled bootprints squashed the impressions of dogs' paws; hundred of paw prints dimpled the mud. There had been only a dozen hounds in the pack, Tommy knew, but it seemed like many more now that they had gone on.

Bobby balked. He kept back from the muddy bank and wrapped his arm around a cottonwood tree as if it offered him some protection from what was certainly beneath the dark waters.

"Come on," Tommy urged as he made the climb onto the fallen tree.

"I don't want to." Bobby remained beside the cottonwood.

"Come on." Tommy was insistent. Demanding. Daring Bobby to step where the men and dogs had stepped, to put the print of his little boot on top of theirs.

"Mama said don't cross over. . . ."

"That was yesterday. You scared?"

"No!"

"Yes, you are! You're scared to come out here and look over the edge with me."

"I'm not!" Bobby shouted.

"Scared as some ol' girl, that's what you are!"

"No!" Bobby let go of his anchor and plunged forward onto the slick bark. "Don't say that no more, Tommy Tucker, or I'll bust you wide open!"

Tommy had won the contest. He grinned haughtily and walked out onto the center of the great log. He sat down, letting his legs hang over the upstream side.

Bobby joined him a moment later and sat beside him. "See," Bobby mumbled, "told you I ain't no girl."

Tommy did not reply. He was too busy peering deep into the waters. Dark shadows moved and shifted with the current. Was that a branch? Or was it something else maybe? Maybe some part of a shackled man? An arm? A leg? The water was deep enough right here that three grown men stacked straight up from the bottom could not reach the surface. No wonder the convict had sunk out of sight.

"You see it?" Tommy pointed to a submerged limb.

"Huh?" Bobby bent at the waist to stare hard at the thing. Long and dark, it was. Swaying in an eddy like an arm waving from the grave. "Let's get Dad." Bobby could not tear his eyes away.

"You suppose it's *him*?"

Bobby shuddered and gulped. "Come on. Let's get Dad!"

"It sure looks like it, don't it, Bobby? You suppose they'll have a reward for finding a dead body?"

Bobby raised his voice angrily. "I want to get Dad!"

"Go get him, then," Tommy said. "I'll wait here—in case it floats away under the log and on downstream. Probably won't, though, because I bet it's stuck on somethin'."

"Come with me." Bobby looked toward the darkening sky. He did not want to make the trip back up the hill to the house by himself. Especially not if that dark thing down there really was a man.

"I gotta stay and watch it," Tommy said. "Now hurry!"

Bobby swung his legs up and planted his feet beneath him to stand on the trunk. Then the unthinkable happened. The mud on the bottom of his smooth-soled boots slipped against the bark. Splinters and bark dug into his hands as he fought to cling to the tree. "Tommy!" he cried as the curve of the tree trunk carried him over the side and down into the freezing water of the James Fork just above the shadowed place.

"Bobby! Bobby! Dad!" Tommy shouted and shouted again. Tommy was on his belly, straining to reach the upraised fingertips of Bobby.

Bobby gasped against the biting pain of the cold and cried out that he could not reach Tommy's hands. The water was taking him, pulling him downward, tugging at his legs like icy fingers.

"Hold on! Hold on!" Tommy was crying as he took off his belt and slung it over the side of the trunk. "Grab it!"

With a desperate lunge, Bobby stretched for the belt and missed by inches. "Tommy, help!" he shouted. Then he was swept under the water, under the giant log, by the current. In panic, Tommy swung to the down-current side of the trunk, expecting to see Bobby pop out. Terror and grief seized him. Seconds passed. Bobby did not reappear.

"Bobby!" he sobbed. "Please don't die! Oh, Bobby! *Don't!* Come up! Please!"

The black waters slipped silently past. Tommy turned to the up-stream side. Was his brother snagged on something? trapped beneath the log? "Where are you?" he called.

It was too long to stay beneath the surface without a breath. *Too long!*

Tommy held his breath as though he could help Bobby somehow. His lungs burned with the effort. Air exploded from his mouth in a wail. "Dad!"

Tommy sank onto the log and buried his face in his hands. "Some-body help! Oh, Bobby!"

Then a muffled voice replied from the oak tree—a deep and resonant voice emanating from between the tree and the waters. "You, boy! You there, boy?"

"Huh? Who's that?" Tommy peered over the edge again. Only the water was there and the dark shadow. Yet the voice of a man had called to him. "My brother fell in! He's drowned!"

"He ain't drownded. I ketched him. But can't hold him for long."

"Where are you?" Tommy could see nothing when he peered over the side.

"In the belly of this here tree. Go fetch your pappy, boy!"

"Bobby? You down there?"

The man's voice said angrily, "Do what I says! Fetch your pappy. Tell him to bring a stout rope 'fore I lose this child!"

"I'm goin'!" Tommy crawled toward the bank. "Don't harm my brother, mister!" Tommy was sure of who it was beneath the oak tree. Now he knew how the man had escaped the hounds.

"Ain't gonna harm him," the voice claimed. "But can't hold him long like this neither. Scat! Call your pappy to come on quick!"

✯ ✯ ✯

"When I say *three*, lift your end," Birch instructed from the opposite end of the heavy oak table. Baby Joe was perched in the center of the table waiting for a ride from the center of the front room to the dining room where a row of windows overlooked the valley. "You ready?"

Trudy nodded. "Ready."

"Okay then. One . . ."

"Dad-dy!" Tommy's voice wailed up and floated away.

"Two . . ."

"Dad-dy! Help meeeee!"

Trudy froze. This was not an ordinary cry for help. "Birch?" She rushed to the window. Had someone fallen from a tree?

"Helllp me, Dad!"

Birch dashed out onto the front step and squinted across the field for a sign of his sons.

Trudy snatched up Joe and ran into the yard. "Tommy?" she called back.

"Mama! Bobby fell . . . the creek! Drownin'!" Tommy's voice was choked by a desperate sob.

Still holding Joe, Trudy began to run down the lane that flanked the field and led to the banks of the James Fork. She wept aloud. "Oh, Lord! Sweet Jesus—help him!"

A moment later Birch galloped past her on the bare back of a mule. He carried a coil of rope over his shoulder, and he whipped the mule into a frenzied race toward the creek.

✯ ✯ ✯

The voice of Tommy resounded far away, across the valley. It was a dream, it seemed to Bobby. Hazy voices and the black hollow underbelly of the mighty oak only six inches above his face. Strong hands had reached out from the blackness to hold his head and grasp his jacket.

Bobby could hear the clank of chains like a melody and a deep, resonant voice from the heart of the tree.

"Hold on, boy. It won't be long. I gotcha. Ain't gonna let you go. Your brother's done gone to fetch your pappy. Hold on now, boy."

Bobby tried to move his numb lips. Tried to say thank you to the hands and the tree. But cold and exhaustion made even that impossible. He wanted only to sleep—to float on the waters, to drift suspended from the limbs and hands of the kind oak. His thanks came out as a groan.

"You gonna make it now, boy. . . . Ain't gonna let you drown nohow. Your pappy's comin'. . . ."

Bobby thought how good it would be to sleep. He could not feel his heavy boots anymore or the water-soaked coat that had pulled him beneath the surface. The tug of the water was still strong, trying to tear him from the hands of the oak. The current pulled one way. The voice resisted the water. It was as if the voice of the oak tree held him above the surface. Only the voice.

"Kick them legs, boy!" The voice was stern—like Mama when she wanted something done now. "Kick them legs! Don't let the cold take you, now! Kick!"

Bobby was so tired, so very tired. He tried to obey the oak, but his legs were small and weary compared to the James Fork. The water rushed on. How could he fight against it? Bobby groaned again to tell the oak how sorry he was that he could not kick anymore. His boots were full of water, his clothing soaked and heavier than he was. Could the oak tree hold him until Dad came? Bobby opened his eyes and tried to see the face hovering above him. There was only a shadow of movement. A glint of white and the music of chains again.

And the voice. "You got a name, boy?"

Bobby knew his name. It was clear as anything in his mind, but he could not make his lips say it.

"Heard your brother shoutin' your name," said the oak. "Bobby, ain't it? You gotta kick them legs, Bobby, else the cold gonna take you."

Bobby managed to flutter his legs once. But it was too hard. What did an old oak tree know about fighting the current in full boots? Another moan. Bobby's eyelids fluttered open to argue with the tree.

"Just a minute now, boy! I heard 'em comin'. Hold on now! I ain't gonna let the water take you!"

Faintly, as if from a great distance, Bobby heard his father's frightened voice. "Bobby! Bobby! Lord! Where is he, Tommy?"

The oak bellowed, "Down here, Mister! I ketched hold of the boy. Got him down here. Need a rope, an' quick 'bout it!"

The hands gave Bobby a stiff shake. "You still among the livin'?"

Dad shouted that the rope was tied off to a tree and all they had to do was grab hold. He'd pull them in together.

"Lord Jesus," muttered the voice; then strong arms closed around Bobby. The weight of his clothes and shoes seemed to be nothing at all. It was dark as Bobby was carried across the waters on the back of a shadow.

Dad pulled him onto the shore, and Mama came crying to kneel beside him. Tommy was crying, too.

The clang of chains rang at Bobby's head, and the shadow from the oak tree crumpled in a heap on the bank. Bobby closed his eyes and slept.

CHAPTER SIXTEEN

Revelation

The telephone rang three times before Mrs. Crowley answered it. The inflection of her voice changed from pleased to disappointed and then to pleading. "But *when* will he be here? . . . Well, what am I supposed to do? . . . Should I *feed* the boy . . . ?"

Through the thin walls, David could hear the entire conversation. Father John was not coming as soon as the old woman had hoped. Some sort of emergency had called him away. David knew about the good priest's emergencies. Maybe someone else was dying at St. Francis. Ah, well. Last rites for some poor soul meant a momentary reprieve of David's sentence. A few hours more, perhaps, before he was taken away.

Mrs. Crowley brought a sandwich on a tray and a glass of milk and an extra large slice of cake. She set the tray down on David's bureau, nudging his belongings out of the way.

"You might as well eat something," she said in a defensive voice. Then, "You see, I made you a cake like I said I would. Since you're leaving early, you might as well have a piece now."

She did not look him in the face. The softness crept back into her voice as though she was sorry for everything that had happened to David and for everything yet to happen. Maybe the cake made up for it?

She drummed her fingers on the tray. He noticed that she was scanning the neat line of gifts that David had left for his friends. "It is very nice of you to . . . I mean . . . I did not mean what I said. Your friends will be happy that you thought of them."

"Yeah." David fixed his gaze on the Model T and the big sock full of marbles with Ralph Johnson's name on it. "Maybe Oink won't be so mad at me." He looked at the cake. "Thanks for the cake, Missus Crowley." He could tell she was not angry anymore, just upset. "It looks real good."

She jerked her head in response and then breathed in deeply and slipped out without saying anything else. She had been okay to him, David decided, eating the cake first and drinking the milk. She had done the best she could. He wasn't angry at her for calling Father John to come early. What did he expect her to do with the school mad and Mrs. Johnson fuming? Poor old Mrs. Crowley. She had called the priest to haul him off, and now she felt bad about it.

"Thanks, Missus Crowley!" he yelled to her. She must have heard him but she did not reply, and a moment later the radio came on. It was his favorite program: *Dixie's Circus and Novelty Band.* He wondered if he could hear it at the children's home. Or was the place quiet like a prison? With lights out at sundown and guards patrolling the halls? Well, he thought, he would know soon enough.

Sitting cross-legged on the floor, David opened his footlocker to check the contents one last time. Beneath the sweater his mother had knitted him was the photo album and the box of letters. His mother's comb and brush and mirror and the little round lace doily she had thought so much of. And the books. There was no room for anything else.

He leaned back on the bed frame and opened the letter box, taking out the first letter his father—his real dad—had written from France. He opened it and read how much Max had loved Irene. The letter relived everything they had said on their last walk through Columbia University after the big dance.

It was a lot of mush, but somehow it made David feel better about Max. It surprised him that a man would write such things. After all, she was his mother. But it proved one thing—Brian had been all wrong about David's father. He really did love Irene. A fella so much in love wouldn't have run out on her and David, would he? David figured that his mother had given him the straight scoop on the story. Max was probably dead. He had to have died, or else why hadn't he been with her when David was born?

He thumbed through the stack, automatically scanning postmarks. All through 1918 and part of 1919. A short break during that summer before the letters started again. He plucked one of the last letters from the box and held it up to the light. An English stamp. The postmark was clearly from London. *September 20, 1919.* David decided that this would be a good letter to read. No doubt Max had died right after he had written her, because . . .

David gasped as he held the letter in his hands. It was still sealed. *It had never been opened!* He stared hard at the envelope, trying to understand why Irene had never read this letter. Plucking half a dozen of the last notes from the box, David fanned them out on the floor. None of these letters from England had been opened.

"Why?" he muttered aloud, suddenly angry at his mother that she had not even bothered to read what Max had written to her.

He emptied his pockets, finally finding his penknife. Carefully he slit the seal of the last letter and removed the thin onionskin paper. It still looked new after ten years—the paper bright and white, the ink black and fresh as though it had only just been written. And the words were strong, full of rage and pain.

A letter from your mother says you are going to marry someone else! Please, my darling Irene, answer me soon! Your mother writes that you do not wish to hear from me again. That you have found a man who will care for you and the child. But will he love you as I would? As I do! Will he be husband in name only? I beg you! Wait for me! I will work to pay my fare back to the States or bring you here with the baby. . . . You must only give me time, and I will make things right between us! Our child will have a name . . . my name . . . Meyer!

David felt sick. So here was the truth. It was not as his mother had told him. Max Meyer had not died.

It was not as Brian said either. Max Meyer had not run out on David and his mother.

No, the truth was much more terrible than either of those stories. His mother had run out on Max! *She* had left *him*! She had not opened his letters or answered them. She had simply punished him by marrying a man like Brian O'Halloran.

Folding the letter, David slipped it back into the envelope. He stared at the half-full glass of milk and the uneaten sandwich. It was his mother's fault that he was here and hurting, wasn't it? If she had answered Max's letters . . . if she had only waited . . . if she had told David the truth!

He glanced in the open box. A fat brown envelope was tucked along the side. It was different from the others. David pried it out and opened it, leaning closer to the light to see what was inside. It was crammed full of newspaper clippings.

He dumped them out beside the bed and picked them up one at a time to read. They were all about Max Meyer. Each one contained a different story about David's father. First was a faded photograph that told of his journalism scholarship to Oxford. David checked the date of the clipping with that of the letters from England. *Autumn of 1919.* Max had gone away to study, not to run away. *Not to hurt her.* The next date was two years later—October 1921. Here was a picture of a dark-eyed, handsome young man standing beside a beautiful young lady in a wedding dress.

"Max Meyer, staff writer for the New York Times, wed debutante Deborah Rothman in London last week. The bride is the daughter of prominent New York financier . . ."

David continued to read the words beneath the picture aloud. He stared at this woman standing beside the father he had never seen before. He shuddered at the thought that this woman knew Max Meyer much better than David did!

The heap of clippings contained accounts of parties they attended. Sometimes long lists of guests followed a story about some charity ball, and way down the list the name Mr. and Mrs. Max Meyer was circled.

And then there were stories written by Max cut from the financial section of a New York newspaper. There were a lot of those with the name Max Meyer circled in ink. Finally, a short article described the death of Mrs. Meyer in a car crash in Connecticut.

Somehow David was glad that the woman was dead. Even though he had never met her, he hated her. She had everything with Max, while David and his mother had . . . Brian O'Halloran!

All these years his mother had been saving articles about—and *by*—Max. She knew when his wife died. She knew David had a *real father* and a *real name*! Why had she not told him? Why had she made arrangements for David to be taken to St. Joseph's Children's Home? She had died without telling him *anything*—without giving him even one shred of hope!

"Why?" David cried. Only when he put his hand to his cheek did he notice that it was wet. He was crying. After everything, finally, he was crying!

Replacing the news clippings and the letters, he shoved the shoebox into his rucksack and then socks and clean underwear and the sweater his mother had knitted for him last Christmas.

Closing the lid of the footlocker, he carefully penned a note to Father John.

Dear Father John,

I am running away. Please keep this box for me. It has all my most important stuff in it. I will send for it when I get there.

Yours very truly,
David O'Halloran

He stared at the signature for a moment. Then he crossed it out until no trace of it remained. In its place he wrote *David Meyer*.

After grabbing his rucksack and baseball glove, he slipped out the window. David did not know exactly where he was going, but he hoped the priest would keep his footlocker safe until he arrived. In the meantime, he had to hurry. And he needed a plan.

All six burners of the new stove rattled and hissed like the steam engine of the Rock Island. Kettles and pots held steaming water that Trudy poured into the tin washtub where Bobby soaked. Tommy refilled the buckets from the well and poured still more water into the hot-water reservoir to heat for the big bathtub where Birch bathed the big black man on the back porch.

When Bobby complained "Too many baths in one week," Trudy knew that he would recover.

The man who had saved him, however, had not spoken since they had hauled him to the house on the back of the mule. It was as if he had used his last ounce of strength holding on to Bobby and carrying him to shore.

The man's right shoulder had been dislocated. Birch set it right while he was still unconscious in the mud of the James Fork. His body was scarred beyond anything Trudy had ever seen. He wore tattered striped cotton dungarees and no shirt. His back was as striped from lashes as the fabric of his trousers. His skin was cold as ice, and the pallor of shock showed through his ebony skin as bluish gray. His gums were white, like a horse's Trudy had once seen die from colic.

Trudy hefted a tepid pan of water from the burner. "Take this to your dad," she instructed Tommy. "We can't warm him up too suddenly, or he'll take shock and die."

Tommy held the pan for a moment and stared at the vapor. "What are we gonna do if he wakes up? He saved Bobby." The boy frowned. "Is Dad gonna give him back to the law?"

Trudy saw the anguish in her son's eyes. How could they turn the man over to his pursuers after he had saved Bobby? "Go on now," she urged Tommy, without answering his question.

The boy shuffled away, carefully balancing the pan so water did not spill. He let the screen door close with a bang.

Birch had set up the camp stove beside the tub, and it was warm enough on the closed porch. If the convict came around, Trudy resolved that they would see to it that he was cared for until he recovered. She did not want to think beyond that.

"He grabbed me up by my hair," Bobby said firmly, putting a hand to his head. "I thought the tree was talking to me all the time. Forgot about the cannibal."

Trudy nudged him forward and poured warm water over his head. "He is not a cannibal," Trudy replied quietly. "Just a man." How could she explain to her son that law in the South meant something entirely different to a man of color? She had seen that terrible truth firsthand ten years earlier and had never purged it from her mind.

"Well, how come they got dogs after him?" Bobby asked. "Like he's a fox they're huntin'."

"It doesn't take much for men to turn dogs loose on another man if he's a different color, Bobby. People have been doing it since slave days, and sometimes it's just because the fellow ran away." She scrubbed his head and he winced "All I know is he saved your life. That should count for something."

The screen door swung back again, and Tommy came into the kitchen with his face screwed into a scowl. "You should see him with the mud washed off, Ma," he whispered. "There's no place on him that isn't all scarred up." He glanced furtively toward the porch. "Dad says it looks like he's been some sort of slave instead of on a chain gang. Do they beat folks so on a chain gang, Ma?"

Trudy shook her head in dismay and turned back to the stove. Selecting the largest kettle for Tommy to carry back to Birch, she instructed, "Bring me back some water from the well."

Gazing thoughtfully at the back of his brother, Bobby said in a solemn tone, "Tommy tried to save me. But I was a goner if that fella hadn't grabbed me and held on. And all the time he was talkin' to me real nice. Tellin' me not to give up and such. Sayin' he knew my mama and dad would be real unhappy if I was to give up." Bobby's brows furrowed as he splashed water on his thin shoulders. "What's goin' to happen to him?"

Tommy reappeared. "Dad says I should fetch the large ball-peen hammer and his heavy chisel so he can strike off the chains. Hard iron cuffs on both hands and feet. Rubbed bloody underneath. Dad says he doesn't know how he held on to Bobby with his shoulder out and them chains. Just don't know."

"We ain't callin' the law, are we?" Bobby asked as Tommy retreated with the hammer. Soon the steady clank of metal resounded from the porch.

Trudy did not reply. She busied herself fixing supper as though nothing unusual had happened. As if the ring of the hammer against shackles was a call to eat.

The warmth of the water and a cup of broth held to his cracked lips seemed to bring a spark of life into the eyes of the black man. He did not speak to Birch as the iron shackles were broken off and piled in a heap beside the back door. Tommy nudged the iron with the toe of his boot. The ponderous links did not yield, but lay twisted and heavy on the floor.

How had this man carried them? How had he outrun the hounds and managed to swim the swollen creek with such a burden?

Here was a fearsome man, but Tommy could not fear him. Beneath the welded flesh of a hundred scars were thick bone and muscle, a barrel chest, and a bull-like neck. His ears were thick and distorted from beatings. His right eyebrow was divided by a scar that ran up across his forehead nearly to his scalp. His face displayed nicks and cuts from countless fights, yet the deep brown eyes followed every movement of Birch Tucker with gentle gratitude.

Tommy nudged the chains again with disdain. It was the shackles that Tommy feared, not the man. Wrapped in a quilt, the man lay patiently as Birch doctored his wrists and ankles with a smelly ointment known as Bag Balm. Meant as a medicine for the sore udders of milk cows, Birch swore by it as a cure-all for every human cut, scrape, or open wound.

The fugitive inhaled the strong scent of camphor and eyed the can as though he knew the stuff well. Had he been a farmer once? His kind eyes observed Birch before turning toward Tommy. He opened his mouth as if to speak, but only a rasping croak came out. He bit his lip and seemed to shake his head. Then he closed his eyes as though some terrible pain had passed through him. A tear escaped and coursed down his cheek.

"You saved my boy," Birch said in response to his wordless emotion. "I'm mighty grateful to you for that, mister."

The convict lay motionless and limp on his pallet. Did he hear Birch's thanks? Could he understand? With a trembling hand, he wiped his cheek and opened his eyes, locking a pain-filled gaze on Birch. Again he tried to speak. His throat constricted, and he convulsed in a violent cough.

Birch looked sharply at Tommy. "Have your mama make up a poultice. It'll be a miracle if he ain't got pneumonia." He placed the back of his hand on the convict's forehead. "Burnin' with fever."

Tommy hung back, chipping at the plank floor with his boot. His young brow furrowed with concern. The black man seemed to be weakening before their eyes. "Pa?"

"Yes, Son?" Birch tugged the arm of the man into a long white nightshirt.

"He ain't gonna die?"

Birch did not answer his question. "Tell your mama to get that poultice and make him up a bed by the stove."

CHAPTER SEVENTEEN

Runaway

Orchard Street. The old neighborhood. Finkel's pickle store. New York City. His mother smiling in front of a Nathan's Famous sign in Coney Island . . .

A jumble of sepia-toned images crowded David's mind as he stepped off the late-night tram and dashed through the rain toward the massive Philadelphia train terminal.

He was going to New York—going to ride the Baltimore & Ohio all the way to Grand Central just as his mother had dreamed of doing a thousand times. *"We'll go home, Davey,"* she used to say. *"You'll love New York. . . ."* And then she had recited all the things in New York that he would love.

Funny that she'd never mentioned Max Meyer among those things.

It was not the Statue of Liberty or the Sears Building or Coney Island or Nathan's Famous hot dogs that David wanted to see in the big city. Not the old neighborhood. Not Finkel's pickle store. Not the university where his mother had studied or the little school where she had taught. No. There was only one thing in the world he wanted to see in New York, and that was the person his mother had left completely out of the picture when she had spoken to David.

"Where to, kid?" asked the man behind the ticket cage.

"New York." David laid his baseball glove on the counter and placed the rucksack at his feet.

"Where in New York?" The eyes of the man twinkled behind his glasses as though he knew a joke and was not telling.

"City . . . Grand Central," David replied with certainty.

"Oh? Well then. Seems you know right where you're headed."

"I want a ticket," David said firmly. He did not like the smile on the ticket clerk's face.

"Round-trip?"

David did not understand the question. He paused and shrugged. "Dunno."

The smile broadened. "I mean, are you coming back? Or only going one way to New York?"

"I'm not coming back."

The ticket seller paused and gave a sympathetic frown. "Ah, I see. Well then, that will not cost as much."

"Good. How much?"

"Twenty-two fifty." The inflection told David that the ticket clerk was positive he would never be able to purchase such a fare to New York. "First-class Pullman."

David tapped his fingers on the counter. The fare was not nearly as much as he thought it would be. He nodded. "Okay."

The man chuckled. "That is, twenty-two dollars and fifty cents, young man." The man leaned closer to the bars of the cage to scrutinize David.

David looked down. His jacket was tattered and rain soaked, the cuffs of his red-flannel shirt were frayed, his knickers were well-worn, and the toes of his shoes were nearly worn through. Was that what the man was looking at?

"First-class Pullman," David repeated, just as he had been told. "That's right."

"Well, how will you pay for it?" The man smiled patiently. There was no one in line behind David. The whole B&O terminal seemed asleep except for David and the clerk.

David fumbled in his pocket, retrieving only one of the priceless World Series box-seat tickets. "You going to the Series?"

The man straightened. "Why, yes . . . I was fortunate enough to get my purchase slip early. . . ."

"Where are you going to sit?"

"Now, see here . . . I don't see what this has to do . . . we're talking about tickets to New York City, not . . ."

David turned the box-seat ticket over so the stub and seat number showed clearly. He had watched the ticket scalpers tantalize the eager purchasers just that way today at Shibe Park. "I got two of these."

"Box seats!" the man exclaimed.

"Right behind the dugout. I was gonna see Connie Mack up close, except now I have to go to New York and meet my father."

"But you're just a kid! How could you get such seats?"

"Lucky, I guess. Not like some people sitting out in the sun behind left field." He shoved the ticket back in his pocket.

"Those are worth a fortune."

"I'm going to New York," David said firmly. "But first I have to sell my Series seats."

"Good heavens!" exclaimed the astonished clerk. "How old are you? You're no kid. You're a midget tycoon—that's what!"

"Yeah," David agreed. He had Brian O'Halloran to thank for his budding business sense. "So, I'll be back."

"Well, wait!" The clerk crouched low and looked furtively from side to side. "Maybe we can make a deal."

"Yeah?" David tapped his fingers on the counter again and thought of poor Oink. "Maybe. So where are you sitting? You got good seats?"

"First game. Second tier along the first-base line."

"About a million miles up," David replied as the clerk spread his pitiful tickets out for David to examine.

"I'll give you fifty bucks for your two." The clerk was perspiring with excitement.

"Maybe I can get more than that. Probably I can."

"Okay, then. Seventy-five."

"Seventy-five and your two crummy tickets. And an envelope and a stamp because I have to mail something to someone."

Without hesitation, the ticket clerk extended his thin hand through the bars. "Done."

And so David purchased a first-class Pullman berth to New York with a little cash left over. Carefully he addressed the envelope to Ralph "Oink" Johnson and slipped the new grandstand tickets into it. He licked the flap, sealed it tight, and wrote in his new name on the return address.

David Meyer
Used to be O'Halloran
New York City

David hated it that he had to put O'Halloran on the envelope, but he figured Oink wouldn't know who sent him the tickets any other way.

An announcement blared over the loudspeaker, calling for boarding of the B&O New York Flyer on track 7. David slipped Oink's tickets into the mailbox and ran to catch the train.

※ ※ ※

The crunch of buggy wheels sounded on the drive as the Tuckers were finishing their supper. Trudy peered out the window into the dark yard just as the voice of J.D. called out, "Howdy! Howdy in there! Birch? We come callin'!"

Trudy ran to the kitchen door in a panic. Had J.D. brought his gun?

"Birch! It's your cousin! Go around and bring him in the front way before he walks in on all this!" Her eyes swept the porch. The leg-irons were piled in a heap by the back door. The unconscious black giant lay wrapped in a quilt next to the camp stove.

"Lord, help," she murmured, and the eyes of the fugitive opened a moment. He seemed to nod before closing his eyes again.

Trudy could hear Birch as he dashed around the house to intercept J.D. before he entered his usual way. Could they keep him away from the porch? out of the kitchen? If J.D. saw the limp figure lying there, he would fetch his rifle and claim he had conquered the convict and saved the whole household.

"Try not to cough," Trudy whispered to the man. She laid her hand on his burning forehead. "Can you hear me, mister?"

Again the eyes fluttered open. A nod. A rasping attempt to reply.

"My husband's kin have come to call. They will not abide this if they find you here. You must try to be quiet." She stood and murmured again, "Help us, Lord." Leaving the man on the porch, she returned to the kitchen, where the boys stood pale and wide-eyed at this development.

Trudy could hear Birch talking louder than usual. "Come on in! Front door's open. Why, Maybelle, what you brought?"

"Apple cobbler. Your favorite, Birch boy. A welcome-home cobbler!" Her high voice skittered across the windowpanes and made the boys' eyes get wider. Was this to be a long visit? What about the big man lying on the back porch?

Trudy leaned down to whisper a warning. "Not a word about it! And don't look so guilty! *Smile!*"

The truth of it was that Trudy looked just plain irritated at the unexpected visit. She enjoyed apple cobbler well enough, but after all, the house was still in the wreckage of moving, and there was a fugitive and a heap of leg-irons on the back porch.

"Trudy!" Maybelle called from the front room. "Trudy! Mercy! Would you look at all this!"

"True?" Birch's voice shook slightly. "You ain't in the tub yet, are you?"

Trudy tossed her apron onto the table and straightened her hair. She still wore the dress she had on down at the creek. Mud was splattered on the front so she put her apron back on. "Coming!"

Tommy whispered her own advice back to her. "Smile."

For a moment she felt like boxing his ears. Then, drawing a deep breath, she smiled and left the kitchen.

Maybelle and J.D. stood in the center of the clutter of table, chairs, and heaped-up furniture. Maybelle had that hungry-for-information look on her face, a sort of frozen grin as if she were standing in front of a camera holding her smile too long. Only this time, Trudy knew, Maybelle was mentally taking pictures that she could then carefully draw for others among their curious neighbors.

"How wonderful to see you both." Trudy indicated the chair still up-side down on the table. "You can see we are not prepared for callers yet."

"Never mind that," J.D. said cheerfully. He snagged two chairs from the heap and placed them in the center of the room beside the parlor stove. "We ain't callers. We's family, girl! Maybelle brung apple cobbler. Where are the boys?"

"In the kitchen. Finishing supper." Trudy's heart was fluttering in her chest. She hoped her panic did not show.

Maybelle said admiringly, "My, my, don't that Miss Trudy talk fine." She said it as if Trudy were not in the room. "That little accent. Ain't lan-guage an interestin' thing? Here the mother talks just like a German, and the boys don't show no trace of it at all."

This was no compliment. Trudy knew that, yet she continued to smile sweetly and graciously took the cobbler from Maybelle's pudgy hands.

Birch cleared his throat uneasily. "You know Trudy was born in the German community over at Fort Smith way. Born right here same as you, Maybelle."

"That's right," J.D. joined in. "Them Germans all spoke their own language till the war come along and nobody took kindly hearin' the kaiser's tongue in these parts."

At last Maybelle addressed Trudy. "But you aren't really German, are you?" So here was the point of this empty chatter.

"No, I am American," Trudy replied. She inhaled the aroma of the cobbler. "Shall I dish this up? How kind of you to bring it. I'll just be a minute." She slipped back into the kitchen and closed the door. With a sigh, she leaned against the wall and put a hand to her head as she tried to regain composure.

Bobby, Tommy, and baby Joe all sat staring solemnly at her. Forks were raised between their plates and their mouths as though all activity had frozen with the first shout of J.D. in the yard.

The hum of Maybelle's buzz-saw voice pierced the door.

"She ain't comin' in here, is she, Mama?" Tommy asked as footsteps approached and furniture scooted around.

Trudy closed her eyes. "Lord."

That was all the prayer time she got.

The door swung open, and Cousin Maybelle pounced in on the boys.

"Well, would you look at the little gents! Your ma done taught you to stay in the kitchen when y'all got callers, but we're just family! No need to crouch back here."

"Hello, Cousin Maybelle," Tommy said sheepishly. He could not bring his eyes up to meet her look. "We're just finishin' our supper here." He held up a biscuit.

"And I brung desert! Apple cobbler!" she announced, again at the top of her lungs. "Your daddy's favorite. You like apple cobbler?" She embraced each boy as Trudy took out her enameled tin plates and dished up the cobbler. This was trial by fire if ever there was one.

"Yes'm," Bobby and Tommy said in turn. Baby Joe gummed his biscuit and happily banged on the plate.

Maybelle spun around and raised her hands in praise of the new stove. Then she looked at the muddy washtub on the floor and remarked that it was clear someone had been in need of a good scrubbing. At that, Bobby piped up, "It was me. I fell in the creek today!"

"Lord have mercy. You fell in that creek! Why, it ain't been so full in twenty years! Practically flooded. And you fell in the creek!"

Tommy kicked Bobby under the table.

"Just the edge," Bobby said. Hadn't Mama told them that liars don't go to heaven? Now here they were, lying like anything.

J.D. crammed into the kitchen just in time to hear the end of it. Birch followed, looking very pale and unhappy.

"So you fell in the creek!" J.D. guffawed. "Bet I know what you was doin' down there."

Tommy's eyes widened. Only baby Joe looked completely happy. Nobody looked at the door to the back porch. Was he still out there?

"Yessir," Bobby answered guiltily.

A hearty laugh from J.D. "Bet you was down there lookin' for that convict! Huh?" He whacked the boy on the back. "Bet you was thinkin' to get that re-ward!"

"They gonna give the reward for a dead body?" Birch asked.

"Naw. Those Oklahoma lawmen want him back alive."

"Well then—" Birch shrugged—"nobody's gonna collect that reward. . . . Trudy? You got that cobbler?"

But it was no use trying to change the subject. J.D. was intent on discussing every aspect of the matter in detail. "They give up and went back to Oklahoma. Say if he shows up like a fox raidin' somebody's henhouse for eggs, just lock him in a shed and call 'em. They say he ain't no danger, after all. Petty thief or some such, I reckon. Jumped a truck and run for the hills. Won't get far for long with them leg-irons."

At the word *leg-irons*, Trudy braced herself against the counter. *Leg-irons!* Even if the man could have slipped out to hide in the bushes, his leg-irons were still on the porch plain as anything.

Birch put himself between the back door and his cousin. Trudy knew he had envisioned the same disaster. *J.D. opens the door and . . .*

"Come on, boys," Trudy said with strained cheerfulness. "Let's go have Cousin Maybelle's cobbler in the parlor!"

They were all herded out of the kitchen to the next room, where the one-sided conversation of J.D. and Maybelle continued for nearly an hour. Two helpings of cobbler later, Cousin J.D. belched and announced that he had to get home because he still was not sure there wasn't a convict lurking in the bushes someplace.

As they rattled off down the lane, Birch gazed into the darkness after them. "We'll have to get ourselves a mean dog. Mean enough so J.D. will have to ask permission to come up on the porch. But in the meantime . . . "

The thought was interrupted by a cry from the kitchen.

"Mama! He's gone! Our convict is gone!"

The pallet on the back porch was empty. The door to the outside was wide open. Like a wounded bear, the man had somehow managed to pull himself out of the light and into the cold, dark night to hide. He had not gotten far, however.

If J.D. had walked around the house, he would have stumbled over the convict sprawled on the ground a mere four steps from the house. He was still breathing, hot to the touch, even though the temperature outside had dipped below forty degrees.

Trudy and Birch carried him in and put him in the bed that had been intended for Tommy and Bobby. Birch rigged a vapor tent of bedsheets while Trudy prepared a poultice for his chest and set the kettle to boiling with a few drops of camphor oil to clear his congestion. Not even old Dr. Brown in Hartford could do more for pneumonia, Birch told the boys when they asked if the black man would live. There was nothing left to do but wait and pray.

TERROR
BY NIGHT

part two

*Although the world
is full of suffering,
it is full also of the
overcoming of it.*

HELEN KELLER

CHAPTER EIGHTEEN

Finance on the High Seas

The high-walled wagons were heaped with cotton that shone like fresh snow in the starlight. Tomorrow morning the cotton gin on the border between southwest Arkansas and Oklahoma would open, and the harvest of 1929 would be sold at four cents a pound. The gin would pay the farmer, the farmer would pay the white straw boss, and the straw boss would pay his army of pickers—after he deducted for food and transportation and his commission for the harvesting contract.

It was 1929, but nothing much had changed in the last one hundred years. The sons and grandsons of slaves still served King Cotton in the South. When all was said and done, they worked for their daily bread and nothing else; then they moved on to the next county and the next field and the next row to do it all over again.

Tonight there was a brief rest. Beans bubbled over the open fires where the pickers camped. Whole families slept beneath the loaded wagons or beneath the stars. The night insects clicked and hummed a counterpoint to the weary voices that returned year after year to this field. The same faces. The same voices. The same songs. Backs bent over the low, lean cotton plants. Hands cut and bleeding from the sharp edges of the cotton bolls. Seven-foot sacks dragging along behind. And only this one last night of rest before moving on.

It had always been the same and always would be. Men and women did their work without complaint or they were banished from the circuit by the straw boss. Anyone who caused trouble was expelled from the migrant army. No work meant no food. There was nothing else to do. Follow the work from place to place or starve.

With a sense of dread the young woman watched the lean, sunburned straw boss stroll to where she sat among the children at the fire. His tall boots crunched against the dry sod. The light of the flames caught in his pale eyes as he looked straight at her. He tapped his leg with the riding crop he always carried.

"Where's that mulatto?" he asked as conversations fell away around him. He knew where she was. He saw her. He simply wanted every head to turn and observe the lesson he was about to give.

The child next to her whispered, "Mistah Mills be lookin' for you, Lily."

Lily Jones nodded once and stood up. She was tall and straight-backed in spite of spending all her nineteen years following the cotton harvest. Her skin was the soft color of coffee with cream, the legacy of some white slaveholder with her great-grandmother. And she was beautiful. Men on both sides of the color line noticed it, and there was the problem.

Mr. Mills sniffed and walked briskly toward her. "You ain't been pullin' your weight around here since that husband of yours died last month."

She lowered her eyes, certain of what was coming. "I been tryin', suh."

"Tryin' ain't good enough. Look at you." He gestured toward her belly, swollen with the unborn child. "I kept you on as long as that man of yours was pickin' for both of you, but he's dead. Ain't no good sayin' it ain't so. Y'all ain't pickin' as much as a small child. It ain't right. I'm payin' your feed and haulin' you round, and there's a hundred men could take your place. I ain't carryin' no deadweight."

"But when I delivers my child—"

"When is that? Season'll be past. The cotton will be baled by the time y'all drop that young'un. I tell you I ain't carryin' *no more* deadweight round the country!"

In the circles of other campfires Lily saw the heads of women nodding as their husbands looked nervously away. There was that matter, too . . . the way husbands and sons looked at her when she passed, the way women called her uppity and high yaller because of the lightness of her complexion. But to be cast out from this society meant there was no place left to go.

Behind her a woman snickered and said, "High-yaller gal. When she has that young'un, she can get work in a whorehouse."

Twitters of laughter echoed the woman's words.

"Please, Mistah Mills, I ain't gonna cause no trouble," Lily pleaded. "I'll work hard. It's just that the sun beats down so fierce in this place. And the cotton is so short! It hurts me to bend way down."

"That's what I'm sayin', gal. Plenty of men round who take no mind how far they got to stoop or how heavy the cotton sack be. I got no place for you, gal. Now don't make me get rough about it. You got no man. You ain't nothin' but trouble for me. We're goin' on south in the mornin', and I expect you to be on the road headin' north. That, or else I'll call the sheriff and tell him you're makin' trouble."

"But where am I gonna go to, Mistah Mills? Since my man be dead, who I gonna be with?"

"Makes no difference to me." He raised his chin and looked around at his audience. "Any one of these folks'll tell you they's lucky to have work. I got ten men who want to take your place. Men who'll pick four hundred pounds of cotton a day to your two. Y'all ain't worth your salt, and that's just the way it is."

Mills turned on his heel and strode toward his trailer. Lily remained standing in front of the fire. She stretched her hands out to warm them, although it was not really cold tonight.

All around was silence. No human voices. Just the clicking and whirring of the insects. When at last she sat down again, she was alone. The children had melted away to blend in with their families at the other fires in the field. It would not be good to speak to her now that she was no longer one of them.

☆ ☆ ☆

Lights from a thousand portholes gleamed against the backdrop of the black Atlantic, giving the illusion that some enormous chunk of New York City had fallen into the harbor and now cruised the high seas.

This was the very image Cunard Lines wished to suggest to its wealthy patrons. *The ship is merely an extension of Manhattan, linking America and Europe like a moving luxury hotel!*

Four giant screws churned the glassy green water. Three red stacks bellowed smoke as the ship moved swiftly toward its destination. Every luxury was available, every convenience. But on this crossing, something new and exciting had been added to the ship. Now travelers had only to walk down a flight of stairs to the promenade deck to find the Cunard Line's first seagoing stock-brokerage office. It was as simple as filling out a form, and any transaction could be made through a direct Marconi linkup to the New York Stock Exchange. This was news!

Three hours out of the port of New York, the Cherbourg-bound liner *Berengaria* had geared up for a raucous Prohibition-free party on board the great Cunard ship. Champagne corks popped like a barrage of machine-gun fire. Glasses raised and clinked in endless toasts as the passengers guzzled the genuine article. The booze they had been drinking in America was stuff fermented in a bootlegger's rusty bathtub. After a few weeks of freedom, U.S. customs agents would be combing their luggage upon their return to confiscate smuggled samples of what they now imbibed so freely. Perhaps this knowledge spurred the vast majority of those on board the *Berengaria* to attempt to saturate themselves with real champagne, real Scotch whiskey, potent bourbon, and a wide variety of flavored brandies.

Tonight no one cared about sliced roast duck or salmon steaks in dill sauce. It was widely believed by the crew that most of the passengers would not have cared much if the *Berengaria* hit an iceberg and repeated the performance of the *Titanic*: "More champagne . . . whiskey, double on the rocks, please. . . . Do you think if I put that apricot brandy in my medicine bottle, they will notice?" What they could not legally carry off the ship in bottles, they would take with them in saturated cells and hangovers.

Life on board the Cunard liner was meant to be an intoxicating experience, to say the least. Nowhere on board the vast floating city was this more true than in the private dining room located on the aft side of the promenade deck. In this room, sixty-eight distinguished members of the world press corps were gathered around a large horseshoe-shaped table. White-coated waiters scurried around the room, pouring champagne with both hands while frescoes of Greek gods scowled down at the group from the high ceilings.

Harry Beadle of the *New York Globe* stood at the podium. His round, red face glowed with gratitude as he raised his glass to honor Max Meyer beside him. "*Extinguished* membersss of the press," he began.

At this, the entire assembly began to shout with one voice: "Press! Press! Press!" From the moment they stepped on board the Cunard liner, the press corps had discovered that the flush toilets had handles bearing the instruction *Press*. What better badge could there be for those members of the press corps?

As if inspired by the same thought at the same instant, the mob reached into their pockets and pulled out the stolen flush levers, holding them high above their heads. "Press! Press! Press! Press!" they chanted, directing their pleasure at Max Meyer.

Max raised his hands in acknowledgment of their gratitude as Harry Beadle tried to silence them so he might complete his speech before he passed out.

At last the chant fell away, and the "press" badges were safely tucked back into pockets as Harry Beadle began again in a much louder voice. "Gentlemen of the press! We are here to honor one of our *own* . . . who is a regular rags-to-riches kind of story himself!"

Harry did not dare mention Max's name yet, lest the wild demonstration of affection erupt again. He leaned down to thump Max on the shoulder, however, just so he would be sure whom he was talking about. "Although he is a member of the staff of a certain newspaper that shall remain nameless . . . and although he has managed to worry our readers by his daily financial columns and dire predictions of disaster . . . we forgive him!"

Again came the wild shouts of camaraderie: "Press! Press! Press!"

Harry shouted over them, "*Why* do we forgive him? Because he has not forgotten the little guys! No! He has not forgotten those of us out here pounding out beats for a story—*any* story! He has single-handedly convinced the *chumps* of the Cunard Steamship Line that *we* belong on this voyage! That somehow we might be able to give them some great publicity for their new stock-brokerage service!" Harry raised his hand for emphasis. "And what do we all say to that, gentlemen of the press?"

To a man, they stood and raised their flushers. "Press! Press!"

"Yes!" cried Harry happily. "We are privileged to witness history in the making, my fellow citizens! This floating stock brokerage is the first of its kind on the high seas. More popular than a floating craps game, more exciting than shuffleboard. We witness the passengers of the esteemed *Berengaria* as they give up relaxation and deck chairs and bridge to stand in line to buy and sell on the New York Exchange. What's the scoop? America is addicted to greed—that's what! And because of the sales pitch of our *extremed* colleague, we are privileged to drop a few bucks ourselves in between wiring in our stories. Other than that, this whole trip is *free*, gentlemen! The booze! The food! Everything absolutely *free*!"

A great cheer echoed in the room as the waiters gaped at one another in amusement and horror. What would happen if the Cunard Line executives could hear this speech?

"Well," Harry persisted. "The Cunard execs may be fools, but *we* are not!"

More shouts of joy.

"And we have this whole round-trip cushy assignment just because of one man . . ."

Out came the "press" levers.

"Drumroll, please!"

The handles banged on the table.

"Members of the press, I give you . . . MAX MEYER!"

Max stood and bowed demurely, accepting their adulation and exultant applause. Gathered in this room were correspondents from every major American news chain, and a few from Europe had joined the journey as well. Hearst was represented. McCormick of Chicago. Ochs had sent a man along. Trump and the *Wall Street Journal* were on board.

Sixty-eight correspondents planned to keep the wireless operators busy over the next few days, filing copy that proclaimed that America's addiction to the stock market need not stop at the water's edge. The businessman who used to get delirium tremens without an hourly fix on the happenings at the Exchange could now travel worry-free. A buy or sell order was only two minutes and the tap of the wireless key away! And the entire scheme had been conceived, planned, and executed by Max Meyer, who claimed to hate sea voyages more than plague or famine. With the unexpected backing of Keenan Brokerage and Cunard Line, the idea had been approved by the commission, and this was the result.

Tonight Max was perhaps the only completely sober passenger on the ship. This was not because he had an aversion to alcohol, but rather because he had an aversion to the ship and the movement of the water. He had once spent an entire sea voyage hanging over the rail because of too much champagne. And he had vowed he would never repeat his mistake.

His shipboard sobriety served to strengthen his reputation among the ship's officers and ultimately with Cunard Line. A dozen crossings over the years had acquainted him with the men in position to make the shipboard brokerage firm become a reality. This maiden voyage was proof that the concept was a sound one. The experiment was a success beyond everyone's wildest dreams. Max Meyer had made believers out of each cynical journalist in a position to write about it. Even tonight's revelry was a part of Max's plan. Every hard-boiled newspaperman might be bombed, but when they returned to their offices they would remember . . . there was nothing bootleg about their up-to-the-minute stock quotations. Max had made certain their every desire was instantly gratified. That was the sort of publicity money couldn't buy.

As he gazed out over the beaming faces of journalism's finest, he did not doubt that they would dutifully report that something new and wonderful had been launched on the sea of high finance. And for each shipboard transaction made, Max earned 10 percent of the Keenan Brokerage commission.

Max Meyer was making money—potentially lots of money—and his colleagues loved him for it! Press! Press! Press!

CHAPTER NINETEEN

Escape to New York

The wail of the train whistle awakened David at the same moment a Negro porter placed a gentle hand on his shoulder.

"S'cuse me, young man." His eyes darted to David's worn-out shoes and then back to his face. "We are arrivin' in Grand Central shortly. You slept all the way from Philadelphia. Slept clean through breakfast." He presented David with a brown-paper sack. "Got fruit in here for you case you be hungry. Banana and two oranges all the way from Florida. Be a pure shame for a young man to ride first class and miss out on these here oranges."

David smoothed his wrinkled shirt, tucking the tail into his knickers. He was plenty hungry all right. He croaked his thanks and took the paper bag, but the porter did not move from the aisle.

"You got folks comin' to pick you up?" asked the porter. His liquid brown eyes displayed a kindly concern.

"Gonna meet . . . my dad." David peeled the banana and took a bite.

"Your pa knows you're comin', then?"

"Gonna s'prise him," David said around the banana.

That seemed to satisfy the porter, who nodded and swayed toward the blue-uniformed conductor waiting at the far end of the car. The two leaned their heads together and spoke in low tones, each casting looks toward David as he finished the banana.

Something was up.

The conductor consulted his watch and then eyed David. He stuck out his lower lip in a thoughtful way and muttered something else to the porter.

David pretended he did not feel their eyes on him. He gazed out the window at the towering buildings of the great city. The highest pinnacles were lit by the first light of dawn, making them glow in pastel colors.

New York City was a big place. A whole lot bigger than Philadelphia, where the tallest thing around was the giant statue of William Penn at city hall. Next to New York, William Penn was a midget and the city hall a dollhouse. A person could probably disappear real easy in such a big place, David reasoned. That is, if a person was able to get off the train without getting pinched by the railroad cops.

The conductor crossed his arms over his chest and glared openly at David, as if challenging him to try to slip past. The banana stuck in David's throat. The porter cocked his head toward David in a pitying sort of way. He passed him again and asked, "You enjoy that banana, young man?"

David nodded, certain that the porter and the conductor knew he was on the run. But did they know he knew?

"You say you gonna surprise your daddy? Your daddy don't know you're comin', then?"

"Sure he knows. He works at the newspaper. Works all the time. He just doesn't have time to come to the station and pick me up. So I'm gonna go right to his office at the newspaper and surprise him."

"What newspaper he work at, child?"

Was there suspicion in the dark, moist eyes?

"The New York paper."

"Hmmm." From under his arm, the porter produced a selection of newspapers. *New York Herald Tribune. New York World. New York American. New York Evening Post. New York Evening World . . .* "You tell me which one, and I'll call down there for you. Tell him you're here."

David frowned at the newspapers. *Which one, indeed?* David had imagined that there was only one newspaper in New York City. How could he find Max if there were so many? He inhaled deeply and pointed to the copy of the *New York World.* "That one."

The porter smiled and straightened. "Well then. That's nice. I'll call your daddy to come fetch you. What's his name?"

"Max. Max Meyer."

"I'm real glad to know that fact, young man. Tell the truth, we thought maybe you was that runaway we got word about. Young man just up and took off from Philadelphia. Lots of folks is worried about him."

"It ain't me," David said adamantly, even though it was. And they knew it. And he knew they knew. . . .

But he had not come so far to be turned back now. What did he have to go back to? An iron cot at the children's home? Father John? Parochial school? Here in New York . . . *somewhere* . . . David had a real father. He would not be stopped by a pig-faced railroad conductor and a white-gloved porter.

The train was slowing down, its brakes squealing as Grand Central Station slid up just ahead.

"I got to use the toilet," David said suddenly.

"Well now, young man. We ain't but a few minutes from the terminal. Can it wait?"

"No." David's eyes darted past the broad-chested conductor, plotting his escape route. The porter escorted him to the tiny cubicle. David slid the bolt closed and glared at his own reflection in the mirror. The clacking wheels slowed to a *tap, tap, tap,* then stopped.

From the narrow corridor the porter rapped on the door. "You 'bout done, young man?"

"No, I'm not!" David hollered back. He narrowed his eyes and waited until he heard the bumping and shuffling of departing passengers outside the door of the toilet. Only then did he unlock the door and make his move.

While porter and conductor were blocked by the disembarking passengers, David ducked and bobbed against the flow of luggage and suits and skirts, finally crowding out the exit at the far end of the car. Behind him he could hear the conductor calling for him to come back and the porter reminding him that he had left his bag behind.

It didn't matter. David did not care about the underwear or change of socks in his rucksack. He had tucked the precious envelope of clippings into the pocket of his jacket. Maybe when he found his father, he would get some new clothes. New shoes. A jacket that fit and a new bag of marbles.

As he dashed through the rumbling crowd of Grand Central Station, the voices of his would-be captors were lost in the din.

David was not such a dunce that he was lured into the bank of telephone booths in the enormous lobby of Grand Central. Nor did he stop to look at the dozens of newspapers displayed at the news vendors' kiosks beside the ticket booth. To have done either of those things might have meant being nabbed by the railroad cops and chained up in the luggage car to be shipped back to Philadelphia. He was in the fourth grade, almost ten. That was plenty old enough to know what he was doing.

He emerged from the great railroad palace into the roar of the New

York City morning. The sun was blocked by the tall buildings, and the wind hooted down Fifth Avenue, making men and ladies alike hold on to their hats and umbrellas as they plowed up and down the sidewalks.

The crowd was vast, moving like a river. David stood elbow high to a grown man, so he walked unnoticed through the morning rush-hour throngs. Nobody looked his way. He was invisible as he moved along with the current.

He did not know where he was going, but that did not matter at the moment. The more distance he put between him and the cops back at Grand Central, the better off he was. He already had planned what he would say if anyone asked him where he was headed. *"Orchard Street."*

And if that was not good enough, he would tell them, *"I am going to Nathan's for a hot dog."* This was a very New York thing to do, his mother had often told him. Everyone ate at Nathan's Famous sooner or later. With a hot dog in his hand, who would suspect that he had come from Philadelphia? But no one asked. He walked for a long ways, and the crowd never seemed to thin out. Groups would break off and go into a tall building at the same time a revolving door would spit out another group onto the sidewalk.

After a while David realized that he was trudging along with his neck so far back that it looked broken. He had been staring up at the tops of the skyscrapers. His mother had also told him that it was easy to spot tourists from the way they wandered around gaping up at the buildings.

David corrected himself, scanning the entrance of Macy's Department Store to see if the on-duty cop had noticed the way he had been looking like a tourist. Luckily, the cop was staring blankly ahead, as if he were sound asleep with his eyes open. Or maybe the guy was just a wax dummy rolled out on little wheels like the one at the wax museum in Atlantic City. David pictured himself tweaking the nose of the wax policeman; then the fellow blinked once and scratched his cheek and yawned. Ducking his head, David moved to the outer edge of the sidewalk, far enough that he could see the other side of the street.

On the corner was a small store with bowfront windows. TOBACCO was stenciled on the glass above enormous gold letters that read: ALL THE LATEST NEWS!

This was just the place David had hoped to find. And there was a telephone booth right beside the entrance.

David would find out which newspaper Max worked for, and he would telephone. *"Hello, Max Meyer, remember Irene? This is your long-lost kid. . . ."* He had not thought out exactly what he would say. First things first.

A bell above the door jingled as David entered the tobacco store. The place was small and warm and smelled like the pipe tobacco that Father John smoked in his old briar pipe. It was a pleasant aroma, and David felt at ease in the place. Racks and racks displayed the latest newspapers and New York tabloids. On the back wall were publications in strange languages that David did not understand. He clasped his hands behind him and tried to stand up straighter, taller, and look older as the bespectacled old man behind the counter puffed his pipe and glanced up from the paper he was reading behind the battered counter.

"You wish somethink, younk man?" The old man clicked his pipe-stem between his teeth. He spoke like a foreigner and looked like one, too. His drooping mustache was yellowed with age. His bushy eyebrows poked up above the wire rims of his glasses. He wore a blue bow tie and a blue jacket stained with tobacco and maybe mustard. He was eyeing David suspiciously. Maybe not many fourth graders came into this place.

"I would like to know which New York paper Max Meyer works for," David said firmly, as though he were an old customer with a right to ask questions.

"Max whooooo?"

"Max Meyer."

"Nefer heardt of dis fellow." He waved his pipe in the air. "He is a delifery boy, mebbe? He bringks d' papers to my shop, mebbe?"

This was bad news. "No," David said, bewildered. "He writes. He writes . . . things. . . ."

"What kind of thingks?"

"Stuff . . . about money."

"Nefer heardt of dis fellow." The old man scratched his head with his pipestem and turned the page of his paper. David could see it was not a newspaper written in English.

David stood in front of the racks and stared at the myriad of New York papers. There were many more here than the old black porter on the train had carried around. How could David pick the right one and find his father's name inside?

Each publication had a different headline:

"NO TRACE OF LOST AIRLINER"

"LINDBERGH TO AID HUNT OF PLANE"

"BRITAIN PROPOSES DISARMAMENT"

"BANKER SOUGHT IN $500,000 THEFT"

David picked up the story about the banker because Max wrote about money, after all. It was in *New York World*.

The eyes of the old clerk lifted suspiciously as David opened the paper and searched for the name of Max Meyer inside.

"You want to read it? You gotta buy it." The old man scowled. "Three cents."

David nodded and counted out three pennies, which he slid across the counter. "Okay?"

"Read it outside," the man insisted. "I don't run no liberry for kids."

David took the paper back out in the cold. The wind whipped at the pages, threatening to tear it out of his hands. Ducking into the phone booth, he closed the glass door and sat down on the wooden seat to peruse the newspaper one page at a time. No Max. But there was a telephone number listed just inside the front page along with names of publishers and editors.

David fished a nickel from his pocket and dialed the number.

A woman's high voice answered, "*New York Woild.* How may I direct your call?"

David took a deep breath and crossed his fingers as he pulled himself closer to the mouthpiece. "Does Max Meyer work for this paper?"

"I am sorry; there is no Max Meyer on the staff of the *Woild.*"

David checked off the *World* and returned to face the old tobacconist with another three cents, purchasing the *New York Herald Tribune* and then the *New York American* and on and on until there was a stack of newspapers in the bottom of the phone booth tall enough for David to stand on to make his calls without straining to reach the dial or the mouthpiece.

Always the question was the same: "Does Max Meyer work there?"

Always the answer was the same: "I am sorry; there is no Max Meyer listed on our switchboard. . . ."

He lost count of how many pennies he gave to the old vendor through the hours. The selection had been whittled down to half a dozen possibilities when David picked up a copy of the *New York Times.* He studied the headlines eagerly, hoping for some clue.

Then he heard the whispered voice of the old man. "This is the boy, Officer Dooley."

David found himself in the stern, scrutinizing gaze of the wax cop from Macy's. David looked away and placed three cents on the counter just like all the other times.

"You like to read, huh, kid?" said the officer.

"I'm looking for somebody." David raised his chin in a fearless way, although he was shaking inside.

"Lookin' for somebody, huh? Gonna find them in the want ads or what?"

"I don't know," he said in as calm a tone as he could muster. He was so close. Would he be arrested, hauled away in a paddy wagon like Brian when he had gotten drunk and broken a window at the greengrocer? "I got to make a call."

David slipped out, the familiar bell ringing behind him. He barricaded himself into the phone booth, propping the newsprint against the glass door as he sat down to hunt through the publication. Nothing doing. No Max. No story. Nothing.

David dialed the number of the *New York Times* and waited for the nasal voice of the switchboard girl.

"*Times.* How may I direct your call?"

"Does Max Meyer work there?"

"One mo-ment ple-ase. I will transfer you."

Could this be? David jumped up and down on the newspapers and laughed out loud. All this work was not wasted! Max worked for the *New York Times*! Of course it would be the *Times*. It was thicker than the other newspapers! It looked better than the rest. It was only right his father would write for the really big New York paper! David felt foolish for not having started at the other end of the rack.

"Hullo . . . Financial Desk. Missus Morgan speaking."

"Hi! I am trying to get ahold of Max Meyer."

"Max?" Her voice sounded busy. "Sorry. He's not here."

"Not there?"

"That's right. Not here. Gone. Get it?"

"But where is he?"

"Well, if it's anybody's business, dear Max has gone to Yurp."

"Yurp? But where's Yurp?" David was desperate. Had he found his father now—only to lose him a moment later?

"You don't study geography in school? He's gone to France, Yurp, that's where. Left last night on the *Barn-garn-ya*. Sorry."

The phone cut off with a click.

David stood very still in the little glass booth. He let his copy of the *New York Times* fall on the heap. Replacing the receiver, he sat down to think what he should do next.

Just then the Macy's cop, who was smoking a cigarette, came out of the little news shop. He began to walk in an official way to the telephone booth, where David had stashed enough newspapers to start his own kiosk.

"What are you doin' in there, boy?" the officer shouted through the glass.

David opened the door and stepped out into the cold. What was the use? Max was long gone to France, Yurp. Now what was David to do?

"Where do you live, boy?"

"Orchard Street."

"You're a long way from home."

"I suppose so."

Good thing the officer did not know how far from home.

"What are you doin' with all these papers?"

"I bought them. They're mine." David lifted his chin defiantly.

The cop looked at his pocket watch and rose slightly on his toes. "I suppose they are. What do you intend to do with them? Open a newsstand?" He laughed and reached to grasp David's coat. "Little scamp. You're playin' hooky, that's what! Little ragged hooligan! Do your parents know what you're up to? We'll just take you down to the station, and—"

David kicked him hard in the shins and tore free of the meaty hands, leaving his coat behind. As the policeman shouted at him to "Halt, halt, halt!" David dashed into the moving mass of pedestrians and disappeared.

CHAPTER TWENTY

Under His Wings

Morning sunlight was no respecter of persons. Dawn crept across the hills and valleys of Arkansas just as bright and clean as if this were the first day of creation. It glowed through the paper-covered windows of the poor tenant farmers just as it penetrated the glass panes of the rich folks. It warmed Trudy's shoulders as she dozed in the rocking chair at the foot of the fugitive's bed. It fell across the pages of the open Bible on her lap.

Far away the whistle of the morning train to Hartford called. Birds sang and cows bellowed in the pasture. Trudy opened her eyes and inhaled the strong vapor of camphor. Her head jerked up as it came to her why she was sleeping in the chair. The labored breathing of the fugitive was silent now.

He was motionless, his face peaceful as he gazed steadily past her to the flood of light and color beyond the window. She could not hear his breath, and a chill coursed through her. Was he dead? Had his soul drifted away with the dawn?

She opened her mouth to call Birch just as the eyes of the man flitted to her face and then to the Bible on her lap.

"Mornin', ma'am," he rasped.

For an instant she could not reply. Relief flooded her. She nodded. "You are . . . better?"

A long look at the Bible. "Guess the Lord ain't through with me yet." He spoke each word carefully, as though he had not talked in a long time.

"We were not sure. You have been unconscious." Trudy took in the crooked nose, the scarred hands folded across the quilt. "I am thankful He saw fit to spare you . . . and for what you did for my son."

He did not reply to her thanks but kept his eyes fixed on the Book. A hungry longing was in his eyes. "He knows when the sparrow falls, the Good Book says. I suppose He knew from always that boy was gonna get into mischief down at the creek. Maybe all along the Lord was savin' me for that child. And savin' that child for me. He is like that, Jesus is. A man just don't know. Gotta trust." He put out his hand toward the Book. "May I hold it, ma'am? Been so long. Ain't held me a Good Book in my hands for nigh on ten years."

Trudy rose and placed her Bible in his hands. He held it like a lost child. His palm covered the entire page in the embrace of an old friend. "He ain't forgot me," he whispered. "Although y'all may have forgotten, the Lord kept me in His hands. He ain't forgot." There were tears streaming down his cheeks as he looked up at Trudy. "You best call Birch Tucker, Miz Trudy. I got plenty to tell him."

Trudy gasped and stepped back, unwilling to believe what her mind and memory shouted at her. "Who—who are you?" she stammered.

From behind her, Birch cleared his throat. She turned and saw him in the doorway.

"I knew a man once," Birch said. "Rode with him on a train from New York City. A homesick soldier. He planned on becoming a preacher. I talked about Shiloh, and he talked about Mount Pisgah and his family. He had hunted on Poteau. Had looked down on the birch trees of this farm from the heights . . ."

The black man closed his eyes and nodded. "Clear as a vision, them trees. Like a white picket fence down below in the crook of the James Fork . . ."

Trudy's hand was at her mouth. She gasped with disbelief. *A miracle!*

"He preached me a sermon and fought at my side," Birch continued. "Saved my life, I reckon. Later saved the soul of my wife, who heard him preaching out the window of his little church. And now . . . you've come back, Jefferson Canfield! You've saved the life of our child! We gave you up for dead years ago!"

"There is a God," Jefferson said through his tears. "He's been alongside me all the way. Led me through the wilderness. Made light to shine on them trees in your field. *Birch!* the Lord said to me when I thought I was done for. And I know'd I wasn't gonna die yet."

"Jefferson Canfield!" Trudy staggered back and sat down in the rocking chair. Her legs would not hold her. He was so visibly changed that she could not have recognized him if they had passed on the street. What had they done to him? Yet his soul was unchanged, his love for God un-diminished. Yes. She could see that plainly in his eyes.

Jefferson held the Bible up to the morning light and began to read. *"Under His wings shalt thou trust: His truth shall be thy shield and buckler. Thou shalt not be afraid for the terror by night; nor for the arrow that flieth by day; nor for the pestilence that walketh in darkness; nor for the destruction that wasteth at noonday."* He paused and looked at Birch. "Reckon He ain't through with me yet."

"I reckon not," Birch agreed.

"Ten years that thought kept me livin' when I wanted to die and be with my sweet gal, my Tisha. It's been ten years since anyone spoke my name."

"Well now, that ain't exactly so," Birch said. He turned and called for Tommy to come into the room.

The boy was as fair as Birch. His blond hair tumbled down over his forehead. He smoothed it back and grinned at Jefferson. "You woke up."

Jefferson studied the child. "You look like your daddy," he said in a wistful voice, filled with longing.

If things had been different, Trudy knew, no doubt Jefferson and Latisha would have had a whole passel of young'uns. Some would look like Jeff, some like Latisha. It had been such a sweet dream. Now there was no calling it back.

Birch cleared his throat. "Tommy, I want you to tell our friend your name."

"Yes," Trudy joined in.

Tommy looked from his mother to his father and then at the man whose feet stuck out from the end of the bed. "My name is Tommy."

Birch urged him on. "Tell him your whole name, Tommy, and where you got it. . . ."

*　*　*

Tommy drew himself up proudly as he always did when the subject of his name came up. "Thomas Jefferson Tucker. I'm named for a real hero. A man my daddy knew in the war. Beat the Huns, he did, practically single-handed. Got a big important medal for it, too, from the Frenchies, Dad told me. Then he come home and got married and the Klan . . ."

Tommy faltered as he noticed that the black man had covered his face with his hands. "Did I say something wrong?" Tommy asked his mother, who was also crying.

"No, Son." Birch wrapped an arm around Tommy's shoulder. Then he said to Jefferson, "We named our firstborn after you, Jeff. Every time we pray for our own son, we pray for you. Didn't know where you were or what had happened to you, but every day . . . *every day* . . . we prayed for you. It hasn't been ten years since anyone spoke your name, Jeff. Me and True spoke it to Jesus every day. You hear me, Jeff?"

Tommy looked up at his father in wonder. Was this the hero? Was this the man in the photograph? The same giant who had whupped all those hooligans in Missouri and saved the life of his father?

"Yes." Birch answered Tommy's question before it was asked.

Tommy's grin returned. He had heard so much about the Preacher! And now to have him right here—right in this room and in his bed! Upright, Jefferson Canfield must be the tallest person Tommy had ever seen, because his big feet stuck way off the end of the bed and his head fairly touched the iron headboard. This was indeed a wonder!

Tommy stepped up beside the bed and stood peering down at the hands covering the scarred face.

Jefferson must have sensed the child's nearness, for he lowered his hands slowly.

"I got a picture of you," Tommy said in an awestruck voice.

"Don't look like me no more, I reckon." Jefferson wiped his cheeks with the back of his hand.

Tommy leaned in closer, searching the dark eyes and the broad forehead. Yes. The face was just like the one in the picture, only now it was pieced together with scars like a jigsaw puzzle. Some pieces were missing. The man's teeth were all broken, and in one place his ear was torn.

"Yep. It's you all right." He beamed. "Boy! Wait till I tell I got a hero right here in my own bedroom!"

Jefferson took Tommy's hand in his enormous grasp. His fingers nearly swallowed the boy's arm as they shook.

Tommy went on. "How-do," he said in a manly way. "I sure been hopin' you'd come back!"

"Me too," replied Jefferson. "I reckon Jesus been plannin' on this a long time."

During the trip to Hartford for supplies, Tommy and Bobby were warned not to say one word about Jefferson Canfield or what had happened at the creek. "*Stick to school, the new mules, and the weather,*" Ma had said.

It was not school or the mules or weather that interested Tommy and Bobby, however, but the lean bluetick hound dog who strolled out of

Brother Williams's livery stable. She had recently had a litter of pups. Her teats drooped and her ears drooped and her tail drooped, giving her a pitiful, worn-out look.

Tommy clucked at her and she wagged halfheartedly, then walked on to plop down in a patch of sunshine.

"You wouldn't know by lookin' at her," Brother Williams said in a proud voice, "but she's pert near the best old hunting dog a man could want. Them pups has near done her in, though. Fourteen of 'em."

Birch whistled low and looked at the sunken flanks. "They've about eaten her, from the looks of it."

"Yup." Brother Williams called soothingly to her, "Ain't that the truth, Emmaline? Them pups of yourn done sucked you to a mere shadow." He confided in Birch, "She's got a reputation to uphold. I bred her to Lucius Worth's big old hound. I swear her pups are big as she is. Most all of 'em are spoke for." He turned to the boys. "Go have a look, boys. They're in the last stall."

Tommy felt the curious eyes of Boomer peering over the edge of the hayloft as they ran into the barn.

"Whatcha want?" Boomer asked.

"Come to see Emmaline's pups," Bobby answered.

"Best pups in the county," declared Boomer. It must have been true, because Boomer had already proved himself to be a truth-speaking fellow. "Don't pick 'em up. Brother Williams don't like when kids pick them pups up." He returned to his work, sending showers of hay down into the troughs of the horses and mules in the stalls below.

The door to the last stall was closed, corralling the troop of fourteen little coon-dog puppies. Tommy peered through the cracks at them. They were as fat as their mama was thin, as full of energy as she was worn-out. All of them were bluetick like her except for one—a bright-eyed female with a red coat, who swaggered through her wrestling brothers with a torn rag in her mouth. The challenge for tug-of-war was issued and the struggle began. Growls and baby yips filled the stall as every puppy joined the rumble.

Boomer called down. "That's the way they practice for huntin'," he declared knowingly. "Like that there rag is a coon, see? They're killin' it good! Gonna be the best hounds in the country. Ain't no coon nor possum gonna get away from that bunch!"

Tommy kept his eyes on the red puppy. Her chest was broad; her long ears pulled the skin of her face downward, giving her a wise, sad look. She was tough, too. She pulled on that rag with the strength of two of her brothers, toppling a larger male, then pouncing on him when he rolled. The ear of the male puppy proved a more inviting target than the rag. She latched on and growled, pulling him sideways until he yipped and tucked his tail in pain.

"She's the best one," Tommy whispered. It was love at first sight. "The little red one. That's for me."

Birch and Brother Williams stood behind the boys, observing the universal love that happens between small boys and puppies.

"You in the market for a good coon dog, Birch?" Brother Williams was stroking his stubbled chin in anticipation of yet another few dollars in his pocket. "Best coon dogs in the country."

Birch laughed. He called to Boomer. "Is Brother Williams tellin' the truth about these puppies, Boomer?"

"Yessir, he is. Brother Williams might lie about a lot of things, but he tells the truth about them dogs."

"Well, how much are folks payin' for them, Boomer?" Birch circumvented Brother Williams, who had the glint of greed shining in his eyes.

"Homer Goodfellow paid him twenty dollars," Boomer reported, tossing down another pitchfork full of hay. "Lemme see. Ha! And Henry Peebles paid twenty-five for that big male—the one the leetle red gal just beat up."

"I want the red one, Pa," Tommy said eagerly.

Brother Williams sniffed pleasantly. Maybe Boomer was not such a bad influence after all. "That leetle gal is gonna cost you. She surely is. Got all the brains of her mama, and she's tough as horseshoes! Leader of the pack, that one. Twenty-five dollars."

Birch scoffed. "No fool gonna pay that for that little mutt."

"Suit yourself . . ." Brother Williams seemed unmoved. "You know what a well-bred dog is worth. Worth more'n a mule. And my Emmaline put everythin' she got into them pups of hers. I ain't gonna let 'em go cheap as fryin' hens. You get a good dog, and you make back your money in pelts the first season—and that's the gospel truth."

Boomer joined in the praises of Emmaline's puppies. "Yessir, Emmaline is a right Christian dog. And she has herself some right Christian puppies, too! Amen to that!"

"You mean that by way of a compliment, Boomer, or as an accusation?" Birch laughed.

Boomer did not appear to understand. "Right *Christian* puppies, Mister Birch! It's true Brother Williams is a liar, but old Emmaline is a right—"

"Shut up, you fool!" shouted Brother Williams.

Silence descended from above. The hay fell down with more vigor. Boomer had said it once and twice and three times, and once was enough.

Birch looked at the yearning faces of his sons. "If these boys will work and pay half, I'll buy that little red one from you for twenty-two."

"Twenty-four."

"Twenty-two."

"Twenty-three fifty."

"Twenty-two."

"Lordy, Birch Tucker! You are a hard man! A hard man, I say! This ain't the way to horse-trade! Ain't fair! Give in a little!"

"Twenty-two and two bits."

"Done." Brother Williams looked as done in as old Emmaline. His face was sagging, and his hat was shoved way back on his head. He was sweating in spite of the cold. "Shake on it. The puppy ain't gonna be ready to go for four more weeks. I'll hold her. You and them boys pay up then."

Tommy and Bobby let out whoops and hollers of joy. Emmaline wandered back in and stood in the frame of the barn door to see what was up, to make sure no human boy-pup came near her little pack. Sad and wise, she wagged a time or two as Birch Tucker shook on the bargain with Brother Williams. Four weeks was still a long way off, and by then, no doubt she would be glad to see the whole bunch of her litter go on down the road!

The day had turned cold. Lily sat on the back porch of the prim white farmhouse and imagined what it would be like to be inside such a place.

She knew the mistress of the house was keeping an eye on her out the kitchen window, but she did not resent the woman's suspicion. After all, she had given Lily a plate of food and let her stop to rest here on the back steps. Beans and bacon and hot corn bread.

This was only the third meal Lily had eaten in six days. She sopped up the grease with the corn bread, cleaning the tin pie plate, and licked her fingers. Her shrunken stomach ached from the meager portion, but she would not let even one drop of nourishment be wasted. After all, she had a precious little one inside her, and she did not know how long it might be before she ate again.

The leather sole of Lily's shoe had flapped loose. She tore a strip of cloth from her brown cotton shift and wrapped it tightly around the shoe and sole to hold them together.

For days she had followed the same general route back north into Arkansas that the migrant cotton pickers had used heading south. Names like Gillham, Grannis, Wickes, Hatton, Cove, and Hatfield stuck in her mind. She could not read the names of the towns on the signposts, but at least the country and the farms were familiar to her.

Towns of redbrick buildings and white-frame farmhouses were surrounded by worn-out fields. For the six days she had been on the road, Lily had slept in haystacks and deserted barns and eaten old apples rotting beneath trees. So in spite of the fact that the woman of this house suspected her, Lily blessed her for this food.

The screen door squeaked open. Nervous and distracted, the farmwife stepped into the cold air.

Lily could feel the woman eyeing her shoes, the thin cotton of her shift, and the swell of her belly.

"Where you goin' to, gal?" the woman asked, taking the plate.

"Thank you, ma'am . . . I was right hungry these days. Reckon the Lord saw how hungry I was and sent me here. Bless you, ma'am."

This thanks appeared to make the woman uneasy, as though she did not want to imagine that such a small thing could mean so much to anyone. "I ask you where you're headed?"

Lily shook her head and bit her lip. "North."

"Just north?"

"Don't rightly know. My man passed on some time ago, up north of here. I s'pose my feet just keep goin' back that way, 'cause that's the last place I was happy." She gave a quick, self-conscious smile. Lily had not meant to give so much away about herself. "But pay that no mind. I surely thank you all for the kindness."

The farmwife looked past her on up the road. "Trees are all in color. It's gettin' cold these days. You ain't got no coat?"

"No'm. It were warm south of here."

She held up her finger for Lily to wait. Retreating into the house, she returned a moment later with a heavy red-flannel shirt. "My son outgrowed it. Put it on."

Lily stroked the gift. Kindness was a rare thing. "You a right fine Christian woman."

"It's nothin'. Now get along." The face was unsmiling in spite of the kindness, as though she wanted to do more.

Was it worth asking? Lily hesitated. "Y'all wouldn't need some help round the place, would you? I can clean up right nice. Scrub pots. Chop kindlin', even."

The woman looked her full in the face. "We don't need no help."

Lily knew she had somehow made the woman angry.

"Y'all in the family way," the woman continued. "I done my Christian duty, but you ain't neither white nor black, and you look like trouble to me. I fed you. Now get on down the road. We don't need the likes of you round here."

With those words, the woman undid the kindness she had done.

Lily's hopeful smile faded. She placed the red-flannel shirt on the top step and backed away. "Thank you all the same, ma'am."

"Well, take the shirt! What? Too good for charity?" The woman snorted and retrieved the gift she had so grudgingly offered in the name of duty.

Lily heard the screen door bang shut behind her as she walked out to the gravel highway.

CHAPTER TWENTY-ONE

Rum Row

When David lost his coat, he had lost everything. News clippings. The picture of his mother. Money. Hope. He had not eaten all day.

He trudged down the street with his eyes on the sidewalk, looking for a coin someone might have dropped. Once when he was eight, he had found a silver dollar lodged in the crack of the sidewalk outside Mr. Heber's market. And then there were those tickets to the Series that he had found on the tram. Was it not possible for another miracle to happen now when he needed it most?

He had no desire to look up at the skyscrapers or to marvel at the bigness of Manhattan. It was bad enough that he could feel the vastness of the city and his own smallness. Fourth grade suddenly did not seem as mature as David had imagined himself to be in Philadelphia. Yes, he had played hooky back home and had ridden the trams all over Philadelphia, never giving it a second thought. Back then he had carried a sack lunch and a nickel tram fare in his coat pocket. Now there was no lunch, no nickel, and no coat. Worse than all that, however, was that there was no Max. All the time David had been thinking that he would find Max, break the news to him, and they would have a hot dog together. Maybe take in a Brooklyn Dodgers game sometime. But Max had gone away on a big ship to Yurp, leaving David alone. The whole deal was rotten, David thought miserably as he searched for a wayward coin. Lousy and rotten!

Tall buildings blocked the sun, creating a false twilight in the street. Was it close to suppertime? David's stomach ached as if it were way past suppertime. He had eaten only one banana all day long, and he had lost his coat. Now he was going to starve to death on his first day in New

York. If he did not freeze to death first. Up ahead, the music of "East Side, West Side" was playing.

An organ-grinder cranked his music box while his trained monkey munched on a pretzel and bared his teeth at passersby. David envied the monkey. He eyed the pretzel hungrily and mentally calculated what it would take to snatch it out of the little creature's hands and take off down the street. Dragging the music box and the monkey after him, the organ-grinder would have a tough time chasing him down! The monkey smiled at David. More a grimace than a smile. Bits of pretzel fell out of its mouth, wasted on the pavement.

"Little creep," David muttered, turning away.

As if it understood his insult, the monkey squawked and put its thumb to its nose in an almost human gesture of disdain. *"Welcome to New York, you little sucker!"*

David trudged on like this for hours, it seemed. The artificial twilight darkened slightly to a purple hue. People went into buildings and people came out of buildings, and no one ever stopped to inquire what a kid was doing without his coat on such a cold day. No one asked why he was bent at the waist searching the pavement. Mostly, no one asked if he was hungry or lost—which he certainly was.

When at last he raised his eyes, David did not know where he was or how he had come to be there. A red electric tram crackled around the corner where David stood. Redbrick warehouses with wrought-iron fire escapes stretched away down the street. At the end, an enormous white-hulled freighter with huge red stacks towered over the shabby structures of the docks. A flat-roofed brick warehouse was topped by a white sign with red lettering just like the freight ship: American Fruit Company.

An open truck was pulling away, laden with giant clusters of bananas. More bananas than David had ever seen in his life. The air smelled of ripe fruit, fermenting pineapples, and smoke from the smudge-pot fire where stevedores warmed their hands. Across from the ship was a green railway coach that had been converted to a diner.

Food and fire!

His stomach churned with hunger; his numb hands were shoved deep into his pockets. He hesitated only an instant on the low curb before hurrying toward the blazing barrel, where two dozen men gathered like kids around a campfire. A bottle of white Haitian rum was passed from hand to hand to be evenly distributed among the coffee cups. David recognized the label on the bottle as Brian O'Halloran's favorite brand of booze. The dockworkers were laughing and talking loudly—the rum bottle had probably been passed around more than once. This fact made David pause before he approached the group. Brian had taught

David plenty about the unpredictability of drinking men, but hunger and cold overcame his caution. The long arm of Prohibition was not in force here on the docks.

Unnoticed, David squeezed in between rubber boots and dirty dungarees and heavy peacoats to inch closer to the blazing barrel.

Six different foreign accents tinged the air blue with raucous curses. "Trow a little of dat rum on de fire. She look like de fire goin' down." This comment, made by a short, muscular Jamaican, was accompanied by a splash of rum in the barrel. The blaze rumbled and floated up, catching a new piece of wood in its heat.

"Blimey, Trevor!" growled a burley cockney. "What you wastin' good rum for?"

"It's gettin' plenty cold out here, all right! Don't let de fire go out, dat's why!"

"Don't need no fire to keep us warm. Just pass the stuff round again, blow on the barrel, and our breaths'll light 'er right up!"

The Jamaican held the bottle aloft. "Plenty more where these come from!" He took a swig and wiped his lips, then blew on the fire. Sure enough, the blaze jumped a bit, causing laughter all around.

David was laughing, too. He stretched his numb hands out and stepped closer to the barrel. This was the best he had felt since he lost his coat and lost his money and lost his father.

But then the bottle passed over his head, and the cockney discovered him. "Blimey, Gus! What's that? A little elf there!"

A giant Swede towered over David. He peered down in amazement. "Naw! Dat's biggest mices I ever seen! Dat's vat!"

A second Swede peered through the flames at David. "Vat big mices dey got here in America!" Much laughter.

"Ain't a mouse, Olaf!" shouted the American with a shock of bright red hair beneath his stocking cap. "That's the biggest water rat I ever seen, though! Hey, little rat! What're you doin' down here?"

This was the first time anyone really looked at David in a friendly way since Father John. And the first time a grown-up had smiled at him since a long time before his mother died. The fire was nice. David felt warm inside. He started to answer and tell these rough men how he came to be lost and why he had come to New York, but they were all talking at once, guessing what would bring a coatless kid in city knickers down to the wharf.

"He come to buy bananas. Right, kid?"

"Naw! Come to buy his mama's rum!"

"Naw! His mama sent him down here lookin' for his daddy!"

"Hey, kid." The Swede thumped him on the back in a friendly way. "Vat your mama say when she know you been down here?"

David saw that this question was one he was expected to answer. "She won't know."

"Vell, mamas haf a way of findin' out! Vere is your mama?"

The ring of faces smiled down at him, expecting Gus's warning about all-knowing mothers to make him shudder and run for home.

David's smile dropped self-consciously on one side. His eyes filled. He hated to say it. He did not want to hear himself say it.

"My mama's dead," he said in a very small voice. He whispered it so quietly that it was a wonder anyone heard it at all, but suddenly everything got quiet, so quiet that David could hear the whirling gears of a loading crane a whole dock away. This silence seemed to last a long time. And no one was smiling anymore.

"No mama?" asked Olaf.

The Jamaican nudged the Swede hard in the ribs. "Shut up, mon. Don't you hear de boy?"

Gus leaned closer. "Vere is your papa den, boy?"

"Gone. I came here to New York to find him, but he's gone to Yurp, they told me. I never met him before, so it's not like I ever had him to lose."

The fire crackled in the drum. Weathered faces looked sorrowfully at one another; then the questions began all at once.

"Where is your coat?"

"Ven you eat last?"

"You got someplace to sleep?"

✷ ✷ ✷

David had not stumbled upon a group of ordinary stevedores or the garden-variety longshoremen gathered for a friendly chat on the wharfs of the Lower East Side.

"And this ain't no Boy Scout troop neither!" growled a burly seaman known as Jumbo. "As for me, I don't think the Boss is gonna like no stray kid hangin' around Rum Row. Little pitchers got big ears, as my ma used to say. What if he hears somethin' he shouldn't?"

David did not explain that he had already heard plenty about the legendary Rum Row. It was one of Brian O'Halloran's favorite topics of conversation with his poker buddies when he was on a bender.

To a man, these fellows on the dock served the great offshore armada known as Rum Row. This fleet of ships was anchored just beyond American waters for the sole purpose of providing bootleg scotch, brandy, bourbon, rum, and rye to thirsty American citizens. The ships came from every sea and flew the flags of dozens of nations. Rusty tramp streamers brought fine champagne from France. Ancient gunboats from England filled their holds with the finest scotch. Trawlers, schooners, and fishing vessels all brought their cargo from afar and anchored as close to shore as the U.S. Coast Guard would allow.

Lit up so bright it seemed as though Coney Island had moved out to sea, these rumrunners waited for small shore craft to buzz out from shore and ferry their cargos back to port under cover of darkness. Once landed, the contraband was transferred to fleets of trucks protected by well-armed strongmen. The convoys of bootleg booze would roar away toward the cities of the eastern seaboard—Jersey City, Newark, Philadelphia.

Then the local bootleggers took over. The pure liquor was diluted with grain alcohol and distilled water. A dash of prune juice was added for color. The goods were rebottled, new labels slapped on. Rubbed with sand and perhaps wrapped in seaweed, the stuff was then sold as the genuine article. A case of scotch that sold for eight dollars on the other side of the Atlantic ultimately brought four hundred dollars to the bootlegger at the end of the chain. There was plenty of profit left over to pay the cops and bribe city hall. When all was said and done, Prohibition had definitely given birth to a thriving business.

All this David had heard before. With talk of ships and the evening run, it did not take him long to figure out that these were the pilots and crews of the shore craft servicing the great flotilla at anchor.

David was dressed in an enormous peacoat and dining lavishly at Big Nel's Dockside Diner as the men talked over his head.

"So vat is ve gonna do vith the little feller?"

"He can't sleep in the warehouse. The rats will eat him."

"Ve take him vith us, den? And maybe tomorrow ve talk to the Boss. Get the kid a job making deliveries to the speakeasies vith the other kids?"

Little Pete, the cockney pilot of a forty-foot Jersey skiff, explained that the kid could not go with him tonight. After all, the Jersey was mostly open, and the kid needed someplace warm to settle in.

One by one, the other members of the shore-boat squad made disclaimers. It seemed as if David might end up sleeping in a warehouse with the rabbit-sized rats, after all.

The two Swedes exchanged guilty looks. "Poor little kid. Vat ve gonna do vith him? No mama? No papa?" Gus said mournfully.

Olaf brightened. "Sure! Ve can take the little *Mice* vith us, Gus." Olaf clapped David on the back as he christened him with the new name Mice.

Gus appeared to like the idea and David's new name. "Vat you think, little Mice? Ve take you on big adventure. You think you like going on the sea?"

The warm glow of David's weariness was replaced by the stirring of excitement. He nodded eagerly. After all, this was something like being thrown in among the pirates of *Treasure Island*, which his mother had read to him twice.

And so the duty of hospitality fell on Olaf and Gus. The two Swedes were brothers, formerly fishermen, who used to stop by Rum Row and top off their catch with one hundred or so cases of scotch. Then someone explained to them that without the fish in her hold, their ancient trawler would hold a whole lot more hooch and make a whole lot more money to send back to their families. Fulton Fishmarket would never miss them. A light had come on in the minds of Olaf and Gus Svenson. They had traded in their fishing nets and purchased two double-barrel shotguns with which to fend off any pirates who might try to jump them and steal their cargo.

They explained all this in detail to their new guest as they walked along the dock toward their trawler. Named *Jazz Baby*, the rust-streaked grand banks looked more to David as if she should have been named *Mrs. Crowley*. He did not mention this, however, because the Svenson brothers were proud of her. She was the slowest of the Rum Row shore boats, but without fish, she could carry twice as many cases ashore as anything going.

The *Jazz Baby* had a comfortable cabin—two berths and a camp stove. Gus and Olaf were live-aboards, living on the little boat full-time with an enormous black dog named Codfish. The dog smelled like codfish, but that was not where he got his name. Gus told David that the animal was a Newfoundland. This meant nothing to David, so Olaf explained further that Codfish was a dog bred to swim in freezing cold waters just like some old codfish! The dog looked ferocious. He stood in the bow and barked and snarled as they approached.

"He looks mean as the devil himself," Gus said.

"But dat is just his vay of sayin' hello." Olaf nudged David. "Ve don't tell nobody he ain't mean, though. He scares pirates better than a shotgun."

And so David came to live on board the *Jazz Baby* with Gus, Olaf, and Codfish. He got on well with Codfish, made sandwiches for Gus and Olaf, even spotted a Coast Guard patrol on the first night out. All in all, Mice was a handy kid. He never was formally invited to stay on board, but when daylight came, no one ever took him to join the corps of underaged delivery boys who wheeled false-bottomed wagons to the back doors of the speakeasies.

Like his hosts, David slept by day and was a watchman in the bow for the night runs to Rum Row. No school. No Mrs. Crowley. No Brian O'Halloran. It was indeed a life right out of *Treasure Island*.

CHAPTER TWENTY-TWO

The Leprechaun's Deal

A team of tugboats, dwarfed by the size of the *Berengaria*, nudged the great liner against the docks of New York City's Pier 54. The quay was an anthill of activity. Customs officers, porters, brass bands, and dockhands mingled with a great crowd of well-wishers who had come to greet arriving passengers.

Harry Beadle, smelling of bourbon and pale from his hangover, crowded in beside Max at the rail. The noise made his wide blue eyes seem even larger behind the spectacles. He nudged Max and pointed at two stern-looking men in business suits.

"Can't fool me. They are plainclothes coppers. Feds. They will confiscate every drop of booze we try to smuggle off this tub . . . and sell it themselves at a profit." He nudged his hat back with his thumb. "It's not fair."

Max eyed him with mock disapproval. "You fellas single-handedly guzzled enough to float the *Berengaria* on the crossing. I would think you wouldn't want to see another bottle of bourbon for a year or two."

Harry rubbed his head. "You think that is what gave me this pain in the neck?" Raising his eyes, he suddenly straightened and nodded toward a cluster of men at the foot of the gangway. "Speaking of pains in the neck—" he nudged Max hard—"there is your new partner waiting to give you a big kiss, no doubt. And his partner and his partner's partner." He snorted. "Mike Keenan has brought the lower half of Wall Street down here. *And—*" another jerk of the thumb—"lookie there. He brought along a radio crew to steal the story right out from under us."

Max could see the crew of RCA men clustered around Keenan,

shouting questions into the microphone. Keenan was a master at publicity. He utilized every means to push his brokerage firm, including large ads in the financial section of the *New York Times*.

Firms like J.P. Morgan and Fisher Brothers considered Keenan an upstart, a carnival barker. Keenan pushed Wall Street to every shop clerk and subway motorman and waiter, as though Cunard-Keenan-Meyer Seagoing Brokerage held the key to all their dreams of wealth. Like Max, Keenan had grown up in the slums surrounding Orchard Street, and so he knew all about the dreams of the little men. He knew just how to phrase a proposal, how to pitch a deal to every bum with a hundred dollars. There was much more to the success story of Mike Keenan, but the small-time investors, whom he dubbed Minnows, had put him on top. From there he had joined forces with David Sarnoff, another old neighborhood boy, who would be the head of RCA radio in a matter of months. They had made millions together in the RCA radio pool and had become fast friends.

Harry Beadle eyed Keenan with disdain. "Why did you ever pick Keenan to approach with this floating-stock-brokerage idea anyway, Max?"

"He's got the brains. He's good with the brass at RCA who set up the technical end of broadcasting from the ship." Max shrugged. "And he was enthusiastic about the idea."

Harry nodded curtly, his lips tight as though he were trying very hard to keep his mouth shut. "Yeah, I guess so." He frowned. "Well, there is RCA, stealing our story. Guess they will want to talk to you on the radio too, huh?" Harry glanced at Max as though any word uttered on the radio would be a betrayal of the print journalists.

"Keenan didn't bring those guys out here to talk to me," Max said defensively, pointing to the gangway where a line of first-class passengers trooped off the ship. "It's those guys he wants."

Keenan greeted the president of General Motors and gestured toward the microphone. Would GM mind giving the listeners a minute?

Clearing his throat and pushing through the entourage of flunkies, the broad-bellied automotive executive moved toward the radio technicians like a moth to a porch light. It was free publicity. He loved it. General Motors loved it. Cunard loved it.

And Mike Keenan, who was asking all the right questions, loved it. Here was his ultimate revenge on the snobbish "old money" brokers of Wall Street. The president of General Motors might have an account with J.P. Morgan & Company when he was on land, but Mike Keenan owned the ocean and the airways!

"A sea voyage is a long time to be away from the tickers, especially when fortunes can rise and fall in a matter of minutes. Did you find the use of Cunard-Keenan-Meyer Seagoing Brokerage convenient?" Keenan asked.

What was good enough for the millionaires of America would certainly be swell for the long list of Keenan's shopgirls and street sweepers and shoe salesmen!

Max could picture it now. In some little kitchen of some little house in a very ordinary neighborhood, some housewife was listening to the radio and calling her neighbor to report that the president of General Motors had the same broker she had. It was just that simple. The concept might have belonged to Max Meyer, but Mike Keenan was playing the game by his own rules and winning!

"I used to shoot craps with Keenan when we were kids," Max muttered. "I don't know. Maybe he was playing with loaded dice, but he was always a winner. You've got to admire him for that."

"Ha!" Harry Beadle scoffed. "I do not have to admire this guy at all. Except I will say this for him. He does not dress like the rest of the swells on the street, like a guy who has fallen into a pot of gold. More like a fat leprechaun who got snagged by a briar bush."

This was indeed true. Keenan was a man of deep superstition. He had made his first million while he was wearing a green bow tie with yellow dots, Max remembered. Once, when he did not wear that tie, his fortunes had turned. *Does he bathe in it? sleep in it?* Max wondered.

Keenan's bald head was forever hatless, rain or shine. Max did not know the tradition behind that oddity, nor what circumstances dictated that Mike Keenan's socks did not match. Not ever. His suit was Savile Row, London tailored, but always rumpled. His paunch tugged at the buttons on his vest, straightening the loop of the gold watch chain across his belly. Everything had some superstition attached to it—from the hatless head to the mismatched socks.

And behind that careless, disheveled appearance was a ruthless businessman with an intellect as sharp as a carving knife. Mike Keenan was far from the harmless eccentric his appearance portrayed. He threw dice and won. He played the stock market and won. He had made a lot of the players rich when they placed their dollars on the line beside his. More than a fat leprechaun, Mike Keenan was a genius, and in a wary way Max did admire him.

"There should be a law against guys like your new partner." Beadle shook his head slowly. "And you should be very careful around this guy. Mind your p's and q's, Max, because really Mike Keenan is no leprechaun. He is a vampire who will suck your blood."

Max clapped his arm around Beadle's sloping shoulders and propelled him toward the gangway. "We'll talk about it when you're completely sober." He glanced toward the policeman stationed below to check departing passengers for violations of the Volstead Act.

"You can tell?" Beadle checked his own breath and winced. "A little morning toddy. Hair of the dog, you know."

"Yeah. A dead dog. Dead for a week or two, from the smell of your breath. Have you got a bottle on you?" Max patted Beadle's pockets, finding a suspicious lump in his overcoat. "Come on, Beadle. You'll get thrown in the clink for carrying that off the boat." He wrestled the bottle of Danzig-made Goldwasser liqueur from Harry's pocket and shoved it into the hands of a grateful ship steward. "A tip," Max said as they descended the gangway.

"I'd rather stay on the ship," Beadle mumbled, pulling himself up straight in a drunken attempt to look sober. "Except that you have forever ruined ocean voyages for me by installing Wall Street on the promenade deck. I intend to write that in my column when I sober up."

"That will be a week or two. By then perhaps the *Berengaria* will have hit an iceberg."

"Or Mike Keenan will have hit one," Harry said too loudly as they stepped onto terra firma, where Prohibition had made the bootleggers as wealthy as the lords of Wall Street.

A policeman met Max by the gangplank. "Mister Keenan says you are a VIP, and he would like I should get you through without trouble."

Harry Beadle at his side, Max stepped past the policeman, who put a large hand on Beadle's arm. "Not you." He stopped Beadle and pointed toward the line leading through the customs check. "That way."

With a shrug, Beadle waved Max on.

A young man in a pin-striped suit leaned close to Keenan, whispering that Max had arrived. An instant later Keenan and his clan of flunkies surrounded Max and ushered him to a small anteroom leading off the pier and past the wall of government officials who searched luggage and coat linings and passengers for contraband.

"Well! Max! Well, well!" Keenan clapped Max hard on the back as though they were great friends instead of cautious business partners. "So! A great success, eh? A hundred thousand shares on the maiden voyage. Everyone is talking about it! Everyone! Calling you a genius." Keenan raised his arm as though to flex his muscle. "And I'm the strongman. Quite a partnership, they're saying. The pressmen you selected to cover the event have all filed impressive stories. The wires are full of it." He leaned close. "It's double the regular business of the firm at the same time."

"The minnows are biting!" cheered the young man in the suit.

"Thanks to your idea, Max, we've managed to land a few big fish as well!" Keenan thumped his back hard again. "At 10 percent commission, you'll soon be a wealthy man."

Keenan was babbling on in his carnival-barker style, not giving Max opportunity to say more than hello. Not one customs officer looked up as Keenan led him out on the street. Max wondered how much bounty had been paid to walk him through the authorities, but he did not question the ease with which he was escorted past the red tape. Sunlight gleamed in his face as he spotted the General Motors president climbing into a limousine at the curb.

Keenan had evidently noted his curiosity. "Money talks. As you shall soon see." With that, he raised his hand and snapped his fingers, calling up a long, sleek Stutz Weyman sedan driven by a chauffeur.

"My luggage?" Max asked, considering that some of the other passengers would be two hours getting to this side of the Cunard Building.

"Taken care of," Keenan assured him as the uniformed chauffeur opened the rear door of the sedan and stepped aside for Max and Keenan to get in. "Everything taken care of." Keenan settled back against the burgundy leather seat with a sigh.

The leather smelled new and clean. There were no ashes in the silver ashtrays, and the walnut trim of the gleaming automobile appeared to have been just polished. As the sedan pulled away from the curb, Max noted that Keenan's coterie remained standing, reduced to hailing a cab as their master left them behind. It was clear that Keenan did not want to wait until tomorrow for his scheduled business meeting with Max.

"We've come a long way from Orchard Street, haven't we, Max?" He sighed contentedly. "A couple of streetwise toughs, shooting craps, making time with the girls." He laughed a short laugh. "I used to secretly date a Jewish gal from your neighborhood while you were busy climbing in the window of that swell little schoolteacher on the Irish end of Cherry Street . . . what was her name?"

Max did not reply as Keenan brought up Irene Dunlap. Keenan knew her name well enough. He had lived in the same tenement building as the Dunlap family. He had often taunted Max as he passed on the sidewalk.

Keenan rubbed his cheek as if trying to remember. "What was her name? Iris? Irene . . . *something*, wasn't it?" He eyed Max knowingly. "Her brothers didn't think much of you; I can tell you that. They would talk, down at Clary's Saloon, about how they were going to kill you if you laid a hand on her." Another amused chuckle. "Those were the days, eh? She married some other guy, didn't she?"

"I lost track," Max said indifferently, as though the mention of Irene Dunlap did not still cut him to the heart.

"Well, the old neighborhood ain't what it used to be. Still, you were a fixture around the old joint for a while. Before the war. But we got out of there. Different sides of the street, but the same dreams, right, pal?"

"Different methods of leaving." Max shrugged, uncomfortable with the way Keenan was trying to make the bond between them stronger.

"Ah, come on, Max," Keenan prodded. "We knew you were going places. I remember you when you were about that high." He held his hand above the level of the seat. "You used to sell jelly apples on Cherry Street. Remember?"

"Of course I remember. But I'm surprised you do. . . ." Max relaxed a bit, somehow flattered that Mike Keenan recalled Max's first business venture as a seven-year-old. "I used to buy them two for a penny and then take them across the Manhattan Bridge to sell to the Italians for a penny apiece."

Keenan chuckled and shook his head. "A brave kid. You're lucky you didn't get killed."

"Not brave. Just too dumb to know the difference."

"Smart enough to smell a 100 percent profit. I was sixteen, maybe seventeen years old. You must have been . . ."

"Seven."

"Right. And there you were, the little Jewish-boy businessman teaching us Micks a lesson in economics."

"Nothing you didn't already know."

Keenan shook his head in disagreement. "No. I'm not talking about just buying and selling. I mean the fact that you had the guts to get out of your own backyard to make it big."

"Candied apples at a penny apiece is hardly making it big."

"But *enough* pennies and you really have something, don't you, Max, boy? It's all there." Keenan gestured at the tall buildings of Manhattan. "The old names of Wall Street forgot that there are a whole lot more people who eat hot dogs at Nathan's than gents who dine on caviar at the Plaza."

"What's your point?"

"I've made my fortune selling penny stocks. Lots of them. Now take this Cunard brokerage deal . . . it put me in touch with the big money. It enhances the image, see? Now our little hot-dog wagon is selling to the big boys, too." He nodded. "The penny stockholders like that. They like the image. I have you to thank for that. I've got some big plans. Another pool mixing the big-money men and the little guys. You mention it in your column . . . you've got respectability, see . . . people listen when you suggest—"

Max raised his hand to stop him. "I don't want to hear about it," he said in a weary voice. He knew that Keenan had bribed half the financial writers in America to tout his schemes. Max did not want to be part of that half. "It's one thing to have a legitimate venture . . . Cunard-Keenan-Meyer Seagoing Brokerage . . . nobody can ever accuse me of selling out if I'm just part of that deal."

"Sure, sure." Keenan sounded eager to appease Max. "Sure. You don't want to hear about it. I get it. The less you know who's involved and how it works the better." He cleared his throat as if to change the subject, gave a nervous smile, and swept his hand around the auto's interior. "So, how do you like the car?"

"A beauty," Max said, grateful to move away from Keenan's talk of deals and schemes.

"Well, I told you . . . just my way of saying thank you. And welcome to Cunard-Keenan-Meyer Seagoing Brokerage, right?" He pulled open a walnut cabinet door, revealing a small bar complete with glasses and bottles of European-labeled liquor. "All the comforts of home, see?"

"That's nothing you'll find in my room." Max laughed, astounded at the sight of illegal booze. "Not that quality."

"Well, it's all yours now, Max." He snapped the bar closed and gestured broadly. "All yours. The whole thing. The booze. The Stutz. And Cueball, who is on the payroll, will be your driver."

"No thanks," Max replied as the chauffeur pulled into the carriage entrance of the Plaza Hotel. "I don't need a car. It's two blocks to the office. A short ride to Wall Street . . ."

Keenan lowered his voice belligerently. "Don't need it? Of course you need it. Everybody knows you got nothing when that society-dame wife of yours kicked you out . . . even the car, huh? She wrecked your car, right? You didn't even get a set of sheets, and that's why you're living at the Plaza Hotel."

"I like this hotel." Max did not like the way Keenan had the facts of Max's life so easily in proper order.

"A lot of swells like this hotel. It's a rich man's hotel, as long as you live in the six rooms on the top floor. But you got one room here, they tell me. No car and no driver. And I'm telling you it does not look good for business if you've got a stake in Cunard-Keenan-Meyer Seagoing Brokerage and you live like some sort of vacationing shopkeeper. Take the car. And Cueball."

"No thanks."

The beady eyes of the driver glanced into the rearview mirror with alarm and amazement at Max's refusal.

"Appearances *demand*—"

"*Appearances* would indicate I was accepting a bribe, Keenan." Max stepped out of the vehicle. "I won't be bribed."

"Sure, sure." Keenan winked broadly at Max as though he had understood something. Maybe Max just didn't want Cueball to overhear the transaction? He dropped the extra set of keys in Max's pocket. "Then you just *use* the car, huh? The hotel valet will park it here. We can't have you going around town in a taxi. It wouldn't look right, now that you're playing ball in the big leagues. The big clients might think something's wrong with the business if you're all over town in a taxi. Use it when you want it. Call the office, and Cueball will drive you wherever. . . ."

Keenan hefted his bulk from the automobile and rattled off instructions to the Plaza doorman for parking the Stutz. Then he slapped Max on the back and pumped his hand as Cueball hailed a cab.

Max had never liked having anyone run his life. Keenan was still a two-bit Orchard Street hustler who had to run everything. With a curt, tight-lipped nod, Max watched him climb into the cab. *Appearances!* How could a man in a green polka-dot bow tie and unmatched socks talk about appearances?

As though Keenan read his mind, he said out the window, "You're right up in front of this thing for me now, Max. The high-society dames will love the leather interior just like they love those suits of yours, eh?"

With that, the cab slid away.

CHAPTER TWENTY-THREE

Partnership

The 1929 World Series had come and gone, and David hardly noticed. He had settled in comfortably with the rum-running Svenson brothers.

"Hey, Mice," Olaf called to David with a grimace of pain. "I got a bellyache—all them Polish sausages and sauerkraut. You go fetch a pineapple at the varehouse."

Fresh fruits were Olaf Svenson's answer to every intestinal ailment from diarrhea, which he cured by eating bananas, to constipation, which he cured by consuming pineapples by the dozen until he needed bananas again.

Gus confided to David that in their native land no one had ever seen a pineapple, except of the canned variety. Bananas were a rarity. Oranges were such a treat that they were given as holiday gifts and remained uneaten until they threatened to spoil. And so the close proximity of the American Fruit Company warehouse was for the Svensons like living next to a candy store. In this case, the candy was free for the asking to any member of Boss Quinn's rummy crews. Still, Olaf could not bring himself to indulge in such delicacies unless he had some good reason.

David hurried across the wharf toward the giant brick warehouse. The place was quiet today. Delivery trucks packed with bananas, oranges, and bootleg scotch had driven from the loading dock early this morning. Two long, shiny black limousines were parked beside the steps leading into the office. The Boss was in residence today, David knew. The strong-arm chauffeurs were nowhere to be seen. Angelo Garducci, the slow-witted warehouse watchman, was not at his usual post beside the door. David decided he would simply fetch an armload of pineapples himself and save a second trip when Olaf decided one would never be enough to cure his ailment.

The heavy sheet-metal door of the loading dock was closed, but David had been shown an alternate way into the building. In the alley, a frosted-glass transom window was left open to provide air for any workman unfortunate enough to need to use the squalid little room that passed for a toilet. The window was too small for anyone larger than David to get through, but standing on a garbage can, he could hoist himself up and through the tiny space.

He took one last big gasp of fresh air and ducked in. He had discovered that he could hold his breath just long enough to escape the smell of the cubicle. But today was different. Dropping from the window ledge onto the floor of the room, he heard a voice, deep and rasping with fury, outside the bathroom door. David had seen and heard such anger when Brian was drunk. The violence of the voice made him stand rooted beneath the window.

"Naw, Boss! Don't! I tell you I didn't mean nothin' by it. Just wantin' to make a couple extra bucks for my kid to—"

The plea was stopped short by the sound of blows and a strangled cry.

The angry voice began again. "*Enough!* We don't want to kill him . . . yet!"

Sobs emanated through the thin wood of the door. "Please . . . Boss . . . I didn't mean nothin'."

"All right, then." The angry voice calmed to a soothing tone. "All you got to do is tell me who was in it with you. You see, Joey, I do not like it when my own men steal from me. I am a generous man. You want to take maybe one bottle, then you ask and I give. You want a bunch of bananas maybe? Maybe a crate of pineapples to take to your old lady?"

Pineapples! David inhaled the stench of the room and began to cough. He had come for pineapples and had stumbled on the Boss fixing Joey the Book—maybe for good.

"What's that?" asked the Boss.

David could feel the man's stare through the door. He backed up a step and scrambled to climb onto the toilet and out the window again.

"I thought you said there was nobody left in the place!"

Reaching the window ledge, David bumped the stick that held the window up. It slammed closed with a loud bang just as the door of the toilet crashed open. Wood splinters flew against the brick and struck David in the back. Strong hands reached out, pulling him down, swinging him around, throwing him out the door and onto the cold concrete floor of the warehouse beside the prone body of Joey the Book.

A circle of shoes closed around David and Joey. Joey was bleeding badly. His eyes were swollen shut and his right ear seemed half torn away. He was breathing heavily.

"Joey!" David said, as scared as he had ever been.

"Hiya, kid," Joey managed to wheeze.

"What are you doing here, kid?" demanded one of the high-booted chauffeurs, who also served as bodyguard and hired gun for Boss Quinn.

David looked up to where the Boss sat on a high stool, smiling calmly down at him. Even smiling, Boss Quinn looked nothing like David's favorite baseball player, no matter if they did have the same last name. Every one of the six other men in the room was pale, shaking— scared-looking, as though David had heard something that frightened them.

David remembered what the Boss had just said about stealing. He looked at Joey the Book with his broken face. Had Joey stolen something from the Boss without asking? A case of pineapples? A bag of oranges, maybe?

The chauffeur gave David a hard nudge with the toe of his boot. "I asked you what you are doing here, kid."

Would the Boss have David beaten for stealing pineapples? "I was in the toilet," David said. The Boss still smiled. The others, including Angelo, looked at one another in disbelief. Nobody used that toilet unless he was desperate.

"You better tell me what you're doing here, kid." The chauffeur became threatening.

"I came looking for Angelo," David answered truthfully.

The chauffeur shot Angelo a hard look. "You know this kid?"

Angelo looked worried. He put his hand on the top button of his shirt as if he were concerned about having his throat cut. "He belongs to the Swedes," Angelo croaked.

"Why is he looking for you?" The chauffeur took a step toward Angelo, who backed away.

"I dunno! Honest." He glanced pleadingly at the Boss, who smiled stonily from the shadows.

The Boss turned his gaze on David. "Tell the truth, kid," he said in a kindly way. Like Old Man Grover at the market when David had gotten caught stealing Beeman's gum.

"That's the truth," David replied in a small voice. Joey the Book closed his eyes and breathed out with a long shuddering sigh. David sat up and scooted away from Joey. Joey looked as if he might be dying, and David did not want to be close to him if he did.

"Why were you looking for Angelo?" asked the Boss, who did not seem to care about Joey the Book anymore.

"Because I wanted to get some pineapple."

"Pineapple," repeated the Boss.

"Olaf has a bellyache again. Pineapple helps him, so he sent me to fetch a pineapple. Not to steal, but to ask Angelo."

Angelo looked hopeful. "He's probably telling the truth, Boss. That Swede has more trouble with his bowels. . . ."

The Boss raised his chin slightly, and at that signal, the chauffeur slapped Angelo hard across the mouth, silencing him. Everything was quiet except for the toilet, which ran all the time . . . and Joey the Book, breathing shallowly.

"I'm talking to you, kid. Understand?"

"Yessir."

David's response appeared to please Boss Quinn, who shifted slightly on his stool and crooked his finger at David. "Good. C'mere, kid."

David rose quickly and stood in front of the Boss. The man's dark eyes glinted beneath the brim of his hat. His nose had a bend in it, as if he had gotten hit in the face with a bat. His lips were narrow and his face full. His bottom teeth were crooked, and David could see them when the man talked.

The Boss put a hand on David's shoulder. "So, you do not want to be like Joey the Book there. You know why he is in such trouble?"

David shook his head. "No, sir."

"That's good. I mean, you got nice manners. You got a name, kid?"

"They call me Mice."

The Boss laughed. " 'Cause you can squeeze in and out of tight places?"

"I guess so," David answered. "I don't know why really."

"You got a real name?" The Boss sounded almost friendly.

"David."

"Yeah? David. David what?"

For a moment David almost replied *O'Halloran.* "David Meyer," he answered firmly.

"I see. But you live with the Swedes." The Boss took out a silver cigarette case, opened it, and offered one to David.

"No thanks," David said, feeling embarrassed.

"You don't smoke, huh?"

"No, sir."

"You scared your mama will catch you?"

Angelo looked as if he might answer about David's mama being dead, but he did not.

"I got no mama," David said. A statement of fact, not self-pity.

"How old are you?"

"Nine."

"Did the Swedes send you to find out about Joey the Book?"

"No, sir. Olaf wanted a pineapple."

"You know why Joey the Book is in such bad shape?"

"I guess he's been fighting."

The Boss shook his head. "That ain't it." His fingers squeezed around David's shoulders. "It's because he has been lying. See? Stealing first and then lying about it." The fingers dug into David's shoulders, making him want to cry out. But he kept quiet. Brian had taught him something about that. The Boss pushed David down to the floor until he was on his knees before the wooden stool. Then he released his grip.

"You got guts, kid." He brushed lint from David's shoulder. "Now, I'm going to let you in on a little secret, huh? I do not like it when my own people steal and lie to me. You ain't lying about the pineapple, are you?"

"No, sir," David replied. "Olaf says he's bloated like an old blowfish."

The Boss raised his hand to silence David. "All right then, I'm going to let you in on another secret." He gave David a gentle slap on the cheek. "Pay attention. If you tell anybody what you saw in here, I will come to your bed at night and take out this." He moved his wrist to the side, and a stiletto clicked out from the sleeve of his suit jacket. He grabbed David by the hair and pulled his head back, then lightly brushed the cold steel blade across David's throat.

David's heart was pumping wildly. He now had to use the toilet for real. He wished he hadn't come in through the window, that he had never heard any of this or seen Joey the Book on the floor.

"I won't." David's voice trembled as he spoke.

The Boss held the boy's head back a moment longer. "I do believe you are telling the truth, kid." He released David's hair and snapped the knife back into place. He flashed a quick smile at Angelo. "Get the kid his pineapple and get him out of here."

☆ ☆ ☆

Appearances.

Keenan had definitely thought of everything in his plan to create an appearance for Max that fit the Cunard-Keenan-Meyer Seagoing Brokerage image he wished to project.

"These are not my rooms," Max said softly to Derby, the day manager of the Plaza, who had taken him personally in the penthouse elevator up to the six-room suite.

Derby looked pleased by Max's unconcealed expression of astonishment. Had the manager mistaken Max's shock for pleasure? "Sorry to disagree with you, Mister Meyer. Your rent is paid for a year." At that he presented Max with an invoice displaying a figure of $40,000, paid in full, from the account of Mr. Max Meyer.

Paid by check
Cunard-Keenan-Meyer Seagoing Brokerage

Max opened his mouth to protest and then closed it again. *Forty thousand dollars?* Max had been living like a miser, counting every penny since his wife left him. And now this! But it was not a matter he could discuss with Derby, who grinned and fussed around the main salon in his gray morning coat. This was something to settle with Keenan, who had obviously taken Max's earnings and tossed in a few thousand more to lease this opulent suite for the sake of the business image!

Derby raised an eyebrow and adjusted the red roses in a large urn. Then his attention turned to a basket of fruit on a heavy white-marble coffee table stationed between the cream-colored sofa and a large pale marble fireplace, complete with blazing fire.

"Of course, your agent negotiated for that cost to include a full breakfast every morning." He tugged proudly on his vest, but his pride turned into cautious alarm as Max simply gaped at the bill.

"My agent?"

"Your real-estate agent. Miss Rutger."

"Miss . . ."

"Rutger." The man gave a nervous smile. "She had the place redecorated to suit you. Said . . . you would be pleased—"

"That is included in this bill?"

Great surprise filled the face of the day manager. "Well . . . heavens no! I supposed you had that all arranged in advance with Miss Rutger and the decorator. Good heavens, they tore the place apart, had it all redone from the crown molding to the carpets! Is it satisfactory?" He bit his lip. What would happen if the room was unsatisfactory? Would Mr. Meyer have the place torn up again? Painters and drapery hangers traipsing up and down the hall?

"I seem to have mislaid Miss Rutger's number." Max's hands trembled slightly. "Would you happen to have . . . ?"

Derby produced the agent's card, plucking it instantly from his waistcoat pocket. "These pale colors . . . is that it? She insisted on all pastels. I told her you would probably prefer the heavier walnut paneling, like in the library. She at least heeded my advice about the library. A man such as you would like a more masculine-looking library, I told her. Besides, it would have ruined the walnut shelves; and if you ever move out, you would have to pay for new installation of those customized walnut—"

Max pushed past him to a set of cream-colored doors and pulled them open, revealing a dark, richly furnished room with floor-to-ceiling bookshelves and yet another blazing fireplace. Two burgundy leather wingback chairs sat before the hearth, giving the illusion of an English gentleman's reading room.

"There's supposed to be a dog on the hearth," he said. "Where's the dog?"

"Oh dear!" gasped Derby. "The *dog*? Oh my! There is a dog in the suite? I haven't seen a dog. What breed of dog is it, Mister Meyer?"

Max thought of Keenan. "Irish wolfhound."

Derby looked close to fainting. "Oh my! Oh dear! *Wolfhound*, you say?"

"And where are the stuffed heads?"

"Heads?"

"For the walls. Heads and antlers. Trophies."

"Well, she simply must have forgotten to have them installed. What sort of heads?"

Max waved the question away. He walked slowly forward to touch the new leather of the book spines that filled the shelves. Classics—Dickens, Scott—mingled together with the latest authors, including last week's release by Hemingway. Brand-new books. He slid *Oliver Twist* from the rank. The gilt pages glistened in the firelight. He cracked the volume open and inhaled the sweet aroma of new printer's ink. *Never opened!*

As Derby whistled and wandered off in search of the nonexistent dog, Max replaced the book and opened another heavy walnut door leading to the bedroom. An enormous four-poster bed sat against the wall opposite a large window facing Central Park. A bowfront, inlaid Italian armoir was beside the bed. To his astonishment, Max saw that his steamer trunk was open and empty beside it. Had his wardrobe been unpacked already?

He stared down at the business card of Miss Edith Rutger, Property Management. She had thought of everything. A typewriter sat on a small desk in front of the window. A neat stack of white-linen paper was in place beside it, a cup of sharpened pencils at the ready. . . .

From the salon, Derby called to him, "Oh dear, Mister Meyer. Have you found the dog? Perhaps you should telephone Miss Rutger. She seems to have thought of everything else. Perhaps she has it boarded somewhere? You didn't have it in your little room on the third floor, did you? Pets were not allowed down there . . . no space."

He was rambling and wandering from room to room, looking under things and behind furniture.

Max shook himself, and pocketing the card, he escorted Derby to the door. "I'll bet my bill does not include gratuities," he said, smiling through gritted teeth.

"No-o-o-o." Derby rubbed his fingers together. "Nor telephone charges either. But daily maid service and linen and—"

"Breakfast. Every day for a year." He pressed a heavy silver coin into the soft hand of the little man and closed the door on him.

Through the door he could hear the day manager exclaim, "But you haven't seen the other three rooms!"

Max rushed to the telephone and dialed for the operator, only then noticing that all his family photographs were arranged neatly across the marble mantel above the fireplace. His eyes narrowed at the sudden awareness that this Rutger woman had to have gone through his most personal belongings to find the pictures. He flushed with anger and a twinge of embarrassment as he repeated the telephone number to the exchange and waited to be put through.

CHAPTER TWENTY-FOUR

The Smell of Money

The sweeping drive leading up to Mike Keenan's Forest Hills estate was lined with marble statues and manicured shrubs. Damon Phelps, seated in the back of Keenan's limousine, whistled softly. He pulled the strap that lowered the leather partition to the driver's compartment. "Say," he observed to the chauffeur, "this is really something. What's a place like this cost, anyway?"

"Mister Keenan don't discuss his personal finances with me," replied the uniformed driver with a hint of frost in his tone.

"Oh yeah," said Phelps. Then another thought struck him. "Keenan—Irish, right?"

"Don't be callin' him a Mick. Mister Keenan don't like it," the driver warned.

"Thought so," concluded Phelps, leaning back and closing the partition again. "Micks all like to throw money around, but this one has done real good for himself."

The chauffeur turned Phelps over to a butler whose starched shirtfront looked as stiff as his countenance. The butler showed the oilman into a book-lined study complete with a world globe in its mahogany cradle, fully four feet in diameter.

"Would you care for a drink, Mister Phelps?" the butler intoned.

"Don't mind if I do," Phelps agreed. "Bourbon and branch?"

"Naturally," said the butler, lifting the northern hemisphere of the globe to reveal a row of crystal decanters.

After placing a heavy crystal glass in Phelps's hand, the butler bowed himself out of the study with the words "Mister Keenan will be with you shortly."

Phelps sipped his drink, savoring the liquor as he gazed around the room. Had he inspected carefully, he might have noticed that the leather-bound, gold-edged volumes had never been opened and that the Tudor-style furniture was actually modern in construction. But Phelps only noted the expense. "Whew," he muttered, clinking the ice in the glass, "this place smells like money."

The door reopened and Keenan entered the study. "Good to meet you, Phelps," the broker said, shaking hands. "Top off your drink for you?"

This was a good beginning. There was no patronizing in Keenan's tone. It was strictly business between equals. "I wouldn't mind," said Phelps, extending the crystal tumbler. "I wish I could meet your bootlegger. That is really prime booze."

"Funny you should say that," Keenan observed. "The gentleman who furnishes my private stock is in fact a client and another participant in the Sabre Oil pool."

The mention of Sabre Oil brought Phelps's attention back to the real reason for this meeting and soured the taste of the whiskey in his mouth. "See here, Keenan," Phelps growled, "is this Sabre thing on the level? I mean, I know that the drop the other day was just temporary and all, but I thought the idea was to get in and out quick. My . . . uh . . . my clients are a little anxious."

Keenan chuckled and poured himself a gin and tonic. "Nothing to worry about," he said easily. "That was all smoke. That nutty Babson . . . just a slow news day, nothing more."

"News, yeah. What's the name of the guy who first spread it around? Jewish name, I think."

"Max Meyer." Keenan nodded. "All taken care of. He's in our corner now. Fact is, Meyer is part of the reason why the Sabre pool can get even bigger."

"What do you mean bigger?" asked Phelps suspiciously. "I thought we were about ready to wrap it up."

"And leave the biggest opportunity lying on the floor? Phelps, you and I didn't get where we are today without milking every drop out of every enterprise. Isn't that right?"

Phelps nodded.

"So, with my new newspaper connection and the extra capital everybody is putting in—"

Phelps sputtered into his drink. "What extra capital?"

"It's like this. My bootlegger client wants to get in the pool in a big way, see, but only if the rest of the pool matches him. I figure each of us—because I'm in this too, personally—each of us needs to come up with another half million. What do you say?"

"What about the half million and more you already got?" demanded Phelps.

"Peanuts," said Keenan lightly. "I mean, we'll cash you out today if you want. But would you rather make 50 percent on a half million or see this thing all the way through to the end? A million will make you ten million."

Caution fought a losing battle with greed. "I want to see this Meyer fellow first," Phelps insisted. "I want to make sure for myself that he'll play ball."

"It's already planned. I'm gonna have both of you at a dinner party. You can meet him then."

✳ ✳ ✳

"No, Miss Rutger is not at home. The office is closed. She is in the country for the weekend. . . ."

Max instructed the servant on the other end of the line to have Miss Rutger contact him the instant she walked through the door. No, tomorrow's business hours were not soon enough to suit him! He was unhappy and demanded a word with her!

Max could almost hear the maid shudder at his words. It would be an unpleasant message to deliver, no doubt.

He had even more dismal luck trying to contact Mike Keenan at his Park Avenue apartment. No answer there whatsoever. Keenan had a large house in the country where he stashed his wife and children. He lived on Park Avenue alone during the working week and then dashed back to Forest Hills to live like a wealthy Irish landlord on his estate during the weekends. There was no chasing him down today. Max would simply have to vent his fury on the unsuspecting real-estate agent who had taken it upon herself to purchase him an entire library of books he had already read!

Weary from the frustration of having his life managed without his consent or knowledge, Max turned his back on the living room and gazed out the window at the view he had not asked for.

Fringed on one side by Central Park and on the other by the enormous mansions called Millionaires' Row, Fifth Avenue stretched toward the Bronx and Harlem to the north. Max knew those humble regions well enough and had to admit that the view of this end of Fifth Avenue was much finer.

On this street, the royalty of America built their homes, mirroring the elegance of Europe's old gilding. Monarchs of industry directed their empires from here. Max could name the owner of each little palace beneath him. Morgan. Astor. Vanderbilt. DeForest. Stuyvesant. Roosevelt— all names that were read from the famous list of Four Hundred in hushed whispers. Max could see the double-decker tour bus driving slowly past the stately homes. Each name was blared out through a megaphone, and a list of fortunes was recited to gawking tourists.

In America, a large bank account was like being born into the aristocracy. The kings of sugar and steel and oil and rubber groomed their crown princes to take over the family kingdoms. And the daughters of these American magnates spoke to one another in French and shared dressmakers and sent out servants to spy on one another. They were linked by bonds of pleasure, drink, school, sport, charitable works, and travel. Very few, if any, knew that Fifth Avenue extended northward into a different city of despair and poverty.

But Max knew. He had come from that foreign land and so infringed on their world of make-believe. His mere presence at the balls and parties of the very rich somehow caused an unpleasant undercurrent in the proceedings. Max had often wondered if it was because he had once been poor, very poor. Or perhaps it was because he was Jewish?

His wife had denied that his origins had anything to do with the stiff smiles and the hard eyes of the older generation. It was his financial beliefs, she explained. His stubbornness in printing warnings that sounded so *negative* . . . almost *un-American*! At first he had been an interesting curiosity but later became an annoying threat. Max had poked tiny holes in their insular society. He had talked about Orchard Street tenements and the dark cellars of Harlem. In the end he had been excommunicated from the congregation of the very rich. That had not kept him from having dinner with their rebellious daughters at the Stork Club on occasion, however. Packaged in designer dresses and fur capes from Paris, these women were empty-headed and frivolous. . . . *"Daddy would be so angry if he knew I was out with you!"*

Max smiled as he looked down the row of mansions and imagined how unhappy the congregation of Four Hundred would be if they knew he could see right into their windows with a good pair of binoculars.

He stroked his chin thoughtfully as he pictured the expression on the face of Mrs. Vanderbilt, who had once publicly derided him for carrying on a conversation in Yiddish with the old news vendor outside the Ritz Tower before a charity ball. . . .

"A breach of etiquette to speak in a foreign language that others cannot understand."

"You do not understand Yiddish, Mrs. Vanderbilt?"

"Of course not. Such a vulgar tongue!"

"Then next time I will speak with my old friend Sam in French so you can hear what the poor think about the charity balls of the rich."

That had cinched it. The story of his exchange with *the* Mrs. Vanderbilt had been passed from one Fifth Avenue mansion to the next, discussed in every parlor and tearoom. Finally, it had exploded in the middle of a civilized supper of pot roast at the Newport home of Max's in-laws.

"Insulting!"

"Rude!"

"Why don't you tell us what the poor think of our charity balls, Max?"

He had told them. And then he had left and moved to the Plaza. Mike Keenan was correct. Max had taken nothing with him but his clothes and personal belongings. A hotel with fresh sheets, maid service, and a fine menu seemed his best choice for living the bachelor's life. Back to basics, he liked to say. His financial column was his wife and mistress. The news staff were his family, and there were beautiful women in abundance in Manhattan. Max was not a lonely man as long as he did not think too deeply or let his memories carry him too far back.

Involuntarily, he turned from his view of Central Park and Millionaires' Row. He scanned the large sitting room of the suite. It felt too big. Empty of companionship. He had not felt so alone in his tiny third-floor hotel room.

The fire was dying. Max tossed another stick of wood in the grate and waited for the flames to lick the bark and crackle to life again. He sighed and sank onto the cream-colored sofa. The fire was pleasant and relaxing. Lying back on the cushions, Max scanned the neatly arranged photographs that Miss Rutger had placed in silver frames along the mantel—images that could, indeed, make a man lonely. Had the woman meant for them to comfort him in this quiet six-room suite?

"I am not comforted, Miss Rutger," he said aloud. "You prying, presumptuous biddy!" He was practicing saying things that he would probably never really say, but at the moment it felt good.

Somehow Miss Rutger had managed to place each family photograph in chronological order, telling the history of his life from left to right. Mama and Papa looking like immigrants right off the boat, which they were. Mama holding baby Max on her lap. Bubbe and Zeyde Fritz in grocer's aprons in front of the old Orchard Street store. Max at five. Max at his bar mitzvah. Max graduated from high school. Max in the army with Ellis Warne and Birch Tucker. Max with Irene Dunlap. Irene. Irene. Irene. Cousin Trudy at her wedding to Birch Tucker. Birch and Trudy and their sons. Max in cap and gown at Oxford. Max in a pin-striped suit shaking hands with President Warren G. Harding. Max with President Hoover at the conference of European Financial Affairs.

Heady stuff. Indeed, Max had come a long way from Orchard Street. But that did not mean he was any happier than he had been in those days.

He closed his eyes and listened to the pop of the fire. How he envied Trudy and Birch! Money? A suite at the Plaza, including breakfast? A photograph of himself beside the president of the United States? What did any of it mean? He would give it up in a moment to have what Trudy and Birch had—kids, each other, love. . . .

"Don't think about it," Max said out loud, sitting up and taking the photographs off the mantel one by one in the order of greatest pain. In the end, he left only the picture of Trudy and Birch and their sons.

The photographs of himself at Oxford and with the two presidents were then spaced evenly across the shelf. Such images were the only accurate reflections of his life now, were they not?

Max stood back and studied what remained, then stashed the rest on the shelf in the empty closet of the spare bedroom. Out of sight, out of mind.

CHAPTER TWENTY-FIVE

A Place to Call Home

Trudy and Birch carried quilts and pillows out to the lean-to beside the barn. The lantern within glowed through the cracks between the boards. Trudy could hear the deep voice of Jefferson Canfield humming a soft, familiar hymn. The singing took her back to those sweet Sunday mornings when the little church at Mount Pisgah had filled the land with praises. Ten years. So much had changed since then!

Birch knocked against the wall of the shed.

Jeff opened the door. He filled the frame, his head bent forward so he would not brush the low ceiling. Dressed in Birch's overalls and shirt, his long arms stuck out from the too-short sleeves. On his feet, however, was a pair of brand-new work boots, size thirteen. Trudy had purchased them last week at Siemon's Mercantile in Hartford and presented them to Jefferson on his first morning out of bed. He declared that he had not worn such fine boots since he was in the army. He did not know how he could repay her, and so he promised he would pray that Jesus would bless her doubly for her kindness.

Today he had announced that he was well enough to move into the shed and had spent the afternoon fixing it up.

"Evenin'." He stepped aside to show how he had arranged the camp stove and the cot within a circle of feed sacks to keep out the draft. "Ain't had such a fine place to call my own in a long time." He took the blankets and ran his hand over the colors of the quilt as though he recognized the prints. He smiled. "Mighty fine," he said gently.

"Your mother gave it to me, Jefferson. For a wedding gift. I want you to have it."

He looked at the pattern as though he could clearly see among the colors a dress that Little Nettie had worn or a shirt belonging to Hock or Big Hattie or Pink. His eyes clouded. "I never expected I'd be sleepin' under one of my mama's quilts again, Miz Trudy. It's mighty kind of you. I'll use it tonight, but Mama would skin me if I was to take y'all's wedding present forever."

"Willa-Mae would want you to have it, Jefferson. I have never used it. It's almost as if I was saving it for you, hoping one day . . . and now, here you are. It's only right."

He held it up and grinned, showing his broken teeth. The quilt was a flower-garden pattern—a work of art big enough to cover even a man as big as Jefferson. "My mama always did make 'em big. She had herself some big chillens."

"I think she intended to give it to you, Jeff. She hoped we would find you in Oklahoma. Prayed we would. So, you keep it."

Jeff nodded self-consciously. "I been warmin' myself on the mercy of the Lord so long, I almost forgot that folks can show His mercy, too. I sure do thank y'all for savin' me this quilt my mama made. It reminds me of her. Yessir, it takes me back." He tipped an imaginary hat to Trudy. "My sisters always said you was a good woman. I brung Little Nettie a doll baby home from Paris, France, and she called that doll baby Miz Trudy. She made it teach the other play-chillens in a school she made up." He shook his head. "Yessir. It's all comin' back like I was there yesterday."

He held the quilt to his cheek. Fragments of Sunday shirts and dresses, memories sewn together with love to keep a man warm. Memories to dream beneath . . .

Trudy wondered about Jefferson's mother. She and Birch had lost track of Willa-Mae and Hock after the Canfield family had been turned out of their farm. And now the son of Willa-Mae Canfield had found his way back from hell to sleep in a shed beneath his mother's quilt. But where was Willa-Mae?

"The Lord will bless y'all. I'll pray He blesses y'all with a mighty blessin'!"

Birch took Jeff's big calloused hand, the hand that had saved Bobby from the James Fork. "We're glad you're here, Jeff."

There was a trace of something in the big man's eyes, an unspoken thought that perhaps he would not be staying on no matter how welcome he was. After all, he should try to find his own family.

"I thank y'all kindly, then." He closed the door slowly and then resumed his soft melody as he made up the cot.

From the window of the big dark house, Trudy watched the light glowing from the shed. She saw Jeff's massive shadow pass to and fro before the lantern as though he were performing a dance of freedom. Like Joseph in the Bible, he had worn his chains a long time. He had waited on the mercy of the Lord for ten years. Tonight she rejoiced quietly with him in her heart.

Jefferson was dreaming again. He knew it was a dream, but the sounds and smells and voices were *so real*. . . . He smiled in his sleep. He played his part just as he had in the three thousand nights that had passed since the real dream had ended for him.

There before him was the hand-hewn log wall of the Canfield cabin, the familiar cuts where his granddaddy's ax had cut the tree and then planed it smooth. All around he heard the voices of his family—the giggles of his sisters as they washed and hung the laundry in the yard, the *clap-clap-clap* of Hock's hammer against the boards, Mama calling out for Little Nettie. The sounds of home!

He felt Little Nettie tap on his shoulder as he lay sleeping in the cabin. "What you brung me, Jeff?"

"I'm sleepin', Nettie. Mama's gonna whup you, Nettie, if you wakes me. Better get on out, and I'll be out directly."

"You awake?"

"Nope. And don't want to be neither. I like this dream. Mama'll whup you if you wakes me."

"You talkin' in your sleep?"

"Yup."

"Will you tell me what you brung me?"

"I can't remember what it was, Little Nettie. It's been so long. Can't remember what I brung you."

"Shoot."

"Get on out, Little Nettie. Latisha's comin'." The presence of his little sister faded away as Jefferson sank into a deeper sleep. . . .

The hammer pounded as Latisha's footsteps sounded on the cabin floor. And then her hands touched his back. Her fingers stroked his face. He could see her, but the vision was faint and misty as though there were a fog between them.

"I come back, Latisha," he whispered, uncertain now if he was dreaming. He did not want this to be a dream. The hammer pounded in the yard. Latisha looked at him in a loving way, but she did not speak. She bent to kiss him and he groaned. "Can I come home now, Tisha?" He sighed. "It's been so long. So long . . ."

She shook her head and put a finger to his lips. He could smell the sweetness of her skin and hear the rushing of the water in the river.

"Let me come home now, Tisha. I suffered enough for ten lifetimes. Won't you let me come home?"

She shook her head and put his hand on her stomach. "There's the child to think about, Jeff. He needs you. Needs to be raised up in the image of his daddy. He's gonna look like you, Jeff. Talk like you."

Jefferson frowned. He could feel the heaviness of Latisha's belly. "But . . . we got no child, Tisha. . . ." He turned his eyes to the door of the cabin and beyond, where his pappy was hammering in the yard. What was he making? Boards all straight and new pine. Hock hammering away. And then he remembered. Hock was making the coffin. Latisha's coffin.

Hock's eyes locked on Jefferson. He shook his head so sadly that all the grief of the world was in his eyes. Hock raised the lid on the box. Latisha lay inside. . . .

"Let me hold her, Pappy! See? She ain't cold yet!" Jefferson shouted and sat up on the cot. He was sweating even though the fire had died down in the little camp stove. He swung his legs onto the cold plank floor and buried his face in his hands.

"I want to go home, Lord." He wept. "Don't make me stay here in this old world no more all alone!"

He was awake now. Wide-awake. He was free and safe on the Tucker farm, yet he was still a prisoner.

From New York to Calais and back to New York in twelve days, the great engines of the *Berengaria* had thrummed Max to sleep each night.

Now a tiny scratching sound echoed in the darkness of the unfamiliar room, pulling Max into groggy consciousness. Why were the engines silent? Had he missed dinner with the captain?

For a moment it seemed as though he could feel the gentle movement of the ship. He coughed and rolled his head to look at the dying embers of the fire and then he remembered. No ship. Manhattan. The Plaza Hotel. And the scratching sound was a key in the lock.

The door swung open, casting a rectangle of light across the dark room.

Strangely detached, Max remained stretched out on the sofa.

This was a hotel, after all. Maids and porters all had passkeys, and Max had noticed he was without towels in the front bathroom. . . .

Then he caught a whiff of perfume. Not the cheap dime-store stuff a hotel maid might wear, but Chanel, straight from Paris. First class, and with a key to this room! Mike Keenan had thought of everything. No doubt this dame, whoever she was, had also been charged to the room account!

There was a second of hesitation; then the intruder closed the door and fumbled in the darkness for the light switch.

Max beat her to it. He reached up, switched on the lamp, and jumped to his feet as the suite flooded with light. There was a terrified scream and the crash of breaking pottery as the woman in the foyer dropped a large oriental vase full of orchids.

Then silence. In the foyer stood a tall, well-dressed young woman. She gaped at him and then down at the shattered vase and heap of flowers at her feet. Clutching at the fox-fur collar of her coat, she stammered, "Y-you're . . . Max . . . Meyer?"

"Keenan sent you?" he asked gruffly.

"Well, I suppose."

Avoiding the broken shards, she stepped into the light. Her dark brown eyes were wide from the shock of finding him here, but she managed a smile. A very pretty dame, the fellas in the office would say.

But Max was not interested. "Well, you can leave your clothes on, sister." Max did not move from behind the sofa.

"I *beg* your pardon?" She clutched the collar closer.

"Tell Keenan I wasn't in the mood tonight."

"Not in the *mood*?" She stepped back, crunching the pottery beneath her shoe. "Whatever are you . . . *what*?"

"Tell Keenan enough is enough." Max growled in spite of the puzzled look on her face. "First the car . . . a Stutz is a first-class car, I'll admit. And then this place . . ."

"What's wrong with this place?" Her eyebrows raised at the question. Her chin lifted slightly, revealing a slender neck. Her head was covered by a close-fitting black hat.

Max wondered what color her hair was. "Nothing's wrong with it." He maintained his air of indignation even though his inner reserve was softening a bit. "Except that Keenan picked it out, paid for it with my money, and hired some daffy dame to decorate it for me, and I never had a word to say about it."

"It seems quite wonderful to me." She let go of the coat and it opened slightly, revealing a red-sequined evening dress, cut low in the neckline and high at the hem.

Perfect. "Yeah. Wonderful. Except I didn't have a word to say about it, sister. And I didn't have anything to say about you either. Tell Keenan I like to choose what books I read. What chairs I'm going to put in my sitting room, and—" he gave her a hard look—"what dames I want to spend my time with. So, leave the key on the table on your way out. I didn't order you for room service."

The woman tossed her head as though she were a kid with braids instead of an elegant flapper with bobbed hair. Brown hair, probably. Dark like her eyes, Max guessed. Too bad women all cut their hair short these days. He imagined her hair must have been very nice when it was long.

"I brought you orchids. But as you can see . . ." She nudged a flower with her toe. "You should ring for a maid to clean it up. Water is not good on a parquet floor." Her cool smile did not waver. She appraised Max as though she knew some secret about him. "You paid a pretty penny for this floor." She reached into her handbag and pulled out a long white envelope. "And here is the bill to prove it."

"What?"

"You'd better call a maid, Mister Meyer. The water is soaking right in. Have her bring floor wax."

"*You!*" Max breathed.

Businesslike, she placed envelope and key on the side table of the foyer. "Yes. Edith Rutger. You have my card, I believe? I thought you were coming after midnight." Her hand was on the door latch.

"Wait."

"If you are not pleased with the furnishings—"

"They're fine." He stumbled toward her.

"You may contact the decorator I worked with. The number is on the bill. I was assured there would be no problem for you to—"

"No! It's fine." Max was blushing as every word, every nuance of the previous minutes replayed in his mind. "I was just—"

"You were just what?" The smile was gone. His insults had finally penetrated her own layer of embarrassment. There was a definite edge to her voice.

"I just thought *you* . . . that Keenan had . . . well, I'm not that kind of guy, see? I thought you were . . ."

"And I am not that kind of *dame*. Daffy dame? Is that what you called me?"

The broken vase lay between them.

Her look told him not to take one step closer. He shoved his hands in his pockets and stayed put. "I didn't mean . . ."

"Yes, you did."

"Well, yes, maybe I did. Yes, I did think that you were . . . that you had come up here because . . ." He shrugged, feeling stupid and clumsy. "Keenan arranged every detail of my life since I stepped off the boat, you see?"

"And you do not like it?" Her eyes scanned the apartment. She was asking him about the place. The furniture. Everything she had done to it.

"No. I mean, *yes*! I do. Beautiful." He was looking at her. She really was beautiful. He was sorry he had been so deliberately rude. "First class all the way." Like her.

"Fine. Then you have no further need of my services."

"Well, yes!" he blurted. "I do. I mean . . . I would like to make it up to you." He gestured in a helpless way at the room and then at the broken vase.

"No need. I have clients who are even more rude than you, Mister Meyer, although that may seem hard to believe."

"Look, can we start over, Miss Rutger? I was not expecting you."

"That is obvious." She looked past him. "Daffy dame."

"An expression. A figure of speech from the newsroom. I thought you would be . . . I did not think you would be so . . ."

"What *did* you think, Mister Meyer? Pray tell me."

There was no explaining this. They both knew what he had thought. Max put a hand to his stomach. He glanced at his watch. Ten o'clock, and he had not yet had dinner. "Have you eaten?" he asked, feeling miserable.

"Hours ago." Her hand pressed down on the latch, opening the door a crack for her escape.

"Could you eat again?"

"I hope to."

"I mean now. With me?"

A pitying, disdainful smile. She shook her head and slipped out the door, slamming it without reply.

"There's your answer, Max, old boy."

Out in the hallway the blast of a trumpet sounded and half a dozen wolf whistles signaled the rapid retreat of Miss Edith Rutger. Max knew company was coming.

He opened the door to the faces of Harry Beadle and a dozen other bachelor members of the newsman fraternity. They crammed through the entrance all at once, pushing Max back as he caught a fleeting glimpse of Miss Rutger making her escape by the stairs. The elevator opened, disgorging another flock of unexpected visitors.

"Hey, Max!" cried Harry, who seemed to have recovered from his hangover. "Who was that gorgeous dame?" He nudged Max in the ribs. "Did we interrupt something important?"

"No such luck," Max said flatly. "Real-estate agent."

Hoots of disbelief replied as still more men and a bevy of giggling flappers crowded into the front room.

"A welcome-home party!" Beadle announced. "Let the festivities begin!"

"Swell joint," cooed a big-eyed flapper to Max. "Who'd he say lives here?"

"I'm not sure," Max answered. "I was just on my way out."

Max guessed that there were at least seventy-five strangers in the suite by the time he found his hat and coat and slipped out. No one noticed when he left. The elevator on the way down was empty, but another mob of revelers was waiting in the lobby to ride up to the party. Pushing through them, Max dashed to the main entrance of the Plaza, then onto the sidewalk in search of Edith Rutger. She had managed to elude him.

"Shall I have your car brought up, Mister Meyer?" asked Sam, the doorman. He held his hand out as though to catch a raindrop. "We're in for a big one. I can smell it in the air."

"No. No car."

"Call you a cab?"

"No, thanks," he said, not bothering to hide his disappointment. "You didn't happen to see a gorgeous lady come out? Tall. Brown eyes. Nice legs in a red dress."

"No, sir. Seen a bunch going in. Said there was a party up at your place."

"So I heard." He stared hard after a taxi gliding down Fifth Avenue. "Maybe she slipped by while you were looking the other way? Red dress. Brown eyes and a really great pair of—" He looked around to see Edith Rutger smiling at his description of her.

"Yes, Mister Meyer? A great pair of . . . ?" She strolled toward him.

"Eyes."

"You said that already."

"So I did." Max rubbed his chin thoughtfully. Had Miss Rutger managed to forgive him somewhere between the top floor and the lobby? "I would like to start over again if you are willing."

Not a chance. "You obviously have not looked at my bill, Mister Meyer. Otherwise you would be quite pleased to see me leave."

At this, the eyes of Sam, the doorman, widened. He fought to suppress a smile.

Miss Rutger looked at him and snapped, "Well, what are you gawking at? I would like a taxi, please." She then gave Max a withering look.

The doorman blew his whistle with extra enthusiasm, hailing a cab and standing at smart attention as the woman climbed into the backseat . . . alone. No tip.

"Nice meeting you, then," Max said cynically.

"I will give you this," she added as a parting shot. "I may have clients more rude than you, but none would be so conceited as to insult me and then expect me to dine with them."

Max held up his hands in surrender. "A hot dog at Nathan's. That's all. I wanted to make it up to you."

She turned her steely gaze to the cabdriver, who pressed his foot to the accelerator before she even told him where to take her.

Max watched as the taillights rounded the corner. "Daffy dame," he remarked.

"Yeah," added the untipped doorman. "But you're right about her . . . eyes."

Max laughed. "Seriously, I'm going for a hot dog. You can get everything on a cruise ship but a good hot dog. You want one?"

The doorman looked furtively over his shoulder to see if a supervisor lurked nearby. "Sure beats a nickel tip on a night like this. Mustard and onions."

"Coffee?"

"Why not."

"We got lousy taste in women, but we sure know a thing or two about fine American cuisine, eh, Sam?" Max grinned.

After a brisk three-block walk to the hot-dog wagon, Max was starving. He hailed a cab and had the driver stop outside the Plaza to deliver Sam's hot dog and coffee through the window.

"Thanks, Mister Meyer." The grateful doorman pocketed his onion-smothered dog. "Where you headed?"

"I'll never get any sleep up there with that party going on," Max explained. "Guess I'll go to the office and spend the night. I know it's vacant because the entire staff is here."

Max kept an extra suit and shirt in the closet of his office at the New York Times Building for just such emergencies. Originally he had installed the comfortable leather sofa for those long nights when his wife had ordered him out of the house. Another daffy dame.

Maybe it was his tenement upbringing or all those months sleeping in the frontline trenches of France, but whatever it was, Max slept better in his cramped cubicle than anywhere else. At any rate, his habit of sleeping at the office had given him the reputation of being a hard worker, a man who loved his job above all other things. Several among the editorial staff had even commented that it was this love of work that made Max Meyer so incorruptible, so dedicated to printing the truth as he saw it.

Max knew the truth about himself, however. It was loneliness that led him to spend long hours researching and delving into the financial maze of Wall Street to see what sense he could make out of it.

Tonight it was loneliness that made him seek out his familiar lair. He kicked off his shoes and devoured three hot dogs down to the last bit of onion. Switching on his radio, he listened to the broadcast of Rudy Vallee singing from the Algonquin Ballroom. Here he felt at home.

CHAPTER TWENTY-SIX

Hired Man

Early morning sunlight topped the rise and illuminated the uppermost branches of the trees, leaving the rest of the world in shadow. Far off a dog barked insistently. Cows bellowed in the fields. The crack of a hammer against a nail echoed in the valley.

Tommy could smell bacon frying on the new stove. He sat up and pulled the quilt close around his chin as he looked out at the awakening world. Something important had happened yesterday, but he could not remember what it was. Something important was happening today as well. He frowned and scrunched his face up. What was it again?

He nudged Bobby awake, and then yesterday came back to him like the sunlight filtering down through the trees.

Tommy scrambled out of bed and pulled his overalls over his long-handles as he danced on the cold floor. "Get up, Bobby."

His little brother raised his head and moaned. "Time for school?"

Tommy grimaced. That was what he had forgotten—they would start school today. Not nearly so exciting as yesterday had been.

"Mama?" Tommy ran to the kitchen. "Where's Jefferson?"

Trudy was poking strips of bacon curling in the skillet. "Gone. Before dawn. Your father took him bacon and buckwheat cakes. But he had already gone."

"Where's he goin'?" Disappointed, Tommy stood at his mother's side and watched the bacon sizzle in the pan.

"Get back. You'll get popped."

"Where's he goin', Mama?"

"As far away as he can get, I suppose." Trudy brushed him off as though the answer did not concern her. "Now go wash your face. Call your father in from the barn."

She called Bobby to get up. "Bobby!" She sounded cross. "Get up, I say! School today!"

Tommy watched from the window as his father carried a feed sack from one side of the barn to the other. He hoped his father would talk more about their strange visitor. Maybe later, after Mama was busy somewhere else.

A cold blast of air hit Tommy as he opened the door to call his father. "Breakfast, Dad! Ma says hurry and wash!"

Birch turned to acknowledge him with a wave, but instead looked past the house and on down the lane. Someone was coming. Tommy heard the hooves against the roadbed.

Birch frowned and bit his lip. He wiped his hands on his overalls and walked slowly out of the barn and toward the lane.

Tommy did not leave the door even when Trudy scolded him. "I think someone's comin', Mama."

Baby Joe in one hand and the skillet in the other, she muttered, "What now? Boys to get off to school and biscuits in the oven and . . . now what?" She peered over Tommy's shoulder as Jefferson Canfield walked into view with his hands held high above his head. Trudy gasped and thrust the baby into Tommy's hands. She put the skillet on the warming shelf before she rushed out.

Just behind Jefferson Canfield rode Cousin J.D. on a big roan horse. J.D. held a double-barrel shotgun aimed at Jefferson's back.

"No!" Tommy thrust Joe into Bobby's arms and followed his mother onto the porch.

J.D. looked pleased with himself. "Mornin'!" he shouted as Trudy and Tommy and Birch all stood apart and scowled at him. "Lookee here what I caught, will ya?"

"What're you up to now, J.D. Froelich?" Birch looked angry as he walked forward.

"Well, this here nigger says he belongs to y'all! Says he works for you, Birch. I say I got me a hundred bucks re-ward!" J.D. shifted his weight in the saddle. "Caught him sneakin' across my field."

Trudy gulped and stepped off the porch. "Jefferson! What are you doing cutting across Mister J.D.'s field! I told you not to go that way!"

Cousin J.D. looked shocked, unhappy. His vision of reward was evaporating quickly. "You mean you know this here Nigra?"

Birch chimed in, "He's a hired man. We . . . I . . . hired him in Oklahoma. Ain't that right, Jefferson? Now step away from that shotgun, Jefferson, and get on with your work."

The black man lowered his hands and, without a word, walked into the barn.

"Whew!" J.D. let the hammers down easy and laid his weapon across the pommel of the saddle. "Why didn't you tell me? And what you doin' lettin' him wander about, anyway? He'll get himself shot and that's the end of it." He wiped his nose on the sleeve of his jacket and spit tobacco juice into the barnyard.

Trudy raised her chin defiantly. "We sent him to buy butter and eggs. Until I get my hens to lay . . ." She looked to Birch for help.

"J.D., you always was trigger-happy. You want breakfast, or are you off to shoot somethin' this mornin'?" Birch laughed, but the echo of his laugh sounded false to Tommy.

"Well, I done ate already. Gotta get, then. Keep that Nigra on a short leash or somebody'll shoot him."

"Jefferson's a hard worker," Birch said. "I'd hate to see him shot before I get those stumps pulled and that scrub oak cleared." He whacked J.D.'s horse on the rump and sent him on his way. His smile remained intact until J.D. rounded the corner of the road.

Then Trudy and Birch locked weary looks. Trudy turned and reprimanded Tommy for coming out without his jacket and promptly followed Birch across the yard and into the barn, where Jefferson sat grimly on a bale of hay outside the mule's stall.

Unaffected by his mother's rebuke, Tommy trudged after his parents. He had gotten his wish. One more conversation with the big man. The day had taken on a new aura of excitement, and it had only begun.

"I ain't walked a mile before somebody was lookin' for a colored man to shoot down." Jefferson frowned. "I had figured to walk to Mount Pisgah and see if'n maybe there weren't some of the old folks around to help me find my family."

"It ain't safe, Jefferson," Birch said in a worried tone. "And it ain't gonna be safe for a long while yet for you to go anywhere near Mount Pisgah. You best stay on here." He looked at Trudy. "And we surely can use us a hired man. I'll pay you wages. I saw how you cleared your own fields and heard you talk about plantin' cotton. I'll leave you to start clearin', and I'll head on out to Pisgah. I'll ask after your folks for you, but you'll surely get yourself killed if you travel."

Jefferson nodded grimly. "I reckon that's the truth." He winced. "I just . . . last night . . . I had a hankerin' to see the old place. I watched a moth fly to the lantern, singe its wings, and drop. And my heart says, *'Jeff, don't be like that moth. If you hightail it home, you gonna get burned.'* It was the Holy Ghost warnin' me, I reckon. But I didn't listen. And now I almost brung trouble down on y'all, too."

"I can handle J.D.," Birch said.

But Tommy saw the look his mom threw his dad. The look that meant, *"I'm not so sure about that."*

The office telephone jangled Max awake just as the newsroom beyond the frosted-glass walls of his office was crackling to life.

"Meyer," he mumbled.

"Hiya, Max!" The voice of Mike Keenan was too cheerful and much too loud. Max held the receiver at arm's length and could still hear every word distinctly.

"Keenan." Max rubbed sleep from his eyes and groped his way around his desk to the chair.

"Got word you tried to reach me yesterday." Keenan seemed uninterested in what Max had wanted. "I telephoned your suite . . . what a joint, eh? How do you like it?" Without waiting for a reply, he continued. "Some woman answered the phone. Said she never heard of you before, but there was a swell bash at the place last night and perhaps there was a Max Meyer somewhere in the rubble. She hollered your name a few times and then said you were either still drunk or dead or not at home."

"Not at home," Max replied, grateful that the Plaza provided maid service and wondering if perhaps an entire cleanup crew would not be needed this morning.

"Glad you survived." Keenan moved the topic abruptly to business. "Hope you'll be in shape for what I have planned tomorrow night. Purely business. Get your dinner jacket out of mothballs. Some high rollers want to meet the genius behind the *Berengaria* scheme."

"No thanks," Max said. His head was throbbing. He glanced up gratefully as his matronly secretary, Phyllis Morgan, slipped into the office and set a cup of steaming coffee right under his nose. She silently opened his appointment book and slid her bony finger down a page filled from eight in the morning until eight at night. And there was Keenan's entry. . . .

"What do you mean, 'no thanks'?" Keenan sounded indignant. "We've had this planned for weeks. Look at your calendar."

Max winced and read the next day's final entry with only one eye. *C-K-M Brokerage Dinner Party—Formal Attire.*

"Right. You're right, Keenan," Max conceded wearily. "I just forgot. Forgot what day it was."

"Well, you had better remember this. We've got some of the biggest men in the country coming. Business does not wait for us to get over our hangovers, old friend. Go take a steam bath. Plenty of coffee."

Max did not bother telling Keenan that he was not hungover. A visit to the Turkish bath did sound good, however. "Sure. I'll be there."

"And by the way—" the humor returned to Keenan's voice—"a certain Miss Edith Rutger will also be attending, if that interests you."

CHAPTER TWENTY-SEVEN

Mount Pisgah

Mount Pisgah, which Jefferson Canfield had once called home, did not exist any longer. Certainly the hills were the same, the valley unchanged at first glance. Birch sat on his mule and surveyed the place from the crest of the hill. But even from this distance, he could see that the old houses and barns of the sharecroppers had been torn down.

Where children had once played in yards or sat in the shade of dozens of porches, the cotton fields kept right on going. Not yet plowed under, the cotton plants looked desolate and ragged since the cotton had been picked. Birch shuddered as he looked over the vast holdings of the old Howard plantation. Absent of people, it seemed lifeless and joyless, like a Christmas tree stripped of ornaments and set outside. The land, once so loved, was now bereft of those who had loved it.

It was good, Birch thought, that Jefferson was not here to see how greatly his home had changed.

Mount Pisgah General Store was still open, however. The paint had flaked, but the sign was still visible. The door was propped open with a rock, and the stovepipe of a potbelly stove was smoking away. Birch tied off his mule and considered what he might say to explain his presence in this out-of-the-way place.

The inside of the store was shabby and dreary. A pall of smoke hung in the place, explaining why the door was open on such a cold day. Smoke escaped from the glowing red stove. Two elderly women stood together back in the corner of the room, where pigeonhole mail slots lay empty behind a metal grate.

They looked up, startled at Birch's footsteps.

"How-do." He tipped his hat. "Saw the smoke of your stove and stopped in to warm myself a bit before I ride on."

"Didn't hear you come in," chirped one of the old ladies. "Mercy! We don't get no customers past pickin' time."

"I reckon y'all don't. I ain't been through this part of the country for years. No, ma'am, not for years. It sure has changed."

"Oh yes, indeed it surely has," said the woman. It was plain she would do all the talking for herself and her companion. "It is ever so much duller round these parts now. Everything's done by machine, except what the migrant workers hire on to do. It's one of the most modern farms in the state, but not to my likin', no sir! Took all the life right out of it. Don't nobody trust them wanderin' darkies who come through to pick the cotton. We don't know their names like we did in the old days."

Birch snapped his fingers as though trying to remember something. "Old Mister Howard used to own this place, didn't he?"

"Yes, he did indeed. But he up and died, and his nephew took it over. The Young Mister is never here more'n once a year. He runs it from Kansas City. Mercy, it has changed round here. Ain't it, Emma-Jean?"

"That's the gospel truth," remarked the quiet woman with a shake of her white head.

"All the sharecroppers?" Birch asked. "Don't suppose ya'll ever hear from them anymore. Place was full of sharecroppers, I recall."

An innocent-sounding question, it sparked an earnest debate about where they had all gotten off to. Birch hoped he might hear some word about the Canfield family without having to ask. The conclusion was that these Mount Pisgah survivors had heard nothing about any of the darkies with the exception of old Miz Young's son, who worked as a short-order cook at Jemima's Eatery over in Little Rock. The first woman had seen him there and recognized him when she went to visit her sister. But that was two years ago, she explained to Birch, and everyone knew how those people came and went. No telling where Miz Young's son was now.

Birch did not push the subject any further except to comment on how he knew *those people* had been here as long as the Howard plantation, and only since being turned off the land were their lives so uncertain.

The woman simply stared at Birch blankly as though she had not understood what he said. "Them darkies who come through here pickin', we don't know a one of 'em by name, that's true. Come and go. Pick cotton and go somewhere's else. Hard to keep track of 'em. Rollin' stones, them darkies . . ."

Birch's hands were warm when he left, but his heart was chilled and without hope of ever finding any trace of Jefferson's family.

✳ ✳ ✳

"Miz Young's boy? Over in Little Rock?" Jefferson smiled wistfully as Birch recounted the trip to Mount Pisgah. The big man's hands circled his coffee cup as though it were the size of a thimble. His massive frame perched on the dining-room chair in such a way that the chair and the table and the entire room seemed small. Indeed, from the expression on his face, Trudy could tell that his heart was striding across the rolling fields of Mount Pisgah as he had done ten years ago.

"He was the only one those ladies knew about. The store was still standing, but little else, I'm afraid."

Jefferson was quiet, as if he were remembering the store. "Bet them old women in the store was Miz Moss an' Miz Digby." He shook his head. "Couldn't be none other. They was always rooted in the same corner of that store."

Trudy laughed in spite of the seriousness of the subject. "I remember them well," she agreed. "And they would know Missus Young's boy, certainly."

"That's right. That little scrawny child . . . his mama worked as a house servant an' cook for Old Mister Howard."

"His name was Washington, wasn't it?" Trudy recalled.

"That's right. Named for a president, same as me. We all figured Miz Young wanted that boy to grow up an' be somethin'. Go on to Tuskegee Institute with the help of the Lord and Old Mister Howard. But that Washington, he paid no mind to school."

Trudy laughed again. "He came a few weeks off and on, but that was only because your sister Lula was there, I think."

"That's right. He didn't want nothin' more out of life than to be a good cook like his mama. That Miz Young could bake an upside-down cake to make a man die from pleasure. Bet that's what killed Old Mister Howard. He was eatin' that upside-down cake at least twice a week. Used to send little Washington on down to the store every day to pick up stuff so Miz Young could make another one. After a while the old man would swear off the things for a day or two. Then he'd get a cravin', an' down he'd send Washington again." Jeff shook his head in pleasure at this one small fragment of a lifetime of memories. "Life was good in them days. Hard, you know, but good." His eye caught Birch's. "I never thought it would ever be no different. Figured I would come home to Pisgah, marry Latisha, an' have me a passel of young'uns raised all the same as me."

Jefferson's eyes clouded as the curtain of reality descended, blocking out the dream. "But it was not to be. Lord had other things in mind, I reckon. Mostly the Lord reminds me how there ain't nothin' in this whole world that a man can trust in except Him." He tapped the coffee cup with his finger. *"Trust the Lord, Jeff, the Holy Ghost says to my heart. And then you ain't never gonna be disappointed."*

Silence descended as his words hit home. Birch knew the truth of it, and so did Trudy. All the same, it was a lesson to be learned again and again. *Trust only in the Lord . . . nothing else is certain!*

Birch slid a slip of paper across the table to Jefferson. "I wrote it down. But I don't know what use it'll be." *Mrs. Young's son. Last seen at Jemima's Eatery in Little Rock. 1927.*

"It ain't much. But it's somethin'. That little Washington Young is cookin' just like he always wanted. Well, my, my. If his mama is still livin', then maybe she knows where my mama is. Or maybe my sisters." Jefferson stared hard at the paper. "If he's still at this place. It's somethin', ain't it?"

It was a sobering thought. Did they dare hope for such a miracle? Trudy took her special linen writing paper from her writing case and placed pen and ink on the table before Jefferson like a meal. And for the first time, Jefferson Canfield feasted on hope as he wrote the letter to Mrs. Young's son in Little Rock.

✷ ✷ ✷

It was a fitting end for the leg-irons. The chains that had bound Jefferson Canfield were dropped down the hole of the outhouse to sink forever out of sight into the muck.

Tommy and Bobby discussed the matter thoroughly as they shared the two-seater toilet. No matter how thorough that Oklahoma sheriff was, and no matter how fierce the old bloodhound, they would never find those chains!

Birch had warned the boys firmly, however, that they held the life of Jefferson Canfield in their hands just as surely as Jeff had held Bobby that day in the James Fork. One slip of the tongue and Sheriff Ring would be back again. A loose word to anyone in Shiloh was much more dangerous than if they laid those leg-irons out on the road in a straight arrow to the Tucker farm. Shiloh was full of snoops who would certainly ask questions. And so Bobby and Tommy practiced the answers.

"Jeff? My daddy and mama have known old Jeff for ten years! Since before we were even born! Jeff? He's come all the way from Oklahoma to join my daddy, to work for us as a hired man. Daddy says we need him, too, what with the terrible mess the farm is in."

All of this was gospel truth, of course. The boys were just instructed to leave out the most interesting parts. Like how Jeff had been tracked down by the Klan and his new wife killed and how he ran away to Oklahoma and got arrested there and thrown into jail, where he had been for the last ten years. These facts, along with the details of his escape from Sheriff Ring and the hounds, all sounded like something out of the penny-dreadful novels that their mother had forbidden them to read. They read them anyway, and the only difference between Jefferson Canfield and the heroes of the penny dreadfuls was the fact that Big Jeff was not white.

All the same, Jefferson was a hero. He was their hero, and they made a vow together: Upon pain of being dropped down the outhouse and vanishing like the chains in a most horrible death, they would never betray the secrets of Jefferson Canfield. When the kids at school talked about how that terrible convict named Cannibal had drowned in the James Fork, they went right along with it. Tommy even embellished the story a good deal, describing the bloodhounds sniffing the blood of the convict and stating that he fully expected the body was going to pop up one of these days and float right past the schoolhouse. His ability to describe such morbid scenes made him instantly popular with the boys and made the girls squeal and then grow silent in terrified contemplation of that gruesome event.

It was only a short leap from there to the topic of possible ghosts and dreadful hauntings in the creek bottom. And so the legend of Cannibal lived on, completely separate from the identity of the hired man from Oklahoma.

The discussion of Sheriff Ring's bloodhounds just naturally wound its way around the topic of that little red puppy in the stall down at Brother Williams's livery stable.

"Exactly how much is half of twenty-two dollars and two bits?" Bobby asked.

Tommy squinched up his face and did the ciphers in his head. "Eleven dollars and twelve and a half cents."

"How we gonna get that much money?" Bobby worried as they kicked a tin can toward the barn. "Nobody's got that much money. I've never *seen* that much money!"

"If we had that pup right now, we could hunt possum. Dad says you can get two bits for every pelt!"

"But we ain't got her, so we can't hunt with her, and if we can't hunt with her, then we ain't gonna have the money to buy her."

This was a complicated problem. "We'll just have to work, I suppose."

"We already work. We don't get but two bits a week each for doin' our chores. That pup is gonna be ready to leave her mama in less than four weeks. That makes . . ."

Tommy added the sum in his head. "Two dollars. I've already been figurin' it out."

"I asked Grandma Amos could I sweep up down at the store every day after school. That old lady's so old she can hardly hold a broom."

Tommy laughed. "Looks to me like she ought to be ridin' a broom instead of sweepin' with one." Then he grew very thoughtful as they entered the barn. He gave a tin can a mighty kick, and it flew up and landed with a loud clang in the bed of the FAMOUS Bad-Luck Wagon.

"Don't say such things about her. You'll give me the creeps. She says she'll pay me one nickel a day if I clean up the store for her. But I ain't gonna do it if you scare me and tell me she's a—"

Tommy silenced him with a slug to his arm. "What's that?" Tommy whispered, staring hard at the space just over the wagon where the sunlight beamed through the missing shingles on the roof.

Bobby gasped with fright. He did not see anything at all, but Tommy had a way of making his voice sound spooky and scary until Bobby just wanted to turn and run.

"If you scare me, I'll tell Dad. Mama will whup the tar out of you, Tommy Tucker, if you—"

"Shush up!" Tommy slapped his hand over Bobby's mouth.

Bobby's heart pounded in terror. What was Tommy seeing? Dead bodies of moonshiners? The wagon filled with ghosts? Bobby trembled even though nothing at all was there. He shoved Tommy's hand away and scowled bravely, although he wanted to turn and tear back toward the house.

"Don't you *see* it?" Tommy cried, taking a step toward the FAMOUS Bad-Luck Wagon.

"Mama don't know about all the horrors been in that wagon!" Bobby spat. "And Dad says don't tell her. But if you don't stop scarin' me, I'm tellin' her everything and then you wait and see what she says!"

"No!" Tommy had not taken his eyes from the wagon. "Hush your mouth, you little fool! It's right there! Right in our own barn!"

"Huh?"

"Our *fortune*!"

"What?"

"*Terror* and *murder* and *moonshiner wars* and *dead bodies* all piled up and old Mister What's-his-name hanging from the *rafters*! Oh, Bobby! It's better'n the carnival side show, I'm tellin' you! It's the red puppy! Eleven dollars and twelve and a half cents right *there*, waitin' for us to pick it up!"

Bobby figured that the strain of the last few days had finally snapped something loose in his brother's brain. He stared and stared but still could not see any money. But he could imagine all the creepy things that had gone on about the FAMOUS Bad-Luck Wagon. And this little glimmer of imagination finally made clear what Tommy was getting at. . . .

Lily knew this place. It was called Shiloh. Her young husband was buried in the woods just south of the road. He had died of pneumonia in just one night, and since there was no cemetery for coloreds close at hand, he had been lowered on a plank into a grave in the forest and buried that way.

There had just been time to make a wooden cross and drive it into the ground; then the straw boss had barked that daylight was burning. Hanging around could not bring the buck back. So they had left Lily's man behind. Sweet William cold in the ground, and they had gone on to the next field.

Lily came upon the woods early in the morning. Autumn leaves had covered the grave and some critter had knocked down the cross, making it hard to find the exact place. She scuffed through the heaps of leaves until her foot struck the fallen cross. Then she sat down beside the grave of William to wait.

To wait for her own death.

The sun slipped across the sky, shining directly down on her. She did not move, although the baby tumbled and kicked inside her womb. Some part of sweet William was still alive, living on as Lily had grown thinner and thinner.

Night came, and the woods howled with cold that penetrated the old horse blanket Lily had found by the road and wrapped around her shoulders. It was cold throughout the night, but still Lily did not die. She stayed beside William all night. She slept beside him and mourned as she had not been allowed to do. . . .

When she awoke the next morning, she was still alive. The baby moved. Sunlight fell in a patch on one small lily poking up through the leaves.

"You ain't gonna let me go, are You, Lord?" Lily asked. "I am considerin' . . . yessir . . . I am listenin'. I ain't but one small Lily of the field. You gotta show me where to go. What am I gonna do, Lord?"

She rose slowly. Her back was stiff—like she had been picking cotton all night. The baby kicked happily now that she was straight again.

She heard dogs barking in a field somewhere and turned her face toward that sound and the light. She would have to find something to eat soon.

CHAPTER TWENTY-EIGHT

The Dream

When Edith Rutger was shown into the Keenans' dining room and seated at the opposite corner of the long table, Max was completely certain that he was to be the main course. This feeling of being a chunk of prime rib in a lion cage had been growing even before Max had taken his place across from the gray-haired man with the drawl and the badly fitting tuxedo. What was his name? Phipps? No, Phelps—that was it. He was some sort of oil baron from Oklahoma.

The man had stared into Max's face when they had first been introduced, as if trying to read some hidden message. And now, through tomato bisque and lobster salad, every time Max raised his eyes he found Phelps studying him intently.

Looking elsewhere was hardly better, because Edith Rutger was at Mike Keenan's elbow, and both of them were also observing Max. A black-uniformed maid removed the salad plates while the white-gloved butler wheeled a silver-domed serving trolley into the room.

The servant stooped beside Mrs. Keenan for her approval. "Prime rib," announced the butler.

"Mister Keenan tells me that you are a newspaper writer, Mister Meyer," said Keenan's wife in a friendly voice.

"Not just a newspaperman, Gladys," corrected Keenan. "A financial writer for the *New York Times*. Very influential."

"A financial writer!" exclaimed Gladys Keenan with a rustle of the beaded fringe on her ornate evening gown. "How marvelous! Isn't finance just the most thrilling thing? Of course, it's far too complex for me, but you men do it so well. Just look at how prosperous we are, thanks to Mister Keenan's understanding of finance."

From across the table came a sharp-edged question that had the sound of being prepared ahead of time and held in readiness. "Why did the market drop so much on the word of that little pip-squeak professor?" Phelps wanted to know.

"It's not so much what Babson said," Max tried to explain. "After all, he's been giving the same warning for three—"

Once again Keenan took over the answer. "That's right. Saying the same things for three years. Only this time the wire services picked up on it and made him a prophet. Power of the press—that's what did it."

"Is that so?" queried Phelps, but he was watching Max for the reply.

"I'm certain that the sudden attention by the press did cause some of the panic selling, but the market forces—" Max tried again.

"There, you see, Phelps? Are you satisfied now?" interrupted Keenan.

Phelps did not look entirely satisfied, but he applied himself to his prime rib and potatoes and left off devouring Max.

Max wondered what it was all about. But no explanation followed. The rest of the dinner conversation revolved around Keenan's golf game and the difficulties of finding a suitable governess for the six Keenan children. Edith Rutger contributed a story about how one of her clients, a matron of an old-money family, was convinced that pink was the in color and was having her entire living room redone in that shade.

But the only color that caught Max's attention was Miss Rutger's blond hair. Max was reminded how wrong his earlier conjecture had been. He had expected her hair to be dark.

After dinner, Phelps cornered Max next to the grand piano. "Okay, enough on Babson," the belligerent oilman said. "But what about Sabre Oil? What about the pool?"

Max took a minute to try to frame a general response about his disapproval of pools that would not sound totally ungracious to his host. "What about it?" Max asked, stalling for time to think.

"I mean, don't you think it's been pushed up as far as it can go? After all, the stock price has already lost all connection with the reality of a two-bit, South American, fly-by-night outfit."

Max could not have agreed more, but he was completely unprepared to hear this sentiment voiced in Mike Keenan's home. "No," he answered truthfully, glancing over his shoulder to see if anyone else was within earshot. "No, if the pool can manipulate enough shares and continue to get favorable press, the little folks who are just beginning to take notice will rush in and snap it up."

Phelps pumped Max's hand. "Now you're talking sense." Grinning, he walked away to refill his glass of bourbon.

Deciding that now was the time to make a graceful exit, Max offered his farewells to the host and hostess. Like Phelps, Keenan also shook Max's hand warmly and thanked him for coming.

In the foyer, waiting for his overcoat to be retrieved, Max heard a voice from behind him purr, "Any chance of getting a ride back into town with you, Mister Meyer?"

Edith Rutger's simple black dress emphasized the length of her legs and the warmth of her straw-blond hair. Involuntarily, Max's eyes traveled up and down her frame as she received her coat and twirled into it with a final flash of silk.

"Sure, Miss Rutger," Max said, feeling tongue-tied and confused by the sudden friendliness. "That is," he said as he took his coat, "if you think it's safe to be seen with me."

"Pooh," she teased. "Safe is so dull, don't you think?"

Max did not question the sudden interest of Edith Rutger in his past, his present, and his future dreams. He simply accepted it, as he accepted her forgiveness of his misunderstanding of her true profession. Nor did he ask her the standard question of *"What's a nice girl like you doing hanging around a guy like Mike Keenan?"*

Edith had explained it. Keenan was a client. She had located his country estate for him. Now she was his client in the stock market. Purely business—real estate and the stock market. Keenan had helped to make a lot of fortunes, and the newly wealthy all needed some place to live that reflected that wealth, did they not? And so Edith Rutger—beautiful, twenty-nine, divorced, and a sensible working girl—was usually available to fill in the odd seat at a Keenan dinner party.

All that being said, she turned her attention on Max. Starting with the row of old photos she had put on his mantel, she probed him for information about each one. By three in the morning she had begun to piece together bits of information into a clearer picture of the man, like a ball of yarn being knitted into something useful.

Max suddenly came to himself, aware of how much he had told her. "Let's take a walk," he suggested, hoping to hide some of his embarrassment under cover of darkness. Hand in hand, they walked on the pedestrian walkway over the Brooklyn Bridge. The tremulous rhythm of the bridge pulsed up from the roads and rails where the late-night trains and trams clacked and sparked above the slow dark waters of the river.

The wind was blowing, but Max barely noticed the cold.

Edith tucked her arm through his and leaned her head against his shoulder. She peered over the edge of the bridge and gazed down at the dark water. "Last night I would have thought you wanted to push me off." She smiled up at him.

"Just shows how wrong even a sharp businesswoman can be."

"Then why did you bring me here?"

"It's mine." He waved a hand across the steel span.

"Yours?" she laughed. "You're really crazy, you know."

"I'm the man who bought the Brooklyn Bridge, see? I bought it all. All this American Dream stuff." He looked at the lights of Manhattan and then toward Brooklyn. "Me and several million others. Ask my grandparents about America, and they would say it was the *goldeneh medina*, the 'golden land.' They bought it. I bought it. Bought the Brooklyn Bridge, you might say. And I look out and still believe in the miracle. Anybody, even a Jewish kid from Orchard Street, can make it big."

"You are a writer, Max." Her voice was soft, admiring.

"An idealist. To the core. But just enough of Orchard Street lives in here that I can also be a realist. And frankly, what I see on the horizon scares me." He looked up into the girders and then to the stars. "Maybe the bridge I bought is falling down. If it does, it will take everything with it."

"A gloomy thought—" Edith pouted—"for such a beautiful moment."

"Chalk it up to Jewish temperament, you know? A tear behind every laugh. A laugh behind every tear. Keeps life balanced if you do it right. Enjoy the moment—" he pulled her close to him—"because tomorrow is never certain." He kissed her gently.

She kissed him back with a fierceness that surprised him. "Some things are more certain than others, Max," she whispered.

CHAPTER TWENTY-NINE

Lily of the Field

Half a dozen dogs held Lily at the end of the walk. The little Victorian house had the look of wealth about it. Every facade was painted fresh. The picket fence was not missing one slat. The windows were shining clean, reflecting a clear sky. Woodsmoke poured out of the brick chimney at such a rate that Lily knew these folks had plenty of wood to burn.

Dogs snarled and barked their warning. She did not move into their territory but waited until someone in the house took notice. A plump-faced woman with frazzled hair glared at Lily through the window and then took to shouting, "J.D! J.D! Get on out there! J.D.! We got us a pregnant Nigra . . . a mulatto out there about to get herself ate up by the dogs! J.D.! Go see to it!"

A long time and much shouting later, a short, bullnecked man with a round red face strolled onto the porch. He leaned against the rail and squinted unpleasantly at Lily. He let the dogs carry on awhile longer before he called them up beside him.

"What you want?" said the man.

From inside the house, the woman asked, "What's that Nigra want, J.D.?"

"Hush up, woman!" he called over his shoulder. Then he turned his attention back to Lily. "What you want?"

"How-do, mistah." Lily tried to sound calm, although she felt light-headed and desperate with hunger. "I . . . come lookin' for some work I might do for y'all. So I can earn a bite to eat. It been a while since I had somethin' to eat."

He patted his fat belly and stared at her. He looked as if he might laugh, but he did not say anything for a full minute until the woman in the house shrieked his name again.

"J.D.! What's goin' on out there!"

Not moving from the porch, he looked up the road and pointed. "Up yonder there. Ain't more'n half a mile . . . there's some folks hirin' on Nigras to work. Yessir. You go on up there, gal. They'll find you a job to do. A place to sleep. All the food you want." He smiled at Lily's expression of hope. "You like the sound of that, gal? Well, just tell 'em ol' J.D. sent you."

☆ ☆ ☆

The morning belonged to Trudy. Jefferson and Birch were out in the field. Tommy and Bobby were at school. Baby Joe was down for his nap. The chores were done, beds were made, and there was bread in the oven and chicken soup simmering on the stove.

Trudy settled down to write letters to Mama and Papa in Montreal, to Cousin Mina in California, and to Max in New York. Each letter contained some added bit of information about the farm and the boys and Birch and the miracle of Jefferson Canfield. What she could not discuss in Shiloh at least had some release in the writing of these letters. It was a good thing, too, because Trudy had the sense that she would break if she did not get to share the news with someone.

Ten years later Jeff spotted those birch trees and . . . , Trudy wrote. It was the stuff a novel was made of. Perhaps one day Trudy would make good on her threat to write a book, but in the meantime family correspondence was a much-needed outlet.

She was so engrossed with the reporting that she hardly noticed the soft rapping on the door of the back porch. The lid of the soup kettle rattled, and for a moment Trudy thought she was hearing only escaping steam. Then the knock sounded again, louder.

It was certainly not J.D. or Maybelle, who had never yet bothered to knock. Probably a neighbor come calling. But why the back door?

Trudy shoved her letters into the drawer of her sideboard and peered out the window. Not a neighbor. At least none that Trudy had seen in these parts. It was a young, frightfully thin colored girl. She had no coat, only a horse blanket wrapped around her shoulders. When she moved a step the blanket parted, and Trudy could see that the girl was heavy with child. Her hair was wrapped in a dark blue rag, and her worn shoes were also wrapped in rags. Her large eyes looked hopefully at the door. The look of desperate poverty was evident on her face.

The young woman did not see Trudy appraise her through the window. She had just turned away when Trudy opened the door.

"I heard you knocking," Trudy said, and the woman turned around, surprised.

She clutched the blanket around her shoulders. "How-do, ma'am."

"Good morning."

Food, Trudy thought. The young woman needed food. Trudy looked past her as if to see where she had come from. How had she come to be in such a desperate condition?

There was an awkward pause. "How-do," the young woman said again. Then, "I don't mean to trouble y'all none, ma'am, but the gentleman on up the road, he told me you's lookin' for help."

"Help?"

"Yes'm." She took a hopeful step toward Trudy. "He say I should tell y'all J.D. sent me. He say since y'all be hirin' help . . . I don't need money. Money don't mean nothin'. Just food . . ."

At the mention of J.D., Trudy's eyes narrowed involuntarily. "J.D.!" she spat.

And in an instant the light of hope vanished from the face of the young beggar. "He told me . . . y'all . . . was lookin' for hired help . . . oh, ma'am! The mistah tell me that and send me here."

"I do not doubt that he did," Trudy said gently, afraid that the woman would weep right there on the step. The flesh of her hands was scarred from picking cotton, her lips cracked from the cold. Her feet poked out from scraps of leather and shreds of cloth, and her arms were thin and spindly in spite of the enormous bulge of her stomach.

"I can work!" she pleaded. On her face was the knowledge that she had been the victim of some cruel prank. "I can do ever'thing! Chop . . . chop cotton or kindlin'. Carry and clean and cook! Oh, ma'am! I needs . . . I was so in hopes . . ." She closed her eyes in despair as the last hope vanished.

"I was just making myself a cup of tea," Trudy said.

"I won't bother y'all, then." The young woman turned away.

"No, I mean . . . would you like to join me?"

"Join?"

"It is so cold out. Would you like to come in and have a cup of tea? fresh bread? It should be done baking."

"Inside?" The young woman clutched the blanket tighter and took a faltering step back. Surely she was hearing wrong.

"Yes." Trudy inclined her head and smiled. "Come in. It is warm in the kitchen."

"No'm. I couldn't. Just put me to work and bring a little somethin' out here after." She scanned the yard for some task she might do to earn her meal. Tea and fresh bread.

"Please." Trudy did not budge. "Come in." Her gaze lingered too long on the pregnant belly.

The eyes of the young woman dropped to her shoes. "I ain't clean enough, ma'am. It's been a long time since I been able to wash my things. It ain't fittin' I come in your kitchen, you bein' white an' all."

Trudy smiled wider. "I'm not white. I'm Jewish. Ask J.D., if you want. But first come in and warm yourself. We're letting all the cold air in."

Lily was called by that name not because her skin was light compared to her brothers and sisters but because her mama had believed in the Good Book. She had come into this world at a time after her pappy had died and there was no food in the cellar to feed nine children.

Consider the lilies how they grow: they toil not, they spin not; and yet I say until you, that Solomon in all his glory was not arrayed like one of these. . . .

She had been a beautiful child, as if to bear out the truth of the Scripture her mama claimed the day she was born. But unlike the lilies of God's field, Lily's existence had been one of toil. She had worked the fields since she was old enough to walk. There had been no schooling. Married off to William at fifteen, she had borne him one baby girl, who died the first winter, and a boy baby, who had been born dead. Lily wondered if perhaps their loss had been the mercy of God. The world was a hard place, lean and hungry. Now, at nineteen, Lily was a widow, alone. She carried this child, but she believed in her heart that the baby would not survive either.

Today Lily had been the butt of a cruel joke. The man named J.D. had delighted in her hopelessness. There was no need of a hired woman at the Tucker farm. Lily was thankful all the same for the bread and the hot chicken soup. She wept with gratitude when Trudy offered her clean clothes and warm water to bathe and later made the offer that she could stay for the night. "You can sleep on the closed-in porch beside a kerosene stove if you like."

If she liked? In her whole life Lily had never been offered such kindness as this. She thought maybe it meant she was going to die. The Lord was giving her one night of warmth and comfort and good food and folks who talked to her like she was human, and then tomorrow the Lord would take her home!

The young'uns spoke to her politely, saying, "Yes, ma'am" and "No, ma'am" when she asked them if they went to school and if they liked it much.

Mister Birch was kind when he asked her how far she had come and how long she had been on the road and how the cotton crop was down south.

Jefferson, the hired man, said hardly anything at all, but he looked at her with eyes that *knew*. . . .

And Miz Trudy talked to her about young'uns all the while. About how wonderful young'uns were to have around and how no woman ought to fear childbirth because it was an easy and natural thing.

Of course, Miz Trudy did not know about the other two babies Lily had planted in faraway fields in Louisiana and Texas. Never mind. It was good to hear such kind words. Good to pretend for just one night that such things were true, even for someone like Lily. That night she went to bed thinking of the words of the Good Book. For this day, those words were true for her. Solomon in all his glory was not treated so kindly as Lily was.

For this reason Lily figured that even J.D., who had been laughing behind his hand at her, had been used by the Lord. What that man had meant for evil, the Lord had turned to a good thing. Of this, Lily was certain.

Warm and clean and fed, she closed her eyes and drifted to sleep with her mind on Jesus. Maybe she would wake up in heaven; that would be all right with her. William was there. Her mama and pappy and those two little babies, too. Heaven would be a wonderful place. Lilies of the field did not toil in heaven. . . .

When the morning came, Lily looked around her at the house and the fields and the barn and these folks, and she thought that maybe she really had died in the night. Maybe this little farm in Shiloh was truly heaven!

It must be heaven—Mister Birch and Miz Trudy asked her to stay on! Jefferson moved out of his room at the side of the barn and went to work converting the feed shed in the pasture into a fit place for himself to live.

And that flower-garden quilt, the one he said his mama made . . . he left it folded on her cot and said she was most welcome to use it if she cared to.

CHAPTER THIRTY

Sacrifice to Mammon

The timid knock on the frosted-glass door of Max's office barely penetrated the clatter of typewriter keys.

"You've got company," said the amazed voice of his secretary as a priest, a plainclothes policeman, and a blue-uniformed cop crowded into the cluttered space beside his desk. Not the usual sort to visit the office of the financial editor of the *New York Times*. These fellows looked more as if they should be next door in the society section, asking for a column or two about the policemen's charity ball or the boys' home charity bazaar.

Max did not stop typing. With a cursory glance, he growled, "Wrong office, fellows. You've got Wall Street here. Charity balls belong to Marian Winters."

They did not move. The policeman cleared his throat as a call to attention. "You are Max Meyer?"

"That's right. Financial page." He finished the paragraph and flipped the carriage with irritation. He did not ask who they were.

"If we could have a moment of your time," began the priest.

What did they want? Tips on the stock market? Everyone wanted to get in the act these days. Max repeated the words he was typing: "With . . . stocks . . . so . . . overvalued . . . the wise investor . . . will think twice . . . before . . ."

Impatiently, the plainclothes policeman tossed a packet onto the keyboard, interrupting Max's studied rudeness.

"What is this?" Max bristled, only now stopping long enough to glare at the committee of intruders. "I'm working here. If you weren't cops, I'd call the cops—"

The priest stepped forward. "Mister Meyer, what I have to tell you may come as a shock."

This was certainly the wrong brand of clergyman to be bringing Max Meyer personal news. A rabbi would have been more fitting. Max started to say as much, but the serious look in the priest's eyes stopped him. "I have a deadline in thirty-five minutes. Shock me quick and get out."

"Did you write that stuff?" The plainclothes policeman gestured toward the packet.

Max opened the envelope to see dozens of his own columns neatly folded. "Obviously. I am Max Meyer. Those are clippings of my articles. So what?" He glanced at his wristwatch.

"Tell Mister Meyer how you came by that." The plainclothes policeman nudged the beat cop.

"A couple weeks ago I discovered a kid in a telephone booth stuffed with newspapers—looked like a runaway to me. Old Man Gruenig at the tobacco shop said this kid had been buying every newspaper in the place, looking for a column by Max Meyer. He called the New York papers one at a time, looking for you."

"You've got my attention." Max leaned back in his chair. "So? Get to the point."

"So, I tried to question him, made a grab for him. I got his coat. . . ." The cop gently placed a child's tan jacket on the desk. "You see, the kid's name and address are right there inside the collar. D. O'Halloran. Philadelphia. A place on Third Avenue."

"Doesn't mean a thing to me." Max tapped his fingers on the desk. "I don't know any O'Hallorans. I'm not from Philadelphia."

"Mister Meyer," the priest interrupted gently, as though he was not sure if Max could understand. "I need to ask you if you have any recollection of a young woman you . . . knew . . . quite well . . . about ten years ago."

"Ten years ago? What is this?"

"Does the name Irene Dunlap mean anything at all to you?"

Max passed his column along to rookie John Murphy to wrap up as he cloistered himself in his office with Father John O'Hara, Officer Dooley, and Detective Kerry with strict orders not to be disturbed.

Irene dead.

A nine-year-old son named David who had come to New York looking for the father he had never known.

It was almost more than Max could take in one sitting.

Father John continued, "Of course you are not responsible for the care of the boy. Irene made it clear to me that she did not wish for you to be contacted after her death. The boy's stepfather is not the sort of caregiver David needed, so Irene made arrangements with me that he be placed in the St. Joseph's Children's Home in Philadelphia." He picked up the clippings and removed a faded photograph of Irene from the envelope. "Apparently the boy was going through some of his mother's personal effects and found the clippings." He took several dozen letters from his pocket and laid them on the desk. "And these as well."

Max simply stared at his own handwriting and the tuppence stamp with the London postmark still plain after ten years. "All this time," he whispered hoarsely. Then he caught himself before his emotions somehow betrayed him.

"You have not heard from him since he ran away?"

"I have been in Europe." Max waved his hand toward his notes. "If he tried to contact me here . . ."

"We thought as much," said the priest.

"That settles it." Detective Kerry gathered up the small boy's jacket. It was much too thin for the cold weather that howled across the city.

"Well, where is he?" Max could not tear his eyes away from the jacket. So small. His son was small, out alone on the streets with no jacket.

"If we knew that, we would not be here," said Kerry.

"Do you have a picture of him?" Max asked. "In case he is hanging around somewhere . . . so I will recognize him?"

With a nod, the priest produced a black-and-white photograph of the boy, which he placed beside the picture of Irene. David looked like his mother—light hair, straight nose. His eyes were intense. Yet the shape of his mouth, his smile—Max recognized himself there! And the cleft in his chin . . . Max had been carefully shaving that cleft for years.

He reached out to touch the flat image. "Yes," he said softly, "I remember."

"He looks some like you, Mister Meyer," said the cop brightly. "I seen the resemblance soon as we come in here. Plain as anything. Kid's got your mouth and chin. Except you're dark and he's fair."

"Like his mother," added Father John.

Max swallowed hard as emotion threatened to close his throat, making it impossible to talk. "What do I do?"

"If he shows up"—the detective fumbled for a card—"give me a call. Keep him busy. Hold on to him until I can get here and take him off your hands."

Father John finished. "Detective Kerry will wire me in Philadelphia.

I will take it from there." A pause. "Irene wanted to be certain that the boy would be raised in a Catholic environment. This is, of course, nothing you need to trouble yourself with. The child will be well cared for. We are certain that he will attempt to get in contact with you. You are our best hope of bringing him back where his mother wished him to be."

What could Max say to all this? He had no claim to the kid. He had never met him. Max knew that Irene had been carrying his child, but he had never heard if the baby was a boy or a girl, if it had lived or died. After so many years, Max had stopped wondering. Until now. *He's got my mouth. My chin. Irene's blond hair. And he came looking for me!*

"We will make this as easy as possible for you, Mister Meyer," added Kerry. He glanced at the priest. "All of us had a fling or two in our younger days. Father knows all about such things. It's just that your fling has come home to roost, you might say."

Kerry's attempt to ease Max's mind did not help. Max simply nodded and stared in silence at David's photograph. So. It was a baby boy. Nine years later Max did not feel like handing out cigars, but he was relieved to know the truth all the same.

"Can I keep this?" Max asked hoarsely as he picked up the photograph.

"Certainly." The priest was grim. He opened his mouth to speak, as though there was much more he wanted to say.

Max knew the priest had read the expression on his face and knew the answers to all those unasked questions. Had the boy had a good life? Had Irene been happy with the man she married? Had David's stepfather treated him well, played baseball with him, taken him fishing?

Ten years meant that none of this was Max's business. He pocketed the snapshot and placed Detective Kerry's card beneath the border of his desk blotter. Max promised to telephone. Promised to hold the kid until someone could come take him away. After ten years, what else was he supposed to do?

✳ ✳ ✳

The bottle of fine French champagne was well concealed beneath the thick pastrami sandwiches and carton of potato salad and carefully wrapped pieces of cheesecake in the wicker hamper.

Edith Rutger had left nothing to chance. She had called Miss Morgan, Max's elderly secretary, with the question, "What does Mister Meyer eat when he lunches in the office?" Armed with the list of the basics, Edith had added the champagne as her own contribution.

When the closing bell sounded on the floor of the stock exchange, she was waiting for Max in the lobby, with basket in hand.

Sobered and stunned by the news about his son and Irene, Max had entirely forgotten their date. He sent word ahead to the office and then took Edith by the arm, propelling her out into the air where he could breathe and think.

"Trinity Church, you said?" She sounded cheerful in spite of his preoccupied gloom.

He nodded silently as they merged with the crowds walking toward Trinity.

"Bad day?" Edith asked, then prattled on. "Mike Keenan says the breaks in the market are nothing more than nervous Nellies who have been reading columns—"

"Like mine?" He looked at her in an amused way.

"Like you used to write." She linked her arm through his. "Keenan says you've joined the right team now."

"He says that, does he?"

"Says you'll listen to reason when you know what's at stake in the Sabre Oil pool."

"Who does he say that to?"

"Everyone. Quinn, my bootlegger. Phelps. Me." She smiled coyly at him. "I've put every cent in it, too. People listen to you."

Max slowed his pace. "Yes, they do, Edith. Little investors who could lose everything if I recommend they buy into Sabre Oil at these inflated prices. Then Keenan pulls the plug, and that's it."

"You're so serious." She shrugged and pulled her hand away from him. "All I know is what Keenan says."

"You should read my column, Edith. It would give you another perspective on the pools—who wins and who loses."

"You're irritable today."

He stood in front of Trinity Church, where they were supposed to have their late lunch. The glazed door reflected the street so that the interior of the church seemed to be full of hurrying people and streetcars. Max glared at the mirror image and then turned his back on the building to look down Wall Street. The sidewalks were crammed with people: brokers, bankers—the high priests to the god of Mammon. Max knew them all by sight and was certain now that the sacrifice these priests were making to their god was the millions of small investors who put their faith in them.

"Edith . . ." Max did not know what to say to her. She wanted him to tell her that he would go along with what Keenan was asking of him. That he would recommend Sabre Oil as the buy of the century.

"Are you all right? Max? You're trembling!"

He lowered his eyes, aware that he was staring off down Wall Street like a madman. "I had some news today. Nothing to do with business." He frowned and shook his head. That was not right either. He had left Irene because of this place. In a way, he, too, had sacrificed everything for Wall Street.

"What is it, Max?"

"I was thinking about my . . . my son."

She smiled curiously. "You didn't tell me about a son."

"He is nine. Just nine. His name is David." He looked toward the Exchange. "I was thinking that all the gold in Wall Street's vaults isn't worth that kid."

"So you're a father, too," she said, too cheerfully. "Hardly the type, Max." She was trying to tease him out of his grim mood. She could not know the emotions that were running through him like tape through a stock ticker. "When can I meet him?"

He did not answer her question. How could he tell her what he had heard today? that he did not know where the boy was?

"He doesn't live with me."

"Too bad. With his mother, then? Divorce is the hardest on the kids, they say. I was always so thankful that Frank and I had no children to involve in the divorce."

"I would give anything—*everything*—if he were here," Max said, and he knew that he meant it.

"In the meantime, please *cheri*, what's the use of wasting a perfectly good bottle of champagne? Come along, Max. Overblown fatherhood does not become you. At least not today, when I want you all to myself."

CHAPTER THIRTY-ONE

The Puppy Plot

It was better than a Mister Bones Minstrel Show, easier than selling lemonade, more profitable than sweeping the floor of Shiloh General Store for old Grandma Amos.

Forty tickets were printed out by hand on sheets of Trudy's special letter-writing paper.

25¢ SEE MURDER AN MISTRY!!!

TURRIBLE FAMOUS

DEATH WAGON!!!

MIDNIGHT SATURDAY!

FAMOUS BAD-LUCK WAGON SPOOK SHOW

Trudy did not know that Tommy and Bobby had made off with her special paper. She did not know about the spook show they had planned in the barn. In fact, she had never yet heard the details about the horrible history of the FAMOUS Bad-Luck Wagon. If she had known, she would have walloped Tommy and Bobby and put a stop to the whole thing.

As it was, the details of the show were kept secret from every adult in Shiloh, even though there might have been a few more tickets sold if the boys had gone after that audience as well. All the same, every kid with two bits had bought a ticket. Thirty-six tickets had been sold in all, putting a grand total of nine dollars in the red-puppy fund!

"Now we gotta deliver," Tommy said sternly as they counted out the last of the nickels, pennies, and dimes they had collected from their classmates.

"Elva Burns wants to know if she can get her money back if she can't sneak out the window."

"I hope you told her—no refunds. We put on the show, but it ain't up to us to get them there. It's just like we said. We meet everybody down at the schoolhouse at eleven-thirty Saturday night. We come back here, and the show starts at the witchin' hour. *Midnight!*" Tommy had put on his creepy voice again.

Even in broad daylight sitting on a feed sack in the barn, it gave Bobby chicken skin. "Don't say it that way." Bobby looked over his shoulder at the bad-luck wagon.

"What way?"

"You're scarin' me. That's what way."

"What? Why, you can't be scared yet. We ain't even fixed the place up. If you're scared and we ain't even got the dead bodies heaped in the wagon and Old Man What's-his-name swingin' by a rope from the rafters . . ."

Bobby shuddered. "Shut up." He kicked at the empty overalls, which would shortly be stuffed with straw and made into the dead bodies of the moonshiners in the back of the wagon. "I don't like this much." He scowled.

Tommy held up the canning jar full of money. "Think about the puppy. You don't like this?"

"How come we couldn't do it in daylight?"

" 'Cause we want them to be good and scared, that's why. Nobody gets scared in the daylight."

Bobby looked out the barn door at the sunlight. "I do."

"Well, I'll give you something to be really scared of." Tommy grabbed his brother by the strap of his overalls and pulled him close. "Just listen to this! You know Fred Woods?"

Of course Bobby knew Fred Woods. He was the biggest kid in fourth grade because he should have been in sixth grade, but he had been held back twice. He was also mean. "What about Fred Woods?"

"When I sold Fred Woods his tickets, he said this had better be good or he was goin' to break your arm—"

"*My* arm?"

"Like a hostage, that's what you are. He said he would break my little brother's arm."

"Why don't he break *your* arm? You sold him the ticket!"

"You know Fred always does things a little backward. That's why he's still in fourth grade." Tommy shook his head solemnly. "So you see?

That's why this has to be real good. Gotta be at midnight. Gotta get this place lookin' as creepy as the Wax Works Chamber of Horrors. We'll get them all softened up. Leave the school and take them home through the graveyard and then—"

"Graveyard!" Bobby moaned and rubbed his arm as if considering that maybe a broken bone or two might be better than walking through the graveyard.

Tommy rubbed his hands together in glee. "I got it all planned out, see? We'll have all the girls practically wetting their underdrawers by the time we bring them in here! We bring them in, put on the show. They'll run screamin' home, I tell you! It will be the scariest thing ever."

"If they scream they'll wake Mama and Dad. Then we'll be in for it."

Tommy shook the money jar. "Think of the puppy."

"Then Mama will find out we made the tickets from her writin' paper."

"You're scared of everything."

"She ain't gonna like it when she finds out."

"She ain't gonna find out."

"Uncle Max sent her that writin' paper from New York City for Christmas. It came all the way from England. Can't buy it in Hartford."

"How do you know?" Tommy challenged.

"Because she said you can't buy it in Tulsa. And if you can't buy it in a big city like Tulsa, it ain't in Hartford."

"We had to use it. Elsewise any old person could copy our tickets on plain paper and cheat us out of two bits. And Mama won't even miss it. Once we get that red puppy and start huntin', we'll have pelts to sell and we can buy Mama sheets and sheets of the stuff. All year long."

"Not in Hartford. Sure not in Shiloh. It ain't here."

Tommy, impatient with his young brother's conscience, snorted and glared at him. "You got no imagination! We gotta think big. We'll send money to Uncle Max and he'll buy it for us. Now quit gripin' and get in the house and sneak that new pair of overalls out here."

"How come I gotta—?"

"Because I'm the oldest and I said so."

"What if Mama catches me?" This was the biggest fear of all.

Tommy scowled. "Don't let her. Act natural. Roll 'em up and stuff 'em in your shirt, that's all." He indicated the clothes that had already been stolen from the clothesline one at a time. "Do like you did with this stuff."

"Yeah? Mama was awful mad about them clothes. She said some old thief just came and stole Pa's work clothes off the line. Then she bought those new bibs and you're makin' me steal them, too. I tell you, Tommy, there's a willow switch at the end of this."

Tommy shook the jar harder. "Naw. There's a red puppy . . . or a broken arm."

Suppertime was quieter than usual around the Tucker table. Tommy and Bobby gulped down their food and then nudged each other and exchanged looks before asking, "Pa? You think it would be okay if we sleep out in the hayloft tonight? Like campin' out?"

Birch cocked an eyebrow at Trudy as a signal that it might be nice to have an evening alone in the house with only baby Joe to worry about. "Don't see why not," Birch replied when Trudy sent the same signal back to him. "But once you're out, there'll be no runnin' in and out of this house all night. Y'all will have to stay put. Not make a racket or disturb Lily . . ."

Perfectly innocent angels, the boys nodded in unison, asked to be excused, then tore off to gather up bedding and a basket of food to last them through the night.

Later, in the kitchen with Jefferson, Lily explained that she had been in her room and overheard the whole thing. Drying her hands on a dish towel, she fished in the pocket of her apron and passed a stiff, cream-colored piece of stationery to Jeff.

"I found this 'tween the feed sacks," she whispered. "Can't read what it says, but them boys is up to somethin'. That there is Miz Trudy's good writin' paper. I knows, 'cause she gave me letters to take down to the post office. What them boys doin' writin' on Miz Trudy's good writin' paper?"

Jefferson tucked his chin and grinned as he read the printing of the ticket to the FAMOUS Bad-Luck Wagon Spook Show. He laughed and refolded the paper, tucking it into the pocket of his big overalls. "If I know anythin', Miz Lily, them boys is out to get themselves a red puppy one way or the other."

"Y'all gonna tell the mister?"

He considered the question. "Naw. You see the way they looked at one another when them boys asked to sleep out? I reckon Miz True an' Mister Birch don't want no ruckus. And I reckon them boys would hate me eternal if I give them away. Mornin' is plenty of time to fess up."

"What we gonna do?"

"I don't know about you, Miz Lily, but I intend on seein' the show for myself."

CHAPTER THIRTY-TWO

Havana Betsy and the Shanghai Girls

Each evening fresh provisions were brought out to the rummy crews of Rum Row—the small community that bobbed on the waters off Manhattan. The daily newspapers were always on hand for those citizens interested in the horse-racing news or the results of the World Series. Vegetables, fresh meat, milk, and butter were provided for those who grew tired of booze and fresh fish caught daily. The larger vessels had happy hours and hauled out entertainers from the New York speakeasies to perform.

But the most precious cargo to be brought out to Rum Row by far were the ladies, known fondly as Havana Betsy and the Shanghai Girls Band. The weather had turned even colder than usual, and the bevy of females from Havana Betsy's all-girl band did not fancy taking a ride out to Rum Row on any of the open skiffs. Carefully coiffed hair had a tendency to wilt badly in the quick-moving Jersey skiffs. Many a velvet gown had ended the journey looking like water-soaked burlap. Fishnet stockings exposed to the salt spray lived up to the name—fishnet.

On this chilly October Saturday night, a dozen shivering Shanghai girls stood beside a heap of instruments on the dock and absolutely refused to ride out to Rum Row with Little Pete and the Jamaican.

"Mutiny," said Little Pete. "The blokes out there will hang us from the yardarms if we don't deliver the goods! It's Saturday night, Betsy, me girl! The customers have been delivered to Rum Row already. If you don't go, the lads will have no music for the dance."

Havana Betsy did not seem to care at all. She planted her substantial foot on the dock and refused to budge. "Your boss promised I could take

my girls out in style this week! No more of this salt spray over the rail!
No more pretending we have come to Niagara Falls! Extra-duty pay, he
promised. And a warm cabin provided for the passage, or we shall not
go! Then see what sort of mutiny there shall be out there!"

Jumbo's face twisted into a threatening grimace. David heard the sullen crewman mutter, "Gimme a minute with one of these here ladies. A
bloody lip or a black eye might make them all repent of their tantrum."

Little Pete overheard Jumbo as well, and he had no doubt that the
bully would carry out the beating if left to his own way. Half the size of
Jumbo, Little Pete stepped in front of him, hurling a few curses, then asking pardon of the ladies for his language. He shook his fist up at Jumbo's
scowling mug and told the man that one more word like that and Jumbo
would find himself wearing concrete shoes and visiting Davey Jones.
Then he turned to Havana Betsy in an elegant fashion.

"Got to overlook that gor-iller, Betsy. The bloke's 'ad no proper bringing up. Don't know 'ow to behave with the ladies."

He nodded and bowed a bit and generally placated Havana Betsy. He
was quite a politician, Olaf and Gus often said of Little Pete. If Pete were
an American, he could run for president. And if Gus and Olaf were citizens, they would vote for him.

David knew that Little Pete would never run for president, but he had
won the vote of everyone on the dock, including Havana Betsy and her
Shanghai Girls Band. Every damsel in distress needed a knight in shining
armor. David observed that Little Pete fit the bill nicely. A cockney Sir
Lancelot.

"Well now, Little Pete—" Havana Betsy shifted her weight on her
high-heeled shoes, and her red lips parted in apology. "It ain't that I
mean to be a hard case in this matter, but I got to think of the damages.
Why, Lillith nearly came down with pneumony last time. She couldn't
play her trombone for weeks."

Cow-eyed Lillith blinked innocently and nodded in agreement. She
raised a dainty hand and gave a dainty cough to prove the truth in what
Havana Betsy said.

"There, you see?" Havana Betsy shook her bleached blond head.
"You shall have to think of some other way for me and my musicians to
get to the fleet tonight."

As she said all this in a very nice way—no longer threatening, but
firm—David watched Little Pete. Clearly Little Pete knew it was time for
negotiation. He narrowed his already narrow eyes and chewed his upper
lip with his bottom teeth.

For a moment David thought that everything had been said that was
going to be said. Then Little Pete's round head lifted as an idea floated

into his brain like a balloon. He smiled broadly at Olaf and Gus, who were standing by as observers, not as participants.

"I got just the thing! A little slow, a little clumsy in the water, but the cabin is first class! Warm! Right in outta the weather you'll be, Betsy!"

"Lovely!" Havana Betsy clapped Little Pete on his scrawny back. "You are a swell fellow, Little Pete. We ought to have you run the country. Business would be booming!"

She did not say what sort of business.

Little Pete strode confidently over to Olaf and Gus. Gus backed away. Olaf raised his hands as though he were about to be shot. Everyone knew that the Svenson brothers turned to blathering idiots whenever a woman even looked at them! Did Little Pete mean to say that the *Jazz Baby* would haul the Shanghai Girls Band all the way out to Rum Row? And maybe even all the way back, too?

It was too horrible to contemplate.

"Ve cannot take the ladies!" Olaf cried. "Ve got a full load of vegetables and clean laundry for Crazy Vinny Vaters! You know how Crazy Vinny is if he don't get his shorts back from the laundry on time!"

"I'll take care of Crazy Vinny Waters," Little Pete said, unconcerned. "And I'll take his shorts out in me little Jersey girl." He gestured toward his open boat.

"Oh *no*!" Gus cried. "You take his things on your skiff, and they'll all get vet, and ve'll get blamed! Crazy Vinny'll *kill* us Svenson brothers for sure!"

Havana Betsy stepped forward to end all arguments. "I shall personally see to Crazy Vinny. He's an old pal."

Gus searched wildly for some other reason why this bevy of females could not set foot on the *Jazz Baby*. "Sure, Missus Havana Betsy, but that ain't the only reason ve vorry."

"Oh?"

"You see, ve gots this big mean dog name of Codfish—"

Jumbo, who hated Codfish, took this opportunity to state his opinion. "Shoot that mangy mongrel! Shoot it! I'll go shoot it myself!"

Havana Betsy laughed and raised her plump hands. "Me and the girls are good with animals. Tame even the mean ones, ain't that right, girls? Music calms the savage beast, you know."

The Shanghai entertainers erupted in a jabber of concurrence.

Still, Olaf and Gus stood in the circle. Why hadn't they loaded up and taken off before they got roped into this?

"So?" Havana Betsy asked. "Anything else?"

Gus and Olaf stared miserably at the planks of the dock. "Vell, there is one thing. Or two things . . ." Gus glanced at Olaf, then continued.

"Me and Olaf . . . ve is married men. Ve tell our wives ven ve come here that ve don't dally with no other vimmen."

"Honorable men." Havana Betsy shook her head in respectful amazement. "Rare nowadays, boys, I tell you. Well then, if that is how it is, I shall lay down the law. Listen up, girls! If these gentlemen are so kind as to aid us in our distress, then hear me. Not one of you shall make a pass or wink or so much as giggle in their direction. These here Swedes ain't fair game. They don't belong to you no more than you can steal a hairbrush or borrow a dress without asking first. Those are the rules of the house, and we shall play by the rules."

She shook her meaty finger like a conductor's baton into the faces of her Shanghai girls in warning before turning back to Gus and Olaf. "Now I've said my piece. We shall be as behaved as though your wives is on board; you have the word of Havana Betsy on the matter, and everyone will tell you that my word is my bond."

Gus and Olaf stood rubbing their chins in identical puzzlement for a long moment. Then, at the same instant, they nodded in agreement.

Gus doffed his hat as though the Shanghai girls were old grandmothers needing a lift to the market. "Vell then, ve are gentlemens, and ve can help you ladies get to vork."

"Why, it's a young boy!" cried Havana Betsy as she hiked her skirt and climbed aboard the *Jazz Baby*.

The sudden attention of twelve women made David blush bright red.

"He is called Mice," Olaf explained, indicating by hand signals to David that he should doff his stocking cap and make with a gentlemanly bow.

David did all this, not because Olaf wanted him to, but because some memory stirred in him and his mother's face came clear in his mind, reminding him to be mannerly.

"And if he ain't the gentleman!" cried cow-eyed Lillith. "This one is too young to be married, Havana Betsy. If I wink at him, am I breakin' house rules?"

"Of course not." Havana Betsy reached out and gave David's cheek a pinch. "He shall sit beside me all the way out to Rum Row!"

Gus caught David's eye. "Sorry," Gus said firmly. "Mice is our lookout! A handy kid, I tell you! Ve gots to have him vit us up top."

David gave a quick and grateful nod, then grasped Codfish's collar and dragged him to the bow, where boy and dog sat sternly among a stack of band instruments and looked out to sea, even though they were still moored to the dock.

"Like hens, they cackle," whispered Gus.

Even enclosed inside the cabin of the *Jazz Baby*, the Shanghai Girls Band sounded like a flock of birds David had heard caged up in the Philadelphia aviary. He was grateful to have a job to do. Pleased that *they* were all inside, while he and Codfish were out among the men.

The diesel engines throbbed to life, causing the trawler to gently rumble and vibrate. Then came the magic that David loved. Lines cast off, the little boat began to move away from the dock. As they picked up speed, the breeze was cold but cleaner smelling. It blew away the lingering scents of too much perfume and the stink of the quay.

The lights were on all over Manhattan. Solid lines and shapes vanished—reorganizing themselves into a vast checkerboard rising straight up from the ground. The bridges, too, were magic. David's favorite was Brooklyn Bridge, the oldest in the city and the most familiar from the Manhattan tales his mother had recited a thousand times:

"Buttresses on lower Madison Street rise like medieval towers. Suddenly a single arch soars out across the water and carries two roadways on its back to Brooklyn! These roads are separated by double lines of tracks that carry trains and trams. Over all this, one hundred feet high in the air, is a wide path for foot passengers. Oh, Davey, one day it is my dream to walk with you across the bridge! I used to go there and toss a penny far down into the water to make a wish. . . ."

"What did you wish for, Mother?" David would ask.

"I was just a young girl. . . . Oh, but I did have such lovely wishes. And now . . . well, I cannot tell you, Davey. Or else they will not come true."

There would be no more wishes for her.

David looked toward the brightly lit arch of his mother's bridge. He had not yet walked up on the pedestrian road, but someday he would. And he would carry pennies in his pockets and throw them over the rail one by one and make a thousand wishes, too. *What will I wish for?* he wondered.

There was a mist coming into shore. The upraised arm of Liberty seemed to be hailing a cab. David drank in these sights, his heart conscious that these had been familiar to his mother. Dear to her heart. If only things could have been different . . . if wishes really did come true.

Like Olaf and Gus, both faithful to their absent wives, David was faithful to the memory of his mother. He did not crave the attention of the preening women inside the cabin of the *Jazz Baby*. To have felt flattered by their attention would have been a betrayal to his mother's memory. All these thoughts were in his heart, but he could not find the words to explain what he was feeling.

So he contented himself with feeling uneasy in their presence.

"Ve mens got to stick together, eh, little Mice?" Gus shouted down from the helm.

David nodded firmly as though this were an explanation of his feelings.

"Keep a sharp eye tonight," Olaf warned him. "Ve gots a big fog coming in. I ain't vorried about no Coast Guards, but I sure vould hate to ram another rummy out there!"

All the shore boats ran the distance between shore and Rum Row without lights so as to avoid the Coast Guard patrols. So even on a clear night, there were occasional accidents.

"Tonight you gonna have to use your ears more than your eyes, Mice!" Gus enjoined. "Listen tight for other engines. Ve gots all these ladies to get there safe, you know."

✶ ✶ ✶

Foghorns sounded in a chorus of hoots, toots, whistles, bells, and bellows. Up on the fly bridge of the *Jazz Baby*, Olaf tugged on the rope of the whistle every sixty seconds, helping to track the little vessel's progress through the fog.

"Ve gots lots of pickets close in tonight," Gus declared, raising his head as a high-pitched bell followed the buzzing of a single gasoline engine on the right, and another answered to the left.

Picket was the term used for the small, thirty-six-foot Coast Guard boats that patrolled the inshore areas. They could make up to twenty-five knots on a flat sea and carried crews armed with machine guns, tommy guns, and rifles. They stood as a last line of defense against incoming rummy boats and, owing to their speed and maneuverability, were considered a dangerous threat to the smuggling operation.

Next up the Coast Guard scale was the seventy-five-foot patrol boat called the six-bitter. Wood hulled, powered by twin gasoline engines, these vessels could make only thirteen knots at best. They each carried eight men and were armed with a one-pounder gun and two heavy Lewis machine guns. Considered by the enemy to be jacks-of-all-trades, the six-bitters were the most hated and feared of all the Coast Guard vessels. Reliable and capable of blowing a rummy boat clear out of the water, the deeper tones of their foghorns announced that there were six-bitters up ahead tonight.

"Two six-bitters," David announced, pointing at the precise locations of the horns.

"And one tollar ship!" Gus added as a deep bellow resounded regularly from out to sea.

By this, Gus meant the steel-hulled, hundred-foot Coast Guard ship given the rugged job of picketing and trailing the large mother ships of the rummy fleet. Forward, they mounted a three-inch, twenty-five-caliber, quick-firing gun and a Lewis machine gun. An impressive arsenal of small machine guns was carried by their crews, and the vessel was capable of trailing a rummy ship for as long as thirty days. Although the Svenson brothers called these vessels tollar ships, they were known in English as *dollar* and the larger *dollar-and-a-quarter boats*. Such names were uttered with respect among the rummy crews. Dollar boats were formidable adversaries to all but the swiftest mother ships.

There was one great advantage that the Rum Row armada had over the Dry Fleet, however. The smugglers outnumbered the Coast Guard vessels by fifty to one. And as long as the mother ships remained anchored outside American territorial waters, the Coast Guard could not board a ship of the rummy fleet . . . unless, of course, the U.S. captains and crews wanted to buy a case or two of scotch!

Everyone knew that the crews of these official vessels were all hard-drinking men themselves. More than once a rummy ship had been confiscated, rummy crew arrested, cargo impounded, and Coast Guard crew returned to port having consumed a good bit of the evidence in the journey. Perhaps they did not approve of Prohibition, but it had certainly given the Coast Guard a big job to do. For the men on board these ships, Prohibition was played out like a child's game of hide-and-seek or Mother-may-I. The trick for the rummy boats was to make it "home" without getting tagged.

In this game, however, there was one additional player feared by the Coast Guard and the Rum Row ships alike. Freelance pirates were also out on the waters. Posing as buyers, or sometimes faking a breakdown, the crews of these boats would board a rummy ship, quietly cut the throats of all on board, and steal the cargo. Murderers and cutthroats without conscience, these hijackers were the reason Gus and Olaf carried shotguns.

If they were captured by the Coast Guard, they would be out of jail within hours, thanks to Boss Quinn. But if the *Jazz Baby* was boarded by hijackers, that would be the end of their rum-running days forever. More than once in the last few months, bodies of their compatriots had washed up on the beaches of Coney Island as a grim reminder that there were those on the seas who played the game for keeps.

David had heard these stories, and the faceless apparitions of these seagoing gangsters haunted his darkest dreams. Hijackers were out there in the fog tonight, waiting until the shore boats loaded up and turned back toward the harbor. . . .

Above all this, the deep, resonant bellow of a great oceangoing ship called from far out to sea.

"Ve gots a big passenger ship coming through, Mice," warned Olaf. "She's coming right down our alley. You gotta look real sharp for her. She gonna look like a big mountain. Lots of lights coming through the soup ven she come. Be sharp, boy!"

David raised his hand in acknowledgment. From the sound of the ship's horn, she was indeed as big as a mountain. The captain of that great vessel knew the waters were filled with Rum Row vessels, Coast Guard, and hijackers. It did not matter to him if he went over the top of them. His ship would not notice any more than the windshield of a Model T noticed an unfortunate bug. It was the responsibility of the small boats to stay out of the course of the oceangoing monolith moving swiftly toward them.

✳ ✳ ✳

Where had it come from? Not a mountain, but a sheer, high white cliff loomed in front of the *Jazz Baby*. Gus and Olaf both shouted in their native tongue. Gus spun the wheel while Olaf laid on the whistle and the great wall sliced through the water headed directly toward the bow of the *Jazz Baby*.

Codfish barked wildly, as though he were trying to scare away the leviathan that threatened to ram them.

David shouted, but his voice was lost beneath the exchange of bellows and whistles splitting the darkness. Inside the cabin, the ladies screamed in unison. The door of the cabin banged open, and the Shanghai girls tumbled out on deck as if they meant to jump before the *Jazz Baby* was split amidships.

"Get back!" Olaf shouted at them. "You vimmens! Get back!"

They did not hear him as the *Jazz Baby* swung hard to port, sending the Shanghai girls tumbling across the stern in a heap of flying legs and dresses and hats among the coils of rope.

Instinctively, David covered his head and pressed himself against the cabin as impact seemed certain. Even Codfish cowered, his tail between his legs and mouth slightly open in a kind of doglike astonishment!

Curses, shrieks, whistles, and bellows were all accompanied by the music of the nearby Rum Row mother ship.

Havana Betsy called down curses on the heads of the two Swedes and then on Cunard Lines and lastly on the Boss, who had not provided them with proper transportation to Rum Row. "If I live, I shall kill someone for scaring me to death!" she proclaimed.

From fifty yards, the anchors of the ship were clearly visible to David.

Portholes gleamed with light. The seagoing beast was about to devour them without slowing, it seemed.

"Dis is vat happens ven ve break our vord!" Gus shook a fist at the liner and then at the heap of females still struggling to get up. "Dis is vat happens ven vimmens is on the boat!"

At twenty-five yards, David could see the faces of people in the portholes. Could they see him? Could they see the little *Jazz Baby* as she rode up the bow wave of the great liner?

The huge swell sprayed up and over the gunwales of the *Jazz Baby*, soaking the instruments and the wailing females in ice-cold salt water. David gasped, taking in a mouthful of brine. The wave knocked the *Jazz Baby* around faster than she could have maneuvered. The wheel spun wildly as Olaf and Gus fought to hold her steady.

David looked up to see the red Plimsoll line of the ship. He could have counted the small flecks of rust penetrating the thick white lead paint of the hull. The *Jazz Baby* bobbed and whirled like a cork, finally ending its spin facing the same direction as the liner. The hull of the great ship bumped once against the side of the *Jazz Baby*, a gentle nudge before she passed on close enough for David to reach out and touch.

Olaf laid on the whistle in a constant blast of outrage as the ship slid away like a giant iceberg. At last David dared to look upward. Even the fog fled before this ship. He could clearly see people on the upper decks as they smiled down at the *Jazz Baby*. Pointing and waving to the drenched Shanghai girls, the passengers of the vessel had been provided with an extra bit of amusement for their last evening on board.

❊ ❊ ❊

Shivering, drenched, and indignant, the Shanghai Girls Band lugged their instruments and followed Havana Betsy on board the enormous three-masted schooner *China Doll*. Registered out of Nassau, the rummy mother ship had been fitted with a dance floor, sumptuous cabins for offshore guests, and a small but well-equipped gambling room.

Crazy Vinny shouted down to Gus and Olaf, "Lucky for you Little Pete got here with my laundry high and dry." He smirked at Havana Betsy as she slogged by. "Too bad you didn't do as good with these here broads!" For this comment, Havana Betsy clocked him across the head with her shoe and threatened him that he had better watch his mouth or the Shanghai Girls would not be playing tonight.

Olaf called, "Crazy vimmens! They almost get us killed! Bad luck vimmens!"

To this Crazy Vinny replied, "Depends on what you Polacks call luck!"

"Ve ain't no Polacks!" Gus roared back. "Ve Svedes!"

Crazy Vinny shrugged. "Whatever. No matter. Lady Luck is with you guys tonight. The Boss is on board. In his office. He says you guys are supposed to come aboard the *China Doll* while we are loading the *Jazz Baby*. He wants to have a word with you about some job down Nassau way." Crazy Vinny smiled. He wriggled his narrow hips. "Moving south for the winter, I bet. You should see the dames down in those parts! *Caramba!*"

"Ve is not Danes!" Gus shouted.

"Ve is *Svedes!*"

Crazy Vinny did not understand their objection. "The Boss says bring the kid aboard, too. Make it snappy."

This was a first. David had never been allowed on board the luxurious *China Doll*. He had heard about the dance floor and the cabins and the fancy clothes of the New York stockbrokers and financial wizards who came out here for an evening of music and drinking. But no kid had ever been in that elegant domain.

Codfish barked wildly as the three boarded *China Doll*. His howls were drowned out by the blare of the jazz music and the buzz of voices. Crazy Vinny led the trio down the crew's hatch and through less opulent quarters, where freshly washed socks and undershirts were strung across the crew's bunks. Girlie pictures were pinned up above footlockers. A Chinese man polished a row of boots in a corner. *Not all that wonderful,* David thought as he scanned the cramped surroundings.

They passed through the kitchen and on down a narrow corridor with small brass-rimmed portholes open to the damp night air. At last they halted before a louvered cherrywood door with light shining through the slats.

"We wait here," said Crazy Vinny. "The Boss's got company just now. Business. Strictly legit, too."

Gus, Olaf, and David stood against the wall of the corridor and waited as the low voice of Boss Quinn penetrated the louvers. Every word was distinct. David listened and felt a tremor of fear ripple through him. The voice, the words, the door between him and the Boss brought to mind the broken face of Joey the Book on the floor of the American Fruit Company warehouse.

". . . I tell you, Keenan, this business is getting tougher every day. Only this morning I got word that the body of one of my best men has washed up on the beach of Coney Island. Joey the Book. He has been dead for long enough that the cops don't figure they will ever be able to identify the body. But what do you know? The stiff's shirt has a laundry mark from Chin Woo Laundry, and they said this is the mark of Joey the Book. . . ."

"Terrible, terrible," the unseen Keenan replied with a shudder in his voice.

Gus and Olaf shook their heads. "Poor Joey the Book," said Olaf. "Maybe hijackers got him?"

David felt sick. He had seen Joey. *"Not hijackers,"* he wanted to say. But if he told anyone at all what he had seen that day . . .

Boss Quinn continued. "So. On one hand I have the Coast Guard and the Feds to worry about. But these pirates. These hijackers. I tell you, Keenan . . . you remember how it was when we were kids?"

Keenan swore in response. "Those Wops—"

"They're all grown up now, and meaner than ever. They're jumping my shore boats. Stealing my merchandise. Killing my crews."

"Terrible," Keenan said in a hushed tone. There was an edge of anger there, too. It was clear he did not like Italians any more than the Boss did.

"I wish to say that the shine is off it, Keenan. All the fun is gone these days. And so, I take a look around me at how the really smart businessmen are going legit. Take Kennedy, for instance. Nothing but a two-bit Democratic ward boss from Boston. But he sold enough rum to buy himself a Palm Beach mansion, and now he thinks he will run for president one day. Sends his kids to fancy schools and walks around New York like a regular respectable gentleman."

Boss Quinn gave a sharp, bitter laugh. "Like he would be welcome in the Protestant social club." There was a pause here. "Like you, Keenan. You have made your fortune playing with other people's money. Dirty money it was, too. Now it's all washed up bright and clean, floating around Wall Street . . . and it is this same job I want you to do with all this."

"That's easy. The Sabre Oil pool is on the way up."

"There have been a few pessimists among the press over that deal. This causes me concern."

"Never mind. I have the worst offender in my pocket, bought and paid for. He'll write what I tell him about the deal. And when he writes something, the minnows believe him, and they bite."

Chairs scraped back. Shadows passed between the light and the louvered door.

"Your word has always been good as gold, Keenan," said the Boss.

The door swung open and the portly, florid-faced Keenan inched past the trio in the corridor as though he did not see them waiting in line.

Crazy Vinny knocked softly on the door. "Boss? I brung the Polacks and the kid off the *Jazz Baby,* just like you said."

"Come in." The Boss seemed in a good humor in spite of what he had just told Keenan about Joey the Book. His thin lips were curved in a slight smile. His hat was off, and the cabin lamp glowed on his rust-colored hair and glinted in his deep brown eyes. He glanced down the line from Gus to David, and then with a wave of his hand he dismissed Crazy Vinny. "So. You boys have done okay for the business. Made a run nearly every night, and you never get nabbed by the Coast Guard or way-laid by hijackers."

"Ve been lucky, Boss." Gus wrung his cap in his hands and spoke sin-cerely, not believing he should accept such high praise without modesty.

"Lucky?" The Boss leaned back in his chair and rubbed his chin as though he did not believe in the word. "Maybe." He paused and looked at David as he spoke. "You have heard about Joey the Book, I suppose."

David's eyes widened. Did the Boss see that he was afraid?

Gus cleared his throat. Should he admit to eavesdropping? "Vell, ve heard a little about it. He was found dead on Coney Island."

The Boss still did not take his eyes off David, who flushed beneath the piercing gaze of the Irishman. "Stiff as a plank. Half eaten by fishes. Wrapped in seaweed. A bit of luck that the coppers found that laundry mark." He cleared his throat. "No, that was not luck, either—it was stu-pidity. Someone fouled up. Whoever did him in should have made cer-tain he would not float back to shore." A slight twitch at the corner of his mouth made David grow pale. "What do you think about it, boy? Who do you think did Joey in?"

"Pirates," David answered hoarsely. "Hijackers." This was the right thing to say, even though David was certain it was not true.

Boss Quinn was pleased by this reply. "You are a clever kid. What did you say your name was?"

"Ve calls him Mice," blurted Gus.

The Boss shot him a withering glance. "I wish to know the boy's given name. His Christian name."

"David Meyer."

"You have the look of the Irish about you. Mayo, is it?"

"Meyer," David corrected.

"You go to church, David?"

"Used to."

"You say your prayers? say your rosary?"

"Sometimes."

The Boss spread his hands as though this was an obvious fact. "Well, there is the reason for your luck, boys. You have a little altar boy on board the *Jazz Baby.*" A frown. "I would hate to see anything happen to the three of you. It is getting hot these days. I want you should take the

Jazz Baby down the coast to Cuba. Make the run from Havana. Fish a little, if you like. An easy spot. Lay low for a while. What do you say?"

There was nothing to say but yes. Gus and Olaf welcomed the change of scenery as if it were a promotion. Only David figured that the Boss had other reasons for wanting them out of New York. Joey the Book washing up on Coney Island had everything to do with it.

"Well then. It is all settled. You can shove off when the weather permits."

"You vant ve should keep running the *Jazz Baby* till then?"

"What would we do without the *Jazz Baby* bringing us the evening news?" The Boss glanced at David with a look that burned through him like a hot iron. "It will be quiet when you are gone."

CHAPTER THIRTY-THREE

The FAMOUS Bad-Luck Wagon Spook Show

It was the kind of night on which the Headless Horseman of Sleepy Hollow might have ridden out. With trembling voice, Bobby told Tommy that he wished Mama had never read him that story. He was scared stiff before they ever reached the schoolhouse.

The wind moaned through the branches of the trees like a thousand voices in torment. Limbs tapped and rattled against one another like the bones of dead men hanging above the lane. Wisps of clouds scudded across the moonless sky. There was no doubt about it. Tommy had picked one doozy of a night to scare the bejeebers out of most of Shiloh School.

Behind every bush, Bobby imagined moonshiners' ghosts following along after them. He tried to cling to Tommy's coat, but Tommy shoved him away and told him he ought not to be such a sissy and that he ought to know not to be afraid because this was *their* show, not real. But they had not created the creepy night or made the breeze groan all around them. They had not made the shadows so deep or the lurking things in the ditches or behind the bushes. It was already a truly "terrible" night!

"Ain't no . . . *nobody* . . . gonna walk through the graveyard. Bet they'll all be too scared. Maybe they won't even make it to our place." Bobby looked all around, over his shoulder, and over his head as if maybe something was about to pounce.

"Ha!" Tommy waved his arm at the shadows. "Think about Fred Woods. He sure ain't gonna break your arm. He'll be sooooo scared!"

Bobby found little comfort in that thought. He could not even think clearly about the nine dollars in admission tickets they had earned, or the fact that his mama's stationery was all stolen. He did figure that now he had done every sin there was, except the bigger ones that he didn't know about yet. He had lied and stolen and lied some more. Then he had snuck out. And Mama hated sneaking!

"I don't like this," Bobby whispered, his voice barely audible above the wind. In the distance he could hear the uneven ringing of the school bell. "Who's ringin' the bell?"

"The wind." Tommy was losing his patience. "Who do you think? Just ringin' the bell. Ain't *nobody*. Just the wind."

There were already a few kids standing on the front step when Tommy and Bobby arrived. They huddled in a little knot and cast fearful glances upward at the school bell and the clouds and the trees that swayed against the purple sky.

Fred Woods and Barney Hocott came together, with little Othar trailing along behind.

"Creepy," said Barney. "From the time we climbed outta the window, I felt it."

"Can't prove to me there's a boogeyman," Fred said in an obstinate way, but his voice shook a bit.

In a spooky voice, Tommy said that it wasn't the wind ringing the bell but the ghosts of the dead moonshiners calling all the children of Shiloh to witness their doom!

His words and tone had a chilling effect on the little congregation. The girls squealed, and one even started blubbering that she did not want to meet her doom. Someone explained that they were going to see the doom of the moonshiners, and that calmed her enough so she could stand up again. But everyone, including Fred Woods, pressed in closer to one another. Those who were on the outside of the ring tried to get inside, shoving the ones who were inside back out again. The whole circle vibrated with panic.

Tommy looked around and winked at Bobby. Bobby knew what his brother was thinking. Thirty-four out of thirty-six were present and scared witless before one step had been taken from the schoolyard. P.T. Barnum could not have done better. The suckers were ready.

"Okay," Tommy said in a voice that made even the older children get goose bumps. "Y'all remember not to say nothin'! Not one word! Just keep quiet and keep in line. I'll take up the lead, and Bobby will come behind."

"What?" Bobby sputtered a protest. This was not part of the deal!

But it didn't matter. There was no end of the line. In fact, the group moved down the lane after Tommy like a human wheel. Arms linked, faces to the outside, they rotated slowly up the road on their way to

Shiloh Cemetery. Bobby just hooked up and joined the group. Sometimes he walked frontways, sometimes backward, but the links were unbroken.

"This is real good," Tommy said, as though he had planned it. "As long as we hold on to one another, ain't nobody gonna get us."

"How does he know such things?" piped Martha Milburn in a quaking yet respectful voice.

Bobby did not want to say that Tommy just made up everything as he went along. Nor did he explain that Tommy Tucker could blow louder than the wind when it came to telling stories.

Fred Woods answered, "Well, it just makes sense, don't it? If we don't let go . . . then if one of us gets it, the rest will, too!"

This sounded something like, *I won't die unless y'all do, too,* but most in the party found comfort in that explanation. In all of history, had an entire school vanished without explanation? No. The closest anyone had come to that sort of disaster was the story about a tornado hitting a school in Mobile. Bobby thought of the Pied Piper, but that was just a story. The real stuff about tornadoes and floods and such was much better.

By the time they rounded the corner and came upon Shiloh Church, everyone was offering up the most gory, horrible tales in turn. They had forgotten Tommy's warning to be quiet. Across the fields, the dogs of J.D. started barking, and Tommy reminded his followers they had to hush or meet the fate of the tornado victims.

Silence fell over the thirty-six. The wind howled louder as Tommy opened the gate to the graveyard. The stone monuments ahead made dark, monsterlike shapes.

"No! No! No! I won't go!" cried Sally-Anne Webb, who was only a second grader.

"Why did you bring her?" Fred asked her older brother, Jed.

" 'Cause she said she'd tell if I didn't," Jed answered resentfully.

Fred took charge. "You come, Sally-Anne, or we'll leave you here alone, and *they* will get you!"

"No! No! Don't leave me here alone! Please!" she wailed pitifully. "Don't let them get me!"

Her brother replied, "Okay. But shut up, Sally-Anne, or I'll smack you. I swear I will!"

Tommy said loudly, "If you don't come now and shut up, they'll get you anyway."

Nobody asked who *they* were.

And so the first step was taken into the graveyard. In daylight these stones displayed the names of grandmas and grandpas and uncles and brothers—all folks everyone knew. But at night, there never was a more dangerous, spook-filled walk than this.

The human circle stretched and elongated, moving around the stones like a glob of oil on water. Shins were struck against granite and small cries emitted. These were honorable wounds, proving great bravery. In future days they would be admired when this battle was recalled.

So far, so good. Bobby did not know how Tommy could be so brave. He seemed undisturbed as he led the way straight to the ages-old broken headstone of the cholera victims in their mass grave.

The group edged around, clutching and shivering and looking everywhere as Tommy told them terrible stories—stories of the moonshiners' battle against the federal agents and the rattle of machine guns and how they all fell on top of one another to be loaded like cordwood onto the dreadful bad-luck wagon. And now, forevermore, they went looking for that wagon each year on this night because this was the anniversary of their death. . . .

They were ready, Bobby knew. Two bits a ticket was a cheap price to pay compared to the sheer terror that rippled through the group. Even boys were sniveling now.

Tommy drew himself up cheerfully. "Well? If you want to see them, we got to get to the barn before the witching hour!"

"Ooooooh!" the crowd said in unison, then shuffled back out the gate and fearfully walked toward the Tucker farm.

This was the truth of it. Even Bobby was believing it. His eyes were bugged out. He was listening to Tommy as if every word were gospel. Like the rest of the troop, his heart was bumping away in his chest at twice the normal speed. He did not remember that they had spent all afternoon stuffing straw into Pa's and Jeff's stolen overalls and shirts. He could not recall how hard it had been to hang up the stuffed dummy from the rafters because the head kept popping off. All of this had vanished from his mind as if the wind had blown in one ear and out the other, taking with it his last scrap of sanity. He tried to think of red puppies and broken arms and Mama with a willow switch. Nothing seemed so terrible as the thought of going into his own barn!

But there it was. Up on the ridge. Across the yard from the still, dark house. The lights in Lily's room were out. Down the way Jeff's little shack was silent. The swing on the hickory tree rocked and spun as if some invisible child were playing on it.

Bobby tried to swallow, but he didn't have any spit. Here and there in the circle somebody moaned unhappily.

Then Tommy started in with his most creepy voice. "Lookit there," he whispered. "The barn door is part open. Bet they're already in there. What do you think, Bobby?"

Bobby was supposed to say he'd run ahead and look. He was supposed to pretend that he vanished—and then he was supposed to hide in the loft and make spook noises. That was the way it had been planned.

"Tommy . . . ," he gasped.

"Go on ahead, Bobby. You go spy it out for us and come back and tell."

"I ain't goin'!" Bobby cried, hanging on tighter to little Othar Hocott.

"Get goin'!" Tommy said firmly.

"If you want to see them boogeymen, you go look yourself! I ain't goin' in there alone. You can kill me dead here in the road. Break my arm. Tell Mama I stole Dad's dungarees, but I ain't goin' in there and that's that!"

Silence. A collective shudder coursed through the crowd. If Bobby, who lived here and owned the bad-luck wagon, was so scared, maybe this was worse than they had imagined. Maybe nobody wanted to go in the barn tonight.

Tommy cleared his throat. "What are you? Chicken?"

"Yes. And I ain't ashamed of it neither," Bobby fired back. "I told you to do this in daylight, but you wouldn't listen."

"I don't want to go in neither," said Othar.

"Me neither," added Martha.

"Me too!" agreed Sally-Anne.

Tommy drew himself up and looked to the bigger members of the assembly for help. "Well then, you little cowards, stay on out. We big'uns will go and see."

But the big'uns hung back, too. "I dunno," said Fred. "You think we oughta?"

"No refunds," Tommy insisted. "You don't go in there, don't come cryin' for your money back."

This thought had the effect of loosening the roots of the fear that held them fast in the lane. One by one boys and girls took a breath or two and squared their shoulders. The young'uns held back at first, but when the wheel began to move slowly toward the barn, they had to go along or be left behind.

The tall black opening to the barn yawned like a cavern before them. Tommy slipped ahead and opened the doors wide. He took the lantern from its nail and bent low to light the match against the wind. The match flared and then puffed out. He tried again. Again the light illuminated his face and blew out. Cupping his hand, he shielded the third match and the lantern beamed brightly. He was going to have to do this without the benefit of Bobby wailing ghost noises in the loft, but the wind was picking up and doing a fairly good job as far as noise was concerned.

The lantern eased some minds, but others squeezed their eyes shut and told their companions to tell them when it was all done.

"Come on," Tommy said in his worst voice.

He stepped over the threshold of the barn door. The milk cow bellowed in a friendly way, making the more nervous members of the audience jump in fear. The mules snorted indignantly that humans were interrupting their sleep. It was the same as any barn. . . .

Then Tommy raised the lantern.

Light fell on the bright green enamel and illuminated the fancy block letters: *FAMOUS*.

So there it was. Above it hung a body swinging with the waft of wind seeping through the cracks. The rope creaked eerily with a steady rhythm. Never mind that the straw that hung out of the sleeves. Never mind that a stuffed head lay on the ground beneath it. It was well worth two bits.

In a hushed voice, Tommy explained how also, on this very night, the first owner had hanged himself from the rafters above the wagon. No doubt he would also fly in with the disembodied moonshiners.

"Come in closer." Tommy wagged the lantern toward the wagon. "Wait till you see this . . ."

Clutching, clinging, giggling, and weeping, the group crowded nearer to the back wheel of the wagon. Tommy removed a canvas tarp, revealing what looked like a whole jumble of legs, like cordwood stacked in the bed of the bad-luck wagon.

"And they hauled them to the mortur-eery just like this."

As he held the lantern higher, the heap of stuffed denims did indeed look real. Very real. Too very real . . .

Suddenly the legs began to move. Above them came the low undulating wail of some dreadful ghost! A hand wriggled up from the mound in the wagon bed, and a low, dreadful voice said, "WHY THEY KILLLLL ME? I AIN'T DONE NOTHIN'!"

The wail in the hayloft grew louder. Boys and girls shrieked and clawed one another on the way out. Tommy screamed louder than anyone, knocking Bobby down as the thing in the wagon jumped out and snatched up the stuffed straw head on the barn floor.

"WHY Y'ALL COME 'ROUND HERE?" The Thing towered over them. "Y'ALL SNEAKIN'! SINNIN'! GONNA END UP LIKE ME!"

Like a herd of cattle stampeding across the screen at the Saturday matinee, the audience tumbled out of the barn and ran screaming down the lane.

Tommy and Bobby fell, crawled, then ran onto the front porch as the giant Thing came out of the barn. It had no head on its shoulders! It turned toward the porch and tossed the straw-stuffed head into the air like a pitcher winding up.

"Let us in! Ohhh! Mama! Let us in! We stole your writin' paper! We sneaked off! Let us in!" Tommy and Bobby screamed.

At that moment, the giant Thing let the stuffed head fly across the yard with a mighty thrust. It bounced once on the top step before hitting the back of Tommy's legs with a thud.

By the time Trudy and Birch opened the door, the Thing had vanished. But the distant screams of the well-satisfied crowds were still plainly heard across the fields of Shiloh.

☆ ☆ ☆

Around the community of Shiloh, there were several qualities that might be considered admirable in a person. A man might be respected for his ability to judge a good horse or train a fine team of mules. A woman might be complimented on her skill in making flaky pie crust or on the manners of her children or her works of Christian charity. The list of fine character traits was as long and detailed as the book of Proverbs and as varied in combination as the folks who lived in Shiloh. But there was one characteristic that was at the top of everyone's admiration list: a sense of humor.

Nothing in Shiloh was admired so much as the ability to pull off a really great practical joke. Therefore, on this bright Lord's Day morning, men and women of every size, shape, and age listened with respect as their still-frazzled young'uns recited the details of their encounter with the FAMOUS wagon in the Tuckers' barn.

"Them Tuckers always did have the best minds when it come to scarin' the bejeebers out of a person!"

Such comments evoked a hundred different recollections of pranks pulled by Tuckers spanning three generations. Ancient tales were resurrected, reinterpreted, and repeated as though they had just occurred. And each of last night's victims had a different story to tell about the same event.

"Then I fell in the ditch and Fred started hollerin' so . . ."

"Sally-Anne lost her shoe in the cow plop, and . . ."

"Little Othar climbed up that ol' hickory tree like a bear was chasin' him to . . ."

Each tale was both hair-raising and hilarious. Except for a few nicks and scrapes and bruises and a lot of terror, no real harm was done. All in all, the folks of Shiloh concluded that those Tucker folks were among the most admirable bunch around. Yessir, a body would have to go some to top that FAMOUS wagon prank!

The fact that the prank had backfired on Tommy and Bobby made it just that much harder for Birch to do what had to be done. But there was the matter of the stolen writing paper and the missing overalls. The fact that Jefferson had been waiting for them in the back of the wagon and Lily had been howling in the loft while Birch and Trudy watched gleefully behind a locked door made no difference.

"Fetch me a willow switch, you two," Birch said solemnly before breakfast.

While Tommy and Bobby hung their heads and traipsed down to the creek to cut their switches, Trudy, Birch, Lily, and Jeff hooted and repeated the details of the mad scramble of the mob to escape. They were wiping their eyes and holding their aching sides by the time the boys glumly returned. Keeping a lid on their laughter, the adults did their best to appear dour and disapproving of the prank.

"Into the barn, boys." Birch sighed heavily as though he were terribly disappointed in his sons. They had promised to make good on the missing stationery out of their profits, but duty demanded that they must also pay with a bit of their hides as well. So out they marched like condemned soldiers to the expected and necessary walloping.

Trudy whispered to Birch as they passed her, "Go easy." She did not need to say that, of course. There would be just enough sting in the willow switch so they would remember the list of thou-shalt-nots they had broken.

Later that morning, the boys sat humbly—and tenderly—on the hard pews of Shiloh Church while members of the congregation grinned and winked at Trudy and Birch when the children were not looking. Preacher Adams preached about the dangers of hellfire and the curse of demon booze. The young'uns all sat solemnly nodding with the apparition of the night before burning fresh in their minds. But all the while, the adults nudged and poked and sent one another jolly signals from pew to pew.

It was a strange and wonderful morning. When it was over, Birch and Trudy had received no less than five invitations to attend the radio broadcast commemorating Thomas Edison's invention of the electric light. This glorious invention had not reached as far as Shiloh yet, but it was, as Trudy said, "the thought that counts."

CHAPTER THIRTY-FOUR

Between Light and Darkness

On the evening of Monday, October 21, billed around the world as the Fiftieth Anniversary of Light, the night sky over New York City was alive with artificial rays. The sweep of searchlight beams twirled along the canyons of Wall Street and played hide-and-seek through the forests of Manhattan.

Fifth Avenue was illuminated with special golden electric globes in honor of Edison and the magic he had brought to the world that drove back darkness. Broadway from Thirty-fourth Street to Columbus Circle was bathed in the golden glow. To prevent any visitor from failing to understand what it was all about, a huge sign had been erected at Broadway and Forty-third. It proclaimed LIGHT'S GOLDEN JUBILEE: 1879–1929.

One hundred thirty radio transmitters made certain that everyone in the United States could be part of the historic reenactment of Edison's invention. Listeners were treated to speeches by President Hoover from the ceremony in Dearborn, Michigan. Congratulatory messages to Edison came from Albert Einstein in Berlin, Germany, and Admiral Byrd in Antarctica.

Breaks in the action were filled with music. Henry Ford's orchestra performed "Oh, Susannah!" an Edison favorite. The band at the Hotel Astor rendered "The Miracle Man," George M. Cohan's latest, as a musical offering to lay at Edison's feet. Obediently following instructions, millions of Americans switched off their lights to relive the drama of the first successful electric bulb.

The lights were off in Damon Phelps's room in the Plaza Hotel, and the RCA Victor radio was faithfully reporting the Michigan ceremony. But Phelps was one of the few Americans not paying attention.

Phelps lay in the darkness of his room, reviewing his experiences in the stock market. Six months before, the market had been a sure thing. Fifty thousand dollars of bank money, "redirected" into stocks, had seemed easy to parlay into a hundred thousand.

But ever since the market had broken on the word of that stupid economics professor, it had no longer seemed so certain. Now all his gains, and more besides, were sunk into the Sabre Oil pool.

Today the market had faltered again. Six million shares had been traded. Pieces of paper representing ownership in nine hundred twenty different companies had changed hands. It was the greatest variety of companies ever to trade on a single day, and almost all of them for lower prices than last week.

Sabre Oil dropped two dollars. Not a huge loss, but it was supposed to go *up!* Despite all the buying by the pool and favorable stories by newspaper shills in the *World* and the *Globe*, the price had dropped!

Hurried phone conferences with Keenan had reassured each conspirator. "Nothing to worry about," Keenan had said. "Sabre stock is still trading higher than what we paid at first. The pool has enough to buy even more shares . . . drive the price up faster."

And what about Meyer? Where was his article? "Not yet" had been the word. "We don't want to waste our big gun and clutter it up with the others. Timing is everything, and it will make even more sense if he recommends buying Sabre after this technical correction. Just wait and see."

Wait and see?! Phelps tossed and rolled on the bed. The glare of a giant searchlight probed into his window, reminding him uncomfortably of the guard-tower lights outside the Oklahoma state prison.

✳ ✳ ✳

All the world was tuning in to the NBC radio broadcast celebrating Light's Golden Jubilee. Certainly all of New York had gotten into the spirit of the anniversary.

Max had declined Edith's invitation to the Candlelight Ball being held at the Ritz. He lied and told her he had work to do. Somehow she'd known he was lying and hung up on him, only to phone again a minute later to try again. *"You know what they say about all work and no play. . . ."*

It seemed to Max that Edith Rutger had made his playtime her own personal crusade. But he was not up for the charade tonight. Not up for the music or the shrill laughter of Manhattan socialites or optimistic conversation about the market from wealthy bankers who spent their lives cultivating the illusion of the American Dream.

Max left work early, walking across the city until finally he found his path headed for the Brooklyn Bridge. Traffic throbbed across the span as people rushed home to tune in their radios. At the far end of Max's bridge was Brooklyn, vast and seemingly impersonal from where he stood. With thousands of dwellings all hooked together by telephone wire, Brooklyn was the place people left at daybreak and returned simply to listen to their radios and sleep. This afternoon there seemed to be more traffic than usual, all moving impatiently toward identical houses to spend their evening in identical pastimes. Was this the *goldeneh medina*? the promised land?

Max turned his back on Brooklyn and looked back toward the rising heights of Manhattan. His world . . .

It had taken him months to understand the diffused grandeur of London and weeks to comprehend the city of Paris. But here in the middle of the Brooklyn Bridge, Max could understand all of New York in less than a minute. He peered up at the web of cables, rods, and girders that crisscrossed the sky above the bridge. Then he looked long and hard at the city he had once loved above all other cities in the world. The buildings seemed to batter the sky. There was no place to go but up or down in New York. The measure of life in this great Babylon was taken by the pulse of the rise and fall of money.

Had Max ever noticed before that every main street ended in a dead end at the water's edge? Up. Down. Dead end. That was all the city of his dreams meant to him now. And so he stood on the bridge above the water. He remembered standing here with Irene when all his dreams were fresh and new and tangible. He'd never thought about dead ends then. He'd never thought about the downside of up.

He'd never thought he would lose the only woman he had ever loved. That she would disappear, along with his unborn child, and leave a void so large in his heart. If only he had known that one day he would stand here in the wind and look at his city and curse it for hiding his son from him!

Max pounded his fist against the steel railing and shouted into the winds, "Where are you, David? Where?"

The moon was a sliver hung above the distant lights of the great city. On this last run out to the *China Doll*, David sat on a coil of rope and looked back at the place that his mother, Irene, and his father, Max, had once called home. All the time he had been in New York, David had still never walked across the Brooklyn Bridge or eaten a Nathan's Famous hot dog on Coney Island. And now he never would.

"Hey, Mice," Gus called over the rumble of the motor. "Vat you think? Ve goin' vere the veather's so varm that we don't have to vear no coat, even in the vinter!"

"Ve goin' to Havana!" exulted Olaf. "Vat you think of such a thing, Mice? You can go swimming anytime! That vater is so clear you can see the fishes you is swimming vith."

"You go swimming with me, Gus? Olaf?" David asked. He knew their reply before they spoke.

"Ve don't knows how to swim! You *knows* this! Ve don't like swimming. Fishermens is to fish, not to swim with the icebergs!"

"I'll teach you both," David promised. "Me and Codfish will teach you how. Like taking a bath."

This drew a big laugh. "Ve don't take no baths neither!"

From the time Gus and Olaf had heard they were being sent to Havana, they had not ceased trying to cheer David up. They spoke of the warm, clear waters, the white sand of Cuban beaches. The sun, the stars, the Latin music. It would be paradise all year round. They would teach him to fish for really big fish, and he would never want to come back to the cold North American coast again.

If going to Cuba had not meant the end of all David's dreams, it might have been a wonderful adventure to look forward to. But he had not run away from Mrs. Crowley and Father John to go to Cuba. New York was where he wanted to be. The place of his mother's stories. The great city where the man named Max Meyer lived and worked without ever once imagining that he had a son.

"How far is Yurp?" David asked.

"Very far avay."

"Very long vay."

"Is it farther than Cuba?"

"It is vere ve come from. Too far to go back to. And very cold place. Lots cold. Turn your nose blue ven you been out fishing in the vinter!"

"Why don't we go there?" David asked, thinking of Max. If Max was in Yurp, how would David ever find him? David did not want to go to Cuba, no matter how warm and clear the waters were.

"Ve don't make no monies there, Mice. Ve just too poor and hungry, too. Someday ve will be plenty rich rumrunners, and then ve going back. Ve vill take you with us, too."

So there it was . . . *someday.* Someday David would go back to Yurp with the Svenson brothers and maybe then he would find his father.

What was the use of staying in New York now? It was just a big, empty, lonely place. Max had skipped.

Besides, the Boss had looked at David as if he were a bug to be stepped on. Then there was that little matter of Joey the Book washing up on the Coney Island beach. Such an event was sure to make a boy's appetite for a Nathan's hot dog disappear in a hurry. And as for the Brooklyn Bridge? He would not like to walk up there alone just now, not knowing what he knew about poor Joey and Boss Quinn. *One little push, and . . .*

Such thoughts made him tremble more than the bleak, cold north wind. These were all reasons enough to leave New York City and never look back.

So why was David looking back? Why did he stare at the grid of the Manhattan lights and wonder? Why did he think about his real father as if he had always known him?

"So vat you think, Mice? Ve going to have a high time, ja? Such a high time, I think!"

"Sure," David replied, although his heart was heavy. "It will be swell, Gus."

✳ ✳ ✳

Dressed in their Sunday best, Birch, Trudy, Bobby, and Tommy had ridden toward Hartford in the FAMOUS wagon to attend the Fiftieth Year Electric Light Celebration at Winters' Drugstore and Soda Fountain.

Lily stayed in the house to watch baby Joe, who had come down with a sniffle. Jeff was up in the barn, keeping a close watch on the spring heifer that was most certainly going to calve tonight.

Jefferson had noticed the gleam in Trudy's eye when she told Jefferson to be sure and eat up at the house. "Lily is such a good cook," she had told him. "Baked an apple pie for me to take to the party tonight, and an extra one for you . . ."

Well now, Jefferson Canfield was certainly fond of apple pie, but he was not interested in the dish Miz Trudy had been trying to get him to sample since Lily had come to the place. He was not looking for a wife. The very thought of such a thing seemed like blasphemy to Latisha's memory. No matter how pretty a gal Lily might be, no matter how good she cooked, no matter how nice she sang when she didn't know he was listening, and no matter how she loved the Lord . . . *no sir!*

Jefferson stayed in the barn, bedded down in the hayloft even though suppertime came and went and the heifer seemed no closer to having that calf. He was no fool. Lily was a beautiful woman. A man would have to be stone blind not to notice that fact.

But Jefferson did not want to notice, did not want to awaken the ache of desire that he felt only in his dreams of Latisha. Not even Latisha's death had separated his heart from hers. If death could not part him from her, Jeff certainly did not want another woman to draw his thoughts away.

The smell of fried chicken wafted into the barn, announcing that Lily was bringing supper to him.

"Jeff Canfield?" She glanced at the heifer that was contentedly chewing her cud. "How come you don't come on in to eat? This heifer don't look no more ready to drop her baby than I am."

He did not look at Lily directly, although he looked down from the loft at the heifer. "It's her first time for calvin'. Don't figure it be wise to leave her alone at such a time."

Lily snorted. "If she could talk, that heifer would say, 'What that fool man doin' up there in the hayloft for? Ain't nothin' happenin' now.' " She held up a covered tray. "Come on down and get your vittles. I'm in no shape to climb up that ladder and bring this to you, man." She patted her stomach. "In case you ain't noticed, me and that heifer got somethin' in common."

"I noticed all right," he mumbled.

"Well, get on down here," Lily ordered. Apparently Jeff did not move quick enough to suit her. "Miz Trudy told me I'm supposed to take care of you. She says you sometimes take to dreamin' and your mind wanders and you just don't eat nothin' a'tall. Not enough to keep a little bitty bird alive, she says." Lily scowled up at him as he picked his way down the ladder. "I made buttermilk biscuits, but when you didn't come when I called, they got cool."

"I don't need special attention," he said with his back to her as he stepped down. "I've had lots worse than cool biscuits in my time, an' been grateful for it."

"Well, you don't need cold biscuits no more, Jeff Canfield. Not unless you just got used to sufferin' so much that you come to like it now."

Her remark stung him. He whirled around. "I reckon you don't know much about sufferin' if you think that."

"I know enough. A person gets to thinkin' maybe she don't deserve to be happy nohow, so what's the use tryin'? She gets to thinkin' maybe there ain't no joy left in livin', so maybe she's better off dyin'." She raised her chin defiantly. "But Miz Trudy say to me, I got this child to live for. I got to bring my mind around to livin' and doin' right by myself so's I can bring up this here baby and give it a life."

She put a hand on her stomach and smiled. "There now, you see? Baby done agreed with me. He's kickin' somethin' fierce!"

Jefferson forgot the heifer and the food and the fact that Lily was good to look at. He gazed in fascination at the obvious movement of the bulge that poked out of Lily's coat. For an instant he moved his hand as if to touch the baby, as he had done in his dream about Latisha. Then he caught himself and put his hands behind his back.

"That Miz Trudy . . . she is good with young'uns." He changed the subject and lifted the napkin to peek at his heaping plate. "Hmmm. Looks good."

"It is good, too. And it would be better if'n you'd quit dreamin' and eat it while it's hot." She motioned for him to sit on a feed sack. "Sit down. I'll keep y'all company awhile, you and that cow yonder. Baby's sound asleep." She looked toward the window of his bedroom. "You ain't said three words to me, Jeff Canfield, since we skeert them young'uns here in the barn. I was wonderin' if I done somethin' or . . ."

He did not look at her as he took a big bite of the chicken. From the corner of his eye he could see that the light of the lantern was all around her and behind her like a halo.

"Mighty good," he said, licking his fingers. And it was good. She was a good cook. Just because she was tempting to look at did not mean he should neglect such a meal. "Good as my mama makes." Another bite. "Miz Trudy's a good woman, but she don't know much about fryin' a chicken."

Jeff was looking right at Lily's belly as he talked and ate. Right at that baby, wondering if it was a boy or a girl. After a time he told Lily all about his sisters and his folks and some about Tisha. Then she told him about William and how he was buried not far from here and how she had come back to die at his grave.

"Then it come to me. Just like Miz Trudy says, there's the child to think about, Jeff. He needs to be raised up in the image of his . . ." Her voice trailed away at the strange look on Jefferson's face.

"I heard them words." He frowned and laid his napkin on the empty plate.

"What?"

" 'There's the child to think about, Jeff.' She said that . . . just so."

"What you sayin'?"

He sat in silence and remembered the dream. "Just . . . I heard someone say them words to me before."

"Which words?"

" 'Bout the child. It didn't make no kinda sense to me. Just broke my heart. I been ponderin' on it a long time. Tried to forget about it because it's never gonna be. Not for me, y'see?"

Lily tucked her chin and raised her eyebrows. "You talkin' like you been out in the sun too long. Only there ain't no sun." She laughed. "You ate your supper all up, though. That's good." She gathered the supper things up to go. "I needs to get on back now."

Jeff put his hand on her arm to stop her. "Please . . . one thing."

"What you want now?" she chided.

"I don't mean to be forward. . . ." His hand stayed on her arm, his eyes on the bulge. He reached out and touched the baby, who kicked obligingly beneath Jefferson's palm. A wistful look spread across the battered features of the big man. Lily did not move. This was between Jefferson and the baby somehow.

"Thank you kindly," he whispered. "I know it don't make no sense to you. But it was a dream I had. I been livin' on dreams for ten years. I just wanted to know somethin' is left that ain't a dream."

Lily nodded as he withdrew his hands. She touched his head as he sat there in front of her. A sort of blessing, the touch was. Then she went back to the house and left him to his dream.

Trudy only glanced at the headlines about Wall Street's unsteady day. Except for the fact that Max was somewhere in all that, she gave the matter little thought. Tonight other things were happening.

There was a sense of belonging that Trudy had never felt anywhere else before. All the congregation of Shiloh Church had traveled into Hartford for the celebration. They and dozens of other farmers from the outlying communities gathered together in Winters' Drugstore and Soda Fountain for their own version of what was a worldwide celebration tonight. Every electric light in Hartford and across all of America had been doused in honor of the occasion. The crowd sat huddled together in the darkness and contemplated what the whole world had been like fifty years ago, before the marvelous invention of Thomas Edison's incandescent lightbulb.

Mr. Winters had hauled his enormous Majestic radio down to the store, and now it boomed out the voice of the NBC commentator as he reported the scene live from Greenfield Village in Dearborn, Michigan.

> *"From the upper windows I can see Mister Edison approaching in an old-fashioned horse-drawn carriage. The streets are laid out here just as they were in the old Menlo Park days. Let me give you the setting for this unique reenactment of half a century ago. Here is the laboratory where the first incandescent lamp was born. . . ."*

Even though electricity had not yet reached Shiloh, the farm families nevertheless huddled together in the drugstore, in awe at the drama unfolding over the radio.

"Below me, on the first floor, is the old office. . . . Just a word about the stairs, ladies and gentlemen. This afternoon I noticed a little cubbyhole leading under them, and I am told that this little dark recess was one of Mister Edison's favorite spots when he found it necessary to take a nap."

Such a personal revelation about the famous inventor was greeted by murmurs of amusement from the little congregation. Who ever thought that famous inventors took naps beneath stairs?

"Here comes Mister Edison, followed by President Hoover and the rest of the party. . . . Can you imagine how this grand old man must feel as he is carried back half a century to the moment of his great triumph?"

Trudy leaned her head against Birch's shoulder in the darkness and smiled as he brushed her cheek and kissed her forehead. Then he whispered, "You make all the electricity I'll ever need."

She remembered the night he had first kissed her at the Fort Smith Electric Park. "That may be all you'll ever get in Shiloh."

"It's enough," he murmured in her ear as the radio blared on about the miracles of the new modern age that still left Shiloh untouched, undisturbed, and perfect in the candlelight.

✶ ✶ ✶

The heavens seemed almost solid with the mass of stars blending together to make the Milky Way. The pitch-black water of the Atlantic seemed as though it did not exist. The *Jazz Baby* floated, suspended on nothing at all between the lights of New York's electric jubilee and the lights of Rum Row and all those millions of stars.

All around, David could hear the hum and rattle of other shore boats moving out to their mother ships, but in this darkness he could not make out shapes or sizes of the crafts. Were they picketboats? Coast Guard? rumrunners? pirates?

Fifty yards ahead a light blinked once, sweeping across the bow of the *Jazz Baby*. The trawler's hold was empty still. There was no reason to fear the patrols or the hijackers. Neither was interested in capturing a rumrunner until the hold was stuffed with bootleg hooch and on the way back to shore.

With this in mind, Gus slowed as the signal light blinked the code for distress. "Is one of our boats, I think," he said.

Olaf returned the signal, which was known only to sister ships of the Boss's crews. Yes. There was a small shore craft dead in the water ahead.

"Ahoy! Is that *Jazz Baby*?" boomed the voice of Jumbo.

"Aye," Olaf returned. "Dat is the *Lollypop*."

"We're dead in the water! Lost our motor. Can you give us a tow to the *China Doll*?"

The *Jazz Baby* moved to the port side as if guided by the voice of Jumbo. Smelling his old enemy in the air, Codfish began a steady, ferocious growl in the bow.

"Mice!" ordered Olaf. "Get Codfish avay from Jumbo. He gonna take Jumbo's face off if Jumbo don't shoot him first. Hold him behind the cabin out of sight and keep him quiet, vill you?"

Codfish was trained to set up a racket at the sign of any potential intruder on the sea. But the dog had a genuine hatred for Jumbo and his fellow crew member Billy Black. Given the slightest provocation, there was little doubt that Codfish would happily bite Jumbo's arm off the minute the reeking seaman reached out to take the towrope.

David sat beside the enormous black animal, with his back to the cabin. The *Jazz Baby* came alongside the *Lollypop*. David hooked his hand in the big dog's collar and whispered to him in soothing tones while conversation between the two boats passed back and forth and the engines of the *Jazz Baby* idled noisily.

"Vat the matter is?"

"Water in the fuel, I think. She died out here an hour ago and we been hopin' you was in our course. Mind if we come aboard?"

The *Lollypop* bumped against *Jazz Baby*. David felt the trawler bob as Jumbo and Billy Black stepped aboard.

"Where is that hell-dog of yours?" asked Billy.

Olaf laughed. "You be better off up here."

Moments passed as Jumbo and Billy climbed to the flybridge. When the *Jazz Baby* moved forward again, Jumbo's tone changed. His words were almost drowned in the rumble of the engine. Then the *Jazz Baby* was thrown into neutral again.

Codfish sat on his haunches and whined once. David jerked on his collar, holding him in place.

"Where is the kid?"

"He ain't here." Olaf's voice sounded frightened, angry. "Vat you doing, Jumbo? Ve gots no cargo! You don't vant the *Jazz Baby*. Ve gots no cargo, I tell you!"

What was this? A hijacking? A hijacking of an empty vessel on the way out to Rum Row? What was the point? Why were they doing this?

"You gots the wrong fellows!" Gus cried. "Put that away! I tell you, ve gots no cargo!"

"Where is the boy?" Jumbo shouted. "Boss wants that little beggar in concrete overshoes!"

"Mice? Vat you saying? Boss wants Mice? He's just a kid! He don't do nothing! Vat you saying, Jumbo? You gone crazy?"

"It ain't me," Jumbo replied. "It's straight from the Boss. He knows *everythin'*, see. He's got it all figured out that you Svenson brothers were tight with Joey the Book."

"Joey? Vat ve got to do vith Joey the Book?" Gus was incredulous.

"Yeah." Jumbo laughed. "He's got it in his head that you and Joey was hijackin'. And so, the Boss wants you dead. See? That is all. He don't like it when citizens is stealin' from him. He wants *you* dead *and* the kid! And . . . where's that dog? Where is the kid?"

"They back at the varf. Ve did not bring them with us tonight. Please, put this avay. Ve ain't done nothing! Ve is going to Cuba! Jumbo! Ve needs to talk with the Boss! Ve needs to tell him ve ain't been stealing nothing! Ve don't know *nothing* about Joey the Book!"

"Yeah? Dumb Swede. You don't know that the Boss gave it to him in the neck? You don't know that the little wharf rat of a kid you picked up was spyin' all the time in the washroom of the warehouse? You don't know none of that, huh?" Jumbo laughed cruelly. "And I guess you ain't figured out that we did not come on here to steal your cargo. We aim to kill *you*. Nothin' less."

"No! Jumbo! Billy Black!"

Two shots rang out.

Something warm and wet fell like heavy raindrops from the bridge onto David's face.

Blood.

David buried his face in the hide of Codfish, who bristled and gave a low growl—as if he would tear out the throat of anyone who came around this side of the boat.

David's heart was pounding like the cylinders of the old motors. "No, Codfish," he managed to beg.

"Let's give this tub a good search before we burn her," called Jumbo. "Dump a little gas on their bodies. These are two who won't be spillin' their guts to the coppers. Check below. I can smell that dog . . . and the kid."

The clop of heavy boots sounded loudly as Jumbo shut down both engines of the *Jazz Baby*. Panicked, David pressed himself hard against the cabin of the boat and held Codfish's collar with a strangling fierceness.

"Nothin' down there!" shouted Billy Black. "Check the bow."

Where to go? How to escape? The smell of freshly spilled gasoline permeated the air. David could hear the sloshing of fuel cans as the *Jazz Baby* was saturated with the stuff. It poured over the side of the bridge, splashing David and the heavy coat of Codfish. It stung David's skin and burned his eyes.

"It don't matter if we find him or not." Billy Black kicked over a crate of fresh fruit that had been bound for the *China Doll*. "He ain't under here."

Jumbo cursed. "Little wharf rat. Ever seen what happens when a warehouse takes to burnin' down? The rats run out first; that's what happens."

"As for me, I don't fancy killin' no kid. These dumb Swedes don't mean nothin' to me. But I don't fancy shootin' no kid."

Jumbo chuckled. "Well then, Billy Black, just strike a match, and we'll *burn* the kid, then. Do you fancy burnin' wharf rats?"

The *Jazz Baby* bobbed again as they stepped from her deck and cast off. The engine of the little shore boat buzzed awake. So they had gained their murderous objective through the old trick: *trust!*

Suddenly there was a rumble as flames exploded from the deck and the ocean around suddenly was bright and horrible. David leaped to his feet as *Lollypop* raced away. He looked up at the bridge, where the bodies of Olaf and Gus Svenson lay over the rail like burning rag dolls placed too close to the hearth. A liquid carpet of flame spread to the bow and rounded the cabin three yards from David.

He screamed in terror, then tumbled backward off the deck of the *Jazz Baby* as the massive body of Codfish slammed against him. Boy and animal hit the water at the instant flames consumed the place where they had stood. David gasped, his mouth filled with brine. The broad head of Codfish glided toward him through the water as David's saturated clothes pulled him under. The dog's strong jaws closed around his arm, pulling him up. Holding him up to draw a breath.

"Codfish is a good swimmer! That is the reason ve calls him Codfish!" Gus's words rang in David's head.

He sobbed in grief as he opened his eyes and caught one final glimpse of *Jazz Baby* and the dark shapes of his friends being devoured by the blaze.

Codfish's legs worked furiously, tugging David away from the sea-borne inferno.

"Codfish!" David cried in anguish. "They killed them! Oh, Codfish! Because of *me!* Let me go, Codfish!"

But the dog did not let go. He merely tightened his grip, to make it clear that he would not let go until they both sank together.

Far away, David heard the humming of motors. Had Jumbo and Billy Black returned to find the rats after they had been flushed out? Would they fire two more bullets into the water and put an end to the desperate struggle?

Like moths drawn to the flame, half a dozen boats circled and moved toward the *Jazz Baby*. The siren of a Coast Guard six-bitter shrieked, frightening the other rummy boats away as it zoomed toward the trawler.

A nasal twang called from a bullhorn. "Any survivors? Ahoy!"

Codfish barked, momentarily releasing David. One more frantic yip, then he grabbed the boy by his collar once again.

"Cap'n! I think that there is a dog! A big black brute, he is! And he is towing a kid along!"

part three

If I ascend up into heaven,
Thou art there:
if I make my bed in hell, behold,
Thou art there.

PSALM 139:8

CHAPTER THIRTY-FIVE

The Windows Open

Shiloh school was canceled for the day since the teacher, Miss Price, had traveled to Fort Smith to have her wisdom teeth pulled. Her absence was celebrated with all the joy of Edison's Jubilee of Light.

The money jar was full to the top, even with the two dollars removed and sent off last week to Uncle Max in New York to buy Mama's writing paper. Tommy shook it loudly with every step they took along the rails of the Rock Island into Hartford. The coins made a chugging sound like a miniature locomotive, and every few steps Bobby cut loose with a loud "Whooooo! Whooooooo!" to add to the effect.

The red puppy would not be ready to take home today, of course, but the boys did not want there to be any mistake about who had bought her.

"Dad says get a bill of sale," Bobby reminded his brother as they scrambled down the berm to the gravel road as the real Rock Island sounded its whistle down the line. "He says tell Brother Williams to write that it's for the red girl puppy, and not for any other."

Tommy knew all this. He had repeated the instructions to Bobby a few miles back. He raised the jar and rattled the coins and gave a little dance in the track as the Hartford water tower loomed above the trees.

It was worth the willow switch. Worth the big scare. Worth the sweeping and the kindling chopping and the shucking of corn.

"We're gonna be rich," Tommy declared as they traipsed past the moving-picture theatre without a backward glance. There was not even the slightest temptation to go inside and waste a nickel on a movie. There was important business to attend to.

Fred Woods hollered from the back of his daddy's wagon, "How-do!"

A greeting from such a prominent bully as Fred Woods certainly meant that all the barriers of newness had been broken down.

"Where y'all goin'?" Fred's broad, ugly face was friendly.

"Goin' to pay for that little coonhound," Tommy replied. "You wanna come to see her?"

Well, of course Fred wanted to see her. He jumped off the wagon and soon enough was joined by half a dozen other boys from the Shiloh school who trailed along as witnesses to this magnificent event.

Brother Williams was in the barn, backside up as he worked on the engine of his old Model T. He cursed Henry Ford and spit tobacco juice and gave the chassis a kick before he noticed the group of boys all crowded together in the barn door.

Tommy shook the jar.

The sound of money lit the eyes of the crafty horse trader. He whirled around with a grin and rubbed his greasy hands together. "Well, how-do! How-do! You come visitin' or for business?"

From the back of the barn, Boomer hollered, "It's them Tucker boys, Brother Williams. Bet they come to look at that there red puppy." Boomer had a way of blurting out the obvious and denying Brother Williams the joy of friendly conversation.

"I can see that, Boomer," Brother Williams called impatiently. "I'll handle this, if you don't mind!"

Boomer replied, "But you said that red pup was the best and that you sure wished you ain't sold her for such a little bit and that you was gonna try and talk them out of—"

"Enough! Shut up! Babblin' fool!"

Tommy held the jar out. "We didn't just come to see her. We come to make a payment on her, Brother Williams. You and Dad shook on it. Twenty-two dollars and two bits. We got our half right here, and Dad says to get a bill of sale for that little red gal, and he'll pay his half when she's ready to be picked up."

Brother Williams scratched his chin thoughtfully and craned his neck as if his collar were too tight. Only he wasn't wearing a collar, just his long johns under his bib overalls.

Tommy could tell that he was irritated because Boomer had given away his entire plan about the red puppy. Now what was he supposed to say with half the boys in Hartford standing around as witnesses?

Brother Williams sniffed unhappily and mumbled something about how Boomer ought to be gagged or locked up. He squinted at the money jar. "How much you boys got in there?"

"Half. Eleven dollars and thirteen cents. One cent more than half, but Pa says he'll make up the extra penny to us."

"Well then—" Brother Williams shrugged—"get on back and look at her. Best puppy I ever see'd. Smart and pretty, too. I reckon I shook on it." A frown. "Even if you did make the cash off that FAMOUS Bad-Luck Wagon I sold y'all."

Behind the door of a stall Boomer laughed gleefully—such a creepy, nutty kind of laugh that Tommy decided if he ever put on another FAMOUS wagon show, he'd hire Boomer to laugh just like that.

"Yessir." Tommy thrust the jar toward him. "You wanna count it first?"

"No. I reckon you're as honest as your papa and mama." Brother Williams spit and grinned. "And fair businessmen too, I reckon."

Boomer could not resist. "Why, you was just cursin' that you sold that wagon 'stead of puttin' on a show yourself, Brother Williams."

The muscles in Brother Williams's cheek twitched as if Boomer's voice made the man's teeth hurt. "Will you shut up?"

"That's what you was sayin'," Boomer whined.

Brother Williams ran a hand over his face and grasped the jar, ignoring Boomer's comment. "Well, I got the money from the spook show all the same now, don't I?"

"Yessir," Tommy said.

"All right, then. Go look at that pup while I draw you up the bill of sale. But don't y'all go pickin' her up none. Emmaline don't take to havin' her pups picked up."

"Yessir," eight boys answered in unison before traipsing back to peer over the door of the stall at the fat round pups heaped in the straw beside their mama.

And there was the red one, sleeping in the center of her dark brothers. Her ears and legs were all tangled with other ears and legs. Her front paw twitched as if she was already dreaming about treeing coons.

"Ain't she beautiful?" Fred Wood whispered.

Little sighs of admiration rippled through the group.

"She'll need raisin' and trainin' before she's any good," Tommy said in a serious voice as he tried not to sound like he was too proud.

They all stood there looking at the sleeping puppies for a long time until Brother Williams called them to the front of the barn, where he kept an old rolltop desk as an office.

The witnesses crowded around as the terms were read aloud and then signed by Brother Williams and the boys and dated.

And so it was done. The red puppy was officially spoken for.

✳ ✳ ✳

The day in Hartford was perfect. Trudy had given the boys a nickel each to spend at Winters' Drugstore and Soda Fountain. They spread the bill of sale out on the soda counter and stared at it in silence as Mr. Winters made the foaming sodas. All the while, Mr. Winters was talking about the bad-luck wagon and how folks had heard about it as far away as Booneville by now.

The bell above the door jingled as someone entered. "You can sure tell these young'uns belong to my cousin Birch, now can't you, Mister Winters? Of course, I think they inherited their mama's business sense, though, if you know what I mean." It was J.D. He slid onto the stool beside Tommy and winked big at the druggist, who did not seem to like the comment J.D. made.

What did J.D. mean? Tommy wondered.

"Howdy," both Tommy and Bobby greeted J.D.

"What y'all up to? Walkin' so far into town without your mama or daddy? Come for a movie?"

"Nope." Tommy slid the bill of sale over so J.D. could see it. "We bought us a pup."

J.D. snorted. "From Williams? That crook. Them dogs ain't worth nothin'. He ought to be givin' 'em away."

Mr. Winters shot him a hard look and set the soda glasses down with a bang. "These boys are celebrating, J.D. They have a right. Why don't you go on now?"

J.D. put a protective arm around Tommy's shoulder. "Why, these boys is my kin. You think they don't want to sit and drink a soda with ol' J.D.?"

Winters shrugged and wiped the counter. Tommy wished that J.D. had gone away as Mr. Winters said.

"So you *paid* for one of them scraggy little mutts, huh?" J.D. dug in and slapped his nickel on the counter. "I'll have a strawberry soda, Mister Winters."

Again the eyes of the druggist flashed. He hesitated as though he wanted to say something but instead turned to make J.D. a soda.

"She ain't scraggy," Bobby shot back. "She's the best."

"Best of the runts, huh?" J.D. laughed. Then, "You tell your pa he ought to be hangin' on to every cent he's got instead of wastin' it on such a pitiful—"

"We earned the money." Tommy was angry now, and hurt. He could no longer taste the flavor of his soda. He wished J.D. would leave.

"Well, your ma and pa are likely to need every cent you paid for that runt, from what I'm hearin'." He was smiling, pleased at the power he wielded over the boys. It was as though he enjoyed smashing their hope with some hint of disaster.

At that moment, Mr. Winters knocked over the glass containing J.D.'s soda. He swiveled swiftly. "Well, that's it! J.D., you haven't come in here for a soda since you started making corn liquor up on Sugar Loaf. And you wouldn't know a good coon dog if one treed *you*. Only thing your hounds are good for is guarding that still of yours. And as for the Tucker family, I can't say I see they resemble any kin of yours. Has Birch Tucker ever asked who it was that fed his old pa booze? I'd say you best not pester these boys in *my* store, 'cause I got your number! I'll ask you nicely now to get on out. This is a good day. A *proud* day! I would have bought that red pup myself. She's the best of the lot anywhere in the country."

Mr. Winters slid two nickels back across the counter to the boys, who sat wide-eyed and dumbfounded. "I'm buying your sodas today, fellows," said the druggist firmly.

J.D. slammed the door of the store so hard the glass almost shattered.

✶ ✶ ✶

The new heifer calf was the color of a doe: soft tan with a black muzzle and large, trusting brown eyes.

"You done good." Jefferson patted the calf's mama and moved the milking stool. "My pappy set great store by a fine Jersey milk cow. He surely did. Although my mama used to say y'all were built too close to the ground for folks as big as her . . . and me." He put the bucket in place, squatted low, and began to milk. "She's right, too, Little Bess. But ain't no cow livin' that'll give the cream like you do! No, ma'am."

The *ting, ting, ting* of warm milk sounded a rhythm in the bucket.

"Got myself a dream someday." Jefferson's words became a melody as he sang to the little Jersey in the stanchion. "Gonna get a little milk cow . . . hmmm. . . . Gonna milk her night an' morn . . . serve up cream an' berries . . . sure as you're born. . . ."

The tiny calf watched him placidly, happy to share her supper with the big man. Jefferson winked at the baby. "My pappy says a man gots to sing an' talk while he's a'milkin'. That way the milk just get sweeter."

The calf blinked at him as if to agree.

"One day, little gal, you're gonna be just as sweet as your mama here. Feed young'uns for a song. . . . Bless the Lord, O my soul!" He sang again as though he could not keep the music in. "The Lord feed His chillens for a song! My, my! Sweet Lord give us milk an' honey! Gots no worries, gots no cares, livin' on milk an' honey, milk an' honey. . . ."

It was a good song. The sweet milk was plentiful, the pail full. Enough to take care of Birch and Trudy and the young'uns and Lily and Jefferson, and enough left over to share with the hogs. There would even be enough to feed that little red puppy when it finally arrived. And Lily's baby, too.

"Can't get no better'n this, Lord," Jefferson said. "Ever'thing a man could want . . . *ever'thing* . . . "

He turned to see Lily standing framed in the doorway of the barn, the light behind her like a halo, just as it had shone around her the other night.

"How-do," she said quietly. She was smiling as though she had heard everything, but she wasn't laughing at Jefferson. Just smiling as if she liked it all. "You always sing while you milks?"

Jefferson looked at the brimful pail. "Yes'm, I do." No apologies. "It works, too." A little milk sloshed onto the toe of his boot.

Lily nodded. "My mama swore by it. Critters like it when folks sing to 'em. Like it when folks pray and such, too. My mama used to say that critters can see things folks can't see, like angels. And when we praise the Lord, the angels come around, sit around the barn on feed bins and the haystacks just so they can hear. Then the critters see all them *bright things,* all shining in halos of light, and the critters like it! Makes the milk sweeter, Mama used to say. . . ."

Jefferson took a step toward her. The light around her was *so* bright! "My mama said the same thing. She said folks is blind. Blind souls, folks is. But when folks sing praises, the winders open up, and the light just comes on in."

"My mama liked singing."

"Mine too."

"Well then . . . ain't that somethin'?" Lily put a hand on her stomach. "I been singin' to this here baby, even though he's got a while 'fore he be born. My mama says babies is like the critters in that way . . . maybe they can see angels too, when folks sing."

"Reckon so," Jefferson agreed thoughtfully. He squinted at the light shining even more brightly around Lily. Was it just daylight coming through the barn door?

"Well then . . ." She was silent for a moment. "I almost forgot why I come down. Miz Trudy say she don't want you sleepin' down at the shed tonight, Jeff. She wants you up to the house, to sleep on the back porch." She gestured over her shoulder. "Miz Trudy says she *never* see'd a blacker sky! Them clouds come rollin' in! We in for a big storm, for sure. And—"

"The sun's shinin' . . . ain't it?"

"Why, man? What you sayin'? The sky's so heavy it's about to bust wide-open, that's all!"

Jefferson frowned and walked toward Lily. A storm brewing? Dark sky? But there was the light all around her, light pouring over her shoulders like gold! Beyond the light, one step outside the barn, the house and yard seemed locked in the shadow of an approaching storm.

Like the critters and like a newborn babe, Jefferson knew he was seeing . . . *something.*

"What you sayin' to me?" Jefferson was no longer talking to Lily. "I can't hear it."

"I *say,* Miz Trudy's frettin' about that roof of yours. She say she don't want you down there if it takes to hailin'. And the rain's gonna bust right through. . . ." Lily's words faltered as he walked to her and stopped near enough to touch her.

Jefferson stood quietly marveling at the light. He was afraid if he spoke it would leave. It wrapped all around Lily like a blanket, warm and peaceful. Didn't she see it? Couldn't she feel it?

"You all right, Jeff?" she asked. "What is it?"

"Surely *Solomon in all his glory was not arrayed like one of these,*" he whispered, remembering Christ's lily. "I reckon the Lord done put His hand on you, Lily."

Her eyes grew wistful, hopeful, at his tender words. "My mama always told me so."

"I reckon I seen you in a new light just now."

"How's that, Jeff?"

"I reckon the same Lord who watches sparrows an' clothes the lilies has led your footstep right here."

"I do believe so."

"Now He's sayin', *Pay attention!* Yessir. I'm listenin'. It ain't what I thought I'd ever be hearin' again, Lord. But I hear what You're sayin'! *Consider Lily . . .*"

Her eyes filled with wonder as she gazed up at him. "Why, Jeff!" she said in a startled voice. "The sun musta broke through! What's all that light behind you?"

Jefferson smiled down at her as the warmth washed over him. "I reckon the winders is opened up some, Lily," he whispered as he bent to kiss her softly.

CHAPTER THIRTY-SIX

A Voice from the Grave

Throwing the switch to rekindle Edison's magic bulb had seemed to put a spark back in Wall Street as well. After Monday's plunge, the market had recovered, if only modestly. Steel was up two dollars, Westinghouse six, and Sabre Oil about fifty cents.

On Wednesday, over six million shares had changed hands in what was the second-largest trading day ever. However, several blue-chip stocks had taken another beating: General Electric's price had dropped twenty dollars a share, and Westinghouse had fallen over twenty-five dollars. Sabre had remained unchanged, but others had gained. The shares of nine hundred sixty different companies were bought and sold. The foundations of the great bull market were shaken.

On Thursday, October 24, Max Meyer was in his usual place in the press section of the visitors' gallery above the floor of the Exchange. It was still fifteen minutes till the opening bell at ten o'clock, but he was studying the assembling players for clues as to what would happen today.

There were rumors of all kinds: President Hoover would act to stem the crisis of confidence; the Exchange would close; a shipment of gold was coming from investors in England. But the most wicked, in Max's opinion, appeared with the phrase "organized buying support." The financial writer was sure this slogan concealed an optimistic fairy tale. The minnows expected the wealthy bankers and brokers to ride to the rescue and support the market with a massive influx of cash.

"Hey, Harry," Max called to Harry Beadle, "what does 'organized buying support' mean?"

Harry looked surprised. "You are joking, right? Everyone knows that the National Bank and the House of Morgan are putting together a hundred million dollars of price supports."

Max sighed and returned to watching the brokers and traders. The next hour would tell the tale, one way or the other. Max could see Mike Keenan at Post One. The broker moved from assistant to assistant, giving instructions, like a commander readying his troops for battle.

The superintendent of the Exchange approached the rostrum and prepared to sound the gong that would open trading. Outside, as Max had entered the building, there had been an expectant hush over the crowds of investors standing silently, waiting to see what would happen. But unlike other days, there was no expectant hush inside the building. The buzz of noise was already loud, and although Max could see the precise moment that the bell was sounded, he never heard it chime. The roar of trading overwhelmed the gong like a tidal wave.

Max watched as the market opened with higher prices. National Foods increased fifty cents a share; Consolidated Copper was up eleven dollars, Sabre Oil higher by a dollar.

The optimism caused by bargain hunting lasted exactly twenty-five minutes. Then the bottom began to drop.

General Electric fell by another twenty-five dollars, Westinghouse another twenty. As Max watched, the stock ticker fell farther and farther behind. By ninety minutes into the trading day it was already running thirty minutes behind.

On the floor, all was panic and confusion. The specialists were prisoners inside their posts as waves of traders, four and five deep, assaulted them with orders. Mostly the confused babble made all conversation unintelligible, but occasionally a freakish coincidence would pile a dozen voices on top of each other. At such moments the visitors' gallery echoed with the shout "Sell at the market!" Nine hundred seventy-four stocks were traded—the third new record of the week.

At twelve o'clock, Exchange guards accompanied the superintendent into the press box. In polite but firm tones they announced that the gallery was being closed. The press would have to leave. Max knew why: on the trading floor, "no bid" responses were appearing. Brokers trying to sell at any price were finding no takers at all.

In the afternoon, a committee of New York banks stepped into the battle. Even though it was widely reported that their effort was intended to return the stock prices to the earlier high levels, their true intent was only to slow the market's slide. No part of the plan was aimed at saving the little investor, and if he or she chose to take the bankers' optimistic words at face value, well, so much the worse for them.

Max decided to fight for the little guy in the only way he could. He went back to his office and began pounding out a story. In it he attacked the false optimism being pushed by some brokers. He took particular aim at pools, using Sabre as an example. *If you are in the market,* he wrote, *get out now. Otherwise you may fall in a pool and drown.*

Already the disastrous trading day had been dubbed Black Thursday. But Wall Street had survived much worse than this. No doubt tomorrow would be better as long as optimism prevailed. . . .

"Absolutely not!"

The voice of Damon Phelps shrieked through the art-nouveau lobby of the Plaza Hotel. The desk clerk thought about mentioning the disturbance to the manager, Mr. Derby, but then he reflected that the shouted conversation was about stocks. These days, who could blame an investor for yelling at his stockbroker? After all, the desk clerk was slipping away every half hour to phone his own broker.

"No, I won't talk to you!" Phelps yelled at Riley. "Get me Keenan!"

The ears of the clerk perked up at the mention of Keenan's name. Everyone knew the Irish Wonder. The chief clerk shushed his assistant, telling the man to stop rustling the financial pages of the *New York Times*.

"Keenan!" Phelps screamed. "Are you crazy? Another million into that hellhole? What do you mean, we need to do our bit? The House of Morgan is placing orders right now for *how much*? Fifty million!"

Phelps's voice dropped abruptly. No matter how hard the clerks strained, they could not hear another word. But what they had heard was enough. They would hold on to their stock and confidently await the market rebound.

In the office of the First Petroleum Bank of Tulsa, Assistant Vice President Penner stared at the telephone in his hand and gestured with it toward the stock ticker. "What can Mister Phelps be thinking of?" the owlish little man groaned. He attempted to wring his hands and found himself wringing the receiver as well.

"What did he say exactly?" asked Tell.

Taking a deep breath, Penner forced himself to stop watching the ticker tape spewing its load of bad news onto the office floor. Of course, looking into Tell's cadaverous face was no better. "Mister Phelps says that we must wire him another million dollars at once. He said that organized buying support would carry the day and that now was the time to buy the full control of Sabre Oil."

"But the prices are all off so badly . . ." Tell's voice sounded like a whisper down a hall, the echo thrown back by an open sepulchre. It made Penner shudder.

"But he insists," the shorter man said. "He said to close all the savings accounts that have not been active for two months and send it all to him. Also, we are to make him a personal loan against Phelps Petroleum for half a million."

"We can't make that kind of loan!"

"He says Mister Keenan's banking connections will make it good," Penner wailed. He sounded close to tears.

"What about the notes and transfers we have been delaying?"

"We are to pay only if they come from another bank, like this one from First Omaha," Penner replied, waving a paper marked URGENT— THIRD REQUEST.

"And personal accounts, like, um, this Tucker fellow, whose bank has been pestering me from Arkansas?"

"Mister Phelps says to lose the records."

There was complete silence in Phelps' private office except for the steady clicking of the stock ticker.

At last a voice from the grave asked, "He said what?"

"That's right." Penner's voice sounded shrill. "He said to eliminate the records. We never heard of those out-of-state accounts at all."

CHAPTER THIRTY-SEVEN

The Minnow and the Sharks

Steam rose from the big washtub that boiled over the open fire behind the house. Lily, her hair done up in a red bandanna, hummed softly as she stirred the brew of sheets and Sunday shirts. She had told Trudy that she dearly loved doing the washing. Trudy had doubted her word for a while, but there was joy on Lily's face as she hung socks and bib overalls and underthings on the line. Perhaps the chore of laundry was a light one compared to the work she used to do.

Trudy was happy to turn the boiling pot, the washboard, and the lye soap over to Lily. She contented herself with ironing in the kitchen and dreaming out the window as the flatiron banged a steady rhythm on the board.

The leaves had fallen away, giving the mountains a brown and barren look. Some gold still clung to the hickory trees, but winter was very near.

It seemed to Trudy that they had always lived in Shiloh. All Birch's good memories had become her memories, as if she had spent all of her thirty-two autumns in this place. She was truly home.

This morning Birch had ridden out in the FAMOUS wagon to fetch a load of coal. Jeff worked alone in the field with a preoccupied fervor as though he could not bear to think about another day without reply to his letter to Little Rock.

Trudy saw the longing on the big man's face: Was his mother still living? his father? his sisters? She had watched the restlessness of Jefferson's heart grow with each passing day. Shiloh was not his home, after all. Until he found his family, perhaps no place could ever be home to him.

He had said as much when Tommy asked him if he would please stay here with the family forever: *"Forever is a long time, boy. A mighty long time for a man to be without his own family . . ."*

Through the window, the clank of harness sounded as Jeff worked the team to uproot a stubborn stump. He worked without his coat in spite of the cold day. Trudy noticed Lily gazing at him. Her brow was furrowed as she checked a heavy flannel shirt still on the line. Not dry yet, but it was plain on Lily's face she did not think it proper for Jefferson to work in his shirtsleeves.

Her belly bulging, she waddled toward the crest of the hill and put her hands to her mouth to holler down. "Jeff! Jeff! Put that coat on! My William took a chill just the same way and up and died! Now put that coat on!"

Jefferson looked at her and considered her warning. Then, retrieving his frayed coat from the root of an upturned stump, he put it on and saluted her.

Well, well. Trudy smiled to herself. He had given Lily the quilt, and now she was telling him how to dress. It was promising. Trudy could hear Lily laugh, a bubbling, really happy laugh. "Well, well," Trudy said aloud. Was something blooming in the barren field?

The morning drifted on like this with Trudy watching Lily watching Jefferson. No doubt about it—Trudy was a matchmaker. Birch had accused her of it, as had Cousin Max and her own mother.

Trudy was in the middle of dreaming up a happy ending for the two lonely people out there when the clatter of a Model T interrupted her reverie.

The unmistakable yodel of Cousin J.D. resounded in the yard. Trudy grimaced and replaced the flatiron on the stove top, determined that he would not get through the front door and interrupt her entire day.

But that was not to be. First the knock on the front door and then the groan of hinges announced that J.D. had not waited to be invited in. Trudy stopped and glared at him as he stepped aside and ushered Delbert Simpson, the pudgy little assistant bank manager, into the parlor as though he owned the place.

"J.D.," Trudy said flatly, "Birch is not at home, and—"

"Not home? Well, Delbert come all the way out here from Hartford to have a word with him."

"Hello, Mister Simpson. You have made your trip for nothing. Birch is not at—"

"No matter." J.D. dismissed her with a wave of his hand. "Delbert, look at this place, will ya? It ain't what it used to be, but y'all can see it's sturdy."

Delbert still had not said a word. Hat in hand, he nodded and scrutinized the house as though Trudy were not even standing there. "Right nice. Right nice."

"Thank you," Trudy replied coolly.

Delbert looked at her as if she had no right to reply to his compliment. "What I'm saying, Missus Tucker, is that as collateral for a loan, this place is right nice. Mister Smith is gonna be pleased—"

"Collateral?" Trudy took a halting step forward. "What are you—?"

J.D. chimed in. "Delbert was sayin' that loan y'all took—"

"Loan? We did not . . . *would* not . . . we own this place free and clear!"

Delbert raised his eyebrows and turned the corners of his mouth down in disagreement. "Y'all don't own it free and clear. Wish Birch was here so I could discuss this with him myself." He shrugged. His eyes glittered with a strange excitement, as if he was overly eager to tell her the next news. "Old Sam Tucker left a heap of back taxes on this place. Near five hundred dollars by now. We were searching the title in case your money from First Petroleum don't come through in time from Tulsa, and we found all these back taxes. The loan department checked at the county, and if those taxes don't get paid, well, this place'll be auctioned."

Trudy felt the blood drain from her face. She grasped the back of a chair to steady herself. "But . . . how?" She looked at J.D., who seemed undisturbed by the bad news. And not at all surprised.

"Well, Missus Tucker, y'all signed a note to mortgage this farm. As collateral for that letter of credit you asked for—"

"No! We never!"

Delbert slapped a thick envelope down on the table. "You sure did. Signed by Birch Tucker, as you can see."

"But our funds were supposed to be . . . transferred. First Petroleum Bank. Tulsa."

"That is the slowest bank I've ever seen." Delbert shook his head. "Two letters we sent, and they don't have the courtesy to reply! I declare. The president of our bank is fit to be tied. He's put up all the cash backin' y'all up, and there doesn't seem to be—"

"Wait!" Trudy cried, fumbling for her purse and the First Petroleum Bank passbook. "It's all right here. Every deposit." She tried to give it to Delbert, who shook his head. "See for yourself. Ten years we have been saving . . ."

"Well, they haven't sent your money. So we've got nothing to back up that letter of credit. Mister Smith says he figured this might be the case, so we began procedure for when the mortgage kicks in."

"When is that?" Trudy was shaking. "When does this note come due?"

"Y'all got another eight days, Missus Tucker. But besides all that, there is this little matter of the taxes. Now the bank'll have to think real hard before we take over land with a tax bill like this." He nudged J.D. "J.D. was saying just yesterday he might pay those taxes. The mortgage on this place isn't so much it can't be worked off."

Trudy glared at J.D., who was looking pleased with himself. "If I buy the place for taxes, 'course I'll let y'all stay on and sharecrop to pay off the mortgage y'all put on the place. I can do that much. . . ."

Trudy picked up the envelope and removed the document inside. And there it was, just as Delbert said. In exchange for a letter of credit, Birch had offered the farm as collateral. If the loan was not paid by November 2, then the deed of trust on the property would be held by Hartford National Bank. Payments would commence November 30, 1929.

"Birch," Trudy whispered, laying the paper on the table. She looked around the room as though suddenly the house belonged to someone else. Then she squared her shoulders. "We shall contact First Petroleum personally, Mister Simpson," she said firmly. "It is an oversight. They have simply misplaced the paperwork. The money is all there, and you shall have it by November second."

Delbert inclined his head. "That may be so, Missus Tucker, but like I said, it's the taxes, you see. The bank will not lend you money to pay property taxes. It's bad business. And those are past due. It's that simple. And we see that the farm is worth holding the mortgage on. We'll transfer your loan to J.D."

Trudy bit her lip and tried to comprehend what Delbert Simpson was telling her. Had J.D. already paid the taxes? Had someone turned the farm over to him legally? "You cannot . . . legally . . . ," she bluffed, not knowing what she was talking about. How could this be happening?

J.D. stood smug and superior in her front room. No wonder he acted as if he owned the place. Very shortly he would.

"I need to ask you to . . . leave." She was controlled, but her voice trembled.

"I won't turn you out," J.D. said too cheerfully, the way he might talk to a snarling dog he was trying to get past.

"You bet you won't!" Trudy snapped. "But for now this is still my house—*our* house—and I have the right to turn *you* out. So get out, J.D.! I have wanted to say that to you a thousand times, and now I shall. Get out of my house!"

✳ ✳ ✳

"I thought we had Max Meyer with us," Phelps complained. "I thought the *Times* was all lined up on our side. How could he do this to us?"

The Sabre Oil pool conspirators were gathered in the dining room of Mike Keenan's estate. After chasing out the servants and locking the doors, they had spread the Friday-afternoon edition of the *New York Times* all over the long dining table. Keenan, Phelps, Edith Rutger, and Boss Quinn revolved around the various stories of Thursday's market plunge like planets of speculators around the sun of finances.

The centerpiece of their attention was Max Meyer's column. Max's headline drew them back over and over with renewed flashes of anger, frustration, and fear: "Sabre Oil Pool a Trap for Unwary Investors." The story attacked pools in general as sucking in unsophisticated and over-eager small investors, but it singled out Sabre as an example of the worst. Max referred them to Thursday's market decline, which had cost Sabre's stock 20 percent of its value, as an example of how quickly savings could be lost by the thoughtless or imprudent. Worst of all, it warned that Thursday was just *"a shadow of the real decline that is looming closer and closer."*

"But it gained back three dollars today," Phelps protested.

"Nobody saw Meyer's story in time for it to affect the market today," Keenan cautioned. "It could hurt us yet."

"It is apparent to me that you still do not get it," asserted Quinn. "Meyer did not make a mistake here. He is a fink, a traitor."

"Does it really matter?" Edith asked Keenan. "I mean, really? Everyone else sounds so positive. Maybe they'll all just laugh at him again."

Keenan was inclined to agree. "Listen to this." He quoted from the front page of the *Times*: "Wall Street Optimistic after Stormy Day."

Eager to find positive news, Phelps also reported with enthusiasm. "Look here, Morgan and Company says the foundations of the market are sound. . . . The drop was due to technical rather than fundamental reasons."

Boss Quinn said, "I wish to observe that we need to terminate our business quickly."

"But everyone thinks that now is the time to grab for bargains," Keenan objected. "A few more purchases by us, and we can run Sabre sky-high."

Phelps winced at the phrase "a few more purchases."

"Do not be guilty of reading only the news you like to hear," warned Quinn, "as we want the suckers to continue doing. But see here, I do not like this man's attitude." He read, " *'Senator King of Utah says gambling in stocks has become a national disease.'* This does not put us in a favorable light."

"One more week?" requested Keenan.

Phelps had a vision of himself behind bars unless the pool made enough money to cover the mess at the bank. He held his breath until Quinn agreed.

"And Max?" Edith asked.

"We can ill afford any further bad raps in the press, now can we? I think it is necessary for Meyer to apologize in print and issue a . . . what do you call it?"

"A retraction?" Edith offered. "Max will never agree to do that. Even I couldn't get him to—"

"It is obvious to me that neither you nor Mister Keenan has been able to deliver the goods where Meyer is concerned. He has been a loose end throughout this project, and I do not like loose ends. In fact, I despise them. Therefore, it is now my responsibility. And now," Quinn concluded, "I have other pressing business. However, you may trust that in Monday's edition, Meyer will sing a different tune about Sabre Oil."

As the bootleg boss left the room, he tore a scrap of newspaper off an inside page. It was from a location that had nothing to do with finances and had come to his attention only by chance.

The small announcement read:

Police are seeking the parents or guardians of a boy, aged nine or ten years, believed to be the only survivor of the hijacking and deliberate scuttling of the rumrunner Jazz Baby. The boy is unconscious and hospitalized with injuries. Those with information may . . .

CHAPTER THIRTY-EIGHT

Expecting the Sky to Fall

The smells pulled David back toward consciousness. Hospital smells. Antiseptic. Overcooked food. Chlorine bleach. Was he back at St. Francis Hospital? Had he fallen asleep in his mother's room and dreamed everything?

This thought jerked his eyes open in the hope that he would see her. It must be so. White ceiling. White sheets. White curtain drawn around the place where he lay sleeping. Sometimes when he had fallen asleep by his mother's bed, Sister Anne had tucked him into the empty bed beside hers.

This second thought made David open his mouth and croak, "Mother? Mama?" Why did his throat hurt so bad? Too bad to swallow. And his mouth was dry, as if he had not had anything to drink in a thousand years. "Mama?" he called again.

But his mother did not answer. Sometimes she was sleeping and could not answer, David remembered. When that happened, he could always talk to Father John or Sister Anne or the nurses. David could hear the clink of glasses and silverware on food trays. Was it breakfast time? Had he slept the whole night through? He was still so tired. Very tired. And his throat hurt.

"Sister Anne," he tried to call loudly, but the name came out in a whisper. "Father John?" And then once again, "Mama?"

A man's voice called to him from outside the curtained space. "Hey, kid? You awake?"

It did not sound like Father John, but who else would be there, sitting beside his mother's bed? "Father John," David whispered.

"The kid's awake. Call the nurse, will you? The kid's awake."

David wanted to ask if he had to get up and go to school since he was so tired, but he closed his eyes and let the gentle comfort of sleep enfold him again.

Everything was all right. He had just been dreaming. Such terrible long dreams. Dreams about his mother dying. About Brian. The children's home. Running away to New York and Olaf and Gus and Codfish and the boat on fire. *All dreams?*

David's eyes snapped open again. "I want my mother," he said in a loud, unhappy voice, as though she could make the visions in his dreams go away.

"Sure, kid," said the man on the other side of the curtain. "Sure. The nurse will call your mama. She's coming, kid. She'll get your mama for you." Then he shouted, "Hey, get the nurse, will you? This kid wants his mama."

The curtain parted and through the white fog a pale, withered face entered his vision. A nurse. She blended with the curtain except for her face, which seemed very big as she leaned close over David. "Well, hello, young man." She smiled with crooked teeth and took his hand. "Finally awake?"

"Where's my mother?"

"You want your mother. A good sign. What is her name?"

Who was this nurse? Everyone at St. Francis knew Irene O'Halloran. "Are you new?" David asked.

She chuckled and stood back out of his vision. "Good heavens, no. Tell me your name."

"David. Don't you know?"

"David. A very nice name. What is your last name?"

David tried to remember. Was it O'Halloran? Or was it the other name? The one in his dreams? "O'Halloran."

"Your mother's name?"

David was very tired. So many questions. "Irene."

"Irene what?"

"O'Halloran, too. Don't you know? Where is Father John and Sister Anne? Do I have to go to school this morning?"

"Where does your mother live, David? We have to know so we can tell her you are safe."

He raised a heavy hand and gestured at the curtain. His mother lived here now, in the next bed over, and she would live there the rest of her life. Why didn't the nurse know these things? "There she is. Mother?"

"What street, dear?" The nurse patted his head. "So we can bring her here."

"St. Francis Hospital," he answered.

"No, David. This is General Hospital. Where is your mother?"

"St. Francis . . ."

Someone came in and stood beside the nurse. A big man with a bald head and a white coat and a thing hanging from his neck to listen to hearts. David could not remember what to call the thing, but the man was a doctor. He mumbled to the nurse about pulse rate and if David could remember anything.

"Hello, David," said the doctor, whose breath smelled like coffee and cigarettes. "How are you feeling?"

"Sleepy. I want Mama."

"What is your address, David. Can you tell us that?"

David licked his lips. He was thirsty. "103 Third Street. Philadelphia."

The doctor and nurse were silent a moment. The nurse repeated everything David had said. She told the doctor about St. Francis Hospital and the name of David's mother and then his whole name. "And he was asking for Father John and Sister Anne."

"Philadelphia. Then he is a runaway," said the doctor. "Contact his mother. No, probably best to contact the Philadelphia police. They can give a run out there and speak with his folks. Tell them we've found him."

Found? David was confused. "Where am I?"

"General Hospital, dear," soothed the nurse. "New York City."

David squeezed his eyes shut. He moaned a low, unhappy sound. "Is this a dream?" He started to cry, suddenly very frightened because maybe he was still in the terrible dream and his real father was gone and Olaf and Gus were dead and the Boss was after him. . . .

"No, David." The doctor brushed back the boy's hair with a cool, pleasant hand. "You are safe now. You had a terrible ordeal, but you are going to get well. But we need to contact your mother in Philadelphia."

"No-o-o-o-o," David groaned. "I remember. Not a dream. Mama is dead. She *died*! And I came here to find . . . to find . . ."

"Who, David? We need to know who."

"My dad. My . . . father . . . Max Meyer. See? I came to find him and tell him. But he left for Yurp, and Olaf and Gus and Codfish . . ."

More mumbling between doctor and nurse. "You don't suppose he's talking about *the* Max Meyer? The columnist?"

"I read his stuff all the time. . . ." The doctor leaned close to David's pillow. "What does your daddy do?"

David could not remember. Enough was enough. Why wouldn't these people let him sleep? His mother was really dead. So were Olaf and Gus. The boat had burned and Codfish had dragged him away. Where was Codfish? "My dog," David said. "I want Codfish."

"He's talking about the big dog who pulled him to the boat. The papers made quite a fuss over it," said the nurse.

"Well, where is the animal?"

"Kenneled, I suppose. I did not think to ask."

"Find out. And telephone the office of the *Times* for Max Meyer's desk. Probably not the same Max Meyer, but give it a try all the same."

The man in the dark brown, double-breasted suit filled the doorway to the financial office of the *New York Times*. It was not that he merely stood in the doorway. He literally filled it, with his shoulders brushing against the doorposts and the crown of his fedora touching the lintel. Miss Morgan thought that if he turned around too rapidly he might become wedged in the opening.

"May I help you?" she asked.

The man breathed loudly through a much-battered nose. It gave his words the ominous sound of barely controlled power, like an evil freight train lurking on a siding. "We wish to see Max Meyer, doll."

"We?" asked Miss Morgan. She thought perhaps he always referred to himself in the plural.

"Yeah, my partner and me, see?" The hand he jerked backward toward the hallway was the size and texture of a football. Miss Morgan could not actually see the partner, but she was willing to take the caller's word for his statement.

"So, is he in, doll?"

"No, he's not. In fact, I don't expect him back today at all."

"Did he say where he was goin'?"

"I'm sorry—what did you say your name was, and why do you need Mister Meyer?"

The human mountain did not reply to the question. Instead, over his shoulder, he said, "How do you like that, Sal? Our old buddy Maxie forgot all about our dinner party."

When Miss Morgan could not hear a reply, she supposed that the visitor's bulk blocked sound as well as sight. "You know Mister Meyer, then?"

"Sure, doll. We was in the war together. Over there, and all that. Sal and me come to town for a reunion, see?"

"I can leave a message for Mister Meyer. Let him know where you are staying. What was your name again?"

"That's okay, doll. We don't want to make him feel bad for forgettin' us, do we, Sal? Naw, no message. If he calls, don't even tell him we stopped by, see? We want to surprise him later. Get it?"

When the two men reached the Plaza Hotel, Sal stopped the big man outside on the sidewalk. "He ain't gonna let us in, ya know, Ham. We gonna just bust in, or what?"

"Leave it to me, Sal," his partner reassured him. "Just leave everything to me."

The Plaza's assistant manager studied the threatening form of six-foot-six-inch Ham and the smaller but leanly sinister-looking Sal. Comparisons of an ax handle and a switchblade came instantly to his mind.

"Excuse me, gentlemen," the assistant manager said with what he hoped was polite authority. "May I be of service?"

"Certainly, youse may," replied Ham mildly. "My friend and me is here at the request of Mister Mike Keenan. To see Max Meyer, the financial col-loom-nist."

The assistant manager was impressed. Despite their appearances, these two were obviously well connected. Not many people knew that Max's suite had been arranged by Keenan. It must be all right.

"Certainly," he said. Then he added in an obliging tone to the elevator operator, "Take these gentlemen to Mister Meyer's floor at once."

Once outside Max's door, Sal and Ham did not bother to knock or ring the bell. Ham did not punch his fist through the panels or kick the door open. Nothing so dramatic. The huge man simply extracted a key from his coat pocket and unlocked the door.

Closing the door behind them, they made a thorough search but found no Max, nor a clue to his whereabouts.

"He ain't plannin' to be gone long," Sal observed. "See, Ham, there ain't but one missin' suit. All his other clothes is still here."

The two displayed all the ease of frequent guests arriving for a weekend visit. They removed their suit coats, took off their shoes, unslung their shoulder holsters, and settled down to wait for Max's return.

The whole world seemed to be falling apart. Faces on every street corner in Manhattan were sullen or gloomy or frightened. No one looked at anyone else. Each man and woman walked alone this Friday with a dark and personal spectre. For many, the dreams of tomorrow's glory had come crashing down yesterday. Instant wealth had instantly been cut in half. Today had been some brighter, but the shimmering bubble had been shown to be "pop-able."

Now what?

In the lobby of the Plaza, a man was quietly sobbing while a worried-looking flapper patted his back and looked around at nothing at all. Others huddled together and spoke in low, urgent whispers, as though they were at a funeral. These were the sounds of uncertainty. Everything else was silent and solemn.

Max hurried to bypass the clerk at the front desk, only to be hailed loudly.

"Mister Meyer!" The clerk held up an envelope. "Messages, sir."

At the mention of Max's name, a hundred pairs of angry eyes turned to look at him. Had he not been part of the cause of the disaster, after all? Pessimism in print had caused the Wall Street collapse.

The sobbing man raised his head and stopped crying long enough to mouth the words, *"Dirty Red Jew! Commie creep. Ruin the country . . ."*

Max took the messages from the night clerk and tried to ignore the eyes boring into his back.

"From your office, Mister Meyer." The clerk seemed nervous. He glanced down as though he were not really talking to the Wall Street doomsayer. "They say it's most urgent."

Max took the messages with a shrug. Everything about the day had been urgent. Max had spent the last twelve hours tracking down rumors that the biggest names on Wall Street had yet another scheme in mind to pour millions into the market come Monday to stem further decline. His notebook was filled with enough information to write six months' worth of articles and now, no doubt, the *Times* was calling to get the copy to them before press time tonight. Max had already decided he was in no mood to answer even one more urgent message.

Then the phone rang behind the desk. Mr. Derby poked his head out from behind the partition. "Ah! Mister Meyer!" Derby said cheerfully. "I thought I heard your voice!" He held out a candlestick telephone. "A call for you. Urgent, he says."

Trapped, Max frowned and took the telephone. "Meyer here."

The voice on the other end of the line was unfamiliar. Not Beadle or Miss Morgan, as Max expected.

"Max Meyer?"

"That's right."

"My name is Doctor Oates. At New York General Hospital. Your secretary told me you might be at your hotel. Of course, I did not mention the purpose of my call. . . ."

Max was growing impatient. No doubt this fellow wanted some advice on the market. "Sell," Max said.

"I beg your pardon?"

"That's my advice. I stand by my story."

"Mister Meyer, I am calling about . . . you may think this odd, but I am telephoning you because we have a small boy here. His name is David. He says—"

Mr. Derby frowned as Max Meyer dropped the telephone and rushed from the hotel, leaving all his other messages stacked on the front desk.

"What's got into him?" mused the clerk.

"The same as has gotten into everyone, I suppose," said Derby. He gestured toward the men and women in the lobby. "It's as if we're all expecting the sky to fall, isn't it?"

CHAPTER THIRTY-NINE

Storm on the Horizon

"Don't you know what's happening in the stock market? what a mess this is?" Delbert Simpson tapped his fingers on his desk at Hartford Bank. "This isn't a good day for this. . . ."

"What's that got to do with us? with our money?" Birch asked.

"We got no more time to spend on the matter today; that's all."

From his balcony perch, the president of First National Bank of Hartford scowled down at Birch and Trudy as they huddled at Delbert's desk. He rattled his newspaper impatiently.

"There's not a thing more I can do about this, Birch." Delbert was sweating as he waved his hand over the wires and forms laid out across his desk blotter. "First Petroleum Bank of Tulsa says they're having some discrepancy with your records and can't release your funds until it's all straightened out."

"But they admit they have our account!" Birch leaned closer and banged his fist on the desk.

"They don't seem to know."

"Why can't you extend our letter of credit so we can pay off the taxes?"

President Henry V. Smith cleared his throat loudly, sending an *absolutely not* signal to his assistant. Delbert's eyes darted up toward the king. He gave a small nod of assent, then answered, "All we have is your word for how much y'all have saved."

"Our word—" Trudy's voice was trembling—"and this." She held the First Petroleum savings book out to Delbert. "Every deposit we ever made. They will certainly have the matter straightened out shortly. It was

Vice President Tell himself who recommended to Birch that our funds be transferred electronically. The modern way, he said. Safe, he said. No one could steal it from us if we—"

"All very true." Delbert held up his hands to interrupt her. "And if the money is transferred—"

"If you do not honor the letter of credit, then we shall lose our home as forfeit to these unpaid taxes," Trudy replied urgently.

"And if we advance that amount to you, combined with the nine hundred you have used in credit, then Mister Smith and the board believe that we will have more cash in the place than it is worth."

Birch's breath exploded in indignation at such a statement. "Every cent we've spent has been only to improve what was already there. Farm equipment, mules, seed, lumber, paint, furniture. All that is owin' on the farm is $511 in back taxes my pa didn't pay. That land is worth a whole lot more than that, Delbert! You know it is."

"Maybe today it is, but farm prices are falling. The economy is shaky. We've got to think about the future." Delbert was unrelenting. He drew himself up in his chair. "Just because First Petroleum Bank is all in a fuddle about your account doesn't mean that this bank has got to take a risk to carry you. You're madder than a wet hen at us, and it isn't us! Look at this! Why, I just sent those folks another letter. They act as if they never heard of you, Birch! It isn't us!"

"We spent nine hundred on that letter of credit," Birch tried again. "You said we could have up to two thousand! You've gone back on your word. You won't cover that five hundred in taxes, and I'm gonna lose my place over it!"

Delbert was silent. He sat stone-faced and stared down at the documents. He tapped his fingers on the loan folder impatiently. He would say no more, argue not one more syllable. The matter had been decided. No doubt it had been discussed at length. If J.D. bought the place for $511 in back taxes, then the bank's mortgage would be for only the amount Birch had used up to now. If the bank loaned the tax money to Birch, however, the mortgage would be that much higher.

"Y'all are sellin' our dreams, Delbert. Don't you see that? Please, lend us the tax money."

Delbert did not look at the couple. The clock above the lobby ticked loudly. There was no more to be said.

"What do you mean he can't talk to me?" Birch was yelling so loud that his voice clearly penetrated the glass of the public telephone booth in-

side Winters' Drugstore and Soda Fountain. "This is urgent! Tell him . . .
yes! Birch Tucker! I need to talk with Vice President Tell! I'm callin' from
Hartford, Arkansas!"

Trudy stood in front of shelves of laxatives and stared unseeing at the
boxes and bottles. Other people in the store glanced nervously at her
and then at Birch. They spoke in low monotones as they paid for their
purchases and lingered on as though to hear the end of the story. Trudy
was already certain that everyone in Hartford and Shiloh knew that the
letter of credit had been canceled. First Hartford National Bank was no
longer backing up any purchases made by the Tucker family. Any merchant who sold to them did so at his own risk.

"You think I care about his meetin'? I tell you . . . get him! Get Tell on
the line, or—no! I am at a public telephone booth! I have been a customer for ten years with First Petroleum Bank, and now you're tellin' me
I can't get my money out because I'm out of state! And it was Tell who
told me . . . well then, get him on the line! Now! Or I'm comin' back to
Tulsa!"

Every head pivoted as Birch's voice boomed through the store. Trudy
stood erect, but she felt the flush of humiliation climb to her cheeks.
Had all the town also heard about the taxes? Did everyone know that
J.D. planned to buy their farm for the taxes? that the county commis-
sioner had given him the right to do so since he was the nearest relative
after Birch? Had they heard that J.D. had refused to lend Birch the
money but had offered to let him stay on as a sharecropper?

Trudy glanced up to see Mr. Winters' pained expression as he rang up
a purchase for Mrs. Hocott. It was plain that the druggist knew every horrible detail of how Birch Tucker was being sold down the river by his
cousin. And there was nothing anyone could do to change it.

The receiver came down with a bang in the booth. Birch stood motionless, staring at the telephone for a full two minutes as though he
were replaying the entire conversation in his mind. No one in the store
spoke. Trudy absently picked up a bottle of aspirin as if she meant to buy
it. Now, of course, she did not even have the money to pay for it. Replacing the bottle on the shelf, she walked toward the telephone booth just
as Birch stepped out.

He took her hands. "How many more times can we telephone, True?
He's always in a meetin'. Or gone somewhere." He shook his head. "We'll
just have to go back to Tulsa. Leave Lily and Jeff to mind the kids and the
place. We've just got to get this straightened out or . . ." He shook his
head. "J.D. . . ."

Trudy pulled him outside and around the corner of the building. He
looked as though he would break. "They'll get this straight." She

smoothed back his hair. "J.D. won't take your place . . . our place. He has so much. . . ."

"He always wanted everything, True. Always. As a kid, he had to win every race. Swim the fastest. Hunt the best. Didn't like if I beat him at anything. Couldn't bear it. He'd pout for days, and this is what he grew up to. He just wants it all. He don't need it, but I reckon he's always liked the thought of ownin' everything he laid his eyes on."

Behind Birch, the voice of Mr. Winters added, "That is for sure, Birch Tucker." And then he told what he knew about how J.D. had bragged around town that Birch's father was going to leave the Tucker farm to him. "Old Doc Brown told your pa to quit drinking or die. And who do you think brought your father jugs of corn liquor? J.D. kept Sam Tucker half crazy, dependent. Then after he died, J.D. was plenty surprised to find your name on the will. Birch Tucker going to get that farm instead of J.D. He didn't like it much. And then he settled into the idea after Judge Harding tracked you down. J.D. said you'd take one look at the place and light out. Said it was such a wreck the way Sam Tucker neglected it that you were getting nothing but dirt and squalor."

"I guess he must want that land pretty bad." Birch's shoulders sagged. "I wouldn't have thought this of him."

"You two were boys together. He was like a brother to you. Closer than your own, the way you two spent time together. But he always was spoiled rotten. Always was mean. You just were too close to see it." Mr. Winters stepped back as though his own honesty startled him. "I didn't mean to intrude, Birch. You know. Your mama was a good woman. We all thought highly of her and the way she raised you boys in spite of everything. I just surely hate to see it all come to this."

Birch's head rose in determination. His chin stiffened. "Well, we're going to Tulsa, then. There's nothing else to do."

Birch drove the little Model T furiously from Hartford back toward Shiloh. Together he and Trudy tried to make sense out of the grim events of the day.

For the first time it seemed to Trudy that perhaps the distant tremors of Wall Street were shaking the ground beneath their little world in Shiloh. She purchased a copy of the newspaper and scanned the pages for some hint of what was happening in New York and why it might affect decisions made at the little bank in Hartford.

"It says right here," she read to Birch, "that the dip is nothing but the stock market making adjustments. Even the president, Mister Hoover, says everything is in grand shape. Nothing to worry about."

"Well, tell that to King Henry V." Birch was angry. "No time for that old coot to think about us or our farm today. He sits up there in the bank like some old buzzard ready to pick our bones. Thinks he's too important . . . pretendin' to think about some big hoopla in New York City that doesn't have a thing to do with us folks or our savin's or the real world!"

"I wish I could talk to Max," Trudy lamented. "He could sort it out."

Birch scowled and steered over a deep rut. "Right," he scoffed. "Dear old Max. Now there's a man who has an answer for everythin'. Every time he opened his big mouth when we were in Paris, somebody wanted to close it for him. I'll tell you what's behind all this. . . ." He shook his fist but did not finish his thought.

"Well? What?"

There was silence from Birch as the Ford rattled on. At last he shrugged. "Maybe I don't know either," he conceded at last. "But I aim to find out. You and I will be standin' on the steps of First Petroleum in Tulsa when they open up on Monday. And I aim to ask that little pipsqueak of a banker, Mister Tell, just what in the—"

"We can't make it by Monday."

"We can if we drive all night tonight. Day and night, we can make it, get our money, and get back home where a farmer belongs. Let the bankers sort out their own messes! I don't want a thing to worry about but the weather and the cotton prices." He glared out the windscreen. "I tell you, Trudy, my old grandpa was right about banks. Never trust a bank, he said! He put all his money into a bank in Atlanta during the war . . . that is, the Civil War. . . ."

"My family missed that one." Trudy cocked an eyebrow at Birch in grim amusement that he chose this moment to hark back to those old family tales of poverty and starvation in the Rebel camp.

"Good for you."

"My grandparents were still in Germany dodging the kaiser, thank you."

"Couldn't have been as bad as those Confederate bankers. Every cent the Tucker family owned went into that bank, and what do you think? *Never* trust a bank, my old granddaddy used to say! Put your cash in land, he said. Or gold. And bury it deep, because there ain't no thief as cruel as a high-toned respectable banker gone bad." Birch shook his head. "That Atlanta dandy took half a million in gold outta that bank when Atlanta fell to the Yankees. Bought passage on a blockade runner and went to live in France. Well, it soured Granddaddy on banks ever since, and you can see why. Ruined everyone in Atlanta. Why, my other granddaddy, Sinnickson, claimed to never trust a bank ever."

"This is hardly the same," Trudy consoled. "Oh, Birch, surely it's just an oversight."

"Huh! *Oversight?* That fancy Mister Tell will have double vision for this oversight if I don't leave Tulsa with our savin's! Just let him try to claim he don't know us and that he mislaid two thousand dollars. The Civil War will seem a small thing if this don't get put right!"

A bank of heavy storm clouds hovered over the Sugar Loaf Mountains in the south. Perhaps it was a warning to her soul, Trudy thought as she turned from the window and placed a stack of Birch's freshly laundered shirts in the scuffed tan suitcase.

"Miz Trudy?" Lily hung back outside the bedroom door as though she did not want to intrude on Trudy's thoughts.

Trudy could not answer. What could she say to Lily, who had come from nothing and had found hope in this place? How could she explain that perhaps it would all be lost? That there would be no more hope for Lily to stay on?

Lily did not go away. She looked at the suitcase and the clothes as though she understood everything already. "Miz Trudy," she began again. "Maybe it ain't my business to say." She paused. "I know maybe you and Mister Birch gonna lose all this. This fine place and all. I know that, Miz Trudy, and I'm right sorry about it."

"Thank you." Trudy did not look at her but busied herself folding underclothes and trousers. "I appreciate that, Lily."

But that was not all Lily wanted to say. She remained rooted in the doorway. "What I mean to tell you, Miz Trudy . . . I mean . . . even if y'all don't have this here farm no more, you still have ever'thin'. You got your man. Your young'uns. Folks like that Mister J.D. been around forever—cheatin' folks, puttin' a cloud over life. I seen it, too. But what I mean is . . . if it don't go right up there in Tulsa for y'all, I surely do hope you remember the Lord is watchin', Miz True. Yes'm. I do believe the Lord is watchin'.'"

Trudy bowed her head and held Birch's shirt against her. "I know all that, Lily," she answered quietly. "It's just that we have always dreamed of owning our own place. Raising our boys here—or somewhere—in a place they could call home."

"I know all about such dreams. The Lord give folks such dreams, I reckon. He don't mind that. He just don't want His young'uns puttin' all their trust in things and places. Don't want His young'uns trustin' in anythin' but that He gonna take care of 'em."

Trudy smiled at her, remembering the ragged visitor who had come to the back porch. "How old are you, Lily?"

"Almost twenty, near as I can figure, Miz True."

"How did you learn such a thing?"

"Reckon it just come to me, Miz True. I ain't never had anythin' to call my own, 'cept my soul. For a long while I hung on to my soul. I said, 'This here is mine! Ain't nobody's to claim!' Then one day I gave my soul back to Jesus. I told Him I can't keep body and soul together no more, so if I was gonna keep on livin' . . . well, *He* was just gonna have to take care of the matter! Ever'thin' I got belong to my Lord, Miz Trudy. I don't have nothin' of my own to worry about. Ain't nothin' in this life I trust but Jesus, if I live or die, if my belly's full or hungry. Well, Miz Trudy, y'all go on to Tulsa and see to that business. But try not to trust in anythin' but Jesus. He is faithful. Yes'm, He is faithful!"

Trudy thanked Lily, who returned to her work in the kitchen. Trudy could hear her humming softly as though today were the same as yesterday, as though no storm clouds loomed in the future. There was no consolation in Lily's words. *Trust only in the Lord!* Was this a lesson that could be learned only by losing everything? by having nothing in this life but a soul to give back to God?

Trudy did not want that to be true. She raised her eyes to the dark clouds. Dread weighted her heart.

Max's hands were trembling as he placed the photograph of David in the hands of Dr. Oates. Bright smiling face, impudent grin, the look of mischief in that nine-year-old expression . . . The doctor studied the image for a moment, as though uncertain that the child in the room down the hall was the same boy. Then he nodded.

"Cute kid," Dr. Oates said, giving the snapshot back to Max. "This is tragic. Tragic." Then, "How long has it been since you have seen your son, Mister Meyer?" He closed the door to his office and motioned for Max to sit in the burgundy leather chair in front of his desk.

How could Max answer such a question? How could he admit that he had never seen David? that he had wasted almost ten years of his life up until the moment Father John had given him this picture? And now that he had found David, was he going to lose him?

Max opened his mouth and tried to explain, but emotion chocked off his words. He pressed his lips together and simply shook his head in

reply—a gesture of grief that the doctor somehow understood. Grief beyond words. Regret beyond expression. Fear that it might be too late to
redeem those lost years forever.

"I see," said Doctor Oates. "You were separated from the boy's
mother, then?"

To this, Max nodded. *Irene!* He could not make himself speak. What
words were left after all this? He cradled the photograph of David in his
hands and simply gazed at the eyes—so like Irene's eyes. At the cleft in
that chin that was so like his own.

"David told us some, Mister Meyer. His mother?"

"Dead."

"He came here to find you, then?"

Max nodded, afraid to look into the probing gaze of Dr. Oates.

The doctor cleared his throat. "He is a fighter, this son of yours."
There was hope in such words.

"Tell me about . . . him." So there it was. A perfect stranger knew
more about David than Max did. It had been that way for nine years. Like
a man dying of thirst in the desert, Max craved some drop of insight.
Who was this boy he had not met? How had he come to be here? "A
fighter, you say. Will he live?"

"He aspirated a lot of seawater. I would not have given him any hope
at all before this morning. But he came around long enough to ask for
his mother. And then he told us about you. Well, I have been a dedicated
reader of your column. I could not imagine that the child was asking for
you, but we took the chance and telephoned the *Times.*" A slight smile.
"On such a day as this . . . *this day* . . . but the operator put us through to
your secretary. She knew at once who we were talking about when we
told her about David."

"David." Max said the name. Yes. It matched the face.

"He calls himself David, you know. David O'Halloran. But his father
is Max Meyer. He made that clear to us. He rallied a bit when I told him
you were coming. That was hours ago. Hours. When you did not come, I
supposed you were in the middle of all that mess on Wall Street. I supposed your secretary would not be able to contact you. They say it is the
end of the world down there. And so . . . I told the boy you would come,
but that he must sleep and get strong for your visit. He seemed quite con-
tent to do that as long as he knew you'd really show up."

"I am here," Max managed. "Nine . . . no, ten years late."

"But perhaps not *too* late." The light shone on the doctor's bald dome
like a halo. In a kind tone he asked, "Would you like to see your son, Mister Meyer? I know he has been waiting for you."

★ ★ ★

The boy lay pale and small beneath the oxygen tent. The bed seemed to swallow his fragile form. Max sat motionless and watched him sleep. He did not take his eyes away from the ashen face for fear David would vanish.

Dr. Oates left Max there alone with the instruction to press the call button if David awoke. That had been two days ago. Nurses came in, checked pulse and blood pressure and temperature, and still the boy slept on. It was late Sunday night, but Max had never felt so awake. On the edge of his chair, Max breathed in unison with the labored breathing of his son. When some unconscious pain or troubled dream wrinkled the child's brow, Max winced as though it were his own pain, his own troubled dreams.

Watching the boy struggle so near to death was, in a way, like watching his birth. Max prayed to the nameless, faceless God he had never believed in. He begged for the life of his son to be spared, asked for time, bargained with heaven, trading off all his dreams if only he could have this one little dream come true. . . .

Beyond these walls, Max knew that the world was indeed breaking apart. Yet here before him was the only world he cared about. Let Wall Street come crashing down like a modern Jericho if only David would open his eyes and call Max "Father."

CHAPTER FORTY

The Father

The headlamps of the Model T illuminated the road sign: Siloam Springs 3 mi. It was still a hard day's drive over bad roads to get to Tulsa from Siloam Springs, but Birch figured they could make it by noon on Monday if their luck held through the night.

Trudy lay sleeping in the backseat while Birch drove through the drizzle on the one-lane road. Sipping a jug of cold coffee they had bought in Fayetteville hours before, Birch fought to keep his eyes open. By dawn he figured they would be out of the twisting hill country and on the flat straight highway that led directly into Tulsa. They would straighten out the mess at First Petroleum Bank, sleep a few hours, and head back home.

The trip back would not seem nearly so desperate as this, he thought, because he intended to have every cent of his two thousand dollars tucked away. He would pay off the taxes, pay off the Hartford bank. There would still be plenty left to live on until the farm began to support them again.

He mentally rehearsed a dozen speeches he would make to that pipsqueak Delbert and King Henry V. Smith at the bank. He pictured himself shoving a wad of bills down J.D.'s throat before pounding him into the ground. He revised this vision several times, leaving out the bills and editing the image to include J.D.'s whiskey still being smashed to pieces with an ax handle while J.D. groveled on the ground.

The truth was out now, in spite of J.D.'s warm, sentimental welcome home. Whiskey and J.D. together had robbed Birch of his father. And J.D. was intent on taking the farm, as well.

A few more hours and Birch would set it all right. He would not leave

Tulsa without the cash that would ransom his home from J.D. and the Hartford bank.

The depth of the pothole in the road was concealed by the glare of the headlamps on the water. Birch slowed as the front wheels dipped down and mud splashed over the fenders and the running board. The engine roared as the back-left wheel sank to the hub and the little Ford jerked to a stop, mired in the bog.

All hopes of reaching Tulsa and First Petroleum by Monday noon vanished. The little vehicle shuddered and strained to escape the muddy trap, but it was no use.

"Oh no," Trudy said as she sat up, instantly awakened by the calamity. No explanation was needed, and none was offered.

Birch sat frozen behind the steering wheel as the captured Ford continued to chatter. "Not *now!*"

Peering out the window, Trudy could see the mud-caked spokes spinning hopelessly in the mud. It would take a team of mules to pull them out of this. She had seen it before, and there was no thought that they could dig deep enough or try hard enough to make it free alone.

"We'll need a team, Birch," she said flatly.

He nodded and switched off the engine. With a sigh of exasperation, he sat back in the seat and moaned, "Why now?"

Trudy did not speak as the quiet sound of the rain drummed on the canvas top of the car. The air smelled clean, like sweet pine. "You need to sleep," she said quietly.

"Oh, True! I need to drive! We need to be in Tulsa tomorrow!"

"You need to rest." She touched his shoulder. "You have not slept in days, Birch." Was she saying that because she was so tired herself that every breath seemed a chore?

"What time is it?"

She peered at her wristwatch, trying to make out the hands in the darkness. "Almost four, I think."

"It will be light in a couple of hours. Then I'll walk a ways and find a farmer with a couple of good mules."

She could hear the slur in his words. The slur of exhaustion.

"Come on, then," she said from the warmth of the blankets in the rear seat. "We'll sleep awhile."

Birch dragged himself back and stretched his long legs over the front seat. He leaned his head against her shoulder and, after one long sigh, fell fast asleep.

There was someone asleep on the hospital bed beside David. No, not *on* the bed. *Beside* the bed. Sitting up in the hard straight-backed chair, a man slept with his arms crossed and his chin against his chest. A dark brown fedora was pulled low on his forehead, casting a shadow across his features. In the dim light of early morning, David could not tell if the man was young or old. Just that he was there, dressed in a dark business suit with his tie pulled loose and his breathing deep and even.

Not a guard, David reasoned. The man wore no uniform—and besides, what kind of guard would be asleep in a chair beside his prisoner?

David frowned as he remembered that all of the thugs who worked for Boss Quinn wore suits and hats like this. Only, if this was someone from Boss Quinn, then why hadn't he slit David's throat and slipped away by now?

Maybe an FBI G-man? David knew that the federal agents would want to talk to him. Someone had said so when he was on the Coast Guard ship. Some sailor had said that it would sure be too bad if the kid, meaning David, died before the G-men got to question him.

Well, David had not died. He did not even feel too bad. His throat hurt, and his stomach hurt as if he might be hungry. How long had it been since he had eaten? The last meal he remembered was on the *Jazz Baby* with Gus and Olaf and Codfish.

He closed his eyes as the faces of his friends flashed across his mind and made his heart constrict with pain. *Dead!* And now this FBI G-man would want to ask him about it. He would get the third degree he had heard the boys talk about. Days without sleep or bread or water to drink and probably with a big light shining in his eyes! David had heard all about it.

Frowning solemnly at the sleeping G-man, David shuddered and wondered if there was any way out of this joint. But where would he go if he left? Even if he managed to give the FBI the slip, there was always Boss Quinn and his goons out there on the street. *Everywhere!* And those guys were worse than the G-men. Never mind the third degree and bread and water and life in Sing Sing! If Boss Quinn managed to track him down, David would end up in concrete overshoes and dumped in the East River. Someday maybe he would break loose and float up like poor Joey the Book. And people would say, *"It's the little gangster kid . . . Mice, they called him. What a big mess he is!"*

David covered his eyes with his hands as the image of his own dead body loomed before him. What a really terrible mess! And what a really, really terrible mess he had made out of his life! What would his mother say if she could see him now? This last thought was too terrible to think about, but he thought about it anyhow.

What would Father John say? David should have stayed in Philadelphia; that was what Father John would say! Now David wished he had stayed. He had sold those wonderful tickets to the World Series and had come all the way to Manhattan to become a jailbird! A rumrunner! A miniature mobster and a witness to murder. *Two* murders! Now he did not have a friend in the world except for maybe Codfish. But where was Codfish? How come they did not bring Codfish to visit him?

A choked sob erupted from David's throat. Not even when his mama died had he felt this lonely and miserable and scared! He tried to stifle his grief so he would not wake the FBI G-man, but the more he tried to be quiet, the more his throat ached.

Oh well, sooner or later somebody was going to get him. He could not stay asleep forever. He might be the worst kind of criminal on the run, but he was still just a kid. He let loose with a mighty howl of sorrow, making the man in the suit jump up and stare bleary-eyed around the room.

"I . . . want . . . Codfish!" David wept.

"Cod? Codfish?"

"I want my dog, you lousy copper!" David struggled to sit up. "What have you done with my dog, you stinking copper?"

"I don't know." The man seemed almost frantic. He fumbled for the light. "Are you awake?"

"I want Codfish!"

"A nightmare?" The light clicked on and the terrified face of the G-man blinked down at David.

David stared back at him. This was a familiar face. Brown eyes, warm and moist, worried-looking beneath the hat brim. The shadow of a beard was on his cheeks. His mouth turned down at one corner as he stared at David. Then his eyes filled with tears.

"Are you . . . a copper?" David managed.

"No, David." The man said the name with difficulty.

"How do you know my name? David. How did you know that?"

"Doctor Oates . . . he called me."

"If you ain't a copper, then what are you?"

The man tucked his chin and pressed his lips together as if he were trying to say a word but couldn't get it out. "I'm . . . *Father*."

David screwed up his face at the word. "Father? How come if you're a priest you got no collar? Like Father John wears."

The man smiled slightly. He took off his hat, and the light shone brightly on his face. "Not that kind of father, David."

Then David knew. He knew who this was. He bit his lip and studied the hopeful expression on Max Meyer's face. "You look older than Mama's picture," David whispered.

"I guess I've aged the last couple days." His voice was gruff, as if he was trying to hold back crying just as David had done.

"I come looking for you."

"I heard. I've been looking for you, too."

"You . . . and my mama . . . you liked her, huh?"

"A lot," Max managed. Down went the chin again. He wiped his nose.

"I'm glad," David said, feeling sorry for this grown man who was his father. The real Max Meyer. Here he was, after all this time and all this trouble, and he didn't know what to do.

The room was quiet for what seemed like a long time. Down the hall, the clatter of a wheeled cart sounded.

If anyone was going to talk, it would have to be David. "Do you know what they did with my dog? Codfish?

The question broke the spell. Max brightened. "I'll find out for you." Max hurried out of the room.

The door clanked shut, and after a moment David could hear him crying softly in the hall.

CHAPTER FORTY-ONE

Sinkhole

The jingle of a mule harness drew Birch reluctantly toward consciousness.

"Howdy in there! Anybody in that automobile? Howdy in there!"

Every joint and muscle in Birch's body ached. He felt as if he had spent the night in a barrel.

"Howdy! I say . . ."

Birch opened his eyes, and it all came back to him. Siloam Springs. The car was stuck. Tulsa was still a full day distant, and it was already Monday.

The sun was up, warming the inside of the Ford and shining through the muddy windscreen. Birch struggled to sit up and slowly unbent his aching legs. With a grimace he straightened his stiff back and checked the watch on Trudy's limp wrist.

"Mornin'! Y'all get stuck?"

"Trudy!" Birch shook her shoulder. "Wake up. It's Monday. It's already seven-thirty. True? Wake up."

Tousled and rumpled and peering through one eye, Trudy managed to sit upright and look out the window at the approaching farmer and his team of gray mules.

"I say howdy, ma'am! Y'all get stuck in the bog?"

Trudy suddenly came alive. "Oh yes! Last night we drove right down into it. It will take a team to get us out! Oh, Birch! Look! *Mules!*"

The little farmer in mud-caked overalls stood beaming as he surveyed the mess. "This here's a bad'un. Ain't seen an automobile sunk this deep since last March after the big rain. 'Course I pulled two out last week.

Reckon they got the roadbed all soft. Must be why . . ." He studied the wheel and clucked his tongue as Birch climbed onto the running board.

"We sure are glad to see you, mister," Birch said. "We got to get to Tulsa."

The little farmer clucked his tongue again. "Can't get to Tulsa this way. Road's out up ahead. Gonna have to go around. That is, if y'all ain't broken an axle. Don't like the look of it. No, sir. And I've done seen 'em all. You musta hit in there plenty hard."

Birch took off his shoes and tossed them into the car. Jumping to the solid shoulder of the road, he looked over the mess. The Model T was mired to the back bumper. The license plate was completely covered, and the back-left wheel had almost disappeared.

"Most folks don't tempt fate," wheezed the old farmer. "Don't drive this track at night in no automobile, do they now?" He looked at his mule as though the animal would answer. "No. Folks don't drive this road at night. Wait till daylight if they got any sense a'tall. Then any fool can see that no automobile's gonna make it through this here bog under its own steam. Some folks try, but they always end up at my door askin' for help." He grinned proudly. "Why, a smart man sees this here hole and takes one look at my mules over yonder in the pasture, and I hitch up and give 'em a tow right on through to safety."

Birch looked across the fields to the little farmhouse overlooking the road. There was a clear view from the front porch to the mudhole. The road ahead was a confusion of mule tracks and tire tracks. The old farmer had quite a business concern right here.

"We're in a hurry to get to Tulsa," Trudy said in a grateful voice.

Birch frowned. He had a feeling about the farmer, and it wasn't good.

"Well now." The farmer spit in the mud. "Every fool goin' down this place is in a hurry to get somewhere." He scratched his head.

"Can you give us a hand?" Trudy asked.

"Sure. For a price." The farmer grinned. "This here is a *toll road.*"

Birch had figured that out after a few seconds. When Trudy's eyes narrowed, Birch knew that she, too, had figured out that this was highway robbery of sorts.

"Yessir, it'll cost y'all five dollars to get your automobile outta that there hole."

"Five!" Birch and Trudy said together.

"That's right. Five. Only cost two for me to haul you on over to the other side if you had come to ask me for help first. I don't get so dirty that way, see. Not such a strain on Bill and Jeb." He patted his mules affectionately. "But y'all got a mess here. Gonna take a heap of work to get this here automobile out."

"Five! But five dollars?"

"I don't charge near as much as them fellas on down the road. They catch automobiles like flies in a spiderweb down there. You'd be advised to take the other highway around Siloam Springs, I'd say."

An hour later and five dollars poorer, Birch and Trudy chugged slowly away from the Siloam Springs tollbooth. They had lost both money and time that they could not afford to lose.

☆ ☆ ☆

Lily was sweeping the front porch when J.D. rode up the lane. He was a proud little man, Lily thought. Dreadful proud. She could tell by the way he sat on his horse. By the way his hat was pushed back and the way he rode with his shotgun balanced across the pommel of his saddle. J.D. was just as proud as any field boss shouting at the hands to hurry along with their picking.

He rode right up to the front steps and sat there looking at Lily. She kept on sweeping, never stopping, going over the same planks she had just swept.

"Where's Mister Tucker, gal?"

"Ain't here." She swept a pile of dust up in a little cloud that circled the legs of the big horse.

"Where is Missus Tucker?"

"Ain't here."

"Well, where are they?"

"Ain't none of my business to ask where white folks goin', now is it?" She felt his gaze lingering on her. The horse stamped, impatient to be off.

"You darkies know more'n you let on." He grinned at her. " 'Course, you ain't but half nigger, are you? I know'd a gal like you. Had this light-skinned baby. And what do you think? That baby grow'd up to be a whore in the same place. You know how that goes. Pretty soon the babies is gettin' lighter and lighter till a man can't hardly tell what he's got aholt of no more."

Lily did not look at him, but she could feel him leering at her. "They ain't here." She ignored his comments.

"Does that mean y'all are alone here, then?"

Lily swept harder, backing toward the door. "No, I ain't."

"The boys are at school. That big black buck is down in the field. Who's here with you? The baby?" The saddle leather groaned as he shifted his weight.

The doorknob was within reach. "You best be gettin' on out of here. Mister Birch and Miz Trudy be back directly."

"Is that so? Mind if I wait, then?" He swung from the saddle and bounded up the steps in an instant. He grabbed Lily by the arm and laughed as she struggled to free herself. "I was thinkin' when all this is settled, I might be needin' a house gal . . . to keep things picked up and such."

"Let go my arm!" Lily winced with pain as he dug his stubby fingers into her wrist.

"What you think, gal?" He pushed her against the wall. "You think you want to work for me?"

"Please . . . lemme go . . ."

"First gimme a little kiss." He smelled of whiskey.

Lily cried out and she heard baby Joe begin to cry from his crib. "Stop! Mister Birch is comin'. . . ."

"No, he ain't." J.D. laughed. "I know they've gone to Tulsa. You been lyin' to ol' J.D., ain't you?"

"What you come here for?" She moved her head to the side as he tried to put his mouth on hers.

"Come on." He was not smiling now. "You know why I come. Got to thinkin' about that light-skinned colored gal on down to the bawdy house in Fort Smith. Whetted my appetite some. So I come on over. Just bein' friendly. Don't you want to be friendly with ol' J.D.?" He turned the doorknob and threw the door back, shoving Lily into the front room.

"Help me!" Lily cried.

"Nobody's gonna hear you cry. You might as well relax and—"

A voice boomed behind him. "That's where you is wrong!" Jefferson grabbed J.D. by the back of his coat and slung him around as if he were a sack of potatoes. "You forgettin' me, Mister J.D.?" Jeff held him off the ground as Lily scrambled away.

J.D. struggled for an instant, then shouted, "You know what happens around here when a nigger lays hands on a white man?"

"Yessir. Sometimes the white man gets his neck broke. 'Specially if the white man don't know how to treat a lady."

J.D.'s expression melted with fear. Jefferson held him up as though he were no bigger than a small boy in need of a whipping. "Lemme down," J.D. demanded. Then, pleading, "Lemme down."

Jefferson did not put him down. Lily went into the bedroom to comfort baby Joe, who wailed louder at the sound of the ruckus.

"You got the young'un cryin'," Jefferson said through gritted teeth. "I don't think the young'un likes when you come sneakin' around with your whiskey breath. Don't think he likes when you bother Lily."

"Just havin' a little fun," J.D. whined.

"Don't think the young'un likes the way you have fun. He's mighty fond of Miz Lily. Thinks highly of her. She's a good Christian woman. The young'un don't like to hear nobody talk to her like she from a bawdy house." Jefferson gave him a stiff shake, jolting him till his hat fell off.

"Put me down!"

"No sir." Jeff lifted him higher, banging his head hard on the ceiling.

"Don't hurt me!"

"You need to apologize," Jefferson said quietly as he banged J.D.'s head again, "or else next time your head gonna go through the ceilin'. An' then maybe I might let go an' your neck break like a stalk of dry cane. Then you just be hangin' there—"

"No! Sorry! I didn't mean nothin'! Didn't mean no harm . . ."

"You done harm." Jeff lowered him to eye level. "That there is my woman, Mister. An' this here is Birch Tucker's farm for now. You'd be advised not to come around till it ain't his place no more. Then you an' me can maybe have another chat."

J.D. nodded. His pale blue eyes were bloodshot. "What you gonna do now?"

Jefferson carried him at arm's length onto the porch and down the steps. With one mighty thrust, he tossed him hard into his saddle. Then, picking up the shotgun from the step, Jefferson broke it over his knee and handed the pieces to J.D.

"Get!" Jefferson said.

And J.D. did.

✵ ✵ ✵

It was the biggest dog Max had ever seen. There it sat, stinking and slobbering and gazing happily up at Max.

"Codfish," Max said. "How do you do." The dog offered a paw, a handshake to cement the friendship. Max had sneaked him up the back stairs of the hospital while Dr. Oates and the staff looked the other way.

U.S. Coast Guard Captain Ronald Geisler paced back and forth in front of Max and Codfish in the nurses' coffee room. "It's out of our hands, of course, Mister Meyer, but if it were my kid I'd get him as far from here as I could go. If it were my kid, I'd resign my commission in the Coast Guard and buy myself a fishing boat in Bora-Bora, if you get my meaning." He shook his white head. "It was my crew who picked the boy up, and I can tell you, those hijackers mean business. If it hadn't been for this dog . . . I guess you have to be there to know just what kind of business they mean. But with that little bit showing up about the kid in the paper, they know he did not go down with the *Jazz Baby*."

"You're telling me this isn't finished?"

"I'm telling you you're going to have a visit from the FBI, and they'll want the kid to testify if he knows anything. And even if he doesn't know anything, I can tell you those hijackers are mighty nervous about the fact that the kid is still alive. You follow me?"

"Perfectly. Will they come here, you think?"

The little banty Coast Guard captain peered around the room as if he were inspecting his ship. "Can't say. They might wait until you take him home. They're bushwhackers. Work in the dark, these types. Slit throats, don't leave witnesses. Yessir. The fact the kid is alive has them plenty nervous. And you're a fairly high-profile type of fellow yourself, what with the newspaper business and all. Easy to spot. Easy to track. Like I said, a fishing boat in Bora-Bora is something you might think about for a while."

Max nodded. "I'm no kind of sailor, but I've got a few weeks' leave coming."

"Now you're talking. And don't let those fancy federal men talk you into staying around. Don't let them lay that on this kid, Mister Meyer. Those FBI men have a nasty habit of losing witnesses. I'd hate to see the boy hurt. I tell you, we're going to catch that kingpin out there one of these days, and we won't need a court when we get him in our sights. A good shot with the cannon amidships will save the taxpayers a whole lot of money and put that wharf rat where he belongs." He frowned and rose onto his toes. "Of course, you can't say I told you this. No sir. I'm not giving you advice. It's just that I was there. I saw what the cutthroats did. And what I'm saying is that if it were my kid in there . . . ."

☆ ☆ ☆

David knew everything about Max's life, it seemed. He had certainly heard every word about the old neighborhood.

"Mama said there aren't any pickles in the whole world like Mister Finkel's pickles." The boy lowered his chin and began to recite the words the pickleman used to use when he spoke about life and pickle making. *"You want to make something good, you got to do a lot of work. That's just the way life is."*

Max laughed in astonishment. Ten years had passed, yet Max's lost son shared the same memories that Max and Irene had shared. It was a wonder and a miracle binding father and son as though they had never been apart.

"Did she tell you about anything else?"

"Everything."

"Coney Island?"

"Nathan's Famous hot dogs."

"You want to go there?" How many years had it been since Max had traveled the subway to Coney Island?

David grinned broadly . . . then, suddenly, his smile faded. "Don't want to go to the beach." He shuddered.

"Well, it's too cold now, but in the summer . . ."

David cast a long look at Codfish, who was sleeping peacefully on the floor. "Nope. I . . . you know . . . did they tell you about Joey the Book?" He lowered his voice to a whisper.

"Joey the Book?" Max tried to remember all those odd names kids had in the old days on Orchard Street. This was not a name he remembered. "Maybe your mama's friend?"

David gave his head a rapid shake. "No. Joey the Book. Not Mama's friend. I knew him. Sort of. Not real well. And then Boss had him fixed. Killed. He washed up on the beach and—" David's chin trembled—"I don't want to go to the beach. Don't want to go to Coney Island."

Max nodded, afraid that the boy would cry. Max was not experienced enough at this fatherhood thing to deal with tears.

"Then how about Atlantic City?" he asked, but a chill coursed through him. "Or Bora-Bora?"

"Huh? Bora?"

"Bora-Bora," Max said with certainty. "That's right. Great place. Doc says you'll be well enough to get out of here in a couple of days, maybe. And then . . ."

✳ ✳ ✳

The tone of Managing Editor Bill Whittaker of the *New York Times* was anything but understanding. His voice boomed over the phone.

"Where are you, Meyer? Drunk? Are you drunk, man, or just out of your mind?"

"I've got vacation coming. And I plan to take it. That's all."

"You're *crazy*! You can't leave now. Do you know what is happening on Wall Street? Any idea? Everything you've been saying would happen eventually *is* happening! There is an earthquake down there. You said yourself that the place is ready to fall off into the sea and sink. You can't leave yet. You've got the most momentous story in all of America's economic history taking place, and you're going to cover it! *A financial Titanic!*"

Max waited until he slowed down. "Look, Bill—"

"NO! You look! I'm not going to let you do this! You and that little Professor Babson! Prophets of Loss, they call you! Sure, I laughed, but

Max . . . you were right! Day by day, a little more of the house of cards is falling in. Financiers are scrambling around down here like ants on an anthill, sinking more dough into the thing to try to save it. It's going to blow wide-open! And you're telling me you want a *vacation*?"

"Yes, Bill. That's what I'm telling you." Max was smiling as he hung up the telephone on the still-hysterical editor. Maybe the world was going down. Well, it could fall apart without Max Meyer there to write Wall Street's obituary.

A fishing boat in Bora-Bora sounded better every minute.

CHAPTER FORTY-TWO

House of Cards

On Monday, October 28, the mood of the Sabre Oil pool conspirators was tense but hopeful.

The visitors' gallery of the Stock Exchange was still closed, but Damon Phelps insisted that he absolutely was not going to stay away. Keenan felt too harried to argue about it. After all, there had still been no word of Max Meyer's whereabouts, and no retraction had appeared in the Monday-morning paper. What had appeared in place of his financial column was a small box containing an apology that Max's commentary would not appear. Anyway, Keenan did not have time to argue with Phelps, so the oilman accompanied the broker to the Exchange.

In a tight cluster of dark suits and briefcases, Keenan, Phelps, and the Irish Brigade marched down Wall Street. Long before the trading day was to begin, the street was packed with thousands of curious onlookers. It felt to Phelps as if the crowd was on hand for a sporting event, and a rough one at that, like football or a no-holds-barred fistfight. Supplementing the normal police contingent were fifty extra uniformed patrolmen, including twenty on horseback. "They expecting a riot or something?" Phelps asked.

Keenan only stared back at him.

Once inside the building, Keenan explained to the Exchange superintendent that Phelps was a visiting dignitary, the head of a large Midwestern bank, as well as an oil tycoon. He had unselfishly placed his resources at the disposal of Keenan's brokerage to aid in stemming last Thursday's market collapse. Could an exception to the no-visitors decision be arranged?

Thus Damon Phelps found himself seated alone in the visitors' gallery. He had enjoyed Keenan's honeyed words and accepted them as being only his just due. They were all true, weren't they? Of course, no one paid any further attention to his presence, but he had the best seat in the house anyway.

Trading began in an orderly enough manner, and except for the occasional reference to Sabre Oil, the flow of prices across the annunciator boards carried no particular significance for Phelps. Sabre, he noted happily, opened up another dollar and soon added two more. Now they were rolling!

The stock-market symbol for steel caught Phelps's attention. It had appeared several times already, and Phelps decided to see if it was rising as rapidly as Sabre. The oilman enjoyed comparing himself to the stock-market barons like the Morgans and the Rockefellers, who could muster the capital to manipulate a stock like steel that sold in the hundreds of dollars a share instead of the teens like Sabre. Someday Phelps would play in that league!

When the next figure for steel was quoted, it was down three dollars. Phelps looked on in surprise, which changed to amazement as it slumped another two dollars and then two more. Down on the trading floor, pandemonium was breaking out. Waves of traders mobbed the specialists, and not just around Post Two, which handled steel, either. Messengers crisscrossed the trading floor at frantic paces, sometimes colliding with brokers and sending both men reeling off on new courses.

In the pandemonium around Post Twelve, where radio was traded, Phelps saw a broker try to get a messenger's attention. Apparently no amount of shouting or gesturing could make the younger man understand, and as Phelps watched, the trader grabbed the messenger by the lapels of his uniform, lifted him bodily off the ground, and threw him.

Stunned by this unaccountable phenomena, Phelps almost missed the next quoted trade for Sabre. But out of the corner of his eye he caught it. It, too, was down—had already given back the entire three-dollar gain.

Phelps gripped the railing and leaped upright. It must be a mistake! Why wasn't Keenan watching? Why didn't he do something? Phelps waved his arms and shouted, trying to catch Keenan's attention. While he was flapping and yelling, steel slipped another dollar and Sabre another two dollars.

Phelps' reeling mind settled on the only explanation he could think of: Keenan must be selling them out too soon! What other explanation could there be? Phelps had to stop the broker before he ruined everything.

When Phelps tried to race down onto the trading floor, a guard inter-cepted him. "He's selling me out! He's selling me out!" chanted the oil-man frantically. "I've got to stop him!"

"Calm down, sir, or you'll have to leave."

Phelps tried to dodge past the guard, who grabbed his arm. The two struggled, rolling onto the carpet. Two more guards rushed up, and Phelps was overpowered. His eyes looked glassy, and he let himself be led away quietly.

The guards appeared unsure of what to do with a visiting dignitary—a guest of Mike Keenan no less—who had gone berserk. Eventually they decided to lock him in a vacant office until the end of trading for the day. One guard was left to look after him, but all Phelps did was stare out the window at the milling crowds.

★ ★ ★

The Monday-afternoon business in the First Petroleum Bank of Tulsa was winding to a close. Senior Vice President Tell had ushered two el-derly lady customers out through the front doors and was heading pur-posefully for Phelps's private office.

Halfway there, Mrs. Jenkins, the senior cashier, called to him, freez-ing him in his tracks. "Mister Tell, may I speak with you for a moment?"

Stay friendly and businesslike, everything normal. This litany had been playing over and over in Tell's mind all day long. "Yes, Missus Jenkins. What is it?"

Mrs. Jenkins's voice lowered to a stage whisper. "I must tell you about a most unusual occurrence that has happened today."

Tell could feel his arched eyebrows peaking nearer to his receding hairline, despite his efforts to lower them.

"Most unusual," she continued, "and it concerns you."

"Oh, really?" Tell croaked his reply in a half-tenor, half-bass quaver that had not been heard since he was fourteen.

"Yes." Mrs. Jenkins went on with a conspiratorial wink. "And don't think the other tellers aren't aware of what's going on also. After all, the last seven customers at my window said the exact same thing . . . even the very same words."

"And what was that?" asked Tell. He could feel the bank swaying.

"All seven said that they were so pleased to have their savings in a fine local bank like this and not mixed up with that awful stock market. Isn't that amazing? It was more than seven, actually, taken altogether, but the last seven in a row. Anyway, as you are an officer of the bank, I thought you'd want to know. Perhaps you'll want to share the story with

Mister Phelps when he returns. Let him know how well we carried on in his absence."

Exhaling sharply and swallowing twice, Tell agreed. "Yes, Missus Jenkins, truly remarkable. I'll certainly bring it to Mister Phelps's attention. Now, if you'll excuse me."

Retreating as quickly as possible toward the rear office, Tell could still overhear Mrs. Jenkins. To another teller she observed in a sympathetic voice, "Poor Mister Tell. He must be working too hard. He looks ill."

On the other side of the oak door was Assistant Vice President Penner. His head was sunk in his hands as he sat staring at the clicking stock ticker.

"Well?" demanded Tell. "What's the latest?"

Penner still said nothing. As Tell watched, the ticker spewed out the last of its stream of tape. Penner made no move to refill it, and the machine continued to chatter aimlessly, printing nothing, its message long since delivered.

"It's all gone," Penner said at last.

"Yes, I see that," scolded Tell brusquely, looking at the heap of ticker tape on the floor.

"No," said Penner, waving a hand around in a gesture that included the room, the bank, Tulsa, and the two men themselves. "No, you don't see. For the last hour the market has gone down, down, down . . . 985 stocks, all lower. . . . It was still getting worse at the buzzer. I think it will get even worse tomorrow."

Tell had stopped listening halfway through. "Down, down, down," he mumbled. "Two million dollars, all gone."

"Tell," Penner said abruptly. No title, not even mister. "Tell, how much cash is in the vault?"

"What possible difference—?" Tell began, then stopped. Something in Penner's words and tone and face made him pause and reflect. "You're right," Tell said. "Fifty thousand dollars, more or less, cannot matter now. They say Mexico is very pleasant this time of year."

The man standing in front of Boss Quinn in his office on the *China Doll* was named Smiley, but it was not a grinning face that had given his name. Smiley's early career had included several vicious fights with rival gangs. In one of these, somebody had almost succeeded in cutting his throat and left him with a wide scar, like a permanent smile, on his neck.

Just now the only thing smiling in the room was the scar.

"These things should not be so complicated," Boss Quinn was say-ing. "Meyer has not showed up either at his home or his office. It is most unlike the man. It is almost as if someone tipped him to my unhappi-ness with his brand of journalism. Furthermore, I was only today able to trace the kid, Mice, to the hospital, without causing undue suspicion on the part of the coppers."

Quinn sighed. "So, Smiley," he continued, "it is up to you. Due to Mister Max Meyer being so unthoughtful as to his whereabouts, I am forced to leave Ham and Sal at his place for the time being, where, no doubt, they are living the life of Riley but of no use elsewhere."

Smiley did not look happy. Even the scar seemed to frown. "You wants me to do a job on a kid in a hospital without no help?" he asked in a voice with the quality of sandpaper.

"Did I say that? Here is the kid's room number." Quinn handed over a slip of paper. "There is a fire escape off the alley that should prove use-ful since the kid's room is on that side also. Be on the ladder at 2:00 AM sharp. At that time an automobile will have an unfortunate fire in the street in front of the hospital. While everyone awake is watching out the window, you should not have any difficulty with this little task."

✯ ✯ ✯

Codfish remained at David's bedside all day Monday. Max had taken the big animal out to walk him three times. Only then did he think about what must have happened during the day on Wall Street. All that seemed remote and unimportant now. Only David mattered to him.

Before Max was introduced to the two men in Dr. Oates's office, he knew they were FBI agents. They were well dressed in off-the-rack suits, lacking the fine tailoring of businessmen or the nattiness of gangsters. Their shoes were well-worn, and bulges beneath their suit coats told Max that they were carrying revolvers. What did they want with David? And why had they come here to meet with Max?

Agent Burns flipped open a folder displaying a photograph of a dead body on the beach. He let the horror of the image seep in before he flipped that photograph over, displaying a second, even more horrible image of two bodies burned beyond recognition.

Max grimaced involuntarily. "Looks like the stuff the city desk passes around the cafeteria for kicks during lunch hour."

Agent Burns did not smile at the attempted levity. "This is no joke, Mister Meyer."

"I did not intend for it to be." Max reached over and closed the folder. "I haven't eaten breakfast yet, if you don't mind. Get to the point."

Agent Allen leaned back in the armchair and smiled a professional, patronizing smile. "The point is, Mister Meyer, that the two well-done corpses in the pictures are the men your son was with the night he was picked up out of the water." He inclined his head slightly at the flash of fear he saw in Max's eyes. "That lump of human fish food you saw in the first picture was found on the beach at Coney Island. A real thrill for the kids making sand castles, I guess." He smiled. "Word on the street is that your boy knows something about the matter."

"Interested?" asked Burns.

"He's nine years old," Max blurted. "What can he know about . . . ?" He waved his hand toward the folder.

"He knows enough that there is a contract out on him. The gentleman who arranged the little bonfire for David's friends was very unhappy the boy got away."

"Very unhappy."

"You see, this gentleman is someone we have been trying to get off the streets for quite some time."

"Slippery. Whenever we get close, maybe find a witness, well, the witnesses have a way of just vanishing." Burns cleaned his nails with a penknife as he spoke. Then he drew the blade across his neck. "You get my meaning?"

"Occasionally they wash up," Allen added. "Like our friend in the file there. This poor chump just happened to have a laundry mark in his shirt. Joey the Book, his name was. A handy man to have around. Might have helped us out if he had lived."

"But he didn't."

"And word is that your boy knows something about it."

Max felt the headache start between his shoulder blades and creep up the back of his neck, finally taking hold of his skull like a vise. "He's nine years old," Max said again. "Too young for all this . . ."

"Too young to die," said Burns.

"What do you want from him?" Max felt angry at the two agents, as though they refused to realize that David was just a kid. A kid who should have been playing sandlot baseball and marbles and . . . maybe fishing in Bora-Bora?

"First, we want to talk to him," Burns jumped in.

"You can't show him those." Max pushed the file from the edge of the desk.

"We don't need to. He saw it all. Chances are he can repeat the names of the men who did this. And if he can, then his only chance to survive is to put us in a position to arrest the bums. Send them up to Sing Sing and let them sit in the hot seat, if you know what I mean."

"He can't talk to you now," Max protested. "Didn't Doctor Oates tell you?"

The two men exchanged looks of frustration. "Yes. But with your permission . . ."

"You're going to have to wait." Max stood up abruptly.

"We can't wait," Burns retorted. "If you love your kid, you'll want the men who are out for his scalp to be arrested. That's the only smart move. If David can give us a statement, we can get a court order. Have the perpetrators picked up. Then your worries are over. See?" Again, the professional smile slid into place.

"He's not up for this," Max protested. "When Doctor Oates gives the okay, then I will. But David can hardly put two words together. You understand?"

"He won't have to." Allen flipped open a second folder of mug shots. "All he has to do is point. Easy, huh?"

"I don't know," said Max again. "He's been scared enough already."

"He'll be plenty safe soon. That priest—Father John, I think—is coming to take him back to Philly. We get the kid's statement and *whoosh*, he's clear out of town."

"All right," Max finally agreed, "but not today. He needs at least one more night's rest."

Burns glanced at his partner. "Okay, but this has got to be done no later than tomorrow. Yeah, okay, Tuesday noon."

CHAPTER FORTY-THREE

Escape to Orchard Street

So there it was. Father John was coming to take David back to Philadelphia. Max crossed his arms and watched the boy sleeping. The honey-blond hair and porcelain skin glowed in the soft light.

Now what? Should Max just step aside and let a stranger take over? Did Father John know about Orchard Street or Coney Island hot dogs or Mr. Finkel's pickles? Could the priest protect David from the men who had slaughtered Joey the Book and the Svenson brothers? Was Philadelphia far enough away to hide?

Codfish whined and laid his big head on Max's knee, telling him he needed a walk. Max patted the dog but did not move from the chair. He sighed and considered what he should do. He remembered the warning of Captain Geisler: *"If it were my kid . . ."*

"That's right," Max said aloud. "He is mine." He stared at the cleft in the boy's chin. "My kid."

Codfish whined again, stood, and stretched. He wagged expectantly at Max. Time for the midnight walk, wasn't it?

"You're right, Codfish." Max tapped David gently on the shoulder. "David?"

The boy peered up at Max and blinked until his eyes focused. "Is it morning?"

"No."

"Huh?"

"Codfish says he needs to go for a walk. You want to come?" He glanced toward the clothes the night nurse had brought for David. Her boy had outgrown them, she said, and he would need something to wear when he left.

David was instantly awake. "Can I? I thought I couldn't until Tuesday."

Max pointed to his watch. "It is Tuesday. Past midnight. You can come with me. But we'll have to be careful not to let anyone see us, you know?"

"Oh boy!" David threw back the covers and jumped from bed, but his legs were shaky and almost gave out on him.

"Go easy."

"I'm okay. Just sea legs, that's all. Olaf and Gus always walked funny on the land, too. Just sea legs." He supported himself by holding on to the bed as Max put the knickers and sweater within reach.

"Take it easy," Max warned again, having a moment of doubt. "I'll be back in a minute."

When Max returned from peering down the hallway, David was completely dressed. Max held his finger to his lips, warning David to stay quiet.

The boy nodded and stood swaying beside Codfish as Max slipped out of the room and walked quietly down to the end of the corridor away from the nurses' station.

The nurse did not even glance up as Max turned a corner into another corridor. He walked into a room where an old man snored loudly and pushed the call button. He could hear the buzzer ring far back down the corridor where the night nurse sat reading the newspaper and eating a sandwich. Max dashed into the room across the hall and pushed a second call button above a sleeping patient. Then a third button in the next room.

Walking back toward David's room, Max met the harried-looking nurse as she walked toward the source of her irritation.

"Good evening, Nurse Day," he told the night nurse.

She hurried past. "Three buzzers all at once. It never rains but it pours."

Max could not help but imagine the kind of thunderstorm there would be when Nurse Day found that David Meyer had flown the coop. That would be an hour or so from now when she made her rounds to check blood pressure and temperature. David's vital signs were perfectly normal now. But certainly his disappearance would raise the blood pressures of quite a few people.

David and Codfish were by the door. "Come on!" Max picked up David, flung him over his shoulder, and counted on Codfish to keep up as he made a dash for the stairs to freedom.

It took three tries before a cab pulled to the curb beside Max, David, and Codfish. "You got money?" asked the driver, eyeing the big dog.

"Enough," Max replied, aware of his shabby appearance and unshaven face.

"Guess you didn't invest in the stock market, then," the driver quipped. "I don't give rides to dogs usually, but if you got the fare, I suppose I shouldn't look a gift horse in the mouth, so to speak. Who knows when I will find anybody in Manhattan who can pay for a taxi?" He scowled at the dog again. "But I tell you, if this dog messes in my cab, it will cost you extra."

David stepped forward indignantly. "Codfish has swell manners. He knows his business."

"In that case, kid, the mutt is smarter than anybody on Wall Street. Those guys have messed all over everything down there." He grinned. "Nice poochie. So get in. Where to?"

"Orchard Street," Max instructed, crowding in next to Codfish, who stuck his head out the window as though he were back on the bow of the *Jazz Baby*.

The driver cast a suspicious glance in the rearview mirror. "Orchard Street? That'll cost you seventy-five cents in advance. Not that I doubt your word about the cash, but normally people who want Orchard Street ride the tramcar, if you know what I mean."

Max paid the advance fare, then put his arm around David, who snuggled close and fell fast asleep almost as soon as the cab slipped into traffic. He did not awaken when the driver jerked his thumb back toward the hospital and piped, "Well, look at that, will you? Some poor mug's car is burning up right beside the hospital! After such a day as this, who deserves such a dose of bad luck, I ask you?"

Orchard Street. Mr. Finkel's pickle store. Even shuttered and sleeping, the place smelled like garlic and cloves and coriander spices. David's mother had told him all about it. If he had not known that Max was bringing him here, David still would have recognized the brick tenements with iron fire escapes and Hebrew lettering on the windows of the shops.

David followed Max down a narrow alley to the back of Finkel's shop. They climbed one flight of rickety stairs, and Max knocked softly on the thin wood of the door.

"Who is there?" croaked a thin, reedy voice.

"It's Max Meyer," Max replied.

This information caused quite a stir on the other side of the door. A man and woman carried on a lively discussion. The door was thrown wide, revealing an elderly couple in nightshirts who pulled Max in.

"We have not seen you since your Bubbe died last year, God rest her soul! And here you are! In the middle of the night, no less! Herbert was just sayin' that a lot of people who left Orchard Street would probably be comin' back, the way the world is headin'! So, Max—" the little pickleman squinted down at David—"what is this? Will you look at this, Vera! Max has brought along a little boy . . . Max! This is *you* when you were ten years old! Only with blond hair! Mama! Look here! This boy looks *just* like little Max! Can you believe it?"

A bed was made for David on a cot next to the warmth of the steam radiator. Codfish, however, was not allowed in the flat because Mrs. Finkel was allergic to dogs. Tied to the railing of the fire escape, the big dog moaned unhappily as Mrs. Finkel made coffee and Max told the couple bits and pieces of the story.

"And so Irene left the boy in the care of a Catholic priest, you see. But he ran away to New York looking for me. . . ."

"What else? Poor boy!"

"And now the priest is coming to take him back."

"*No!* To take him from *his own father!* Such a world, I'm tellin' you!"

"But I intend to take him away from here for a while until we can get all the legalities sorted out."

"What else! You have a good lawyer? You know Sam Lasky's boy is a lawyer. *Such* a lawyer he is supposed to be, too. Of course, I think he is some sort of a copyright lawyer. Maybe not so good for custody cases such as this, but who can say? We should give him a call."

"We will have to keep this very hush-hush," Max warned them. "If anyone at all should get wind of the fact that I have the boy here, the police will come and . . . that is the end of it, I'm afraid."

"Such a rotten thing. Of course we should keep our mouths shut. Not a word!"

Max continued. "You were always good with kids, Mister Finkel. And Missus Finkel, you and Bubbe were such close friends. I knew it was the right thing to bring David here. Bubbe whispered in my ear tonight . . . 'Finkel's.' "

"Such a fine woman, your grandmother, God rest her soul. *Of course* we will do this for her grandson!"

"I can pay you some."

"*What?* Not a penny!"

"I've got to get back to my hotel. Get cleaned up. Pick up a few things.

I've got some cash in my safety-deposit box. We'll need it if we're going to survive for long."

"A smart boy you are, Max! I was thinkin' how smart you were the other day when I read your column. I should have known you would have cash put aside for a rainy day. Your Bubbe would be proud. Such a *good boy*! She always said so!"

David was sleeping when Max left that morning. He took Codfish with him, but David did not feel lonely when he woke up. After all, he ate blintzes for breakfast in the little kitchen and listened for hours as Mrs. Finkel talked about when Max was a boy. Then she took out an old photo album and flipped through the pages. All the pictures looked familiar to him. He had seen the same scenes in his mother's photo album, after all.

CHAPTER FORTY-FOUR

The Pursuers

A thin plume of steam was rising above the radiator cap of the Model T, and two of its tires sported fresh patches before Birch and Trudy rolled into Tulsa. The redbrick buildings they passed gave the city a prosperous feel.

A muscle twitched in Birch's jaw, and his grip on the Model T's steering wheel tightened. "Birch," Trudy cautioned, "don't do anything to get yourself thrown in jail. I'd hate to have to drive all the way back to Shiloh without you."

Birch grinned sheepishly at being so obviously upset and apologized. "Reckon I was gettin' riled, all right. Maybe just showin' up at the bank will be enough for that fellow to stop messin' with us." He did not believe his own words, but it was a comforting thing to say anyway.

One thing he was also thinking but did not say was that he hoped Old Man Phelps, the founder of the First Petroleum Bank, would not be anywhere around. Birch never wanted to have anything to do with him again—ever.

On the corner just before the turn for the bank was a church. It, too, was built of red brick, and its tall steeple rose four stories above the carefully groomed yard. "Seems like a far cry from Shiloh Church, don't it, True?" Birch asked.

"I'm not so sure about that," Trudy replied. She pointed to a large marquee that announced Pastor Harvey Hines's next sermon: Choose Ye This Day Whom Ye Will Serve. Only one line, but it preached a sermon to Trudy's heart.

When they rounded the turn half a block from the bank, Birch and Trudy knew immediately that something was wrong. The street in front of the bank was crowded with people, and more were hurrying along the sidewalks, coming from both directions.

A policeman with a drooping mustache was trying to keep order. He stood in the middle of the street, urging the milling crowd to move out of the roadway. Birch pulled the Model T up alongside him and leaned out. "Is it a run on the bank?" he asked, fearful of the reply.

"Nope," replied the officer. "Bank is temporarily closed for an investigation. Now y'all move this crate on outta here."

✳ ✳ ✳

At the end of the tether, Codfish looked like an enormous black bear being led into the lobby of the Plaza Hotel. From behind the front desk, Derby, the manager, gasped and frowned, then looked up to see that it was Max Meyer attached to the other end of the leash.

The manager wiped his brow and summoned Max across the nearly deserted lobby. Codfish eyed the potted plants with an interest that made Max tug him along harder before he had opportunity to mark the Plaza Hotel as his territory.

"My heavens, Mister Meyer," breathed Derby, "where have you been? Not that it is our business, but since you disappeared, you have been the most sought-after guest in the hotel!"

Derby retrieved a stack of messages and mail and handed the bundle to Max. "The whole world has gone mad—absolutely mad! It seems that everything is coming true. Doom. Like the end of the world. And everyone wants to talk to you. To see you."

He waved his pale hand across the too-quiet foyer of the hotel as if it were full of visitors anxious to confer only with Max Meyer. "Your newspaper has been calling. Mister Beadle has come and gone a dozen times. Miss Rutger was here three times. Everyone is quite concerned." He leaned in. "There is talk that if things don't turn around today, there will be more than ticker tape flying out the windows on Wall Street."

"I'm not the type to kill myself." Max grinned.

"Oh no, Mister Meyer." Derby's face wore a deadpan expression. "Not suicide. My dear no. I meant quite a few brokers were saying they would *throw* you out a window. You and that Professor Babson and the other financial writers who didn't cooperate."

"Murder. Ah. A different story. Kill the prophet, eh?"

"You'll see when you read your messages." He sighed. "It is already like a morgue around here. The dining room closed early last night, and the orchestra went home. No one felt like dancing."

"I suppose they are learning how to pray," Max said dryly, thrusting the unread messages into his pocket.

"Oh yes! What else? Everything is ruined. Or close to being ruined. Everyone is down on Wall Street this morning! Just the end of the world. The stink of death is over all—" He sniffed and leaned over the desk, "What *is* that dreadful smell?"

"Codfish," Max replied. "My Irish wolfhound. Remember?"

Max did not tip the frantic little man. The last shred of Derby's reserve had faded as he had watched the superwealth of the Plaza Hotel residents slipping away over the last days. Many of the hotel guests were nearly broke or completely broke. At least Mr. Derby still had his job. He dithered and fussed behind the front desk and peered at the empty lobby as if he were the only survivor of some dread disease.

Max gave him a last look as the elevator doors slid closed and the elevator attendant began talking.

"What do you think? I've been taking grown men up to their rooms, and they bawl all the way. Don't come down, neither. What do you think?"

Max rubbed a hand over the stubble on his chin. "I think I need a shower before I come down again."

"Those men from Keenan I took to your floor? They didn't come down neither, Mister Meyer. The whole weekend. I figure they want to talk serious business with you. Either that or they've killed themselves up in your room."

"A fitting tribute to my career," Max replied as the elevator stopped on his floor.

"Nice-looking mutt, Mister Meyer," the attendant called after him. "You better give him a shower too, though."

"Codfish," Max answered, taking his key from the pocket of his overcoat.

The elevator bell chimed and the doors closed just as Codfish balked, blocking the entrance to Max's apartment. The thick black coat bristled, and a menacing growl sounded deep in the throat of the beast.

"Come on, Codfish." Max gave the leash a tug, but the animal leaned against it, nearly pressing his nose against the door. The rumble sounded again, and the fangs bared.

Max stepped back and stared at the latch of his door. The dog snarled again, more violently. He sniffed the latch, and saliva dripped from his teeth as Max pulled him back from the entry.

What had the elevator attendant said about men waiting in his room? Men sent by Keenan? And the comment Derby made about Max being thrown out the window?

The hairs on the back of Max's neck prickled like Codfish's ruff. The dog knew Max's uninvited guests well enough to dislike them.

So much for a shower and clean clothes. Max ducked into the stairway and left the Plaza through the employee entrance into the alley.

With two hundred dollars in his wallet, Max was better off than the majority of yesterday's Wall Street millionaires. In addition to this, he kept two thousand dollars stashed in his Wall Street safety-deposit box. Max walked toward the corner of Wall Street along the East River. The breeze off the river was chilly and moist, and an unpleasant drizzle fell out of the leaden skies.

With the collar of his overcoat turned up, his hat brim pulled low, and several days' growth of beard, Max was scarcely recognizable. It occurred to Max that he could have walked through a group of his friends without being recognized.

That is, if he had any friends left. Right now his only friends seemed to be a son stashed away on Orchard Street and this brute of a black dog straining at the other end of the leash.

When Max rounded the corner onto Wall Street, he was still six blocks from the Stock Exchange, but his progress was drastically slowed. From one side of the roadway to the other, as far down Wall Street as Max could see, the boulevard was packed with people. No cars or buses or trucks could get through the massed bodies. Not today, the twenty-ninth of October.

Not that the people seemed to be hurrying anywhere. They all appeared to be waiting for something. The overcoated throng with their hats and umbrellas were not noisy or unruly. They did not punch or shove or in any way deserve the title of mob, although there had to be at least ten thousand of them.

Strangest of all was the sense Max had of having been somewhere and seen this before, this silent waiting in anticipation of some dreaded unpreventable happening, the silent agony on so many faces.

Then it came to him. In 1922, Max had been in Rome when Pope Benedict XV, the Pope of Peace, had died. There had been thousands gathered there, too, with the same sort of voiceless, expectant fear.

A stranger came toward Max, tottering down the sidewalk. When he was still some distance away, Max sensed that the man had singled him out and focused on him. Max attempted to dodge around him.

Glancing down at Codfish, Max could see that the dog had also detected the steady approach. But, while attentive, the dog gave no signal of danger.

The stranger reached Max's side and grasped him by the arm as one might greet a long-missing friend. "Did you know?" the man said. "I lost a hundred thousand dollars."

Max flinched, wondering if some sort of blame attached to the statement might lead to a punch being thrown.

The man's eyes were moist. "I can never go home again. I lost a hundred thousand dollars." He peered into Max's face and shook his head as if suddenly realizing that he did not know Max, after all.

The man reluctantly released his grip on Max's coat sleeve and resumed staggering toward the river. Max heard him stop another pedestrian and murmur, "Did you know? I lost a hundred thousand dollars."

The unknown man moving toward the East River and away from the Stock Exchange was an exception. Like iron filings toward a magnet, lines of dark-coated men and women flowed up Wall Street toward the Temple of Mammon.

Max heard scraps of conversation amid the silence. A woman in an expensive fur coat was remarking to everybody and nobody how she had asked her broker for an up-to-date quote. "The man wasn't even polite. He snapped at me."

Two men walking arm in arm were openly passing a bottle of bootleg hooch back and forth. They wore strands of ticker tape twined around their hats and streamers of stock quotes over their shoulders. One said, "Have you heard the latest joke? A guy says, 'Poor me, I got heart trouble at thirty-five,' and his friend says, 'You think you got trouble? I got RCA at 140!' " The two went off laughing uproariously and offering their bottle to others.

Opposite No. 64 Wall Street, Max heard someone call his name. "Hey, Mister Meyer." It was Joey Fortuna at his shoeshine stand.

Max made his way through the stream to Joey's side. "How'd you recognize me, Joey?"

"Easy, Mister Meyer. I been watchin' for you. But what are you doin' down here? You shouldn't be here."

"What do you mean, Joey? I used to work here, remember?"

"Yeah, well, not no more. Not if you're as smart as I think. Word on the street is, see, Boss Quinn is after you."

"Quinn? The bootlegger? Why should he be after me?"

"On accounta the oil pool, Mister Meyer. Word is, Boss Quinn figgers you for a double-crosser. You gotta get outta here, Mister Meyer. I ain't the only one who'll figger on lookin' for you around here."

"Thanks, Joey. You're a pal."

"Ain't nothin'. You was always straight with me. Wish I'd listened to you about gettin' outta the market."

"Why, Joey? How much did you lose?"

"I didn't do so bad. I sold out last Thursday, so I got back fifteen hunerd outta my five grand."

Max shook his head. "Sorry, Joey."

"Ain't your fault, Mister Meyer. You tried to warn us. We just didn't listen."

Max turned to leave, then decided he had to know. "How bad is it today, Joey?"

"Word is, it's the worst. All the stocks are gettin' beat up bad. Over a thousand have fallen. A thousand falling in one day! Who'd ever have believed it?"

Birch and Trudy joined the vigil in front of the First Petroleum Bank. Birch spotted a man dressed in the bib overalls of a farmer and approached him with the same question he had asked the cop. "What's wrong with the bank?"

The farmer removed his "goin' to town" straw hat and wiped his bald head with a neatly folded red handkerchief. "It's a robbery," he said with authority. "Gangsters."

There was a burst of oil-field profanity, followed by "Excuse me, ma'am" from a man who reeked of sulphurous crude oil. The oil-field worker's face was stained with grease, and his work boots oozed tar onto the sidewalk. "That ain't it," he said. "I heard at shift change and I come straight here. Phelps has been messin' with somebody's wife, and the fella up and shot him."

"That is malicious gossip," said a short, primly dressed woman whose high-buttoned collar matched her high-button shoes. "Mister Phelps is not even in town. Besides, he has always been a member of First Church and a pillar of this community. This closure undoubtedly has to do with the mess up in New York."

This last suggestion was largely discounted. Few in Tulsa could see how the troubles with the stock market could affect a locally owned bank in Oklahoma. The farmer said, "Now, Miss Pine, you know folks here are glad that our money ain't mixed up with those slick New York folks. Don't you be startin' any rumors, neither."

Trudy clung to Birch's arm. She studied the drawn green window shades and the Closed sign on the door as if they could provide clues as to the truth.

"Maybe Phelps stole the money and run off," the oil-field hand offered.

"Why would he do that?" asked a young woman with a baby in her arms and two small children clinging to her skirts. "Why would he rob his own bank? He's already rich as Croesus. But when are they gonna open up? I want my hundred and twelve dollars. I gotta buy groceries."

This refrain was taken up by the crowd:

"My thirty-four dollars."

"My six hundred dollars."

"My seed money."

"Tryin' to buy a car."

"Eighty-six fifty."

Even if the original trouble plaguing the First Petroleum Bank had not been a run, it was about to become one.

The cries of "I want my money" and "When will they open up?" were reaching a crescendo when the doors opened. A tall, gray-haired man in a dark blue suit appeared, flanked by two state troopers.

The official-looking man studied the crowd over his sharp-pointed nose until the noise subsided. When all was quiet at last, he spoke. "My name is Lerner," he said. "Bank examiner." A groan rippled through the group as if everyone already knew what Mr. Lerner was about to say. "Certain irregularities have come to light. The state of Oklahoma is now in charge of the bank, but pending a complete investigation, this bank is closed."

With that, the floodgates of comment and protest opened wide:

"How about my money?"

"My savings?"

"All I got is . . ."

"What am I supposed to live on?"

"My husband's out of work . . ."

To all these entreaties Lerner turned a deaf ear. "The bank is closed," he said again. "Move along. There's nothing further to be done here today."

"Mister," Birch called with an edge of desperation in his voice, "we drove for three days to get here, and all our savings is in that bank. Can't the state or somebody help us now?"

Trudy saw the shake of Lerner's head that was the only answer. In her mind rang the refrain of Lily's words: *"Trust only in the Lord. Only He is faithful."*

* * *

Max prepared to make his dash for the bank and his safety-deposit box. "Look, Joey, I came down here to get some stuff out of my bank. Have you spotted any of Quinn's goons?"

The shoeshine scanned both directions on Wall Street before replying. "Yeah. Guy by the name of Smiley. Ugly kisser and a big scar on his throat where somebody tried to carve him an extra mouth. Got it?"

The newly completed bank building at No. 40 Wall Street was only another long block away, but Max could not stand out from the crowd by hurrying now. He fell in with the line of drifting pedestrians, many who seemed to be sleepwalking. No one took any interest in Max or Codfish.

At the corner of Wall and William streets, Max stopped to inspect the crowd ahead. He was looking for anyone who was watching the entrance to the Bank of Manhattan. Everyone seemed to be waiting for something, but no one cared who came and went at No. 40.

Stepping out to cross William Street, Max heard the shout, "He's going to jump!"

Instantly, faces pivoted to look upward toward a ledge on the eighth floor of Max's bank. A man was walking on the ledge. Others took up the cry: "He's going to jump!"

In that moment each neck on Wall Street craned back. Each, that is, except Max's. Perhaps this was the chance he needed to make it inside the bank in safety. Max cut through the rooted spectators. He imagined that this first despondent man might be the beginning of a rash of suicides as the depth of the stock-market plunge became apparent. Max found himself looking into the upturned faces, wondering who among them might decide to become the next jumper.

Then he spotted something that made him halt midstride. There, below narrow-set eyes and the angular chin of a man, was a purplish, puckered scar that stretched across a thin throat. *Smiley!*

Max turned slowly to walk away. The killer was no more than a dozen feet from him. If Max ran now, he would certainly draw attention to himself.

At the same instant, the man on the ledge saw that the interest of the crowd was focused on him. He shook his head broadly, then stooped and held up a bucket and a trowel. The man was a workman, finishing up some caulking on the rain gutter of the recently finished skyscraper.

The crowd in the street gave a collective sigh, but there was no chuckle at the misunderstanding. Nothing could relieve the tension and anxiety of this terrible day.

The mob was starting to look around again. How recognizable was

Max from the back? What if Smiley had a confederate who even now spotted Max and was signaling to Smiley to close in?

The half block back to William Street was an agony. The corner seemed to recede. Were the footsteps behind him speeding up? Was the killer moving purposefully through the crowd to overtake Max?

Don't turn around! Don't look back! Max told himself.

A woman confronted Max. "Don't I know you? Aren't you that . . . ?"

"No, sorry," he said without looking up.

When Codfish went one way around a signpost and Max went the other, Max's feet tangled in the leash. As he stopped to straighten it, Max wondered if in the next instant he would feel the press of a gun barrel against his backbone. Or would this killer lean around Max from behind with a knife?

Despite all his best intentions, Max began to jog back down Wall Street toward the East River. Codfish caught Max's anxiety and strained at the leash. Max was certain that the footsteps behind him also increased their tempo. What if the gangsters had more killers in place at the end of the street? What if Max was heading straight into their arms?

By the time they reached Joey Fortuna's shoeshine stand, they were almost running. They swept past Joey, who looked up in amazement but did not call out to Max. Around the next corner they swung, away from Wall Street, away from Max's savings. Running to . . . *to where?* His apartment had been invaded, his bank account was known, his office was undoubtedly shadowed. Where was there a place of safety for him and David?

Max could not resist any longer. He turned around abruptly, ready to look his pursuer in the face. There was no one following. Just the ever-increasing crowd of mourners, grieving the death of their dreams.

CHAPTER FORTY-FIVE

Giving All for the Cause

As they had done every day, Tommy and Bobby climbed the hill to Shiloh General Store to collect the mail and hear the news from Grandma Amos.

The old woman was in the back room, bent over her ledgers when the boys came in. "Is that the Tucker boys?" she hooted.

"Yes'm," they replied in unison.

"Your pa done phoned up from Tulsa." She shuffled out, waving a slip of notebook paper. "They said to tell y'all they's doin' fine and on the way home. Said things didn't go so good down to that bank. The place done closed up tight. Can't get the money out. Somethin' to do with all that mess up North with them Yankee stockbrokers, your pa said. He don't understand all of it neither, but they sure got trouble up there!"

All the while Grandma Amos talked and talked. Getting the mail, she kept right on talking and waving the message all around while the boys waited quietly for her to finish up.

"When I was just a little gal no bigger'n y'all, them Yanks come blazin' through Atlanta! Burned the banks. Well, they burned near ever'thin'. We ended up eatin' rats, it was so bad. They cleaned out ever'thin' decent folks had. Didn't have money left 'cause we give it all to the Cause. Weddin' rings and silverware—we give it all to the glorious South. Didn't do no good, though. Y'all listenin', boys?"

"Yes'm."

"The more we sunk into the Cause, the more it needed. Like a big ragin' fire, it was. Never enough, though we give all we had." She paused to sort through the mail. "And I reckon that's what happened up in New York City in that Wall Street place, from what I hear. Well, now it's gone. Nevermore to rise. The South ain't a'gonna rise again, I reckon." She snorted and handed the note to Tommy. "And I reckon that Tulsa bank ain't gonna rise again neither."

Tommy blinked at her. Was she done? "No'm."

"Y'all won't be eatin' rats, though. Lose the farm, I reckon, from what that no-good J.D. is sayin'. But y'all ain't gonna be eatin' rats as me and my kin did back there in Atlanta."

Tommy scanned the note. All it said was: *Tell the boys we are on the way home and well. Send love.*

It was a wonder and a miracle that the old woman could take such a small message and make it go on for so long. Then, with a pitiful look at the brothers, she reached her gnarled hand into the penny-candy jar and pulled out two lemon drops. Maybe this was her way of assuring them that rats were not on the menu this time around.

"Thank you, ma'am," the boys said together. They hurried out of the store before she could get onto another long tale about the Civil War, which she said had been a *real* war, and make no mistake!

Nothing else mattered to Tommy and Bobby except that their folks were coming home. They walked slowly and sucked on the lemon drops without giving much thought to what old Grandma Amos had said about the bank in Tulsa. Somehow the real news had gotten all muddled up in the story about Atlanta being burned by the Yankee gangsters.

"But what did she say about the farm? about J.D.?" Bobby asked his brother.

J.D. himself answered the question. He rode up at a trot as though he had come looking for them on purpose. Neither of the boys was glad to see him. After all, he might be kin, but nobody had to like it.

"Well, well, if it ain't Cousin Birch's boys. How-do there!"

"How-do."

"I heard your bad news." He slowed his horse to keep pace with them. He seemed awfully happy for a man who had just heard bad news.

"Mama and Dad are comin' home," Bobby offered. This was the best news ever.

"Home." J.D. grinned and looked toward the knoll where the Tucker farm would be. "Well, I reckon y'all still can call it that. It'll be my place, but y'all can still live there. Still call it home."

"It's our place." Tommy shoved the thick shoulder of the horse as it moved too close.

"Well, y'all know that granddaddy of yours was a terrible drunk. Drank up all his money. Reckon he paid for his liquor with money that should have gone for his taxes. And now y'all got no money."

"What's he talkin' about?" Bobby was angry. He wished J.D. was not a cousin and not an adult, because Bobby wanted to tell him a thing or two.

"What I'm talkin' 'bout is the fact that your daddy and mama been runnin' all over the countryside tryin' to get money to pay them taxes. But I'm gonna pay 'em next week, see. And then the first thing I'm gonna do is run that big nigger of yours off my place."

J.D. sneered. "That's right. And y'all can tell him that when you get on home today. Tell him that J.D. is gonna go on into Fort Smith to pay up those taxes. Then I'm gonna make a special telephone call to a certain Oklahoma lawman about a certain nigger convict who drowned in the James Fork some time back. And after I make that call, that Oklahoma lawman just might want to come on back here and take a look around my new place. He might want to look right into the face of that nigger y'all keep there."

J.D. drew himself up straight in the saddle. "Y'all be sure and tell him what I said. And tell that pappy of yours, too. Bet he'll find it real interestin'."

Spurring his horse into a gallop, J.D. lifted his hat with a whoop of victory.

✱ ✱ ✱

Poor Codfish was stuffed onto the fire escape in the back alley, hidden away lest any of Boss Quinn's goons or the FBI G-men spot the dog and close in.

But Codfish was not hidden far enough away, as far as Mrs. Finkel was concerned. Lying on the groaning bed, she sneezed and moaned and sneezed again. It was just like in the old days, Mr. Finkel explained to Max, like when there were dray horses up and down Orchard Street. The old woman had taken to these fits of allergy back then, too.

So it was not that they did not like David. It was not that they did not wish to help Max in his hour of need. It was the dog. Max and David and Codfish would have to find another place to hide out until this thing with the Catholic kidnapper blew over.

Of course, if Max wanted to take the mutt out and turn him loose on Orchard Street, that was another matter. But he could not sleep on the fire escape. Better he should be in a zoo or something. A dog of this size? It was like putting a bear in a birdcage. . . .

"Never mind," Max told the downcast pickleman.

"And you will come back to see us, David?" asked Mr. Finkel, presenting him with a parting dill, the giant of all pickledom.

David nodded and gave the old man a hug. Codfish wagged and woofed once, which was followed by the echo of violent sneezes and coughs nearby.

"That is just fine, David," said Mr. Finkel. "Just you and your papa next time, *nu*?"

And so the trio slipped from the flat of the pickleman just after dark with the sneezes of Mrs. Finkel ringing in their ears.

Two blocks up Orchard Street, Max was showing David this store and that apartment and telling him about who had owned what.

Then David asked the question: "Where are we going?"

Max pressed his hand to his forehead and sighed. "Somewhere," he replied with a frown.

"Your friend's house?"

Max looked down at the dog and then back the way they had come. "The question these days is, Who do you trust?"

He shook his head and ducked into a tiny flophouse hotel around the corner on Cherry Street. It had been a last refuge for winos and aging prostitutes in the area from the day when Max was a kid. Called the Red-eye Resort, it would serve as a place to get off the street for a few hours until Max could decide what to do. In such a place, Max figured Codfish would hardly be noticed at all. Most of the guests were just as shaggy and smelled somewhat worse. All of them had fleas. Most would think that the enormous black dog was nothing more than a figment of imagination brought on by too much bootleg booze. A slight variation on pink elephants.

Tonight, with several days' growth of beard, Max also looked the part.

"We need a room. Me and the kid. We lost everything in the stock market, see."

"I can see you was a real big spender," said the corpulent, frazzled woman behind the counter in the tiny lobby. "That'll be two bits a night. Second floor. One bed. Toilet at the end of the hall."

"You got a telephone?" Max played his role as a down-and-outer to the hilt.

The woman pointed to the grimy booth across from the desk. "Nickel a call. No long distance." Then to David, "Take care of your old man, kid. You know people who went bust is jumpin' outta windows all over town." She slapped the key onto the counter.

✴ ✴ ✴

Sleazy and stinking, the Red-eye Resort was a long way from Bora-Bora. But at least it did have one bed, which Max and David shared. Yellow neon lights blinked on and off outside the window, bathing the sleeping boy in a golden glow.

Max watched David for a time before turning his gaze to the peeling, water-stained wallpaper and the spider that lived in the corner of the ceiling.

No doubt about it—the kid had certainly picked a doozy of a time to show up in Max's life. Why hadn't he come along last week, when Max could have put him to bed in satin sheets at the Plaza and fed him room-service filet mignon and fudge sundaes and listened to the radio? Or taken him to a motion-picture show at the Roxie?

Now there was no going back. Boss Quinn's goons were ordering room service at the Plaza and putting it on Max's tab while they cleaned their revolvers and waited for Max to walk in. No doubt they hoped to kill both Max and David in one blow. Father-and-son execution. Touching, but hardly the kind of event Max wanted to participate in.

Cement overshoes. Wasn't that the term David had used when he told Max about Boss Quinn's solution for traitors? Max found it remarkable that he and David were both being measured for Quinn's peculiar shoes.

There was also the little matter of the FBI, not to mention the priest from Philadelphia. This had to be some kind of record. How many people could claim to be wanted by such a diverse spectrum of the population?

Life had become very complicated, indeed. The Plaza was definitely off-limits. The bank was certainly being watched by Quinn's men and the FBI. As for the priest, no doubt he was waiting in the wings to snatch David the minute they were apprehended.

Max reached out and touched the boy's soft hair. *What an incredible kid!* Like a rubber ball, this kid bounced back and came up ready to take on the world.

"My kid," Max said, feeling fiercely proud. It was not by accident that David looked like Max . . . or that the boy held himself with that same self-confident swagger.

"My son," Max whispered. For ten years Max had wondered, and now here was the truth right in front of him.

No room at the Plaza. No satin sheets. No room service. No movie at the Roxie. But that still did not change the truth of what Max wanted to be for the boy.

"I'm a father," Max said with all the wonder of a man looking at his newborn child for the first time. "We got to make it, kid," he said in a hushed and hopeful voice.

Damon Phelps wandered through the New York City streets. He had lost his suit coat. His tie, unknotted, hung limply around his shoulders.

Passersby heard him mumble to himself, "Two million dollars or twenty years in jail. What will it be?"

A cop near the East River saw him walk into a puddle of crankcase oil in the street and stoop to touch it. When he stood up, he was rubbing his fingers together. When the cop yelled at him, asking what he thought he was doing, Phelps shouted back his reply: "Gonna drill a dozen more wells today, every one a gusher."

Phelps tried, unsuccessfully, to snap his greasy fingers. "Two million dollars? Nothing to worry about. Made money in oil before. Just hafta do it all over again."

Phelps set off toward the bridge with its brightly lit towers and cables. "Drilling rig," said Phelps with admiration, "already working." He began to run toward the bridge.

The cop flagged a fire truck returning from a fire. "Think we got a jumper."

Phelps had already climbed up on the railing of the bridge. He was addressing an imaginary driller when the cop arrived. "Down another hundred feet," Phelps instructed. "Don't stop till we hit the pool . . . the pool."

The firemen saw him look up at the bridge tower and speak to an imaginary derrickman. "Get back up there!" Phelps ordered. "Do I have to come up and show you how it's done?" He began to climb a spindly ladder till he reached one of the suspension cables.

Phelps looked around at the bridge towers and the shining windows of the skyscrapers. He began to name each flickering tower with the name of an Oklahoma oil well. When he came to Old Glory, Well No. 49, he stopped, took his fist off the cable, and shook it at the sky.

"Who told you to come down?" he threatened in a loud voice. "It should be you that's dead, not my boy!"

And he stepped off into space.

Three dollars and twenty-two cents was all that remained in Birch's wallet as they stood beside the little Ford and waited for the decision of the car dealer.

"She ain't worth more'n seventy-five." The little man studied his notebook.

"But we paid almost three hundred for the car last year!" Birch exploded. Yet this offer was twenty dollars more than the last place.

"This is *this* year," the man said firmly. He was unmoved by their story. "As a matter of fact, I reckon that today is going to be a day that a whole lot of hard-luck folks date the rest of their lives from." He shook his head. "Just how easy you think it's going to be for me to sell this pile of junk after what happened today? And I'm not talking about the bank closing, either. What I mean, mister, is that there's a whole lot more that just went wrong with the world than you or I can see right now."

"Seventy-five?" Birch looked at the mud-spattered car.

"Take it or leave it. Tomorrow I may be sorry I offered that much." He kicked a patched tire. "Y'all better make up your minds before I change mine."

"Just a minute." Birch turned to Trudy, who stood looking at the sunset. There was a strange, faraway smile on her lips.

"What do you think?" Birch asked.

"About what?"

"Seventy-five. It's twenty higher than the last fella. And we can get train tickets one way for ten dollars. Not have to worry about the repairs . . ." Birch ran a hand over his unshaved face. "Help me with this, True."

"All right, then," she agreed. The automobile had meant something special to her, a tenuous link with the modern world of 1929. But suddenly it did not matter at all anymore.

Birch turned and extended his hand to the car dealer in a bargain. The deal was struck, the papers signed, and they left the car lot with seventy-eight dollars and twenty-two cents.

"Well," Trudy said softly as she took her seat in the second-class Pullman car. "Here we are, back where we began."

Birch stowed the luggage in the rack above the seat and plopped down wearily to stare bleakly at the darkening countryside. "Full circle." He winced. "Ever sorry you got on this merry-go-round with me, True? Ten years later you come around again, and still no brass ring."

"You call three sons and a handsome husband 'no brass ring'?" She smiled. "I was just thinking . . . how we have lost everything—what we thought was everything. But it doesn't mean anything at all to me. I have you, Birch. And the boys. And I have the Lord in my heart. All the rest is . . ."

She waved her hand toward the sky. "There is nothing left for us to do but believe. Like Lily told me: 'Trust the Lord; only He is faithful.' So I must. And you must trust, too. He sees us, Birch." She looked at a flock of birds rising from an empty field. "There is nothing left but trust."

Birch leaned his head back against the seat and gazed above her head. "Such hope we had! Ah, True . . ." His voice choked off as he struggled to contain his emotions. "It was . . . home to me. A place to raise the boys with all the love I wished my father would have shown me. A way to rearrange the picture I had of my boyhood. Make the birch trees a place to climb and rock and holler for joy, instead of a place to aim the plow or cut switches for a whippin'. I just wanted to give them . . . what my pa never gave me."

"But, Birch, you have done that! And all without the Poteau Mountains or the James Fork or the birch trees! Oh, Birch!" Trudy took his calloused hand in hers and kissed his fingers. "You have given them . . . and me . . . *yourself*! Your *love*! And isn't that the only safe place for them to hide their hearts?"

Tears welled up. He looked away from her. Such beautiful words. Were they true? Somehow he had always connected loving his family to his dream of having a *place*. Now that the dream was gone, what remained? Only love.

"Love *is* enough, Birch. And I think . . . maybe that was what Lily was telling me. When there's nothing left to give the Lord, then you have to look at what you have. Your soul. Yourself. And that is the only gift He wants from His children. Your sons love you, Birch. They trust you. All that was true before Shiloh. It will be true after. And maybe that is what the Lord wants from us. For us to look to Him. To trust Him like a Father."

"My Father . . . ," Birch said, "loves me. I will not . . . be afraid." He closed his eyes. *"A thousand shall fall at thy side, and ten thousand at thy right hand; but it shall not come nigh thee."*

Trudy moved to sit beside him. "Truth. We still have that."

The eastbound train from Tulsa chugged across the dark landscape. No longer did Trudy and Birch feel that it was taking them home to a *place*. They were going home to their family. It was enough. It was everything.

CHAPTER FORTY-SIX

Whom Do You Trust?

The Tucker boys huddled together on the bed and placed their most precious belongings in a row on the quilt.

"How much you think we can get?" Bobby asked, his eyes shining in the lamplight.

A penny whistle was just a penny whistle. A pocketknife for whittling was worth a few cents, Tommy figured. The magnifying glass had been free with coupons from Quaker Oats. Other items added up to something under half a dollar.

"What about this?" Tommy reached under his pillow and removed the slip of paper that had been the focus of all his dreams. The bill of sale.

"The red puppy," Bobby said, staring at the signature of Brother Williams.

"He'll give us our money back," Tommy said confidently.

"But, Tommy . . . that's . . . the red puppy. The best puppy in these hills, they say."

"I'm glad she's good. Brother Williams ought to be real happy when we ask him to take this and give us our money back."

"But what about the huntin' we were gonna do? What about everything we talked about?"

"Dad needs the money now, Bobby. Dad needs us to help. We don't need that pup. Just got to help Dad; that's all."

Bobby studied the paper for a long time. The dog did not mean even half as much to him as it meant to Tommy. That was all in the world Tommy had talked about. He talked about her in his sleep, talked to the fellas at school about how it would be when that pup was raised and Tommy took her hunting possum in the woods. And now here he was going to give her up. Just like that.

"For Dad," Bobby agreed.

✳ ✳ ✳

"I seen his kind before." Jefferson paced the length of the small kitchen. "I seen 'em, Lily. Men like J.D. killed my Tisha an' run off my folks from the place."

"But, Jeff, you hear what he told the boys? He gonna call up that Oklahoma lawman to come on back here."

"I reckon he'll just have to do that."

"You got to go, Jeff."

"That's just what J.D. wants me to do—hightail it out of here an' leave you all alone. Leave Birch and Miz Trudy, too, when they need me."

"You go on. I'll follow after."

These were words that Jefferson had heard before. He had run away once. He did not want to run again.

"Hear me now, Lily. I'm a man. I got to stand here like one. I feel it in my bones. The Lord's sayin', *Jeff! Pay attention! You got to stay here an' do battle against the powers of darkness. Got to pray before the storm comes that's gonna wipe the slate clean!*" He clenched his fist and looked out across the dark land of Shiloh. "Folks around here need me to stay an' pray. Somethin's comin'! You hear me, gal? Tonight. Like Daniel in the lions' den. We can't bend our knee to the god of fear. We got to stand an' pray. We got to wait for the hand of the true God to pull the teeth out of the lion! This little place is in powerful need of a miracle. I can't see no miracle on the way. But the Good Book says the Lord inhabits praises. So I'm gonna watch an' pray an' praise the Lord until that miracle comes on the wind across the mountains!"

He took the milk pail with him when he left the house. Lily sat silently beside the window and listened as Jefferson's bass voice boomed out hymns through the night.

Even if no miracle came to Shiloh, their hearts would be ready for whatever the morning brought.

✳ ✳ ✳

Max could not sleep.

He spread all his rumpled mail and messages in a row on the foot of the bed. And he asked the question: Who do you trust?

There were several frantic notes from Edith Rutger. The first read:

Max, darling! Where are you? Help me sort out what has happened between us.

Edith

The second message was much longer. It contained veiled references to the fact that every cent she had was tied up in Sabre Oil, and she needed Max to give her advice.

The third message was laden with accusation. It oozed from the page. Max had broken her heart. He was not chivalrous. He made her love him and then had slipped away without a second thought. . . .

Max did not feel guilty, but he did consider Edith as he wondered whom to call. He placed her notes in a neat pile to the side.

Then there was Keenan. A dozen messages, each more hysterical than the last. By now Keenan was undoubtedly dead broke. Possibly dead. Max wadded his memos up and tossed them at Codfish, who snapped at them when they flew through the air.

There was another thick packet of stuff from the paper. Entreaties from Managing Editor Bill Whittaker progressed to warnings and finally to the words YOU'RE FIRED. Max decided that this meant his paid vacation was off. Whittaker was not the one to call at such a moment.

Max's secretary dutifully called to remind him of this meeting or that appointment. If Max involved her, the sweet old lady could end up hurt or fired or in jail for aiding and abetting.

"So long, Old Faithful." Max dumped Miss Morgan's notes onto the discarded pile with assorted bills and notes from various females he would never see again.

Ah! But Harry Beadle! Beadle had been around longer than any managing editor. He was a faithful friend, always there when Max needed him. And he owed Max a number of personal favors. Max had bailed him out of jail three times in the last year after raids on speakeasies. Beadle was no doubt as pickled tonight as Mr. Finkel's cucumbers, but he would do everything he could to lend Max a hand.

"Yes, Beadle, you owe me, old buddy, and I shall collect!" Next to Edith's letters, he placed the Beadle notes about meeting at this gin joint or that. Definitely a winner.

Now, who was left in Max's who-do-you-trust file?

He recognized the envelope immediately. The stationery belonged to dear Trudy, although the handwriting was that of little Tommy, no doubt. The address? Something new. Shiloh, Arkansas.

While David slept, Max opened the envelope and grinned as two dollars tumbled out onto the bed. Chuckling softly, Max read the confession of Tommy and Bobby that they had misused the paper Max had sent Trudy for letter writing. And if he would be so kind as to pick up more, here was the money for it and it ought to be enough for mailing, too, they hoped.

In tandem with that was Trudy's account of their move to Shiloh and the tale of the FAMOUS Bad-Luck Wagon Spook Show, including what paper the tickets had been made from.

With a laugh that made David stir and Codfish perk his ears, Max reread the story, then folded the letter and carefully replaced it in its envelope.

Nobody could tell a story quite like Trudy. Like Mark Twain, this deserved to be read aloud to David when they found a quiet moment together. Max slipped it into his coat pocket and wondered if there would be any danger in picking up new stationery.

That was the least he could do for the lady who remained at the top of his who-do-you-trust file.

CHAPTER FORTY-SEVEN

Judas Kiss

"Edith," Max said over the lobby telephone, "you are the only one I can trust to help me."

She sounded surprisingly wide-awake at the other end of the line. Her voice was brittle, almost frightened. "Of course, Max, darling. Anything. Anything at all. Just tell me."

"My place at the Plaza is being watched."

"By whom, darling?" Such a shocked tone. "What do you mean? Watched?"

"You don't want the whole list . . . just . . . you remember I told you about my son?"

"He's with you?"

"Yes. And that's part of the mess. I need to leave town for a while. But I can't get into my place. And I was thinking . . ."

"Where are you, darling? What do you need?"

Max sighed loudly. "I can't tell you how swell it is that you're still here for me, Edith. After the way I've neglected you lately. First, tell me you forgive me."

"You know I do."

"Thank you. I'll sleep easier at night knowing that. And until I send for you—"

"Where will you be?"

"A little island I heard about. A paradise . . ."

Outside the dingy glass of the phone booth, David glared at Max and put a hand to his stomach. He was hungry. *Hurry up,* he mouthed.

"Yes, yes, Max. How can I help?" Edith was eager, approving of his plan.

"You've got a key to my place. I want you to go up there. Pack a few of my things: suits, shoes. And my family photographs. Funny. I put them all up in the closet, but now that I'm leaving . . . will you pack them for me? And my shaving things. Whatever."

She sounded emotional, as though he had touched her when he asked for the photographs. "You know I will."

"And, Edith . . ." David was making faces now. Codfish slobbered on the glass. "Put in a picture of you, too."

"Oh, *Max!*" He could hear the emotion in her voice. "Yes. Where do you want me to bring it? Where are you, Max?"

Max glanced at his watch and nodded at David. Yes, Edith was going to help them! David made the sign for okay.

"Grand Central Station. Under the clock in the main lobby. We'll be there at noon today. Does that give you time enough?"

"I'll be there," she promised. "You can trust me, Max."

Boss Quinn was smiling as he stepped toward Edith Rutger.

She sat on the couch and stared at the telephone. She finally raised her eyes to Boss. "Well, you heard everything."

He nodded and sat down beside her. "You are a swell dish. I especially am impressed with the stuff he says about his family photographs. Very good. Very good."

"You've got what you wanted. Max and the boy."

"Pardon me for the disagreement, but I do not have what I want until I have them in my hand. And for this I am still in need of you, doll. You will be paid handsomely, I might add."

Edith reached around him for her coffee cup and sat back to negotiate the business deal. "What do you want me to do first of all?"

"I will have Ham and Sal bring his suitcase over from the Plaza. They do not need to pack it, of course, since where he is going he will not need clothes." Quinn smiled appreciatively at that thought. "But you will need to carry the suitcase into Grand Central Station like he says. And stand there looking pretty and worried under the clock until he comes with the kid." Quinn shrugged at the simplicity of it. "Then we take over. A gun in his ribs and he will not run away. A gun in the kid's neck and he will be like a quiet old dog, if you take my meaning."

"I don't want him to know that I . . ." Edith's words faltered.

"That you betrayed him?" Quinn needled. "He will not suspect. Although it will not matter one way or the other to him in a short while."

"I just have to live with myself; that's all. I don't want him to die knowing."

He shrugged broadly and smoothed back her hair. "Sure. Done."

"So, how much will you pay me?"

Boss Quinn's smile did not fade. "You are in a bad way after what has happened. I am not in such a bad way. I put up a fortune, but I still have a fortune in booze to sell. Contracts. Sure things. I can pay you enough that you can live well. Say, five thousand?"

"Five? That's nothing. Nothing."

"No, doll, five grand is five grand. Nothing is what you have now. Is this correct?"

"All right, then. Five thousand. But . . . I want another five for the boy."

"You are a hard-nosed businesswoman, Edith Rutger. I admire that in a woman." He nodded and snapped his fingers. "If it goes well, sure. Ten grand for the both of them. You can trust me."

He picked up the telephone and dialed. After two rings, he issued the orders. "Meyer and the kid will be at Grand Central at noon. Pull the boys in. A man at every entrance. You heard me! I would not like it if he got away."

✵ ✵ ✵

Beadle sounded surprisingly sober as he pleaded with Max over the phone. "Look, Max, you are wanted by everybody—the FBI and the Catholic church and the meanest gangster in New York. Don't you think it is wise to turn yourself in?"

"I'm not going to put my son in danger by hanging around New York until he can testify against Boss Quinn."

"But there is the children's home in Philadelphia. The priest, Max! He says he can take the kid there and hide him."

"You know Boss Quinn has connections in Philly the same as here," Max explained. "I can't chance it."

Beadle sounded worried and unhappy. "You should not do this, Maxie. I am telling you as your old friend now. You should bring the kid in before you get nabbed. Listen to me—would I steer you wrong? I know whereof I speak, Maxie! Please!"

"You owe me." Max was adamant. "Are you going to help?"

There was a long silence before Beadle answered in a sorrowful voice, "I don't have a choice in this. You are putting me in a very bad place. Maxie, you don't know what you are doing! If Quinn catches you, he will kill both you and the kid!"

"Are you going to help me?"

A reluctant grunt. "Yes."

"All right, then. Taped to the bottom of my desk drawer is an extra key to my safety-deposit box at No. 40 Wall Street."

"Bank of Manhattan."

"Right. Box 242. Your name is on my card. I put it there in case anything ever happened to me."

Beadle's voice trembled at that revelation. "Thank you, Max. I mean . . ."

"I'm trusting you to get my dough out and the rest of the stuff I have in there. Put it in a bag and meet me under the clock at Grand Central Station at noon today."

"Ah, Max! Just come on back. The G-men will look after you. Come on in! Whittaker is a forgiving kind of guy. He will give you your job back, just like that!"

"Beadle!" Max said sharply. "Are you going to do it or not?"

There was a long silence followed by a miserable sigh. "All right, Maxie. Just remember, I didn't want to do this. Just remember that, will you?"

"Great. Twelve noon under the clock at Grand Central." Max hung up the telephone and sighed with relief as David tapped on the glass again.

"Can we eat now?" the boy asked. "You got it all fixed up?"

"We're on our way, David!"

✳ ✳ ✳

FBI Agent Burns pulled the safety-deposit key from the bottom of Max's desk drawer and handed it to Agent Allen. Father John looked on with satisfaction as the key was then passed to Beadle, who sat miserably staring at the telephone.

"Take it," Burns said with a smile.

Beadle glared at the tiny key. "After all Max has done for me—now this. He will not understand. He won't believe it when I tell him you listened to the whole thing on the other phone. He will think I have ratted on him to get him and the kid picked up."

Father John puckered his brow in concern for Beadle's conscience. "He will one day thank you for it, Mister Beadle."

"I don't think so, Father. But it would make me feel better to think that." He took the key.

Burns towered over him, barking orders to Allen, who telephoned a call to deploy two dozen G-men to pick up Max and David at Grand Central Station.

Burns returned his attention to Beadle. "We will go with you to the bank. Better to have the money on hand to give him in case he stashes the kid some place until he gets the money. If the kid is not with him, we can trail him easily enough."

"You mean I have to be there?"

"He'll never know your connection to the pickup."

Beadle winced. "Like Judas. I have to be there."

"He will thank you for it," Father John said again, but Beadle still did not believe it.

CHAPTER FORTY-EIGHT

The Death of a Dream

It was not as if Tommy had ever even held the red coon pup, after all. She was penned up in the back of the livery stable with her mama and her brothers, and old Brother Williams had hung up the sign: Do Not Touch!

So nobody touched the pups except folks who were given permission. Now Tommy was glad of the restriction. It would have been a terrible thing to have cuddled her and felt her wet puppy licks on his cheek, then had to give that up forever. He had only dreamed of such things. Only in his imagination had he run across the fields of Shiloh with her galloping after him. Only in his mind had he and the red pup possum-hunted in the persimmon patch.

It was a dream he could give up . . . for Dad.

Reaching down at his feet, he felt for his overalls, which he had put under the covers to keep them warm for morning. Bobby had left his clothes slung over the chair, and they would be cold as ice when he put them on.

"Wake up!" Tommy shook his brother from a deep sleep.

"What? What you want? It ain't light yet."

"We got to get to Hartford." Tommy was dressed before he put his feet on the ice-cold floorboards. "Get up, or I'm goin' without you." He threw Bobby's clothes at him.

Bobby shuddered and moaned. "It's so cold. . . ."

"Get up."

"Why do we have to go so early?"

Tommy had no answer for that except that he wanted the business settled before Mama and Dad came home from Oklahoma. He wanted to have all that money stashed in the mason jar, and he wanted to come right up to his folks and tell them that he and Bobby wanted to help pay the taxes.

Bobby dressed himself in the predawn light, gasping and shuddering as the touch of cold denim on his bare legs woke him up.

They could hear Lily breathing softly in the other bedroom as they sneaked through the kitchen. Without making a sound, they slipped out the back and hurried down the road five miles to Hartford.

"This is a dark day," said Brother Williams as he looked at the bill of sale that trembled like a leaf in Tommy's outstretched hand.

"Yessir, it is!" shouted Boomer from the tack room as he polished a harness. "It's a black day! Looks to me like we's in for a mighty big storm, Brother Williams!"

"Will you shut up?" Brother Williams shouted back. "That ain't the kind of black day I'm talkin' about, you old fool!"

"All the same," Boomer went on, "big storm. Black dark clouds. Big black dark . . . biggest darkest black . . ."

Brother Williams kicked the door of the tack room shut, mostly shutting off Boomer's weather report.

"As I was saying to you Tucker boys—" the old man breathed a sigh and shook his head—"we all heard what's gone on with y'all's folks. Dirty business! That lousy no-good cousin of your pa's had his eye on that place since . . . well, just about as far back as I recall. And now this."

"We're helpin'," Bobby said. "Eleven dollars and thirteen cents. Thought we ought to help pay them taxes."

"How much is owin'?" Brother Williams was not trying to be a snoop; he was one naturally. Tommy had heard his father say so, and he did not blame Brother Williams for wanting to know everything, because it was his nature.

"We don't rightly know," Tommy answered truthfully. "But Dad and Mama went on back to Tulsa to get their money—"

"I heard all about that!" He was shaking his head and clucking his tongue. "It was all over the radio. Went on down to Mister Winters' store to hear it. I told him that's where your mama and papa done gone to fetch back their life's savin's. Well, I mean! Never was such a terrible calamity to come upon undeservin' folk since Job." He looked around his place as if he were seeing spooks. "Make a man shudder to think what unexpected things could happen! Stopped me right in my tracks when I heard all about it. Folks is mighty sorry for y'all."

"It'll be okay," Bobby comforted the old horse trader. "We just need back our eleven dollars and thirteen cents to fix it up."

Brother Williams considered the boys with his watery blue eyes shining in a sad way. "You young'uns . . ." His voice sounded like he had a frog in his throat. "That Birch Tucker has got to be the richest man I know, and that's the truth of it."

He took back the bill of sale. He counted out the change and put it in the jar, even though it would have been easier to give the boys paper money. Perhaps Brother Williams knew that young'uns take more pride in a heavy jar full of coins than in paper money of any denomination.

The jar was almost full when the puppies started growling a mock battle back in their stall. Bobby looked at the toes of his shoes, and Tommy felt the color rise on his cheeks. He wanted to go look at her. He surely did. He wanted to pick her up and feel those sloppy puppy kisses on his face, but it was not to be. Thinking about it would not make it so. Taking a last look at her would just make it harder to bear.

He raised his chin and listened to Boomer still going on about the weather behind the door.

"Smells like rain . . . no . . . ain't rain . . . smells like . . . biggest blackest clouds! Don't want to be out in that. No sir. Don't nobody want to be out in that there storm. Wind. *Whoooooooo!*"

Brother Williams' eyes got wild. "Shut up, Boomer! It's too early in the mornin' for this gibberish!" He booted the door again and went back to counting out quarters as if it were nothing at all.

Then it was done. ". . . and thirteen cents. There it is, boys. Every penny of it." He eyed them both. "Y'all had breakfast?"

Bobby's eyes brightened. Tommy's stomach growled. "No."

"I see you ain't." His mouth turned in an upside-down *U*. "Y'all get on over to Zelda's Café. Get yourself some breakfast."

Tommy nudged Bobby—a firm no. Of course they could not spend good money on breakfast.

"Well, well," Brother Williams said, "if I give you money for breakfast, y'all aren't gonna eat nohow. So . . ." He dialed the telephone and instructed Zelda at the café to fix the Tucker boys the best breakfast she knew how and put it on the livery stable tab. He might send them home without a red puppy, but they would not walk all the way back to Shiloh with empty stomachs.

✳ ✳ ✳

Miss Zelda wiped off the counter and eyed the clean plates of the Tucker brothers with admiration.

"You Tucker boys even eat like your daddy. That man! When his mama used to say, 'Clean your plate' at the church potlucks, she never had to worry about leftover gravy on his dish. No sir."

"Thank you, ma'am," Tommy replied. "We was hungry."

"You come a long way since before sunup, Brother Williams tells me." She smiled sadly. "Real good of you boys to help your ma and pa thisaway. Real shame what's happened." She took their plates.

"Yes'm," Tommy agreed, although he did not want to talk about it. He picked up the money jar. "They're comin' in this mornin'. We'll be gettin' on now so we can be home when they get there."

Miss Zelda drew herself up and waved the dishrag toward the window. "Y'all best stay here awhile. Looks like a bad storm is comin' in. No sir. Y'all best not be out on the road when it hits."

"Thank you, ma'am." Tommy shifted the jar and grimaced apologetically because he was about to contradict Miss Zelda. "But if it was to go to stormin' and me and Bobby wasn't home, and if Mama and Dad should get home when it was stormin' and then find we wasn't there . . . you see? They would be terrible worried."

"We'd get a lickin'," Bobby added with certainty. "We'll run fast, Miss Zelda."

"It's not even rainin' yet," Tommy assured the large, ruddy-faced woman as she eyed them doubtfully.

"Well . . . wouldn't want you boys to get a lickin'. Hurry on home, then. But don't forget who told you so if y'all get rained on."

"Yes'm." The boys backed toward the door and thanked her one last time. Then they lit out across the street and through the alley toward Shiloh as the sky glowed yellow beneath the clouds.

It was a busy morning at Grand Central Station. Railroad stocks might have tumbled off a cliff over the last week, but the trains still came and went. The loudspeakers still called out departures and arrivals. The big clock in the lobby still ticked toward noon, eastern time.

Among the mass of travelers this morning, the thugs of Boss Quinn and the plainclothes FBI agents mingled with New York City policemen in civilian dress who were on hand as backup. Each man carried photographs of Max Meyer and David O'Halloran Meyer. Like vultures and hyenas, they perched and waited for their quarry to enter the building. Eyes darted from entrances to the place beneath the clock and then back again. Soon Edith Rutger would stroll into place. Quinn's men were advised to be careful of the doll in case there was gunplay. Boss Quinn had taken a liking to her and would not like to see her damaged.

Beadle, too, would soon arrive. Allen and Burns had already decided that once the deed was done, poor Beadle deserved a good stiff drink. They would treat.

The tiny stationery store was located on a side street two blocks from the enormous dome of the train station. On the window, gold letters were stenciled in Old English script: Rule Britannia Fine English Stationery.

There was time enough before their train for Max and David to drop in and purchase the special writing paper that Max had been buying here for Trudy for ten years. No other would do, Max explained. And since they were leaving New York for a very long time, Max could not say when he would ever have a chance to buy Trudy's paper again.

The little English shop clerk did not recognize Max at first. He peered at him over his glasses and squinted down at Codfish in an unpleasant way.

Max pushed his hat back on his head and smiled. "It's me, Mister Fuller. Max Meyer."

Surprised, the little man leaned closer over the counter as though he could not recognize the ragged countenance of one of his most faithful customers.

"Good heavens! What has happened?" He held up his hand. "No, no! I know what has happened. The same as has happened to everyone. The crash. A black and bottomless pit this morning, I hear. Down and down. I shall lose my best customers, I fear. Who will be able to purchase such fine goods as these after what has happened?" He sighed. "Now the gentlemen who bought Swiss fountain pens from me shall be selling pencils in a cup on the street corner." He frowned. "And as for my little shop . . . ah, well. I suppose I can sell pencils as well." He managed a half smile. "It was lovely while it lasted, this American dream of mine."

Max had not thought about Wall Street much or considered what effect it would have on little businesses, but no doubt this would be the last chance Max would have to purchase special paper for Trudy. The prosperous, elegant decade of the twenties had just come to an end.

With that in mind, he placed an additional two dollars on the counter along with the funds from Tommy and Bobby.

"This may have to last her awhile," Max said. "Two hundred sheets of the Berkshire linen. One hundred envelopes. Boxed. Don't bother to wrap it. We have a train to catch."

CHAPTER FORTY-NINE

Black Storm Coming

Somewhere behind the brooding clouds, Jefferson knew the sun was shining. Before breakfast he was at work in the lower field, hefting cut firewood into the FAMOUS wagon. The aroma of bacon mingled with woodsmoke. Pausing from his chore, he peered toward the house as the smoke from the chimney grew more dense.

Lily was up. By the time he got to the house, she would have the boys at the table and the platters heaped high with eggs and wheat cakes and grits and most likely a thick slab of ham along with the bacon.

He had hoped to finish hauling the wood before she called him in, but it would have to wait now. Wiping sweat from his forehead, he looked to the hills at the heavy sky. The day had started off cold, but a strange, sultry feel had moved across the land.

"Big storm a'comin'," he muttered, glancing at the woodpile with regret. The rain would come before he got all the wood to cover if he stopped to eat now. Even if he kept hard at it, there was no guarantee the heap would not be caught in a downpour.

"Jefferson!" Lily called him from the porch. "Jeff! Breakfast on the table!"

He waved broadly and tossed another log onto the wagon. "Comin'!"

"Those two boys down there with you?" she called back.

"No, they ain't." Hands on his hips, he surveyed the fields. *Where could they have gotten off to?* he wondered. It was still hours till school.

"Tommy! Bobby!" Lily cupped her hands and called until their names echoed across the valley and down in the hollow.

Jeff slung his coat over his shoulder and headed back to the house.

No sign of the boys in the persimmon patch. Not in the birch trees. *Maybe in the barn?* He gave a look in the barn and called for the boys. The sweet Jersey cow bellowed a reply.

"Not here?" Jeff asked as he took his place at the heavily laden table. "You know how young'uns is. Most likely imagined they'd catch a fish before breakfast."

"Ain't like the boys to miss breakfast, Jeff." She glanced at the glowering sky. "Especially not wheat cakes. Those two take great store in a big breakfast."

"They ain't gonna catch any fish on a day like this. Not with such a sky. Storm comin' . . ."

Lightning flashed, cracking the gloom above Shiloh with a brilliant light. Thunder rolled down the mountain, rattling the windows of the farmhouse and causing baby Joe to look up from the wheat cake he was playing with.

Jeff sat very still as the rumble died away. "I don't like this, Lily." He rose and returned to the porch. Cupping his hands around his mouth, he sounded like a different brand of thunder. "Tommy! Bobby! Y'all come on back to the house!"

No reply. Again lightning flashed in the far distance. The clouds were moving overhead, and yet the air had grown still. The birds did not call. Shiloh was silent, waiting for something. Waiting for the miracle Jeff had prayed for? or for disaster?

Lily came out with baby Joe on her hip. "Don't like the looks of it," she whispered. "I seen this kinda sky before. Down in Texas it was. Twister weather. All still and heavy, like somethin' evil done sucked away the cool breath of life."

Jeff lowered his head in agreement. "I seen it, too." His eyes darted to a distant explosion in the sky. Light shattered the gray backdrop in a hundred silver veins, finally forking to the ground. The boom followed a few seconds later.

"Where are those boys?" Jefferson shouted. "I *felt* it comin' last night. Lord knows *I felt it*, Lily. And I prayed!" Another burst of lightning interrupted him. "But I pictured the boys *here* when it come down." He stepped into the yard. "Tommy! Bobby! Where . . .?" The blast of thunder drowned out his cry.

"Maybe it's goin' past us, Jeff," Lily said hopefully. "Just because the sky looks bad don't mean . . ."

Jefferson raised his face and sniffed the stillness. "The breeze comes first." He looked at the first stirring in the top of the hickory tree. "The big wind will come soon."

"Jeff! What is it?"

"I *got* to find those boys, Lily." He scanned the horizon. "Lord? Not them young'uns, too! Got to help me find 'em, Lord!" A single drop of rain fell on his cheek like a tear. Jefferson did not wipe it away. "There ain't much time now, Lily. You know what to do."

"You can't leave. They'll come back, Jeff. When they see what's comin', they'll hightail it right on back here!"

"They ain't comin' back, Lily," he said urgently. "Listen to me, gal! Tell me you'll do what you got to do."

"Jeff! Nothin' but a thundershower comin'! Please don't go! Jeff?"

Baby Joe began to cry, as though he sensed that the distant wind had begun to coil high above them. The child buried his face in Lily's shoulder.

"You got this young'un to think of, Lily. An' your own baby. Stay here, gal. I ain't no kinda man if I don't go to hunt for them. . . ."

The Rock Island wailed long and loud as it pulled into the Mansfield station.

The conductor appeared at the door of the Pullman. "Bad weather ahead, folks. This is as far as she goes for a while."

"We ain't goin' on to Hartford?" asked a traveling salesman with a scowl. "I got to get to Hartford! Don't look like bad weather to me." He gestured out the window at the cloudless sky.

Birch looked over the rooftop of the station. The sky had a yellowish cast to it, as though the color was being sucked away.

"Doesn't matter what the sky looks like here, mister." The conductor was adamant. "Strong winds, rain, and hail reported out toward Hartford. Tornado weather ten miles up the track, and the Rock Island has decided better late than never, if you catch my meaning."

Birch and Trudy exchanged stunned looks. Birch put his hand on her arm. "You know how it is. Nothin' comes of it. Better to play it safe."

"I just wish it could have held off until we got home. You know I don't mind the scare of a good storm as long as we're all together."

"Jeff and Lily know what to do if it comes to it. Which it won't."

The conductor called out, "Breakfast at the Mansfield Café will be served for all passengers heading to Hartford. We will keep you advised of any change in conditions."

"What will we do when we get to that place we're going to?" David asked Max as they strolled toward the massive New York City rail terminal. The rumbling locomotives rattled the roof of the train shed. The echo of the loudspeaker could be heard distinctly even half a block away.

"Fish, maybe. If you like fishing."

"Oh yes, I do! Only . . . I haven't ever been. But I know I will like it."

"And play baseball, if you like baseball."

"Baseball is my favorite. I found box-seat tickets to the World Series at Shibe Park but sold them so I could come here."

"You sold box-seat tickets to the Series?" Max laughed in wonder.

"Yes. To the man at the train depot. I got to ride first class and had a bed on the train with sheets as clean as the hospital sheets. But then when I got here, the copper stole my coat and all my extra money, so I was hungry for a while until Gus and Olaf took me in." David reached out and touched Codfish on his broad head. "Codfish, too. Will Codfish have to ride in the baggage car? If he does, then I want to ride in the baggage car with him."

"No. No baggage car for either of you. We'll go first class. Private compartment all the way."

"All the way to Bora-Bora?" David was grinning up at Max with wonder. He had not thought of Boss Quinn or the G-men or the children's home all morning. Everything would be swell.

"All the way to the end of the line. And I'll wash up and borrow a razor, and we'll see the world from the dining car." Max winked. "How's that?"

"Codfish too?"

"Codfish may have to stay in the compartment. But he'll have clean sheets and a big window to look out of." The dog wagged his tail as though he knew he was the topic of conversation.

"Are there kids at Bora-Bora?" David asked quietly. He had missed the old gang even though Gus and Olaf and Codfish had been good company.

"Lots of kids. And school."

"I'm glad. Mother would not like it the way I haven't been in school and the way I've been saying *ain't* so much. She used to say such language was like cursing. I sort of fell into it."

"It can happen." Max was understanding.

David ducked his head as though the next question embarrassed him some. "Will you . . . read to me?"

"Your mother used to read to you, did she?" Max nodded. "Let me see. What would Irene have read?" He ticked off a long list beginning with *Oliver Twist* and ending with *Treasure Island*.

Exactly, perfectly right! It was amazing!

"How did you know?" David breathed in awe. The shrill wail of a train whistle sounded as they approached the building.

"It is my business to know such things. How about *Huck Finn? Tom Sawyer?*"

"Nope."

"Then those are the two we can read together." He slipped an envelope out of his pocket. It was the same kind of stationery that they had just bought. "But I will begin with this. The story of the FAMOUS Bad-Luck Wagon. Ever heard of it?"

"Nope."

"You soon will," Max said with a twinkle in his eye as they pushed through the revolving door and entered the echoing lobby.

CHAPTER FIFTY

Twister!

No time to lose!

The soft breeze quickened and came to life, suddenly bullying the leafless trees through the valley. Lily watched as Jefferson's form jogged down the lane and disappeared around the bend. Thunder boomed like a thousand bass drums.

Baby Joe wailed louder as she dashed into the house and put him in his crib. She poured a kettle of water over the glowing coals of the stove. Steam hissed and filled the kitchen. Lily called soothingly to baby Joe as she tried to raise the windows. Old paint and new paint held the sash closed.

"Help me, Lord! Give me strength, Lord!"

An instant later the stubborn window moved upward, and the first stiff rush of air burst into the kitchen. With two more windows and the back door wide open, the wind tore at the curtains and banged against the door into the parlor. Lily ran into the front room, heaving the windows open and propping them up with Trudy's books.

To the bedrooms! The window in the boys' room would not open, so Lily smashed it with her shoe just as the first rattle of rain sounded on the rooftop.

So much to do!

"Oh, Lord! Mighty Jesus! Ain't no time! Not yet! *Not yet!*"

Raindrops pelted harder as the gale began a low howl in the distance.

"Remember Jeff! Remember them boys! Don't forget us, Lord! Help me now, Jesus!"

The boom of thunder sounded like cannons just over the rise. It was coming! No holding it back. Lily grabbed the baby and turned a full circle in the room. What to take? She tore a blanket from the bed and Trudy's Bible from the night table. Then she ran through the house and out to the root cellar in the backyard.

The heavy wooden cellar door seemed weighted by the force of the storm that whipped Lily's clothes and stung the baby's skin. From the barn the milk cow bellowed in terror. Lily heaved on the obstinate panel and prayed all the while. At last a split-second release of pressure flung wide the path to safety.

She scrambled down the steps and placed baby Joe on the blanket at the farthest wall of the dark, dank cellar. He screamed hysterically as she mounted the steps again, to stand trembling at the top, searching the countryside for some sign of Jefferson and the boys.

✯ ✯ ✯

The force of the gale seemed like a hand, driving Jefferson back. He leaned into it, each step harder than the last. He could not see Shiloh Church for all the dust that swirled around it. But it was still there. The bell clanged wildly in the tower as a warning of coming calamity.

"TOMMY!" Jefferson shouted, then, "BOBBY!" But he knew his voice was lost beneath the roar.

The church bells seemed to call to Jefferson, an appeal for him to come find safety in the shelter.

"Not these young'uns, Lord! Not those boys! Sweet Jesus, have mercy on us today!"

High above him, the sky began a low rumble, like a distant freight train moving down the tracks.

Jefferson looked up, spotting dark, fingerlike formations protruding from the bottom of the clouds. He could plainly see the slow rotation as that ominous grip pointed downward and then pulled back, only to descend again.

The church bell clanged once more in wild alarm before the wind tore it loose from the tower and sent it hurtling against the oak tree, then skipping across the ground like a stone across a pond.

Trees bowed and whipped back and bent again to snap and tear away.

Where were the boys? Jefferson continued to shout for them, but his voice was drowned out by the roar of the storm. Hands lifted heavenward, he called out to the Lord. Would the hand of God take the good away with the evil? Would He crush the innocent along with the guilty?

"Take me, Lord! Not the young'uns! Hold back until I find 'em, Lord!"

Behind the clouds the furious rumble grew louder, like a hundred freight trains preparing to barrel into Shiloh, ready to wipe away every-thing . . . *everything*!

Jefferson pushed on, although the rushing torrent of air tried to block him, to push him back like the broken church bell.

✼ ✼ ✼

Crouched on the cellar steps, Lily watched the black sky as dark fingers twisted and spooled closer to one another beneath the cloud. For an in-stant she thought she heard the desperate ringing of the church bell, but that was lost beneath the terrible roar that filled the air.

It seemed as though the storm would suck her breath from her lungs and yank her up from the cellar. The cellar door flapped like the wing of a wounded bird, warning her that, in a moment, it would be too late.

"JEFFERSON!" she screamed, praying that he would somehow mi-raculously appear on the lane with the boys under his arms. "Dear God! Help him now!" she sobbed, crawling up to grasp the handles on the heavy wood door. She could wait no longer. Baby Joe wailed frantically as the dreadful howl quickened and deepened.

And then the outstretched hand in the cloud coiled into a writhing black snake. *Twister!* It swayed high above the earth, as if it were a living thing, searching out someone to destroy.

The funnel turned toward the farm, as though it could *see* the cellar and Lily and baby Joe. It hung there a moment longer, bent around to look toward the church and the school, then toward the store and J.D.'s farm. It stretched out, drew back, spiralled, and contorted.

Lily stared, transfixed by the evil of the thing. And then the twister be-gan its descent to earth. Too late for Jeff! Too late for the Tucker boys! Would Trudy and Birch come home to find everyone dead? Would they find the broken bodies of Lily and baby Joe and curse her for waiting too long?

The tormented air shifted, lifting the cellar door and slamming it closed, knocking Lily to the floor. She cried out and managed to pick herself up as the rumble grew impossibly louder. The inside locks were not in place! The twister could seek her out and suck the cellar clean!

The darkness was total. She groped back up the steps and felt for the wooden bars to slide through the metal handles.

Outside she heard something explode. There was a high screaming sound, almost human, as wooden planks were ripped from the founda-tions and nails flung away with disdain by the tornado.

Where are the bars? Lily groped in panic along the stone ledge. The crack around the door widened, slammed shut, then gapped again.

The hand of the storm yanked at the puny protection.
The bars! The bars! Lord! Help me!

"We shoulda listened to her!" Bobby shouted as the first sharp needles
of rain pelted them from behind.

"You want to stay around that café? listen to them ladies gossip all
day? We got to get home."

"We shoulda stayed until the rain passed."

"We'll make it home before it hits." Tommy tried to reassure his
brother. At that instant a cannonade of thunder boomed and boomed,
piling noise upon noise and shaking the ground beneath them.

Bobby stopped in the middle of the field, transfixed by the roar and
the light that flashed all around them.

Tommy grabbed him by the shirt. "Come on! We can make a run for
the trees!"

For an instant this made sense—take shelter beneath the thick trees.
Then a huge oak branch snapped and buckled, plummeting to the ground.

Bobby shook his head fearfully and held on to his hat as the tempest
howled louder and the limbs of sturdy hickory trees convulsed as
though they were as supple as the birch trees on the farm.

BOOM! The sky's agony resounded from the ridge. The rain became a
driving, burning force, tearing at their skin and their clothes.

"We shoulda stayed on the road!" Bobby wailed, suddenly certain
they were lost.

Tommy linked his arm in Bobby's and dragged him forward. But forward to what? Where were they? If there was a farmhouse nearby, surely
their Shiloh neighbors would let them wait out the storm.

Bobby stumbled and fell. The rain fell harder, more biting, turning
into hail the size of raindrops and then the size of mothballs.

Tommy dragged his brother along as hail bounced against the road
and struck them from every angle. "To the trees!" Tommy shouted. Better
to take their chances in the woods than to be stoned in an open field.
Hard like rocks, cold like ice, the hailstones struck the boys as they ran,
raising welts on their backs and causing them to cry out in pain.

Bobby's cap flew off. Caught by the grasp of the wind, it twirled high
and flitted across the sky like a leaf. White hailstones clung to his hair
and slipped down the neck of his shirt. "We shoulda stayed in Hartford!"
He shook a small fist at the leaden sky.

Then he heard the rumble. Like a train above them, in front of them,
behind them.

"It's the Rock Island train!" Tommy shouted. "I hear it!"

"But where?" Bobby was confused. He did not know anymore where the tracks were. Where home was. There were only the wind and the hail and the roar of the train that seemed to be everywhere all at once.

"We'll go toward it!" Tommy called to his brother. "That way, I think." He pointed through the woods. If they could make it to the tracks, they could find their way back to the farm. Tommy linked his hand in the strap of Bobby's overalls, and Bobby did the same with him.

"Don't . . . let . . . go . . . !"

The berm of the railroad track loomed before the boys like a shadowed wall. But there was no train. The roaring enveloped them, shaking earth and trees and sky. Tommy looked upward as the cloud broke into four spinning tops that formed a crooked black rope.

Wind and hail whipped his face as he fell to the ground, pulling Bobby down with him. A high whistle and an explosion sounded as the terrible arm reached down and hammered the earth. Churning, thundering, it sucked up fields and tree branches and animals. For an instant the image of a cow appeared, then vanished in the whirling fury.

High at the top of the funnel it seemed as though birds flew in circles. Not birds, Tommy realized in an instant of horror—the dark things were parts of roofs and fence posts and a thousand other things that had been torn loose and carried away!

Bobby was sobbing, unable to tear his eyes away as the tornado seemed to glide across the countryside directly toward them like a giant spirit!

Tommy could not hear his brother's cries. He dragged him closer to the berm, wrapped his legs around him, and prayed. "Don't let go! Don't let go!"

CHAPTER FIFTY-ONE

The Miracle

The silence that followed was profound and absolute. No bird sang. No calf bellowed. The trees did not stir.

In the darkness of the shelter, baby Joe lay in Lily's arms, exhausted from terror. She sat with her back pressed against the wall and watched as shafts of light gleamed through the cracks where the cellar door remained partly ajar. She had not managed to bolt it closed, yet she and baby Joe were somehow still here. Still alive.

The infant blinked at the light and put his thumb in his mouth. He gave two sucks, then sighed with relief and closed his eyes to sleep.

If only peace could have come so easily to Lily. She stared at the light and imagined the destruction that surely lay beyond the quietness of this tiny refuge. Could the tornado have vanished so quickly? Was it truly gone or simply lurking above Shiloh until she climbed the cellar steps and pushed back the barrier?

Lily touched Miz Trudy's Good Book and closed her eyes in grief and yet in thanks. By some miracle she would be able to lay this child in the arms of Trudy and tell her, "You have this one young'un left to you! You can go on livin', even if it's only for one child!"

Lily placed her hand on her own belly as the baby within her womb danced for joy. "I hear you. I know what y'all are tellin' me," she told the baby. Then she looked skyward. "I can go on, too. Even without Jefferson, if You've done took him, Lord. I can go on for this young'un You give me. And for You, Lord, if'n that's what You want!"

She buried her face against the perspiring form of baby Joe and wept for a moment, allowing herself to release the tears. But only for a moment.

Placing the sleeping baby on the blanket beside the Bible, Lily slowly climbed the steep stone steps toward the light. Flecks of dust swirled in the golden shafts, a gentle reminder that the fields of Shiloh had been plowed up by a mighty hand.

Lily pushed against the planks, expecting the hinges to swing open. They rattled and resisted, not yielding even an inch. She lifted both hands and strained against the door. Something heavy, immovable, was resting on the opening. Lily and baby Joe were trapped. Someone would come along sooner or later to free them. But for now, Lily sat on the steps and leaned against the cool stone wall to wait and listen for some sign of life above.

Minutes passed, and Lily heard the clucking of a chicken. Then another. Not all of Miz Trudy's hens had been killed. That was something. A small consolation, but something.

Minutes later she heard the clopping of hooves on fallen planks and then the bleat of the calf, answered by the mournful bellow of the Jersey milk cow. Another miracle!

"Oh, Lord, Lord!" She clapped her hands.

If God could save the hens and the calf and the milk cow, couldn't He somehow wrap His great arms around Jefferson and Tommy and Bobby, too?

For the first time, Lily dared to hope. The words of Jefferson came back to her: *"Like Daniel in the lions' den. We can't bend our knee to the god of fear. . . . Stand an' pray, Lily. We got to wait for the hand of the true God!"*

She answered that memory audibly, standing in the center of the shelter like Daniel in the lions' den and raising her hands to the one true God.

"I can't see what You done, Lord, but I hear them hens, and I believe. Yessir, Lord! You ain't brought us so far to break us to pieces. Don't matter what's out there or what ain't out there no more. I'm believin' You, Jesus. You see when *one* sparrow falls. You spin clothes for the lilies. You done pulled the teeth out of that lion for us, and I ain't gonna fear nothin'! Ain't gonna fear *hunger*! Ain't gonna fear *bein' poor*! Ain't gonna fear *what men do to me*! Ain't gonna fear *bein' alone*!"

And there was one more thing. "Ain't gonna fear the terror of night nor the arrow by day, nor pestilence nor plague! No sir! You said it, Lord. You done *promised.* My eyes are gonna see the downfall of the wicked. A thousand shall fall, but it ain't comin' near us! No sir! You said it! And *I believe it!* No plague shall come nigh thy dwellin'!" Lily's face was washed in the light. "Hallelujah, Jesus! Hallelujah! Amen!"

"AMEN!" boomed the voice of Jefferson from above. "You havin' a private revival down there, gal?" he called joyfully. "Just you an' the Holy Ghost an' baby Joe? Or can me an' these here Tucker brothers join y'all?"

Bobby and Tommy laughed. "We're okay, Lily! Got the money back for the red pup, too." The rattle of coins in a jar sounded like a tambourine. "The house is still standin', too!"

"Well, say Amen, somebody!" Jefferson's voice rolled high with joy. "Amen an' Amen!"

Lily could not speak. She could only weep with the exuberance of an unexpected miracle. The miracle of life that went on through disaster. The miracle of laughter and small boys with a mason jar filled with coins to give to their parents.

"The Lord is good, ain't He, Jeff?" she managed as she picked up baby Joe.

"Unlock that shelter, gal," he called to her. "I just gotta move this here FAMOUS wagon off the door. . . ."

"It ain't locked. I couldn't lock it, Jeff."

Heavy wheels groaned across the boards. "Then the Lord done locked it for you, Lily! He lifted this wagon up from the field and set it down right on top." He was laughing. "Still full up with wood."

And then the portal opened, and daylight beamed into the hole.

Lily emerged into the light with the baby asleep in her arms. The FAMOUS wagon, still heaped with its cargo, was unscathed. The house seemed untouched. Trudy's books still propped open the windows. The barn was mostly down, and Jefferson's shed in the lower field had vanished, along with the outhouse.

"Glory be," Lily whispered. "If that don't beat all!"

Just then a naked chicken strutted across the yard. Every one of the creature's feathers had been sucked off.

Lily shook her head in wonder.

"Ready for the stewpot," Jefferson said admiringly. "If you get to it, gal, we'll have chicken and dumplin's for supper by the time Birch and Trudy get home. And the Lord already done the pluckin'!"

"*Don't* that beat all!"

✯ ✯ ✯

It was lunchtime in Manhattan.

Max bought six hot dogs from the Nathan's Famous Franks cart in the main lobby of the terminal.

"Four with everything for me and my son. Two without for the dog."

David was gazing solemnly at the empty space beneath the huge clock at the far end of the vast room. It was five minutes until twelve. Edith Rutger had not shown up with Max's suitcase, and Beadle had not arrived with the money.

"It's almost noon," David said as Max gave David his hot dogs and then dropped the two naked franks into Codfish's open maw.

"That's right. Lunchtime. Eat up. Our train will be boarding in five minutes." Max checked the first-class tickets that protruded from his pocket. "Two more minutes. Eat up. Last chance to have a real New York hot dog. They are meant to be eaten on the run."

Kraut, onions, mustard, pickles, catsup, and other unidentified stuff was crammed onto the bun. David opened wide and fit his mouth around the thing, taking a bite just as the boarding call echoed over the PA system: *"B&O Washington Express now boarding on Track 22."*

"That's us," Max said. "Come on. Bring it. We'll eat it on the train."

David tried to speak around the bite but could not get the words out. He looked toward the empty space beneath the huge bronze clock at the far end of the lobby. Still no sign of Miss Rutger or Mr. Beadle. It was only minutes until noon! How could they leave? What about all the stuff? David chewed fast as Max nudged him toward the wide corridor leading down to the loading platforms.

All Trains, a big sign read, and an arrow pointed along a side corridor toward Gate 22.

David swallowed and almost choked. Had Max forgotten? "What about all your stuff?"

"Don't worry about it," Max answered calmly. "I'm sure we can pick up a few things when we reach Shiloh."

David walked backward, trying to see a lady with a suitcase and a man with a money sack beneath the clock, but they still had not come!

Max did not seem to care. He patted Codfish. "Bora-Bora would have been too hot for Codfish, I think. Very humid, hot places, these tropical islands. He is a Newfoundland, used to cooler climates. Trudy writes that the weather is wonderful in Shiloh. Cool and mostly mild. A little snow sometimes, but nothing like New York."

"But what about your things? Isn't that Edith lady bringing your coat?"

"I suppose she is. Yes. But we just don't have time now."

David gawked up at his father, who was proving to be either a little nutty or full of surprises. "But that was just the first call. We can wait! You don't want to leave behind . . . clothes. Do you?"

"They won't fit in Shiloh, anyway. Bib overalls, Trudy says. The boys stole all of Birch's bib overalls and stuffed them full of straw."

David eyed him suspiciously and scratched his head. Okay, so business suits would not do. "But what about the sack of money?" David insisted, juggling the hot dogs.

Max stopped in the center of the corridor, turned around, and gazed back for a minute. "No, let Beadle have it. We'd never make the train, David, I'm telling you."

"But . . . but . . . that's more money than I ever heard of except maybe for what the bootleggers have." He tugged at Max's sleeve. "I'll go back. I can get it and run fast and catch up with you and Codfish."

David stopped and Max stopped. Codfish wagged his tail in confusion.

"You couldn't run that fast, David. It's not possible." Max shook his head firmly.

"I could. Except maybe I couldn't carry the suitcase."

"You couldn't." Max looked at his watch. "Even in a taxi it would take you fifteen minutes to get there."

David glanced back at the lobby and then at Max. "A taxi?"

"On foot it would take much longer. Trust me. Let's get on the train and go to Shiloh."

"But . . ." David waved his hot dog wildly at the lobby and the place beneath the clock. "But it's just right there! What taxi? They will be right there in just a couple of minutes! I heard you tell them to meet you at noon beneath the clock at Grand Central Station!"

"That's right." Max grinned and pulled another frank from the roll and fed it to Codfish. "They are all over at Grand Central Station, waiting beneath the clock. That's right."

"But . . . but . . . but . . ."

"This is *Pennsylvania* Station, David!"

"Second call. B&O Washington Express now boarding on Track 22."

Max resumed walking down the corridor at a faster pace. "Come on, David, our train is waiting!"

CHAPTER FIFTY-TWO

Granddaddy's Legacy

Chicken and dumplings were served up hot around the kitchen table as one by one the family members shared their story about the miracles that had saved them during the storm.

"First I saw J.D.'s house blow up; then his barn exploded, and the twister was comin' on! I spotted them boys an' then the culvert under the railroad track," Jefferson said. "An' the Lord told me what to do!"

Tommy joined in. "He grabbed me up, and I was hangin' on to Bobby so tight that he caught us both at once and jumped for the culvert."

"So in we goes!" Jefferson clapped his hands. "An' that twister is movin' just on the other side of the railroad track like it was lookin' for a way to cross over."

"The water was over my head," Bobby said. "And cold, too."

"But that twister just sucked all the water up!" Jefferson said in a voice full of wonder. "Just like the Red Sea an' the Hebrew chillens! There we was, standin' on dry ground!"

"Well, I do declare!" Lily exclaimed. "I just grabbed the baby and the Good Book and a blanket and made a run, not knowin' what to take nor what's gonna be standin' in the end! Don't we all got ourselves a heap of miracles?"

Birch and Trudy agreed. They had not had exactly the miracle they had been praying for. J.D. had vanished, but the Tucker house would still be auctioned for the taxes; that was certain now.

Still, the Lord had not let them down.

Birch opened Trudy's Bible and removed the age-yellowed envelope of the letter his mother had written to him in this very kitchen when he was fighting in France. He placed it in the center of the table for everyone to see, then tapped the return address and the postmark. He turned it over so they could see it had never been opened.

"All this time I have been savin' Mama's letter in case some great disaster happened. Somethin' in case I couldn't go on anymore." He picked it up. "That's why I never opened it. Like money in the bank, this letter has been to me. But I know now the only thing a man can bank on is the Lord Jesus."

"Somebody say amen!" declared Jefferson.

And the tiny congregation did so. Loudly.

"Well now, it looks to me like we won't be livin' in this old house," Birch continued. "I reckon that means the Lord has another place for us to be. He did not see fit that we should have that money, and I guess I'm just fine about that. Where He leads we're goin' to follow, and that's a fact." He breathed in. "But my mama wrote this letter here. A sort of legacy for me. I figure there's not a better time to open it than now, surrounded by my family, by my friends. And I want to read it right here, like she is here with us all, talkin' to us. She was a mighty good woman."

Birch smiled and slit the envelope with a butter knife. Unfolding the lined notepaper, he smoothed it out before him. His chin trembled as he took in the handwriting. His eyes clouded with tears. "How-do, Mama," he whispered. "We're all here." He could not say more, so he passed the letter to Trudy.

She smiled gently as though she were meeting a much-loved friend. She winked at her boys, who sat wide-eyed at this event. They knew how their daddy had treasured that old letter, how he had hoarded it and saved it and never brought it out except to hold the envelope in hard times and shake his head and put it back in the Bible.

Trudy began to read in a clear voice:

"September 24, 1918
Shiloh, Ark.

Dear Son,
It come to me in a dream last night. I seen the row of birch trees down to the crick standing tall in the moonlight. . . ."

Every face turned to gaze out the window toward those same trees. The moonlight shone brightly on the white bark. Trudy continued to read:

"A great wind was blowin', like to bust them trees. Then a mighty voice said to me out of that wind, 'Clara, I planted them trees. They are rooted deep. No need to fear any wind can bust them.'

The winds are blowin' mighty strong these days, Son. I don't know that I'll be here when you come home. But I know if you stay rooted in the Lord, deep like them trees, no wind that blows will bust you.

Don't put your trust in nothin' else, Birch. All else is shiftin' sand. Just you read Psalm 91 when you are feelin' scared. It'll tell you all you need.

You're in the trenches tonight, I know. And I am leavin' you with this prayer from the psalms. 'A thousand shall fall at thy side, and ten thousand at thy right hand; but it shall not come nigh thee.'

Your loving mother,
Clara Tucker"

When Trudy lowered the paper, there were tears on every face. Had the Lord given Clara Tucker a vision of this day? of this time? Had He so long before seen these hearts gathered around this table? It was something to consider.

They sat silently for a long time and considered the birch trees in the field and the wind that had passed over them today. And then Bobby piped up, "Hey, there's a P.S. on the back. Read that, too."

Trudy flipped the page and read aloud:

"P.S. Almost forgot. Your granddaddy Sinnickson set great store by that psalm. He always said it got him back here safe from California. Anyway, he give me somethin' to give you for your twenty-first birthday. On account of the way things is, I've hid it away for you, Birch. It's under the bottom step in the root cellar.

God bless you, Son. "

Birch grinned. "That old man. What a character he was. Andrew Jackson Sinnickson. Named for a president too, Tommy! Filled my head with his tales about his adventures in the Sierras." He shook his head. "Well, I'm way past twenty-one years old now, ain't I? Suppose we ought to have a look at my legacy now? or wait until mornin'?"

Protests erupted from Tommy and Bobby. They said they would not go to bed unless the mystery gift under the step was uncovered at once.

The lantern was lit, and the entire crew traipsed out to the root cellar. While Trudy, Jeff, Lily, and baby Joe remained aboveground, Birch and the boys descended.

"What do you suppose it is?" asked Tommy as Birch pried up the stone step.

Birch laughed. "Granddaddy Sinnickson had a chunk of a shooting star I always admired. Quite a story to it. Don't know what became of it after he passed on."

The hollow clunk of the crowbar scraped against the slate, and then the stone rolled back. The boys crowded in closer as Birch dropped to his knees and brushed away dirt from a tin bread box. The lid was rusted shut, so Birch pried at it with his pocketknife as the boys pushed in to see. The tin snapped open.

They stared at the contents a moment. "Unwrap it, Dad," Tommy urged.

Birch pulled back layers of oilcloth, revealing a thick cardboard-bound volume. "Well, I'll be."

"Is that all?" Bobby sounded disappointed.

"What is it, Birch?" Trudy called down to him.

He hefted the massive volume. "Granddaddy's stories! All written out for me!" He traced his finger lovingly across the glued label displaying the old man's spidery handwriting.

Sierra Tales
Life and Travels
for Grandson Birch
from Grandfather Andrew Jackson Sinnickson

"What a treasure!" Trudy cried.

"Is that all?" Tommy clucked his tongue. "Where's the star?" He reached past Birch and pulled up an edge of the oilcloth in the tin box.

Birch's smile of pleasure grew as he glanced into the bottom of the box. "There it is . . . and . . . what in . . ." He gasped and blinked in astonishment at what he saw. "Glory! Praise be!" He held aloft a black, fist-sized hunk of stone.

Tommy chimed in. "Does this mean we can get the red puppy, Dad?"

"It surely does," Birch breathed.

Bobby reached into the bread box and grasped something. "Lookit here, Mama! Great-granddaddy kept all his money stored in canning jars, just like us!" He hefted a glass jar and held it up for Trudy to see. It glistened with gold coins filled to the top. "Two of 'em! Two quart jars! Real heavy, Mama!"

Bobby gave it a shake, and it rang like the sound of a tambourine.

A Thousand Shall Fall

"My Father . . . loves me. I will not . . . be afraid. . . . *A thousand shall fall at thy side, and ten thousand at thy right hand; but it shall not come nigh thee.*"
—BIRCH TUCKER (p. 374)

Have you ever felt like the whole world has turned against you? Have you felt hopeless? alone? afraid? abandoned?

Birch Tucker certainly felt that way upon arriving home in Shiloh and discovering that his cousin J.D.—a man he had trusted—had taken nearly everything from the Tucker farm. We see Birch's hopelessness when he realizes that he could lose the farm—the one hope he has always carried with him.

David O'Halloran Meyer felt abandoned when his mama died and left him with his abusive stepfather and when he learned that he would live in an orphanage. He feels that way again when he arrives in New York City and can't track his birth father.

Jefferson Canfield has to make a desperate, lonely run for his very life. Although he's never given up on God's mercy, after ten long years on a chain gang, he has forgotten men can be merciful.

When Lily Jones is cast out from the cotton pickers, she's ready to give up on living. Yet after receiving kindness from the Tucker family, she chooses to believe and to hope for the sake of her unborn child. As a result, she brings comfort into Jefferson's and Trudy's lives. When difficult times come, Lily pleads with God:

"You ain't brought us so far to break us to pieces. Don't matter what's out there or what ain't out there no more. I'm believin'

You, Jesus. You see when *one* sparrow falls. You spin clothes for the lilies. . . . I ain't gonna fear nothin'! Ain't gonna fear *hunger*! Ain't gonna fear *bein' poor*! Ain't gonna fear *what men do to me*! Ain't gonna fear *bein' alone*!" (p. 404)

Because of Lily's faith, Trudy realizes anew: "When there's nothing left to give the Lord, then you have to look at what you have. Your soul. Yourself. And that is the only gift He wants from His children. . . . Maybe that is what the Lord wants from us. For us to look to Him. To trust Him like a Father" (p. 374).

Do you—can you—trust God like a Father? trust Him to provide for you in the midst of loneliness, fear, and prejudice? trust Him to plant you deep, like a tree, so that no "wind" can "bust" you? (p. 410).

Dear reader, when you are feeling scared and alone, why not follow Clara Tucker's advice?

Don't put your trust in nothin' else, Birch. All else is shiftin' sand. Just you read Psalm 91 when you are feelin' scared. It'll tell you all you need. (p. 411)

Life will always be complicated. We trust that the following questions will help you dig deeper for answers to your own daily dilemmas. You may wish to delve into these questions on your own or share them with a friend or a discussion group.

Most of all, we pray that through this Shiloh *Legacy* series you will "discover the Truth through fiction." For we are convinced that if you seek diligently, you will find the One who holds all the answers to the universe (1 Chronicles 28:9).

Bodie & Brock Thoene

SEEK . . .

Prologue

1. If you were going to write the story of your life and "time was running out" (p. vii), what would be the most important tale for you to tell?

_____

_____

2. "Samuel Tucker would leave a legacy of harshness, of distance and cruelty, for his sons" (p. ix). What legacy are you leaving?

_____

_____

PART I
Chapters 1–2

3. When Birch was unjustly blamed for his boss's son's death, how did he respond (see p. 10)? How would you respond?

_____

_____

4. Can you identify with young David O'Halloran's grief in losing his mother? his loneliness? the abuse he suffers at the hand of his stepfather? (See chapter 2.) What happened in your own childhood that lets you identify with David?

_____

_____

5. "Prince Davey, Irene Dunlap O'Halloran called her nine-year-old son" (p. 20). Who has made you feel like a prince or princess because of the way he or she treated you? believed in you? Explain.

_____

_____

6. "Wall Street was a universe apart from the poverty and squalor of the old neighborhood, yet Max had found a different variety of squalor planted firmly in the hearts and minds of the men who controlled the finances of the entire world" (p. 22). In your experience, do outside appearances match hearts and minds? Why or why not?

_____

_____

Chapters 3–5

7. "For ten years, Birch and Trudy had saved for this day, lived on this dream, looked forward to coming down this road and saying at the end of it, 'Well, boys, we're home'" (p. 28). What are you longing for? working hard for? Why is this dream important to you?

_____

_____

8. "Birch had never been a boy, but he had told Trudy that he was determined his sons would be everything he had not been allowed to be" (p. 48). Because of his own difficult boyhood, Birch wanted his three sons to have what he did not. What would you change about your growing-up years, if you could? How could you carry that longing into other children's lives?

_____

_____

Chapter 6

9. David's "stamp collection represented his mother's life" (p. 51). What item, to you, represents a loved one's life? Why?

_____

_____

10. David had "prayed that she would wait just one more month to die, but she had not waited. God had not heard his prayer, and he felt cheated somehow" (p. 52). Have you ever felt cheated by God? In what situation? How has that situation affected your perspective of God?

_____

_____

11. "David hooted and laughed and jumped harder than the others. But the whole time he wished his mother were near to tell him how he was *supposed* to act. How he was *supposed* to feel. Sometimes he saw the other kids looking at him strangely, almost fearfully" (p. 54).

   When have you wondered how you are supposed to act? how you are supposed to feel? When have you felt different from others? Or when have others treated you differently because of something that has happened?

_____

_____

12. When Birch regrets that he doesn't have much to give his family, Trudy replies, "Oh, Birch! I'm not talking about *things*. I'm talking about *you*! (p. 55). Which do you put a higher value on—things or people? How does your life reflect that priority?

_____

_____

13. "Birch knew his mother had packed her spiritual bags long before she passed from this place into heaven. *'Gonna be home with Jesus someday, Birch. Don't you worry none about me. My soul is ready for the journey. Hallelujah!'*" (p. 57). In what ways is your soul ready for the journey? not ready for the journey?

_____

_____

Chapters 7–9

14. "When his mother died, the hole inside him filled up with hating Brian O'Halloran. This was much better than crying for his mom, David thought. He dreaded the sadness that lurked everywhere around him. He knew that if he ever let it come in and push away the anger, the sadness would sit on his chest at night and choke him to death. He did not want to hurt. Did not want to think about his mother. It was much better to sit in the dark and hate Brian through the walls" (p. 67).

   What things in your life have made you sad? How have you dealt with that sadness? Have you replaced it with other emotions—anger, revenge, bitterness, something else?

   _____

   _____

15. Mrs. Crowley "never seemed to look at David's face. He wondered if she would recognize him if they passed on the street" (p. 73). Have you ever felt invisible? When? How can that experience help you to really see others?

   _____

   _____

16. "David shrugged. He had already told a million lies today. What harm would one more lie do?" (p. 76). When have you told a lie to cover up another lie? What was the result?

   _____

   _____

17. "Birch simply gripped the wheel. He did not look at Trudy or the evil serpent-train that had tempted him and enticed him to such a terrible fall" (p. 83). When have you been enticed to do something silly or dangerous? Tell the story.

   _____

   _____

Chapters 10–12

18. "[J.D.] was a coarse little man. It was hard to believe that he was in any way kin to Birch" (p. 93). What relative do you feel this way about? Do you think any relative feels this way about you? If so, why? What step could you take toward reconciliation?

_____

_____

19. "Mrs. Crowley was off at the market buying bitter chocolate to bake him a going-away cake. The old woman felt guilty, David knew" (p. 102). When you feel guilty, how do you make it up to others?

_____

_____

20. "The look Trudy gave Birch made it all clear: No, she did not like the attitude of little Mr. Simpson and King Henry V. Still, it was a man's world, so she herded her little flock gracefully out of the sacred halls of Hartford finance and left Birch to complete the business" (p. 116). When have you faced gender prejudice? How did you respond?

_____

_____

Chapters 13–14

21. Did you, like David and Oink in chapter 13, ever play hooky from school? If so, what did you do on your "day off"? Was the day off worth it—or not? Why?

_____

_____

22. With the history the FAMOUS Bad-Luck Wagon had, would you have bought it? Why or why not?

_____

_____

23. David was shocked when he unexpectedly received box-seat tickets to the World Series (see p. 132). Have you ever received a surprise that meant the world to you? If so, what was it?

_____

_____

Chapters 15–17

24. When Tommy dared Bobby to go out on the log above the river, Bobby took the dare because he didn't want to be "some ol' girl" (p. 137). Yet the results were nearly tragic. Have you ever taken a dare that turned out badly? Tell what happened.

_____

_____

25. Why do you think David's mother didn't open Max's letters? Why didn't she tell David the truth about what had happened between her and Max (see p. 143)? Would you have made the same choice—or a different one—in similar circumstances? Why?

_____

_____

PART II
Chapters 18–20

26. If you were Lily—pregnant, alone, and out of work—what thoughts and emotions would you have (see p. 161)?

_____

_____

27. "He knows when the sparrow falls, the Good Book says. I suppose He knew from always that boy was gonna get into mischief down at the creek. Maybe all along the Lord was savin' me for that child. And savin' that child for me. He is like that, Jesus is," Jefferson

Canfield says (p. 174). Do you believe that God is actively involved in our lives in such ways? Why or why not?

_____

_____

28. When Trudy Tucker realizes that the scarred man in front of her is Jefferson Canfield, the Preacher, she wonders, "What had they done to him? Yet his soul was unchanged, his love for God undiminished. Yes. She could see that plainly in his eyes" (pp. 174–175). How have the difficult things in your life changed you? What things about you have remained the same?

_____

_____

29. If you were starving and cold, as Lily was, would you have taken the gift of the red-flannel shirt from the farmwife (see p. 181)? Why or why not?

_____

_____

Chapters 21–26

30. "When David lost his coat, he had lost everything. News clippings. The picture of his mother. Money. Hope. He had not eaten all day" (p. 183). Yet hope, help, and food come from an unusual source: two rum-running Swedish brothers and a dog, Codfish. When have you received help from an unusual source? Tell the story.

_____

_____

31. Keenan—who was from the same old neighborhood in Orchard Street as Max Meyer—tries to bribe Max to be on the "right side" of the stock-market information (p. 195). Yet Max insists that he

won't be bribed. Has someone ever tried to bribe you? Did it
work? Why or why not?

_____

_____

32. "Max was not a lonely man as long as he did not think too deeply or
let his memories carry him too far back" (p. 209). He "knew the
truth about himself. . . . It was loneliness that led him to spend long
hours researching and delving into the financial maze of Wall Street
to see what sense he could make out of it" (p. 219). Are you, in any
ways, like Max—living life in the fast lane, addicted to work, etc.—
to keep yourself from thinking too deeply? If so, how?

_____

_____

Chapters 27–29
33. When Birch goes to visit Mount Pisgah, his heart is chilled by the
way the women talk about "those people" (p. 228). Do you tend
to group people into categories or see them as individuals? Give an
example. During the coming week, in what way(s) can you change
your own thinking?

_____

_____

34. Max explains his life philosophy to Edith Rutger: "A tear behind
every laugh. A laugh behind every tear. Keeps life balanced if you
do it right. Enjoy the moment . . . because tomorrow is never certain" (p. 238). Do you agree with Max? Why or why not?

_____

_____

35. Contrast the "welcome" Lily got at J.D.'s home with the one she received at the Tucker farm (see chapter 29). If a pregnant woman
showed up at your doorstep, what would you do?

_____

_____

Chapters 30–34

36. Put yourself in Max's shoes. You have just found out that you are the father of a nine-year-old boy. What would you be thinking? feeling? (See p. 247.)

_____

_____

37. What "scary tales" do you remember being told when you were a kid (see p. 251)? Why do you think these have stuck with you?

_____

_____

38. After Max realizes he has a son, his entire life changes:

"Had Max ever noticed before that every main street ended in a dead end at the water's edge? Up. Down. Dead end. That was all the city of his dreams meant to him now." (p. 279)

Has a single event in your life changed everything for you? If so, what was it, and how did it impact your life?

_____

_____

PART III
Chapters 35–38

39. In chapter 35, Mr. Winters defends the Tucker boys against J.D.'s prejudice. Have you ever found yourself in a similar situation? Either as the defender or the one who needed to be defended? What happened?

_____

_____

40. "Jefferson took a step toward [Lily]. The light around her was *so* bright! 'My mama said the same thing. She said folks is blind. Blind souls, folks is. But when folks sing praises, the winders open up, and the light just comes on in'" (p. 298). Whom do you know who is surrounded by bright light? What folks do you know who "sing praises"?

_____

_____

41. During this time in history, the world was a scary place:

The whole world seemed to be falling apart. Faces on every street corner in Manhattan were sullen or gloomy or frightened. No one looked at anyone else. Each man and woman walked alone this Friday with a dark and personal spectre. For many, the dreams of tomorrow's glory had come crashing down yesterday. Instant wealth had instantly been cut in half. Today had been some brighter, but the shimmering bubble had been shown to be "pop-able." (pp. 315–316)

If this were to happen today, how would you respond to losing part—or all—of your wealth?

_____

_____

Chapters 39–41

42. "I surely do hope you remember the Lord is watchin', Miz True. Yes'm. I do believe the Lord is watchin'," Lily tells Trudy when hard times come. Do you believe the Lord is watching over your life? that you should "Trust only in the Lord!" (p. 324)? Why or why not?

_____

_____

43. When the farmer offers to help Trudy and Birch get out of the hole, it costs them something (see p. 336). When has someone offered you a "kindness"—but it cost you something? Explain.

_____

_____

Chapters 42–45

44. When the stock market crashed, how did the following lives
    change? What does tragedy reveal about these individuals' motives
    and top priorities?

    *Damon Phelps (see pp. 345, 372)

    _____

    _____

    *Tell and Penner (see p. 346)

    _____

    _____

    *Max Meyer (see pp. 358, 362, 364)

    _____

    _____

    *Birch and Trudy Tucker (see pp. 363, 373–374)

    _____

    _____

45. "The question these days is, Who do you trust?" Max tells David
    (p. 370). Whom do you trust—and why?

    _____

    _____

Chapters 46–52

46. Tommy and Bobby Tucker gave up something they really wanted—
    the red puppy—to help their father (pp. 375, 386). When has

someone given up something precious for you? When have you
given up something precious for someone else?

_____

_____

47. Edith Rutger betrays Max Meyer, yet she doesn't want him to know
(see p. 380). Have you ever experienced the betrayal of a friend?
When? What happened down the road in your relationship?

_____

_____

48. Have you ever faced a natural disaster, such as a tornado, a flood,
etc.? Tell the story. How did you respond to it at the time? What
thoughts do you have now, as you reflect on the experience?

_____

_____

49. "You said it, Lord. You done *promised*. My eyes are gonna see the
downfall of the wicked," Lily says after the tornado passes over the
Tucker farm (p. 404). Do you believe that God can spare you? that
He can provide miracles for you? Even in the midst of disaster?
Why or why not?

_____

_____

50. What keeps you hoping for the best, even in the midst of sorrow?
How can that hope become a legacy for those around you?

_____

_____

BODIE AND BROCK THOENE (pronounced *Tay-nee*) have written over 45 works of historical fiction. That these best sellers have sold more than 10 million copies and won eight ECPA Gold Medallion Awards affirms what millions of readers have already discovered—the Thoenes are not only master stylists but experts at capturing readers' minds and hearts.

In their timeless classic series about Israel (The Zion Chronicles, The Zion Covenant, and The Zion Legacy), the Thoenes' love for both story and research shines.

With the Shiloh Legacy series and *Shiloh Autumn*—poignant portrayals of the American Depression—and The Galway Chronicles, which dramatically tell of the 1840s famine in Ireland, as well as the twelve Legends of the West, the Thoenes have made their mark in modern history.

In the A.D. Chronicles, their most recent series, they step seamlessly into the world of Yerushalayim and Rome, in the days when Yeshua walked the earth and transformed lives with His touch.

Bodie began her writing career as a teen journalist for her local newspaper. Eventually her byline appeared in prestigious periodicals such as *U.S. News and World Report*, *The American West*, and *The Saturday Evening Post*. She also worked for John Wayne's Batjac Productions (she's best known as author of *The Fall Guy*) and ABC Circle Films as a writer and researcher. John Wayne described her as "a writer with talent that captures the people and the times!" She has degrees in journalism and communications.

Brock has often been described by Bodie as "an essential half of this writing team." With degrees in both history and education, Brock has, in his role as researcher and story-line consultant, added the vital dimension of historical accuracy. Due to such careful research, the Zion Covenant and the Zion Chronicles series are recognized by the American Library Association, as well as Zionist libraries around the world, as classic historical novels and are used to teach history in college classrooms.

Bodie and Brock have four grown children—Rachel, Jake, Luke, and Ellie—and five grandchildren. Their sons, Jake and Luke, are carrying on the Thoene family talent as the next generation of writers, and Luke produces the Thoene audiobooks. Bodie and Brock divide their time between London and Nevada.

For more information visit:
www.thoenebooks.com
www.familyaudiolibrary.com

THOENE FAMILY CLASSICS™

✪ ✪ ✪

THOENE FAMILY CLASSIC HISTORICALS
by Bodie and Brock Thoene
Gold Medallion Winners*

THE ZION COVENANT
Vienna Prelude*
Prague Counterpoint
Munich Signature
Jerusalem Interlude
Danzig Passage
Warsaw Requiem*
London Refrain
Paris Encore
Dunkirk Crescendo

THE ZION CHRONICLES
The Gates of Zion*
A Daughter of Zion
The Return to Zion
A Light in Zion
The Key to Zion*

THE SHILOH LEGACY
In My Father's House*
A Thousand Shall Fall
Say to This Mountain

SHILOH AUTUMN

THE GALWAY CHRONICLES
Only the River Runs Free*
Of Men and of Angels
Ashes of Remembrance*
All Rivers to the Sea

THE ZION LEGACY
Jerusalem Vigil
Thunder from Jerusalem
Jerusalem's Heart
Jerusalem Scrolls
Stones of Jerusalem
Jerusalem's Hope

A.D. CHRONICLES
First Light
Second Touch
Third Watch
Fourth Dawn
Fifth Seal
and more to come!

THOENE FAMILY CLASSICS™

✪ ✪ ✪

THOENE FAMILY CLASSIC AMERICAN LEGENDS

LEGENDS OF THE WEST
by Bodie and Brock Thoene

The Man from Shadow Ridge
Riders of the Silver Rim
Gold Rush Prodigal
Sequoia Scout
Cannons of the Comstock
Year of the Grizzly
Shooting Star
Legend of Storey County
Hope Valley War
Delta Passage
Hangtown Lawman
Cumberland Crossing

LEGENDS OF VALOR
by Luke Thoene

Sons of Valor
Brothers of Valor
Fathers of Valor

✪ ✪ ✪

THOENE CLASSIC NONFICTION
by Bodie and Brock Thoene

Writer-to-Writer

THOENE FAMILY CLASSIC SUSPENSE
by Jake Thoene

CHAPTER 16 SERIES
Shaiton's Fire
Firefly Blue
Fuel the Fire

✪ ✪ ✪

THOENE FAMILY CLASSICS FOR KIDS
by Jake and Luke Thoene

BAKER STREET DETECTIVES
The Mystery of the Yellow Hands
The Giant Rat of Sumatra
The Jeweled Peacock of Persia
The Thundering Underground

LAST CHANCE DETECTIVES
Mystery Lights of Navajo Mesa
Legend of the Desert Bigfoot

✪ ✪ ✪

THOENE FAMILY CLASSIC AUDIOBOOKS
Available from
www.thoenebooks.com or
www.familyaudiolibrary.com

have you visited
tyndalefiction.com
lately?

Only there can you find:

- ⟶ books hot off the press
- ⟶ first chapter excerpts
- ⟶ inside scoops on your favorite authors
- ⟶ author interviews
- ⟶ contests
- ⟶ fun facts
- ⟶ and much more!

Sign up for your **free** newsletter!

Visit us today at: **tyndalefiction.com**

Tyndale fiction does more than entertain.

- ⟶ *It touches the heart.*
- ⟶ *It stirs the soul.*
- ⟶ *It changes lives.*

That's why Tyndale is so committed to being first in fiction!

TYNDALE FICTION